Shadow Over Loch Ghuil

A Redferne Family Adventure

Pattison Telford

This novel's story and characters are fictitious. Certain long-standing institutions, agencies, and public offices are mentioned, but the characters involved are wholly imaginary.

Acknowledgements

Thanks to my advance readers! Samuel Alfrey (hiding the magic), Brady Burkett (removal of *that* cheesy line), Norm Finlayson, Audrey Jacques, Deb Livingstone, Ansar Mohammed ('Somebody dead'), Mary O'Neill, Audrey Platteel (put the pronunciation guide at the *beginning*), Gabrielle Scott (clarity for readers that missed book one).

Impeccable editing by vickybrewstereditor.com

Cover design by Darin Morrison-Beer

Redferne Family Adventures

You can find out more at www.pattisontelford.com

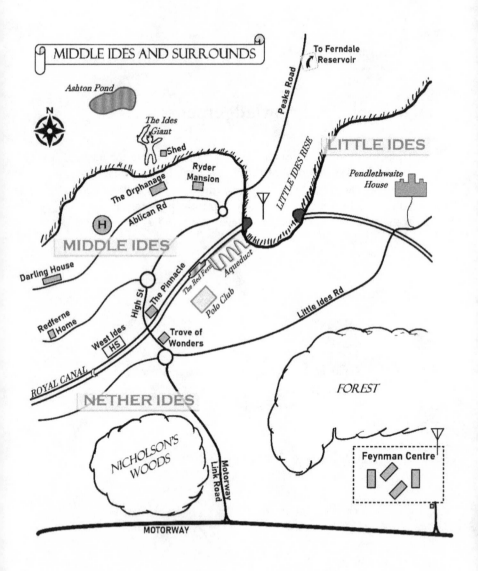

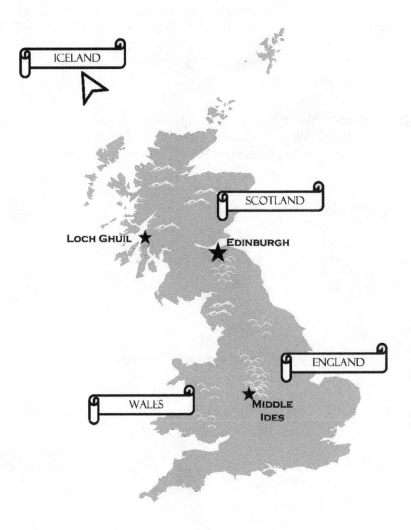

Pronunciation Guide

The Scottish Gaelic and Icelandic names in this book have not-so-obvious pronunciations. Here is a short guide.

Loch Ghuil – LAWkh GYUil
Ruaridh – ROOree
Ena – EEna
Ragnhildur – RAHgnHEYdush
Úlfursdottir – ULLfirsDAHteer
Sgian Dubh – SKAYan DOO

CHAPTER 1 - INTERLOPER

Faraday

The other helicopters were toys. One had crashed in a ball of flames into Nicholson's Woods. Another had whisked us away from the battle at the gates of Pendlethwaite House, under the direction of the Unusual Powers Defence Agency's Scarlett Thorisdottir, who I believed had ordered the killings of my parents.

It had been 3 months since I had last noticed a helicopter pass over Middle Ides. This one refused to be ignored. Its presence announced itself before I saw or heard it. Up through the soles of my feet, the vibration preceded the resonant bass and the first hints of downdraft. I stood, face upturned, at the Ides Giant's foot. Literally the foot—the misshapen chalk outline of a barefoot giant carved into the hill behind my grandmother's care home. Flying low, the double rotors of the military Chinook burst into view above the Orphanage. Sheep scattered, leaving the Giant unadorned. I glimpsed my grandmother's profile in her window in the Orphanage's blonde stone face, head inclined, one hand cupped at her brow in the angling morning sun. The ground protested as the helicopter reared its nose and prepared to settle on the grassy field between my grandmother and me. The Ides Giant complained, ejecting wisps of powdery dust and scattering its tiniest chalky pebbles. Lengths of grass rippled in whorls, every blade attempting yet failing to flee the vicious wash.

Settling, the helicopter's wheels bit into the dewy ground. The engine's whine became a decelerating rhythm, and the spinning blades and the grass below transitioned from frenzy to dance. As the rotors' counter-rotations slowed from disc-shaped disturbances to 2 triplets of chunky rotors, my mind split into 2 fact-finding teams. In the background, I estimated how many more rotations the blades would complete before they halted. I began to count. My primary concern was the figure that dashed down the angle of the rear cargo ramp, navy blue uniform contrasting with the helicopter body's drab olive. Only a single person, so it wasn't an invasion of Middle Ides, but my jaw clenched at the implications. I almost lost count of the rotor revolutions.

Middle Ides was ostensibly a sleepy town, and I had lived through enough excitement in the spring to last me a decade. I instinctively rubbed the lump on my collarbone, and the vivid recollection of my sister Higgs turning into a tree threatened to derail my inspection of the emerging figure.

After 11 rotations, the blades were making their last lazy turns. No longer thrashed by the downdraft, the figure strode further onto the field, glanced at a ruggedised handheld device, and then turned in my direction. Unbuckling the chin strap and pulling the helmet back, my dread turned to scorn and fury. As I half-expected, a shower of blonde hair appeared, falling to the approaching figure's shoulders.

As the Chinook military copter came to stasis after the 17th turn of its blades, Scarlett Thorisdottir strode toward me, unsmiling. When I had last endured her company, on that other helicopter, I could not restrain myself from striking her. The impulse to do worse coursed through me as I drew myself to my full height and glared at her approach. Time hadn't softened my emotions—quite the reverse.

In my peripheral vision, I noticed my grandmother standing pressed to the glass in her room, gazing across the field at us.

Scarlett slowed and halted in front of me, but two steps away, as if she detected my radiating desire to do her harm. She waited for me to speak.

"Last time, you said you—"

A nod. "Never wanted to return to this godforsaken town? Still true. Don't worry, we'll be leaving shortly." An almost imperceptible ripple of her eyebrows inferred she meant 'we' to include me.

"No, no, no. I'll only join you if one of us is in handcuffs. Preferably you. You're a killer, and we both know it."

She advanced a half step. "You're as stubborn as your father. But not half as wise. Get it through your head. I had nothing to do with whatever your overactive imagination is conjuring."

"We found something in Mum's grave. Once we analyse it—"

"Listen. I don't have time for this. I wouldn't be here if it wasn't important, and I need your help. People across England are dying, and I suspect only the nanotech that you and Iain Vanderkamp have been working on can halt it."

"What do you mean? Iain and I aren't working on anything."

"Faraday! Cut the crap. Do you think just because I don't pay you social visits, I'm not deeply invested in monitoring the nanotech you have been developing?"

She had me there. After our whippet Disco kept worrying at the back wall of our basement, I uncovered a *second* secret lab of my mother's. I had dedicated every day for the last 4 months to the treasures within, working with Mum's lab technician Iain to finish work on a range of what we called nano-killers. Nanotechnology that seeks other nanotech and disables it. When my family endured multiple technological attacks, an interest became a compulsion.

I paused before answering. Although I had strong suspicions about my parents' deaths and my gut told me that Scarlett and the UPDA instigated both, I had struggled to uncover concrete proof. My inner cynic worked against my suspicions, too. Maybe if I could restrain myself in her presence, she'd slip up and feed me the evidence I yearned for in every waking—and slumbering—minute.

"If there's a nanotech threat and you need us to help, you'd better explain. And be quick. My patience with you is paper-thin."

She stepped closer. Within striking distance now. But I saw her position her feet, ready for fight or flight—one of the things Newton taught me to watch out for in an escalating situation. Did that indicate a flicker of nerves on her part?

"Kids are being killed in London. And we think unidentified nanotech is causing it. It's coming from one of two sources, but we may well need your tech to neutralise and contain the outbreaks we've seen so far. Come to Edinburgh with me. We need to talk face-to-face with the man most likely to know something relevant."

Gears whirred inside my mind. This was straightforward emotional blackmail. Kids being killed? *Really?* But if she only wanted to snatch our technology—or snatch me—there would be troops swarming my lab and this field beneath the Ides Giant's watchful gaze.

"Let me talk to Newton."

I motioned with the back of my hand, shooing her away, and turned my back to offer an illusion of privacy as I phoned my brother.

Outlining the situation, I told Newton this was an opportunity to watch Scarlett at close quarters. He felt she must genuinely need my help, agreeing that the UPDA wouldn't be this subtle if they only wanted to grab the nanotech for their own use.

"Do you have the anti-tracking kit?" he asked. "If you need to run for it, you can't have them tracking you."

"I'm wearing Dad's watch. Remember we found it had the same anti-tracker as the cars?"

There was a pause. "And how do you *feel?*" Another pause while he let the unspoken reference settle in. He meant my tendency to become paralysed when faced with complex decisions. "Can you keep a grip on things if Scarlett pressures you? I should come along too."

"You've seen me, Newt. I'm not a child anymore. This is our chance. And if this kid-killing thing is true, we'd never forgive ourselves if we didn't help. I'm fine to go alone. Let me call you every 4 hours if that helps you rest easier."

"I'm setting my timer, brother. Don't miss a call. And be careful—she's a crafty one, that Scarlett."

I focussed on keeping a straight spine and a smooth gait as I walked from the Ides Giant's foot to the cargo ramp at the Chinook's rear, where Scarlett leaned her wiry frame. She pushed herself erect as I approached.

"Okay, I'm in. We'll need to go to the lab and—"

"Already got it," she said. "The vials and new nano-containment kettles are ingenious. Much more portable. We persuaded Iain to hand them over."

UPDA. Damn them. How could I help when they had so much power already?

I almost shook my head in disbelief, but a black SUV wheeling around the end of the Orphanage jolted me from my musings. It sped across the grass toward the helicopter. I was spooked and prepared to run, but Scarlett was unfazed and strolled toward its approach.

The SUV came to a swift stop, carving a short, earthy arc in the damp grass. Scarlett raised an open palm and called to whoever was behind the tinted windows. "Got him?"

A brawny man with close-cropped, dark hair emerged from the passenger door. He had *security* written all over him. Polarised sunglasses, a deep navy blue suit that could conceal a bristling arsenal, and boots that looked too bulky to not have steel toes. "He's here, ma'am."

Turning, he opened the rear passenger door, and out sprang Grover Mann, the stable boy from the Middle Ides Polo Club. He looked puzzled at first, as he often did, but his face brightened into a beaming smile as he turned toward me and rescued thick glasses from the precipice that was the end of his nose. He limped forward at a pace that belied his permanently twisted leg. "Furry-day! Is Disco here?"

Scarlett intercepted him, taking his arm gently. "No Grover, Disco isn't here. But you can come for a helicopter ride with me and Faraday. We brought a special helmet you can wear during the ride."

She ushered him up the ramp as the thud of the closing SUV doors behind us preceded the sound of a reversing car engine. I followed her, raising an eyebrow.

"Oh. There could be magic involved, too. We might need Grover to help with that."

CHAPTER 2 - GLEN GHUIL

Higgs

Loch Ghuil was a magnet. It attracted me from afar and then held me, even as I yearned to escape. The flurry of contesting powers that grappled throughout our week in Scotland would cast a long shadow over my friends, my brothers, and me.

Even as my brother departed Middle Ides in a helicopter, the mist hung over Glen Ghuil like a sheet covering a sofa in a dusty, abandoned mansion. It approached but dared not quite close the gap to the steep, heather-lined contours of the valley that cradled the loch's dark waters. Despite the dismal atmosphere, Dot, Lars, and I pitched our tents enthusiastically, glad to be spending time in this remote part of Scotland, away from the mounting pressures and creeping memories in Middle Ides.

This was the first day of our long-anticipated camping trip, and we had chattered across the peaty earth into the valley from the lonely bus stop on the single-track road behind us. When we spotted the level ground skirted by a stand of Scots pines and a rushing burn leading to the distant loch's headwaters, we took only a few seconds to declare it our tent-pitching location.

Dot shook her head, rippling her long, glossy black hair. "Whoever wrote the instructions for putting up this tent made it *look* like English, but it's basically a bunch of random words and a diagram for something that clearly isn't a tent."

"You actually read instructions?" Lars asked. His ululating Swedish accent rippled in mock amusement. "Look, my tent is ready, and you're still holding a pole and a piece of paper."

"Okay, clever clogs, use your tent superpowers over here."

Lars sprang over and scooped up the remaining poles from the spongy patch of green and violet where Dot had emptied the tent bag. He started piecing parts together. "You're going to owe me a favour now."

I stayed out of their way and used a hybrid of intuition and glances at the assembly diagram to set up my lightweight, domed orange palace. I glanced at Lars as I worked, seeing if I could outpace him. This was a familiar pattern, I mused—later kindnesses from Dot would repay Lars's chivalry.

"Maybe there's some magic that makes tents pop up with a wave of a mandrake root," I said.

They both smiled at the idea. Dot's lips curled up at one corner. "Judging by the rate that we're learning how to use magic, you'll be too old and stiff to get into a tent by the time either of us learns that kind of spell."

Ah, the dastardly voice of truth. Yes, both Dot and I had been learning a few rudimentary bits of magic. But we progressed slowly, often frustrated. After the shattering events at the gates of Pendlethwaite House, Dot's father had reconvened the cabal of Middle Ides witches. They vowed to not only adopt a healthier set of ethics but also to help Dot and I discover our magical potential in a more open forum that didn't involve wearing grotesque metallic animal masks.

And so, a pair of modern witches had brought us under their wings. Not actual wings—contrary to folklore, there was no fluttering around from our tutors. Not even broomstickery. Nor warty chins trailing strands of blackened hair. These were witches beautiful in their own ways.

Granny got into the spirit of our education. She doled out snippets of guidance when Dot and I visited, although she clearly had a gold mine of magical experience that she withheld. It was Emeline Grey who spent the most time with us. Yes, *that* Ms Grey, our history teacher at West Ides High School. It was her grey ponytail I had seen peeking out from behind a brass stork mask on the ultimate fateful day of Beauregarde Device's grip on the cabal. Her measured tutelage in the roots and techniques of magic pushed Dot and I to better understand our powers.

And did I mention she was now my brother Newton's girlfriend? Or at least, friend who is a girl. I'm not sure how formal their arrangement was, but they seemed pretty cosy, and Newt always hung around our lessons at Pendlethwaite House or in our back garden in Middle Ides as Emeline tried to tease magic from our very hesitant reserves.

"Whoa! Hairy cows!" Lars's enthusiasm was often contagious, but his voice expressed an order of magnitude more excitement than normal. A trio of highland cattle emerged from the pines. Their quizzical faces turned toward Lars's voice, and wisps of mist clung to their shaggy orange coats and looming horns. One had a fringe covering its face long enough that it could have been cropped and used as a makeshift toupee.

"Look at this guy's horns. I'm going to touch them." He stooped and sidestepped closer, brandishing an outstretched handful of long grass as a show of goodwill.

Dot and I lingered by our tents and observed the show, but her voice had a slight wobble as she called out, "Be careful, Lars! I know he's just a funny-looking cow, but he's still eight times your size. Don't make him angry or anything."

"Shh. I'm fine. Watch—he likes me, I think."

The trio clearly knew they outmatched us and regarded Lars with glassy eyes the size of billiard balls, unmoving as he approached. They showed no genuine interest in the grass stalks and were unperturbed as Lars reached out his empty hand. But just as his palm converged on the lead cow's yellowing horn, they turned in unison and galumphed into the trees. A scattering of small birds fled the canopy, and their wingbeats lingered longer than their images in the foggy ceiling.

"Yow! Next time they'll let me come closer." Lars sounded

only mildly disappointed, and his laugh was joyous.

* * *

Our camping skills were better than I expected. By the time the diffuse sunlight turned orange and gave way to a darker night than Middle Ides ever offered, we had our sleep nests arranged, had dined on sandwiches, and were sipping steaming tea from metal cups beside a sparking fire.

Lars returned to one of his favourite topics. "I still love parsnips, and so does half the town, so I know your magic is real, Dot. But Higgs, what about the Pendletoad? Did we really hear it? Is it real, what your *mormor* said?"

I chuckled at his earnestness. "You heard what Granny said. The story of the spell to protect the witches' bodies that had been sunk into Ashton Pond. And I heard the croaking noises too, that night when Beauregarde kidnapped Dot and me. I keep asking if you want to come up to the pond with me to check it out."

"I'm not going up to the pond," he said. "You go. And take a video. That's good enough for me."

Dot chimed in, "Yeah. Imagine the size of the wart you'd get if you touched a toad that big. But I'm with you, Lars. I think Higgs should go without us."

"Thanks for the show of solidarity, guys. I suppose you want me to dress up as a giant fly too when I go hunting the Pendletoad?"

Lars laughed, then broke into a deep whisper as he smiled through his version of a scary fireside story. "Did I ever tell you about the *hunt for the Pendletoad?* This tasty looking morsel of a girl was taking a shortcut around Ashton Pond one night when—"

"'Tasty looking morsel'? You're referring to me? I think the remains of Dot's spell are soaking too far into your imagination."

"Okay, okay. How about *a girl that smelled like an insect* crept toward the pond when she heard a monster croaking …?"

* * *

From inside my tent, I could tell the fog had lifted overnight. Slanting sunlight streaking along the glen lit the east wall of my tent as I half-woke to the sound of Lars calling in a soft lilt, "Nice cows. Good cows. Don't run away this time. I'm just being friendly."

His footfalls rustled the grass and faded as he walked further from our campsite. A muffled mooing accompanied a louder call. "No, don't run away! It's okay."

A second voice drifted to me, quiet and indistinguishable at this distance, nothing but a jumble of tones. Lars replied to it, tickling the edge of my hearing. I think he said, "Oh, hello," followed by something indistinguishable, and then, "Yes, yes. I'm Swedish."

Not hearing more conversation after that, I drifted off into a basking slumber.

* * *

It wasn't much later that a zipper sound intruded on my doze. Dot's head poked into my tent, scraping the low-slung top of the V made by its entrance flap. "Where's Lars?"

"Meh. He was off chasing highland cattle last I heard." I looked at my phone. We had put our phones into airplane mode to save battery as there was absolutely no signal here in Glen Ghuil. "I heard him talking to someone twenty minutes back, and then drifted off again."

Dot's head disappeared from my tent flap, and I could see only up to her elbows as she stood on tippy-toes, rotating in a slow circle.

"Well, I see the shaggy cows, but no shaggy Lars."

A rush coursed through me. This wasn't right. Cattle, but not Lars? I erupted from my half-unzipped sleeping bag and executed a high-speed crawl that military recruiters would have been proud of, especially since I wore only a striped T-shirt and knickers.

Clearing the flap, I sprung up beside Dot. Even on tiptoe, I still only rose to her jawline as she stood flat-footed. I scanned frantically. Dot gripped my shoulder, seeming to echo my tension. "He's bound to be nearby. Maybe over in the trees there. Lars! Are you here?"

That was a feeble attempt at shouting. I added my voice, which rang out with a wobble and a hint of panic. "Lars! This isn't funny. Answer us!"

We heard nothing but a hint of echo from the glen's rising slopes and then silence, broken only by munching sounds from the cows at the treeline and the burn's cascading water. It had settled into our consciousness as background noise to ignore, but seemed louder now.

Dot pointed to Lars's tent door. "He's not wearing his shoes. He won't have gone far."

Without a word, we scrambled into trousers and hiking boots and started circling the campsite in opposite directions. Dot checked the burn's banks, its icy waters coursing relentlessly toward the loch. I skirted the trees, still calling out. The cows looked on, nonchalant.

Nothing.

"Circle wider," I called to Dot, who nodded grimly.

I zig-zagged through the trees, looking for signs of passage. It was from this direction that the earlier conversation with a stranger drifted to me. Nothing obvious here, but I was hardly a bush tracker.

I started to run, head swivelling, even looking up to the treetops. Dot's footfalls went from a trot to a canter as she too covered more ground on the flanks of our campsite.

I mounted a slight rise at the edge of the pines that offered a better vantage point. Aside from the clutch of trees, the glen's primary landscape was low-growing plants. The clear skies presided over a view as far as Castle Ghuil, miles away at the loch's far end. A yellow flag danced above its ruins. I could see everything. Everything except my friend.

Dot ran up, leaning over, breathless. "He's not here. I

checked his tent again to make sure he hadn't zonked out in his sleeping bag."

"He must have gone off with whoever he was chatting with. But where could they have gone? He would have told us if he was going far. Or at least come back for his shoes. We need to get help."

It's hard to say if we were being practical, but we grabbed our phones and embarked toward the lonely stretch of road where the bus had deposited us. We knew there wasn't any mobile signal there, but maybe we could flag down a passing car. We left everything else at the campsite.

"Wait, wait. I'm forgetting something," Dot said. "I can try the finding spell."

"Jeez. Of course. Here, I'll clear a space."

I scraped aside an arm's length of loosely-rooted heather, revealing a sandy layer of dirt beneath. Grit insinuated itself beneath every fingernail. Dot foraged and scampered back with a twig. She eased herself into a cross-legged position on the heather, closed her eyes, and traced the lines she had memorised. Triangle, triangle, wavy line, triangle, arrow.

When she had practised the spell back in Middle Ides, I could feel the magic at this point: a tingling sensation in my calves, and the symbols would stir into cautious motion. But in this remote glen, a place where the earthly powers underpinning her magic should be strongest, nothing happened. No tingle, no fluctuations in the dirt. I watched Dot relax her shoulders, adjust the angle of her elbows and furrow her brow. Nothing.

"Dammit. I'm *good* at this spell. It's one of the few things I can do properly. But I'm getting nothing. It's like a hand is reaching in and clenching my heart whenever the magic surges."

She rapidly scanned the horizon. "I'm scared, Higgs. We have to find help. Now!"

The twig dangled in Dot's listless hand, then dropped. She sprung up and grabbed my hand, pulling me along. Wordless, we sprinted into the pines, following the path that led to the bus stop, a mile or so away.

Our onrush continued as we lunged through the other edge of the pines and rounded the last bend before the grass took over. The bus stop would be straight ahead, following a path through the heather. But I stopped dead at the trees' edge, and Dot clattered into my back, nearly toppling us both.

It wasn't the path to the bus stop. An unexpected change in the path confronted me. A few paces before me glittered the widening loch's edge. Not possible. The head of the loch was further from our camp than the bus stop, and this path met the waters part-way along its miles-long, fingerish contour.

Dot gaped. "What? How'd we get here?"

I silently turned and reversed course along the path. We must have taken a wrong turn. Dot paced me as I found a fork in the path that we missed earlier and took its side branch. The path rose, telling me we were back on track, and then curled through the pines' fringe.

But again, we emerged lochside, closer to the sea. On the opposite bank from where we had emerged earlier! Castle Ghuil was clearly visible now. It was the old flag of Scotland flying. A yellow field with a rampant red lion rippling in the salty breeze. How could we have accidentally crossed to the far side of the loch without an hour-long trek? A tingle ran through the base of my skull, and it wasn't a surge of excitement.

"Dot—it's the trees. They're doing something to us. We've got to stay out of them."

Our breath rasped from our panicked run. I scanned the loch's surface, wondering whether we ran here insensate or some devious power had moved us like pawns. Dot clasped her hands behind her head, her chest heaving. "The trees are over there, Higgs. There aren't any on this side."

A clenching knot in my stomach confirmed an accelerating fear. She was right. Although we had broken the treeline at a sprint, a glance at the path behind us revealed nothing taller than gorse bushes.

Dot closed in on me, arm to arm, and nodded upwards,

pointing at the steep-sided purple rise of the glen. She whispered, "Let's go *over*. At least from the top, we should get good mobile signal, and hopefully, we can spot Lars."

I set off at once, although my chest still burned from the earlier exertion. The going was tough, with spongy peat giving way to tangles of heather as we crested hillock after hillock that formed the glen wall. My legs grew leaden.

Halfway up, Dot overtook me, and with a burst of speed, clambered over a hump. Before I crested, I heard a groan of despair. "No. Not possible. This isn't happening."

My heart raced with more than the exertion. The smell of my sweat felt acrid in my nostrils. I reached Dot's vantage point and despaired.

The hump before us coasted in a lazy, rock-laced amble down to a sandy swath a few steps shy of the approach to the crumbling grey walls of Castle Ghuil. The castle stood on a tidal island, a connecting bank of sand laid bare by the retreated tide. We had climbed half the glen's side but ended up at the mouth of the loch, on its other side.

Despite the morning sun's radiance, a chill traversed my body as a quiver invaded my hands. Wrongness coursed around us.

Dot was more practical. "Clearly something wants us to visit this castle—what's left of it. But look, there's a flag flying. Maybe someone is inside and can raise the alarm."

Dot was already in motion. She took three steps, half turned, and beckoned for me to follow with a jerk of her head. We skirted the loch's edge and crossed the sandy tidal isthmus to the oft-island home of Castle Ghuil. Its ancient, dilapidated, lichen-mottled stone walls towered above a boulder-strewn base slab of quartz-marbled granite. But the ivy-clad walls were untopped, the roof long disintegrated. The royal flag of Scotland fluttered above, its stylised red lion gesturing out to sea from its yellow background. Unfaded, it looked to be a fresh addition to the castle. At close range, I saw the blue tongue and claws of the flag's upright lion, its majestic tail snaking above shoulder height behind. The rippling fabric made a soothing sound, a root of reality in a confusing situation.

Dot and I tiptoed side by side up a sandy and pebble-strewn path to reach the castle's level. We could hear the murmur of voices and slowed as we approached the entranceway. Still unnerved, we crept to the edge of the iron-bound wooden gate and peeked around the edge of its bulk where it hulked, ajar. The wood smelt fresh, unbattered by seasons of pelting rain and salt spray.

The integrity of the walls belied an interior that was wide open and mostly overrun with vegetation. Grassy patches surrounded a scattering of low stone buildings with slate roofs, showing signs of sympathetic upkeep. Archways punctuated slabs of curtain wall, hinting at the possibility of entering remaining parts of the towers and cellars. A few National Trust plaques dotted the interior walls, but it appeared the philosophy here was to leave the castle ruins largely untouched.

A recent incongruous construction rose at the centre of the space. A modest but modern chalet's straight lines contrasted with the time-worn castle's ambience. Its wide eaves overhung a slightly tilting expanse of flat rock in the castle grounds. A grey metal corrugated roof led me to imagine hunkering down beside a wood-burning stove with oversized raindrops beating a rhythm overhead.

The casement windows were partially open, and the voices became clearer as we allowed our inquisitive ears to eke around the gate. Lars's outraged voice rang out.

"You can't keep me in this cage! What the hell are you planning to do with me?"

A rumbling, raw-throated voice replied, "Och, put a sock in it. You're here until we dinnae need you any longer. We're not gonnae cause you any hurt, so just sit yourself down and resume waitin'. The sofa in there is nicer than anything we have out here."

I felt my ire rise. Dot gripped my shoulder tightly as we continued to eavesdrop.

A second voice carried across the gap to us after a pause.

This one had a Scandinavian lilt and sounded like a woman. "Sundalfar! Are we free and clear now? Are we protected from the prophecy?"

A strange voice replied. It was scratchy and childlike but with a vein of musical depth woven in. "I tell you, I tell you. I only deliver the prophecy. Me don't understand it. Hear me. That part for you to figure out."

"Then let's hear it again."

A keening sigh of exasperation was audible even at this distance. "Again? Very well. Very well.

A Viking boy will roam the Glen,
He must not pass beyond your ken.
Your new nation will be born,
Unless he touch the Ghuilin's horn."

The grumpy voice spoke up again. "We have the lad noo. Viking or nay, I think the prophecy is a load ay bollocks. But he's no going anywhere any time soon, so there willnae be any touchin' the horns of those shag-faced coos. He's nothin' but a bit ay insurance as far as I'm concerned. But let's get on wi' proper business. Our wee blue pal here did excellent work at Pentland Hills—it's time to move on Ferndale. And we chose another person on the kick-the-bucket-list, aye?"

The woman's voice replied, "Yes, yes. We know the next one we can send along so they see we're serious about everything. It's a Mr Roderick Simpson from Penicuik. Saturday afternoon—tomorrow—at two-thirty-six."

Lars spoke again. He sounded proud and unafraid, giving me a surge of energy as I imagined him forcing himself against the bars of whatever cage they had him trapped within. "I'm not some insurance policy. Let me out now, and we can go our separate ways. No harm done. I have to get back to my friends, or the police will swarm over this place before you know it."

The deep voice rumbled with laughter. "They willnae be goin' anywhere, either. I dinnae care about them, and you shouldnae hold your breath for two wee lassies to save you."

Umbrage tinted Lars's reply. "Just wait until they bring their magic down on you. Lassie that!"

It was the woman's turn to chuckle. "Magic is even less of a worry for us than the police. We have that covered."

I'd heard enough. Nobody was going to keep my friend caged. The rage and magic bubbled up in tandem. I stepped into the gap and strode toward the hut. A red-veined leaf erupted from the thumb of my clenched right fist. Dot still held my shoulder and trailed me through the gate, hissing, "Higgs! No. Don't do this."

I turned my head to face her, intending to throw off her hand so I could bring my anger and magic raging down on Lars's mysterious captors. Before I had swivelled halfway, I felt the magic drain from me, and the single leaf retracted. It was like someone had thrown a damp blanket over me, quelling both my desire and my magic.

And then I could no longer see the gap in the gate behind her. I saw the loch opening up into the sea. We had somehow appeared on the castle's far side, heels almost dipping into the lapping waves. Although something had funnelled us to Castle Ghuil, that same force didn't want us to enter it.

Dot's lips parted, but before uttering a single word, she whipped her head around to squint into the shadows beyond the seaweed-encrusted portcullis that beckoned boats along the channel into the castle's bowels. In my peripheral vision, I sensed furtive movement there too. A glimpse of a wiry, blue-skinned figure, knee-high and clad in rags. Hands bound in front, the shadowy form beckoned us into the dark confines of the passage in the rock.

But when I turned to gawk at the odd little creature, it had disappeared.

CHAPTER 3 - DARLING HOUSE

Newton

"That boy, he's got a lot going on."

My grandmother, Angelina Redferne, had an eternal soft spot for my brother Faraday. I think he reminded her of my father as a child. I suspect that neither quite fit in, in the traditional sense, each an outlier in the way he thought and behaved. And both owned their divergence, with respect for others' ways of thinking without bowing to a pressure to conform.

Granny had perked up since the traumatic events that took us into combat with dark magical forces at the gates of Pendlethwaite House. Before that, she had retained the sprightliness of a younger woman, but her mind often wandered and she seemed to be slipping away from reality like an untethered freight train car rolling down the slightest of inclines. But recently she seemed to be more present than wandering, and we were all gracious. Maybe it was the flexing of her magical knowledge that brought her back.

"Where did that helicopter take him again?"

Emeline Grey and I were paying a visit to the Orphanage, the imposing yet comforting care home overlooking the hills at the northern margin of Middle Ides. My grandmother had been in residence here for several years. "Scotland, Granny.

Remember, we told you about Dad's boss, Scarlett Thorisdottir? The one who swept in when we were rescuing Higgs and Dot from your old friend Beauregarde? He went with her."

"That Icelandic thing? Was that who I saw talking to Faraday out there? I never trusted her."

Neither did any of us. Especially Faraday. Although we lacked concrete evidence, it seemed like Scarlett and the Unusual Powers Defence Agency had their greasy fingers all over the deaths of my mother and father, and possible attacks on Faraday, Higgs, and me. It bordered on unbelievable that Faraday would go anywhere with her, but he fancied himself a rogue insider now that the UPDA wanted his help.

Emeline chimed in. "Don't worry, Angelina. He's only gone to Edinburgh, and he's checking in with Newton at regular intervals. It might have looked like a kidnapping, but this is a government agency. They wouldn't just whisk him away."

I hoped Emeline was right. The UPDA sure whisked away Mr Shinoto, the science teacher at West Ides High School. Not only snatched him but also pinned a sequence of crimes on him which we later discovered were caused by a veil of magic drawn over the town by the Knights of the Drowned Cabal. The same cabal that Emeline belonged to and my grandmother had hidden from us.

Granny gazed over the back lawns to the Ides Giant's chalky outline. "And they took that boy from the stables at the polo club too. You know. What's-his-name."

That was weird. "Grover? Grover Mann? He went in the helicopter too?"

"Oh yes. They drove a big black car right across the grass, and he hopped out near the helicopter. It made an awful racket, that whirlybird."

I could see the tire tracks out the window. Strange. I wondered if his parents knew anything about it.

Emeline drew closer to the upholstered wing-backed chair that was my grandmother's favourite observation perch. "But just in case, Angelina, is there something I could do to keep a trace on Faraday?"

The implication was unspoken, but the request was clearly to see if Granny knew any magic that could help us. It was hard to get used to the idea that magic was woven beneath the surface of everything that occurred, but I couldn't unbelieve it now that I had seen it first-hand, in both my sister and Emeline.

"I've heard of witches who can do things like that, but I wouldn't know how," Granny said. "I'm beyond all that nonsense, anyway. You know that."

My grandmother ladled cryptic tips as Higgs learnt more about magic, but she didn't handle the more practical teaching, leaving that work to Emeline. But many signs pointed to her abilities. Semi-believable stories my father told us as kids. Emeline's insistence that Granny had a renowned past in witching circles. Even the fact-obsessed Faraday's recollection of unusual events on a day out with her when he was ten. Many things about her eluded me.

I chided her, adding a playful tap of a punch to her shoulder. "Granny, you're a dark horse. Even if you say you're past it, how about you explain why Higgs has magical powers, but neither Faraday nor I have an ounce? There must be some explanation."

I nestled in beside Emeline and hoped for a comprehensible answer. Granny remained silent, but Emeline looked between us and offered a starting point. "I mentioned that certain people have an aptitude for magic, right, Newt? Like Dot. We managed to teach her simple spells because she's an attentive learner and has a natural instinct for bringing out her latent magical talents. But an aptitude and good tutors aren't the best way."

My grandmother couldn't resist the dangled temptation and continued the story. "Heavens, no," she said. "The best magic comes from bloodlines. That's why Beauregarde grew deranged and jealous of us Redfernes. He knew that real power is amplified with each generation of magic practitioners. I don't know how long magic has been trickling down the line to me, but my mother and grandmother had strong powers too. My Nan was so tuned to the earth that her garden spotted fruits and veg from every corner of the world; even crops that had no business growing in our weather. Those powers passed through my mother and into me, even stronger—although my preferences tended to fire, not earth. Everything springs from the natural world."

"So Higgs takes after *your* grandmother? All that tree stuff?"

She nodded. "It seems so. She has a lot to learn before she can control her magic. There's more to draw on for her than Dot, but she needs practice to feel out how to release the magic. She's almost the reverse of Templeton; your father had the most complete *feel* for magic I've ever seen, but he couldn't summon a lick of it himself. Maybe that explains the weird split between you and Higgs."

I must have looked puzzled, because Granny emitted a hearty chuckle before continuing. "Higgs can *express* the wild magic, but she doesn't have the reserve of magical power that you possess. It's odd—Emeline told me you can't muster even a glimmer of magic, but my thoughts jump straight to you when I sense Higgs using her powers. I get tingles, and can feel energy flowing from you to her. You are the engine and she's the headlights, Newton. She's not going to do much without you being close at hand."

This was all news to me, and my natural reaction was to dismiss it. I felt no magical heritage stirring in my veins. If anyone other than my grandmother told me this story, I wouldn't have given it a second thought.

The implications and emotions swirling were stunted by the vibration and ring from my mobile. It was Terrell Mohammed, my Detective Sergeant. His Trinidadian accent and quick-talking second syllable emphasis always sounded amused, despite delivering serious news. "Redferne? Somebody dead. Can I pick you up?"

It flustered me. "Wait. What? Who?"

"Patience. I'll go tell you when I come by. Be ready."

"I'm at the Orphanage. Can you grab me here?"

"Not a problem! I'm just up the road. There in two minutes. I'm gone."

I made my goodbyes to Granny.

Emeline and I were in a light embrace beside her car on the gravel forecourt when Terrell swung in at speed. There was a crunch of gravel as his car came to an abrupt stop. "Hop in, man!"

* * *

Our destination was Darling House, a low-rise block of council flats on the western edge of town. I could picture them— distinguished-looking red brick with contrasting sooty tuckpointing, the doors to the flats on each level fronted by an arched external hallway. The upper levels faced sweeping views over town toward the aqueduct and the Little Ides canal tunnel.

Terrell shook his head. "It's been like eight years since the last murder. I couldn't let you miss this."

"What do you know so far?" I asked.

"Well, it sounds like a teenage girl was killed by a friend, up here visitin'. The gal mother heard commotion and went into she bedroom to be confronted with a real horrendous scene. The friend jump out the bedroom window, and they found her body where she landed, on the bonnet of a car out back."

I felt sick already. Wasn't I supposed to be investigating token acts of mischief and missing dogs? If the victim was a teenager from Middle Ides, there was every chance that Higgs or Faraday would know them. My hands shook.

I felt a need to respond. "Are you prepared for a crime scene like this? Not as a police officer—I know you are more than competent. I mean psychologically. It sounds pretty grim."

"You aksin' me? Sounds like you're questionin' yourself," Terrell said.

"Yeah. Me, I guess. I've seen nothing like this outside of movies."

"Hey, I moved from Trinidad to get the shockin' violence

behind me. In the islands, I've seen a body dismembered by a chainsaw, a gal whose foot got gnawed off by a caiman, and a man who was accidentally shot in the face by his two-year-old daughter. So yeah, I'm prepared—although I wish I wasn't."

We slowed and parked behind a squad car. "Any tips for a first-timer?"

"Yes, man. If you spew, mind me shoes. And your own."

* * *

Terrell said he'd break me in gently, so we didn't go up to the flat immediately. Instead, we followed a uniformed officer to the back of the block where the visiting teen had flown from the third-floor window. A woman from the forensics team snapped a few photos as we lifted the caution tape and approached the body's ultimate resting place on the car's bonnet.

I wasn't prepared for the minute details that flashed to the forefront of my perception and will remain with me forever. All four corners of the bonnet were curled skyward, and one headlight was smashed, glinting fragments littering the rough pavement below the radiator grille. A fracture in the windshield wove a jagged path, nearly to the top.

There wasn't much blood, although a congealed rivulet had given up its quest to find the bonnet's front edge less than halfway there. The trail emerged from somewhere under the jawline of the wavy-haired south Asian girl who stared at me with accusing open eyes. She appeared to have turned her face just before impact but still hoped her hands would break the fall. They weren't up to that job, though—one arm had popped free of the shoulder socket and gave her silhouette an air of complete wrongness. That palm remained pressed to the bonnet, its elbow pointing to the cloudy sky above, shoulder a twisted wreck. The other arm sprawled overhead as if reaching for the windscreen wiper.

I dry heaved four times, and Terrell gave me a few light, absentminded slaps on the back as I doubled over. After a series of deep breaths, I looked away from the girl's corpse.

Terrell clutched his notebook and sketched the relevant aspects of the scene. "Look at the distance here, car to wall. Gal musta really launched from up there." He gestured at the window that gaped above. "But there's no doubtin' she dead. Nah, let's leave this one to forensics—thanks there, Sally—and cruise upstairs."

I nodded, still breathing deeply through my nose, and followed him as he climbed the outside staircase to the block's third storey. A sheen of sweat on his bald head sparkled, contrasting with the film of grunge and incoherent graffiti in the stairwell. A well-practised flourish of handkerchief from back pocket to scalp and back again mopped as he climbed.

"So, Redferne, put your gloves on. We're here to notice anything the usual crime scene folk might miss. Anything outta place. And pay attention to the mother. You've got good feelers—it's the people lollygaggin' around the edges of the scene should feed your instincts. Here endeth the lesson." A low, belly-powered laugh erupted, calming me.

As we topped the stairs, I saw a uniformed officer standing with his hands in his jacket pockets beside a long-haired woman who leaned, shaking, elbows planted on the walkway's cement sill. Although she faced a picturesque view over the town, with its meandering, leafy roads, canal, and patches of woods backed by the rising hills, she was looking down at her feet, hands on her forehead blocking the view. The officer gave us a tacit nod, and we slowed as we approached the open flat door behind her. Terrell had a quick glance at his notepad. A pair of mop-haired boys in their late teens eyed us from the far end of the walkway. They surveyed the flurry of police activity from a distance.

Terrell gave her the barest of touches, his palm grazing her shoulder as we inched past. "My man Detective Redferne and I are here to check inside, Mrs Antonov. No need to come in, you can stay here with the officer."

Her hunched shoulders heaved, and she gave a hint of a nod, not raising her head from her hands. I snapped on latex gloves, and we crossed the threshold into the flat.

Another uniformed officer stood inside the doorway. It was her job to control the crime scene. She nodded to Tyrell as we entered, saying, "In there, sir," as she pointed to an open doorway leading to a bedroom at the back. "They were apparently giggling and singing along with some boy band, then suddenly ... well, you'll see."

I dreaded what we would experience in there, but I was momentarily spared as I walked into Tyrell's back. He halted in the middle of the lounge shortly after entering. "Wait nah, big fella. Lewe absorb what's at hand before we dive in. Sometimes the best detection happens when you pause and allow the world flow over you."

I looked around the lounge. It was tidy but spartan, with the few decorations being photos of the woman outside and her daughter at various ages—signs of a hard-working single mother who was proud of what she had accomplished with limited opportunity. A half-drunk mug of tea perched on an Ikea coffee table at the edge nearest the settee, next to a face-down and folded-open copy of a current bestselling novel. A pendulum swung in a small arc below a clock shaped like an owl, the ticking audible over the sound of a radio intruding from the bedroom.

Terrell scrutinised the ceiling and squinted at the threadbare regions of the well-worn carpet. He closed his eyes for a good thirty seconds. "G'wan. Let's check the girl's room," he said, exhaling hard through his nose.

His decisiveness gave me the sliver of courage I had lacked all morning. I trailed close in his wake, only managing to half-stifle a gasp, and I saw beads of sweat burst from his scalp.

"Weys!" he exclaimed, mostly to himself. "Dutty business. Not nice."

The girl from the photos in the lounge lay in a blood-splattered sprawl, frozen in a last act of self-defence. Stab wounds had turned her white nightgown into a patchwork of crimson blotches, with a quick count tallying at least eight strikes ranging from her neck to her abdomen. The final violence done to her required no imagination—the knife had pierced the girl's left palm and pinned her hand to the right side of her chest where it remained embedded. Trails of brilliant red droplets desecrated the sheets, the carpet, and two trails of bloody morse code adorned the ceiling.

My stomach rebelled, so I looked away. There was no need to examine the girl's corpse any longer—I was certain every tiny detail would return to me in my nightmares. Instead, I tried to distract myself by following Terrell's instructions and scanned the surroundings for anything that seemed out of place. If only I could take before and after photos for Faraday's analysis. Spotting the minute differences would be a perfect task for his powers.

Nothing looked unusual to me. Aside from the dead girl and the carnage, this could have been a textbook photo, if there was such a thing as an advanced course on teen girl bedroom organisation and décor. A pair of boy band posters, an eclectic array of makeup and nail polish containers worshipping at the foot of a mirror leaning against the wall, and a portable speaker connected to a mobile phone was still sending BBC Radio One to unlistening ears.

"Well, we know who did this. Did you see the blood splatter on the one out back? On she pinkie finger's outer edge? Where she gripped the knife overhand? And the two drip a blood either side of she left eyelid?"

I hadn't. Would I ever be a proper detective?

"But we know *why*, eh? Mum out there told uniformed it was she girl's best friend, visitin' from London. When she opened the door to that commotion, the friend was wide-eyed and panicked, and lunged head-first out the window. 'Twas barely open too. It go be real pressure today."

I remained unable to form words and took one last glance at the mutilated girl on the bed. I didn't know it then, but I had already noticed the clue that would lead us to unmask a threat to the entire country.

CHAPTER 4 - NORTHWARD

Faraday

The roar subsided once I donned the helmet Scarlett handed me. "Is this thing on?" I flexed the microphone stalk, so its bulbous metal tip hovered before my lips.

Scarlett's commanding tones sounded as if they were inside my head. "Of course it's working. Let me get Grover settled, and then we can talk."

She cut over to another channel, and I could see her gesturing to Grover, showing him the 5-point restraint, which she buckled up for him before gesturing out the window. Then, with a click, she was back on my frequency.

"Why'd you say Grover would help us if we needed magic? You didn't ask about Higgs—wouldn't you want her?"

Scarlett turned fractionally toward me. "First, Higgs isn't in Middle Ides. We lost sight of her as she got out of range in the Scottish Highlands. And second, let me show you something. Have you seen this device before?"

I wasn't sure how she knew Higgs was away, but the UPDA seemed to have significant snooping capacity. I parked that detail for now and concentrated on the device Scarlett pulled from a khaki satchel stowed beneath the metal struts supporting her seat. It looked like a field radio from the Vietnam War era, modified to contain a modern display screen. Antennae with rugged connectors to the body could flip up from either end, and the clunky olive frame had rubberised handles at each end with a column of four multi-position dials to either side of the vivid screen. Scarlett toggled a power switch protected from accidental knocks by a criss-cross of thin tubing that arched over it.

"This is the UPSCALE. It stands for 'unusual powers scanner and learner'. As co-inventor, your father named it."

"He made this? Doesn't seem like his kind of thing."

Scarlett chuckled. "That's a polite way to put it. He didn't invent the device itself—you'll meet that man shortly. But he developed its most specialised capability, the part that detects and learns how to assess magic. Look, Templeton's creation is this section here."

She turned the UPSCALE side-on, revealing a section with controls quite unlike those on its face. A rectangular patch of what looked like grey fur abutted a second rectangular area made from slate. A smooth hole drilled into a weathered molar the size of a wine cork allowed it to travel up and down the device's side, brushing against the slate or fur as it moved. An inscribed strip of gold-coloured metal indicated positions along the run of the massive tooth's path, but not in any language I could identify.

"And the funniest part? Here's what powers the magic detection." Scarlett flicked a stubby clasp, and the slate section popped open to reveal a claustrophobic compartment beneath. A gnarled whorl of unpeeled ginger root hid within, impaled on a delicate silver spike.

"I have no idea how it works, but we have to replace the ginger every three months, or the magic detector stops working."

My intrigue must have been palpable. Scarlett handed me the device, and I inspected it. The high-tech screen worked intuitively, in similar fashion to a smartphone. Navigation was straightforward, using one finger, with the other hand reserved for clutching the handle to balance the device's bulk.

"Use this menu *here* to switch from magic learning mode into nano-detection mode," Scarlett said. The screen showed a map, with a tiny X moving across the rough and hilly terrain north of Middle Ides. "Scoot down to London, and you can see some hot spots of nano activity in East London."

Indeed, I could. Zooming in, there were patches of graduated red over Hackney and the Isle of Dogs. Only a fog, though—when I zoomed way in, I didn't see any higher level of detail than the most vivid red illuminating a cluster of 3 or 4 streets in each region.

"Wow. How does it work?" I asked.

"We have nanotech discovery enabled on most CCTV cameras in the country now. A little mist of nano-hunting devices circles each camera, reporting any nano in the vicinity. Look at Edinburgh."

I zoomed out and panned north until I could see the city on the map. Then I zoomed in again.

"See that intense patch there? That's where we're headed today: Caledonian Nanotech. The guy who invented this part of the UPSCALE runs his business from an office there, tucked close behind the castle. He's always testing his creations. It's not strictly illegal; the laws on nanotech are so far behind the curve it's embarrassing."

"And what about the magic detection?" I toggled the switch and navigated 3 menus to activate a distinct style of map on the toughened display. Various indecipherable sigils hovered over different parts of the UK.

"It's somewhat imprecise. That's where the *learner* part in the name comes in. Templeton told me he catalogued only a fraction of the magical powers that we know exist, and the device could detect the ones he catalogued. Once detected, this little patch of goatskin can track the source of magic from several hundred miles away. That part works amazingly well. Higgs shows up as a golden tree, normally. But it's not finding her right now. This part of the UPSCALE is temperamental compared to our nanotech intelligence database. But look, it's working for our friend here," she said, motioning toward Grover. Our location showed a circular green icon containing a trio of animals—horse, dog, and fish.

"Sounds like Dad programmed in a bunch of his knowledge. But I don't get what that has to do with learning."

"Right—if you move the walrus tooth away from the goatskin and tap it on the slate seven times, if magic is being exercised very close to you, the thing can learn about the new magic, and then track it."

"As long as you have fresh ginger, I guess." I smiled slightly, the first time anything resembling happiness had crept into my consciousness when thoughts of Scarlett Thorisdottir were front and centre.

"But hang on. Why did you say Higgs disappeared? The UPSCALE can't track her?"

"Yeah, it's odd. I'm guessing you sent the anti-tracking device with her, so we can't—"

I cut her off, clipping my words, "Of course I did. We don't want your snoopy little people-tracker following us around!"

She turned her head fully toward me and glared but held her temper. "We can't track you *that way*. But with Higgs, the UPSCALE can always see where she is. And her sigil glows slightly when she practices magic. But if you scroll back through the history of her movements—wind back the timescale, there, two days, and then click on that little gold tree over your house—you can see that it tracked her up into Scotland but then winked out early this morning."

I rolled the timeline back and forth, following her trip up the motorway and then the slower drive to the glen's head. "Well, that's Glen Ghuil, where she planned to camp. It could detect her all the way up there, so it seems strange it lost track of her. Maybe she went further up the loch, and she's too far out of range now."

Scarlett let me fiddle with the UPSCALE until I got familiar with its controls. There may have been more ways to manipulate the magic detection system than she let on—there was nothing intuitive about sliding a walrus tooth across goat fur and slate—but I committed its range of movements and its odd inscriptions to memory. As I handed it back to her, my simmering fury toward her resurfaced.

"Tell me again how it wasn't you, or the UPDA, that sabotaged my father's car and then tried to kill me."

Her helmet shook slowly from side to side as she turned to face me once again. "Faraday, Faraday, come on. Templeton was a good friend, and I have absolutely no reason to kill you. We're a government agency, not some band of rogue assassins."

"I know my father was on his way to the Feynman Centre because he suspected foul play in Mum's death. And Newton and I know there were UPDA visitors on-site at the time of her death. You aren't telling the truth."

I wondered if I could push her out through the helicopter door. It would be a bit of a challenge to release her 5-point harness, but then I'd have to open the sliding door and push her past Grover. It seemed unlikely, but I considered it further.

"Give me a chance to prove it wasn't me. I'll grant you left an unpleasant taste in my mouth—along with a welt—last time we met, so I avoided putting much credence in your angry stories. But tell me what you discovered, and give me a chance to find out what *really* happened," she said.

And she was right. Hard evidence of what really happened was the only way I could ever release her from my accusations. I described what I knew about Mum and Dad's deaths, the jeep sabotage that nearly killed me, and the attack on Higgs and Newton by the mechanical dragonflies. I kept a few things back of course, that I could use later to verify her evidence, but it took the rest of the two-hour flight before I finished talking.

CHAPTER 5 - BACKTRACK

Higgs

Dot leant a fraction further forward as if that would help her eyesight penetrate the gloom of the water channel leading beneath the castle's foundation. "I swear I saw something in that tunnel."

"Me too. A little blue guy? Weird looking?"

"Exactly. But as soon as I looked in there, he disappeared."

We both surveyed the tunnel. Shaded by the overhanging slab that formed the foundation of the castle walls rising above, it was hard for our eyes to make out much detail in the gloom's depths. A broad inlet from the shore reached the rocky archway, wide enough to accommodate two rowboats passing. The downward spikes and grate of an ancient portcullis peeked from a slot in the rock above the arch, leaving considerable headroom. Judging by the state of its corrosion, it may have already seen its final raising. Whatever mechanism controlled it was likely well beyond its operational lifetime. But beyond the portcullis, our only impressions were rippling black water, a cool draught of tomblike air, and an uneven footpath skirting the slip. No stunted blue figure.

We inched forward together until we were in shadow. Without the sun in our eyes, we could see the path led further into the gloom, but still no sign of the flickers of movement we had seen earlier.

Dot's voice trembled. "We need to get out of here and find

help. At least we know where Lars is and that he seems safe."

"For now, yes. But something wants us here, although not inside the castle. Look how long the loch is—we're miles from the bus stop. And I don't know if you felt it, but my magic was bursting into action up there at the castle gate, and then suddenly, it bled from me. I've never felt that before."

"Same as during my finding spell back at the campsite," Dot said.

We crept further into the shadows beneath Castle Ghuil, both scanning the passage, but Dot was so jumpy I turned to give her a reassuring nudge. As my head swivelled, I saw it again—the blue figure, beckoning.

I whipped my head back to face the tunnel. Gone again. "He was there. Did you see him?" I pointed to nothingness.

"What? No. I was looking the whole time."

The germ of an idea formed. I eased my head in a lazy swivel and cautiously returned my gaze to Dot's face. There! I could see him again. But this time, I didn't snap around to look directly at him.

I released my words slowly and quietly. "Dot. I can see him again. Right now. But I'm looking away—I can only see him from the corner of my eye."

"He's not there, Higgs. You're scaring me."

I grabbed her hand and squeezed it, lifting our clasped hands up to my chin. "Trust me Dot, he's not threatening us. And his hands are bound in handcuffs. Turn to me slightly until you see him."

Dot jumped back a half step. "Oh lord, Higgs. I can see him. He's just inside the passage."

Resisting the urge to look at him directly, I drank in his appearance as best I could. He looked fully grown but was a twisted, stunted-looking man with an elongated chin and a tuft of thick blue hair, darker than his electric skin tone. His eyebrows were prickly and windswept, matching the rough nature of his sparse clothing. Barefoot with rangy legs and knobbly arms that dangled to his knees, he looked like a twisted, shrunken version of an old man with an incongruously young-looking face. The handcuffs binding his hands together at knee height were unusual. They looked similar to the police handcuffs Newton sometimes carried, but they were as black as space and oddly blurry. It was like they commanded me not to see them, even in the periphery, but my brain jarred me into acknowledging their presence once every few seconds, anyway.

He gestured at us, motioning us into the cave with his shackled hands and spindly, long-nailed fingers.

"I'm okay now, Higgs; let's see what he wants. But go slowly, or I think I'll have a heart attack."

We inched forward together, still holding hands. We faced each other, both for reassurance and to keep him visible. The tiny blue figure retreated ever more slowly into the gloom to crouch, hunched, on the path next to a tethered and worn dory, allowing us to get closer but seeming to signal that he would give us space. Worried to pass the portcullis, lest it come crashing down and trap us in the castle's belly, we stopped a step outside the slot in the slab-strewn path.

Still looking slightly away, I ventured a question. "What do you want?"

He lifted his shackled hands in front of his bare cobalt blue chest and jiggled that still-blurry chain, shrugging the bony points of his shoulders. A clink of heavy metal links accompanied the gesture. Then he raised a finger to his lips before pointing to the rocky ceiling above.

I couldn't resist turning my head to look at him directly, but of course, he disappeared until I returned to peripheral glances.

Dot whispered to him, her grip on me relaxing. "You want us to remove the handcuffs? To free you?"

The tiny blue creature nodded, his blue hair waving oddly as if he was underwater. It parted and reformed lethargically, exposing then re-hiding the rising pinnacles of his ears.

"Come with us. Let's see what we can do."

He shook his head and took a couple of steps forward, gesturing to the slot on the floor where the portcullis would descend if its mechanism worked.

I too whispered, "Oh. You can't leave the castle? They have

you under some sort of restraint?"

Another nod.

"I don't think we can get those cuffs off. We need to find help. But we can't get back to the road that brought us here. Every time we try to go there, it brings us closer to the castle. We're as trapped as you are."

The diminutive thing perked up, telling a story with a series of gestures and expressions. He nodded, raising an eyebrow before tapping his temple. Then he pointed at us, mimicking a walking motion with two narrow fingers. I noticed he had an extra knuckle on each finger, making their spindly length look even more alien.

I kept to my whisper. "Yes, we've tried walking away. We keep reappearing near here."

He held up a palm, paused, pointed both thumbs over his left shoulder, and then repeated the finger-walking while taking quick strides backwards, retreating from us. He repointed over his shoulder to emphasise his point.

Dot chuckled quietly beside me. "Of course. We retrace our steps. Literally stepping back into them. Higgs, let's try it!"

I turned to look directly at where our odd acquaintance should be. Although I couldn't see him now, I figured he could see me. "You're as much a captive here as Lars, but in a different way, aren't you? If we can get out of here, like you say, we'll be back soon. My brother is in the police. He'll know how to get a rescue team out here before you know it."

Dot took my hand, and we both kept the blue man in our peripheral vision as we took a tentative step backwards. Then another. We were still on the path from the sea to the rock below Castle Ghuil. A wide-eyed gaze followed our progress. With raised eyebrows and slight nods, he urged us on. He strode right to the grotto's edge, but no further.

Dot gripped my hand. "If this doesn't work soon, we'll be dipping our heels into the—"

I glanced behind us to see how far away the lapping waves were. Then I shouted.

"Bus stop!"

We were at the road where we had made our first steps into Glen Ghuil yesterday afternoon. The midmorning sun angled across the peaks to the silent pavement of the single-track ribbon.

Our hands parted, and we both pulled out our mobile phones.

"Grr. I forgot to charge mine last night. Totally dead," Dot said.

And my phone was not much more use. It showed two per cent charge, but there was still no signal here. I returned it to airplane mode to save battery.

"The bus comes just twice a day, right?" Dot asked.

I scanned the timetable teetering from the weather-blasted signpost. "Yeah—we've missed the morning one, so it's a long wait until the late afternoon one."

I contemplated walking but couldn't visualise the last house we passed on our way here. There was no habitation in sight as I looked both ways along the snake of the road. We came here for absolute peace, but I wished now for a ribbon of traffic.

Maybe my wishing worked. Not thirty seconds later, the plaintive song of a diesel engine preceded the appearance of a Land Rover over a rise in the road in the middle distance. As it meandered closer, we got a better look. The rugged vehicle that bounced toward us looked like the victim of an attack by a flailing octopus composed of rusty and grime-encrusted chains. The paintwork may have been green at some point but had devolved to a cross between dirty and unsafe-looking.

Dot and I stepped into the road and waved our arms over our heads. The vehicle had no choice but to stop.

As the car wheezed to a halt, a dishevelled nest of hair topping a puzzled face craned through the driver's window. We got our first sight of Ena McTavish. She would prove much less and also much more than we had hoped for.

CHAPTER 6 - CALEDONIAN

Faraday

With reluctance, the twin helicopter rotors slowed as we settled onto the massive letter H on a military helipad. The rocky outcrop holding aloft the castle's regal outline rose above the jumble of grey buildings between us and the city centre. As I scanned a wider arc, I noted a pair of green-topped hills flanking the castle and the Forth Rail Bridge's matte red tips in the distance to the left. We must have landed on the western edge of the city.

We left our helmets on our seats as Scarlett gestured with the hand clutching the UPSCALE, ushering Grover and I toward a waiting car. The downdraft was no longer a hurricane, but it whipped our hair around as if at the whim of a laughing toddler. Even Scarlett's blonde ponytail flitted from one shoulder to the other in a syncopated rhythm.

As the SUV's heavy doors clunked shut, I called my brother to check in. "Hey Newton, we just arrived in Edinburgh, and Scarlett is taking us to visit a nanotechnologist up here. All good."

"Okay, keep updating me. This is all a bit weird, what Scarlett is doing. But you should know, something bad's happened here," Newton said.

"What? It's not Granny, is it?"

"No, no. She's fine. But I had to attend a murder scene today. God, it was horrible."

Newton explained more about the circumstances.

This kind of thing didn't happen in Middle Ides. We left these horrors to Birmingham or London. "Jumped out of a third-storey window? That's terrible!"

Scarlett was mid-buckle in the front passenger seat, but her head jolted to face me at those words. "Hang on—let me talk to Newton."

I glared at her, but her outstretched hand coaxed me out of my hesitation. I passed her my mobile. "Newton? Hi, it's Scarlett. Did you mention to Faraday that a teenage girl was murdered in Middle Ides?"

I heard a few snatches of Newton's voice, but nothing distinct.

"And it was her friend that did it? Are you sure?"

More rumbles from Newton.

"Listen. Keep this quiet, but I have seen seven cases like this over the past two weeks, all in London. We haven't released all the details to the public, but there have been a series of savage attacks by young women on their friends. You may have read about a few of these incidents—they have been in the papers. But what we haven't told the press is that analysis showed nanotech infestation in four of the attackers' brains."

My brain raced. Was this why Scarlett brought me here? She paused for breath while Newton asked something.

"No. They don't remember what happened. They don't remember anything unusual leading up to the violence, just snapping back to reality to face the carnage. And the victims that survived reported the same thing. No arguments, nothing unusual, just a frenzied attack from out of nowhere using whatever was at hand as a weapon."

Newton's volume rose. I could hear him saying he had to tell these details to Terrell.

"No, Newton. You can't tell anyone. Not until I give the okay. But I'll assign some agents from the UPDA who will work through the autopsy process with your chain of command. Let me know if you find anything that could explain what happened, okay?" She paused with a furrowed brow. I counted the passing seconds. Almost 7 elapsed while Scarlett waited. "Come on Newton, give me an okay."

She nodded. "Good. Faraday will call you again in a while."

She returned my phone. I got into the car, and we glided toward the city centre, the driver silent in his sunglasses. Grover pointed out a man on the pavement, strolling in a light windbreaker. "Look. That guy has *three* dogs."

I was less impressed than Grover, but I automatically replied while I considered Scarlett and Newton's conversation. "Yeah, three dogs is unusual. I wonder if they all belong to him."

"I think so," Grover replied. "They're happy." He swivelled in his seat to track them through the rear window as we passed.

Scarlett seemed to anticipate the question forming in my mind. "The man we're about to visit is Angus MacFarland. He's Scotland's finest nanotech expert, but he runs his own company. He's not a researcher like your mother is. Was. Sorry. And I need to ask him some questions about the material we found in these London attacks."

* * *

Our car rattled across the uneven cobblestones of Victoria Street. Its graceful arc of shops and flats towered in multicoloured glory and ultimately obscured the view of the castle walls directly above. We came to a stop outside a red-fronted jeweller's shop.

The location confused me because I had expected to visit an industrial-looking lab building. "Hang here, Zee," Scarlett told the driver. "Angus has an office upstairs," Scarlett said, pointing to a row of large windows above the jeweller's. She turned on the UPSCALE and briefly zoomed in on our current location while in nano mode. "Hmm. Interesting. But nothing too dangerous," she muttered. I wasn't sure if she was speaking to me or trying to reassure herself.

I was already out of the car when she opened the door on Grover's side and clicked his seatbelt release. "Now Grover, we're going to visit my friend Angus for a bit. After that, we'll be going to stay at a hotel. Come with us."

She crossed the pavement and opened a drab door, nondescript other than the small black lettering that read CALEDONIAN NANOTECH. A flight of carpeted stairs beckoned, and I followed in Grover's and Scarlett's footsteps. Before pushing open the door at the summit, Scarlett paused and turned, letting her pointer finger home in on me before saying, "Oh, and Angus has a strange way of speaking. Make sure you don't laugh."

The office beyond the door was larger than expected; a wide expanse of wooden floor seemed almost too vast for the pair of desks and wide oak conference table ringed with high-tech office chairs. The room's three occupants looked up in unison from their conversation.

One sat behind the desk backed by the window. Beyond him lay a direct view across the curved street into someone's kitchen. A short crop of dark, receding hair skimmed his scalp, setting off his pale and pitted complexion. A hawkish nose hung over his unlined mouth. It suggested a habitual expressionlessness that evaded the accumulation of ridges adorning his forehead, giving his eyes a harsh demeanour.

The other two faced him, their heads now turned our way. Although dressed differently—one in a leather jacket and black jeans, the other in a striped shirt topped with a woollen peacoat and loose cotton trousers—they were otherwise identical. Their skin was as dark as shadows at midnight but seemed to glow as if there was a flickering torch lit deep beneath. Long eyelashes capped doe-like eyes and fine cheekbones that threatened to derail the twins' obvious masculinity. Even the length and neatness of their truncated and loosely braided dreadlocks appeared identical, flirting with their broad shoulders.

The two boys remained in their angled half-seated spots on the second desk's edge as the older man rose to his feet, grabbing a pommel-headed walking stick and stepping around his desk. "S-S-S-Scarlett! What're you d-d-doing here? It's been a l-l-l-lang time."

The twins appraised us, moving only their eyes. The man took another two steps toward us, leaning on his stick to support a leg that swung instead of stepping forward.

"Angus. Nice to see you too," Scarlett replied, a chiding twinkle in her voice.

"Ahm s-sorry. That came out a b-bit rudely, didn't it? Good to s-see you."

I thought it strange that Scarlett warned me not to laugh at Angus. Did she really think I would find someone's stutter amusing? But I'd discover shortly, when he stopped stuttering, what she meant.

Scarlett began introductions, saying, "These are my friends, Grover Mann and F—"

She was interrupted as Grover slinked past her, taking his own twisted but quick steps over to Angus.

Angus shrunk back a little at the odd approach from this unfamiliar boy but resumed his stance, leaning on his stick as Grover went to one knee before him. Grover put a hand gently on the knee of Angus's grey trousers for a moment, then looked up, his glasses amplifying his sincerity. "Your leg is hurt too."

The boys to our right shared a glance with the merest eyebrow raises. It seemed they possessed an array of ways to communicate without saying a word or lifting a finger.

"Ah, yes, Grover," Angus said. "She's a b-b-bit crook."

Eyebrows definitely rose when Grover added, "Since you were a little boy. A horse saved you, but your ankle broke."

Angus laughed with a hint of bitterness. "You're right. Horse. It happened when I was a bairn, six years old. These boys here, their ma saved me. But how'd you ken that?"

Grover didn't reply and turned away from Angus, almost as if he became suddenly bored. But he fixated on a new target and stepped over to the boys, who remained in their laid-back positions despite the approach. He grabbed each by a languid, unresisting hand, and they grinned back at him. He looked from one face to another, then back again. "Hi. I'm Grover."

They smiled wider. "I'm Darren," one said. "And he's

Duncan. Nice to meet you, Grover." But then the smiles vanished, and they snatched their hands away from Grover's grasp at almost exactly the same time.

"Oh!" Darren said. Duncan narrowed his eyes and peered at Grover intently. They both shuffled to more erect sitting positions. It was then that I noticed they were not entirely identical. Duncan's left eye matched his brother's hazelnut brown, but his right eye was a blue so light it verged on grey.

There was a brief pause, into which Scarlett continued, "As I was saying, this is my friend Faraday Redferne. Faraday, this is Angus MacFarland, Chief Scientist and owner of Caledonian Nanotech."

The taut line of Angus's mouth broke a little at the corners into what perhaps passed as a smile. "Aye, I see it. I knew your dolphin mother pretty well, and I can see her charm in your face too."

Wait. Dolphin mother? What was he on about? Was that some sort of obscure Scottish slander?

While I puzzled over that, he continued, "Is he into nanotech too? Is Alison here somewhere? I'm guessin' ye're here on some sort ay official UPDA porcupine business. Always happy to solve your nano problems."

I glared at him, further confused about what UPDA porcupine business could be. But was he mocking me about my mother?

"Um, I guess you haven't heard," Scarlett said, lowering her voice. "Alison died. Almost a year ago."

His mouth hung open momentarily. "Och, I'm so sorry, lad. I didnae have a clue. Really, really sorry to hear that. She helped me design *that* tadpole thing, did you ken? And yer father did the real hard work."

I wasn't sure what 'tadpole thing' he could be referring to, but he pointed his walking stick at the UPSCALE in Scarlett's hand.

"That's right. I didn't tell you, Faraday, but Angus is the UPSCALE system's principal designer. He and your mother worked on the signalling and the nano detectors woven into the surveillance systems around the country."

Angus laughed again, his eyes softening as they closed slightly and his lips rising another notch. "Did she show you the ginger? I dissected that part of the handheld buffalo unit three times and couldnae make any sense of it. You'd better fire it up, girl. It's not long before you won't be able to use it in this country. Ye'll be confined to England, else it'll be international espionage."

Scarlett shook her head, still smiling slightly. "As you will no doubt hear at great length, Angus here thinks that Scottish independence is both inevitable and imminent. Me, I don't see any signs he's right. Anyway, Angus, we have some business to discuss. Maybe in private?" She glanced toward Darren and Duncan.

"Nah, they're alright. They work for me and trustworthy. What exactly can I mosquito help you with?"

Grover hobbled back and stood beside me, leaning with the barest of touches against my arm. He continued to regard the twins, pushing his glasses up from their precarious but familiar position at the very end of his nose.

Scarlett alluded to the situation in London, revealing only that a murder suspect was shot and killed by the police and that the autopsy had revealed some unidentified nanotech in her brain. "Look at the schematic here. Maybe you can help me figure out who made it."

She fiddled with the UPSCALE until its vivid screen glowed with a detailed diagram showing the rogue nanotech. I shuffled myself to Angus's side, Grover following me but still watching the twins. He kept his arm touching mine as if magnetised.

Over the last few months, Mum's lab assistant, Iain Vanderkamp, had been working with me most evenings and weekends in a lab concealed at the end of our basement. Using my mother's notes and the secret lab's equipment, I had learnt a lot about her nanotechnology side projects. We developed a prototype of anti-nano-nano, a mist that would detect common forms of nanotech, moving and latching onto it with destructive intent. Scarlett had collected samples of this from

Iain before picking me up. I considered asking if Angus thought it might work against this emerging threat.

Angus, intent on the diagram, moved his face closer to the screen. And I was right there with him. My breathing must have been right in his ear, but he showed no signs of annoyance. The diagram's style was engrossing; the way it illustrated common nano components would be familiar to any scientist in the field. After a good 30-second pause, Angus pointed to an array of interfaces at the illustration's right side. These were connectors—how the tiny technology sensed and interacted with the gargantuan world around it.

"See this interface array here?" Angus said. "They're neurotransmitters, and not dead revealin'. Many labs can produce them, mind. But antelope see what's backing them? Each is fed by its own logic unit. Only the Russians make wee high-density computing like that. You should talk to—"

"Vladishenko! If the Russians are behind this, we're in a whole new world of trouble," Scarlett said. "I really hope you're wrong."

"Och, come on, Scarlett. You come to me because I'm always r-r-right. And you know how much that lot want to s-s-stir up crap here."

"You're calling London 'here' now, are you Angus? See, you're in favour of the British union after all!"

"For now, lass, for now. Anyway—want to see what I've been working on? You should fox come across to the Duddingston lab."

* * *

As we left Angus's office, with a promise to meet him later at his lab, Scarlett scanned herself and us thoroughly with the UPSCALE. An extensible wand touched our shoulders, presumably releasing the same detection nanotech that apparently bathed urban areas across the country. It took 2 minutes and 11 seconds before it reported back.

"Yeah, I've worked with him on several projects, but he's

still a sneaky bugger. I'd rather feel confident that he hasn't planted anything on us."

As we waited for the scan results from Grover to come back, I asked Scarlett about the twins. "Have you met those two before? Angus implied they work for him."

"No. Never seen them. They don't really strike me as nanotechnologists, though. Not like you, who has geek written all over. Sorry! I'll ask Angus what they do when we visit the lab."

"Did you see them recoil, together, when Grover was holding their hands?" I asked.

Grover answered, "Those boys were strange. They said some friendly things at first, but then I saw something."

Although they hadn't said more than 20 words the whole time in Angus's office, Grover often seemed to communicate without a word being spoken. "What did you see?" I asked.

"They only said how they loved each other. Told me about their mother, and how that other man helped them after she helped him. And I saw some weird green and blue and grey stuff. And yellow. It made me a little scared, and I think it frightened those boys too when they saw it. I wished one of my horses was here. And I thought you might want to see your dog, Disco, too, Furry-day, so I talked to her. And I'm hungry."

I still struggled to grasp whatever subliminal communication occurred between Grover and other people or animals. Was there something in his touch? His explanation was always that watching movements, positioning, and behaviour was as good as words for communication, but I boggled at how he might have interpreted those specifics just by the way the twins perched on the desk edge. But he wasn't wrong about me. I had been thinking of our whippet, Disco, probably curled up on a sofa, sniffing the air for a hint of toast or essence of cat. I glanced at Scarlett, who shrugged. "I know a wonderful fish and chips place," she said. She turned to the driver. "Zee, let's grab something at the chippy in Meadowbank. Remember that one? After that, we'll go over to Duddingston to see what Angus has been inventing. Grover, you can tell us about the green, blue, and grey things while we eat."

CHAPTER 7 - DEPARTURES

Disco

I had to run. To protect the pack. Faraday needed me. So did Higgs. How could I escape the house?

I raced around looking for an open window. My claws clicked on the wood floors. Nothing. I saw that the sliding glass door to the back garden was half open, a screen door the only barrier between me and the outdoors. Seven steps backward and a burst of power—the screen bulged and ripped, proving no obstacle. I ran my fastest. Along the drive, then turned right onto the pavement. Since the jeep crashed and I sniffed that tube, I could run faster than any other dog. My ears rippled.

I sped through the town centre, toward the hills. That was the direction I needed to go. A sandwich crust lay at the foot of a hedge, so I paused long enough to swallow it. Then continued. The pavement gave way to gravel as I ran into the hills, dashing along the road's shoulder. My feet fell like a drum roll, and I caught up with a car that ascended the hill beside me.

The passenger rolled down his windows and shouted something to me. I couldn't understand it, but he laughed and laughed before the car pulled away from me, honking. I was alone on the road as it flattened out and headed north across the peaks.

I ran for an hour, two hours. Cars passed, sometimes slowing to look at me. Then I heard cantering hoofbeats and looked up to see a horse ahead of me, heading in the same direction along the road. I sped up a little and caught up. It was a horse I knew from the polo club, a sweaty black mare with a braided mane.

When the horse noticed me, we both slowed to a walking pace. I came to understand that we were going to the same place.

We turned off the main road and cantered for a distance along a gravel track. A blinking deer drank from a tiny stream, hidden in the long grass, so we approached slowly and quenched our thirst. When we continued our journey, the deer ran along with us.

Higgs

Ena McTavish lived in an isolated croft on the southern slope of Glen Ghuil. Marketers could have used her Land Rover in an advertisement for the brand; it looked to have survived every terrain, mud patch, and pothole thrown at it and would continue stubbornly for another twenty years. Despite—or maybe because of—her isolated existence, she waved Dot and I into the car without a second thought.

Her hair would have made Medusa's snakes jealous, questing in every direction. Bushy eyebrows knitted as she took us in. "It's a braw day, but you lassies look as if ye've other things on your mind than the weather hereabouts. Are youse okay?"

I babbled before taking a deep, calming breath. "We're fine. Well, worried, but not hurt or anything. Our friend Lars, though—somebody kidnapped him. We need to get help. To rescue him."

Dot, as ever more practical, interjected, "Hi. I'm Dot Pendlethwaite. We're really glad you stopped to help us."

"Och, hen. Around here, we help each other, nay questions. Let's see if we cannae find some help. I'm Ena McTavish, by the way. Nice to meet you girls." The letter R rippled off her tongue as if the word 'girls' had an extra two syllables.

"Oh, my chattering friend here is Higgs Redferne. Does your phone work here by any chance? Ours are kaput," Dot said.

"Phone? Och, no, I dinnae keep a phone. I'm no even on the phone at my place up there." Ena pointed out her open window to a barely discernible stone building perched among the greens and purples colouring the distant slope. "But there's a pay phone a ways up the road, mind. Let's get you there."

The Land Rover clunked into gear and rattled as it set forth. I didn't bother asking if she had a charging cable. "Sorry to make you stop like that, back there. But we're really worried about our friend. Somebody took him to that castle at the loch's end, and they're holding him there. Three of them—we got close enough to hear them. A man with a gravelly voice, and it sounded like a woman that he was plotting with. And a third... person."

"In Castle Ghuil? Your pal's in there? He's gone too far, this time," Ena said.

Dot jumped in again. "Wait—you know who has Lars?"

"I've kent Ruaridh McRaven since I was a schoolgirl. I never thought he'd kidnap someone. And it's weird that he would capture a Swedish boy, wi' two English girls at hand."

I took a sharp breath through my nostrils as my teeth clenched. "You think he wants to kidnap young girls? What kind of monster is he?"

"No, no, lassie. I didnae mean it that way. Ruaridh's passion isnae women—unless you count Mother Scotland—it's Scottish independence. If he's got a wee plan, I just figured he'd take an English hostage, not some Scandinavian. Weird. He's always writing to the newspapers and yanking the ears of anyone within hailing distance about our heritage and rights. How the Sassenachs don't understand us and never will. He's obsessed."

"What's a Sassenach?" Dot asked. "Sounds like some sort of hill monster."

Ena cackled. "Exactly what Ruaridh might say. Sassenachs *are* monsters, if you consider the English to be monsters. I keep telling him, 'how much more independent are you going to get? I'm already independent, living in this glorious spot'. But he willnae cock an ear to me anymore. In primary school, he was full of joy. He might've tugged on ma ponytail fae the desk behind the odd time, but who's to say I didn't secretly like it? It was only after his parents send him down to a posh Yorkshire school that he soured. Full of piss and vinegar when he came back to do his Highers. It was like a different boy—a charming twelve year old left to be replaced by a moping fifteen year old. Spouting anti-English rubbish and Scottish independence tropes. He probably just missed the Glen something fierce, mind, while he was away. I get antsy if I'm gone even one night."

I flicked my phone in and out of airplane mode as we drove, probably once a minute. It skipped directly from two per cent battery to off, likely to compensate for all those times it remained at one per cent for an hour. I tapped my right heel with rapid abandon as Ena pointed out subtle features of the expansive landscape while we bounced along the uneven road. My scanning for public phone box came to fruition after what seemed like a lifetime but was likely only ten minutes. Ena swung the car to a rumbling stop on the tiny lay-by's gravel.

Dot and I leapt free and crowded into the phone box together, before realising our predicament. A sheepish walk back to the car ended well—without a word spoken. A smiling face topped an extended palm with a smattering of ten and twenty pence pieces.

"Oh my goodness, thank you, thank you," I said before sprinting back to the phone box.

"Wait, can't you call 999 for free?" Dot asked.

"Good point," I replied. "But I'm going to call Newton. He'll know how to get the quickest response. It's not like PC plod can ride his bicycle along the loch and spring Lars free with his billy club. You heard Ms McTavish, this Ruaridh character has some plot up his sleeve. Or his kilt. Wait, it's ringing.

"Newt, it's me."

He sounded surprised. "Higgs? Whose number is this? I didn't recognise it."

"I'm at a pay phone, my mobile is dead."

"Are you okay? You'll never believe what happened here. There's been a murder. A weird one. You may even know her."

"Stop, Newton. I need help. Someone's taken Lars hostage."

I explained the situation at Castle Ghuil, how we eavesdropped on Ruaridh McRaven and some unknown woman, and that we heard Lars, caged. I mentioned Ena's comments about Scottish Independence and how this was politically motivated. But I kept the information about the little blue person and the magic that drew us in and then let us escape to myself. It seemed like something that I could manage instead of bogging Newton down with unnecessary details.

"Why does all the terrible stuff pile up at the same time?" Newton said. "Anyway, listen—here's what we'll do. Did I mention that Faraday is in Edinburgh with Scarlett Thorisdottir? I'm going to call them and let them know. You saw what Scarlett arranged with your science teacher when they claimed he was a terrorist? I never really want to talk to her again, but that's the help we need right now. She can get those wheels moving. They'll be swarming all over Castle Ghuil before you know it. Just get to Edinburgh and meet up with Faraday. I'll feel much better if the two of you are together. Take a taxi if you need to, I can pay it with my credit card. Can you remember an address?"

Dot tugged at my sleeve and moved closer, if that was even possible in the phone box's cramped confines. But I ignored her as I thought about the logistics. "I'm not sure I can get a taxi to grab us way out here, and I'm not sure the woman who picked us up will take us all the way to Edinburgh. She looks like she's seen nothing bigger than a village for years. She said she's headed into town to grab supplies."

"See if you can persuade her. Faraday can give her petrol money or pay her for her time. Maybe that will help. If you can't, get a taxi and call me. I'll pay on our credit card."

Dot was more insistent and hissed in my free ear. "Tell him about the blue guy. You promised!"

My best friend made me realise I was reverting to behaviour that had caused us so much heartache in the past. As a family, we had pledged to keep no more secrets. "Newt, wait. I need to tell you something else. There's magic. And a little blue guy that you can only see in your peripheral vision. I think he's being held captive by Ruaridh too."

* * *

It could barely be called a village, Ena's destination, but it possessed a small shop with an amazing array of goods. It seemed you could get everything from fishing rods to heart medication, and the scent of home baking made Dot and I buy some still-warm miniature meat pies and Coke in glass bottles. We retreated to lean on the Land Rover while Ena McTavish finished her shopping.

"Dot. Do that thing where you can persuade someone to do you a favour. Look—I can see the remnants of a bird's nest wedged between the downspout and the gravel over there."

Although not really under my control, I think my magical ability was much more powerful than Dot's, but she was a better student and accomplished more using the simple techniques that Emeline Grey had been teaching. There was a supposedly simple spell—although I had never been successful with it—that used the remnants of a bird's nest to influence someone's decision-making process. You couldn't make someone do something outrageous, but faced with a choice, it would bend in your favour.

Dot teased some grassy threads from the nest and wound them into the two small circlets that the spell demanded. She overlapped the rings like a magical Venn diagram and placed them on the Land Rover's tire, in the shadow of the wheel well.

Holding one palm over the hand-woven artifacts and closing her eyes, I remembered the sequence of images Dot must be summoning. She would envision a small bird hovering over Ms McTavish's shoulder, making subtle twitterings. I always imagined a hummingbird, but I had never asked Dot what she pictured. Maybe *that* was my problem.

I felt the familiar tingle of nearby magic that had been quashed in Glen Ghuil.

Dot opened her eyes. "It's done. I did a good job, so it should work."

We munched our pies, only now realising how hungry we had become since our last meal yesterday evening. Our gracious rescue driver emerged with four bags of shopping as we drained the dregs from our bottles. Dot swung the rear door open for her so she could relieve herself of her armload of who-knows-what.

After the door clunked shut, Ena turned to us. "Now lassies, no need for all that nonsense," she said, gesturing vaguely to the front wheels. "Ye just have to ask properly. Like I said, around here, we help each other. I wouldn't say 'no questions asked', because we'll need something to blether about during the trip, but where is it you want me to take you?"

CHAPTER 8 - REGENERATION

Faraday

"So what's with all the porcupine, dolphin, and mosquito business?" I remained confused about some of Angus's statements.

"You did a good job of not laughing. I've been part of many disastrous conversations where people reacted poorly. Did you notice him stuttering at first, when we surprised him?" Scarlett said.

"Yeah—he was stumbling, and again for a brief spell in the middle of our conversation, but then it disappeared."

"When he's calm, it's like there is a separate thought stream going on behind the scenes where he's imagining—or at least listing—animals. If he mentions them every once in a while, it holds the stuttering at bay. But when he's startled, his stammer resurfaces."

Grover licked some batter grease from his fingertips. He had been absorbed in surveying the meadows and rocky green peak of Arthur's Seat, the lumpen, scrub-topped hill that graced the sightlines over Edinburgh. Now that our conversation had turned to animals, he swivelled toward us and his eyes focussed on his more immediate surroundings.

"That man, he is always thinking about those horses. I've never seen that kind of horse before," he said. "They were hard to see properly, and they were sort of *green*."

A year ago, I would have glossed over Grover's comments

as impenetrable. Although Disco and I visited him often in the stables at the Middle Ides Polo Club where he groomed and chatted with the horses, I know this sounds like I trivialised him. Maybe I did, a little, although I felt a strong kinship to him. He was adrift in a sea of confusing people and insulated himself in the best way he knew, by retreating to the unjudging company of his animal companions. Similarly, I could shut the world out by focussing on any of my obsessional technical pursuits. For both of us, it was focus that softened the sting of the incomprehensible tempest of life that surrounded us.

After the magical and nanotech attacks against my siblings and me, my mind was more receptive to things a flurry of logic failed to illuminate. Scarlett's comments, and the readings from the UPSCALE, suggested that Grover had a secret reserve of power similar to Higgs. Although I couldn't begin to analyse them, my sister had done things at the gates of the Pendlethwaite estate that stretched my belief in the world which quivered beyond what I could see, touch, or calculate. And if Grover showed some sort of innate magical power, why should my logic ignore it?

Although I wasn't sure what his powers might be, he had a special relationship with animals, apparently shared with Angus. "Grover, how did you see the horse Angus was thinking about?"

As usual, direct questions didn't work very well, and he jumped to another thought. "Wait. Is Disco here yet?"

I tried another tack. "No, Disco's not here. I left her at home. What about those boys—what did you see? You said green, blue, and grey?"

Grover closed one eye and his brow furrowed. He ran his freshly licked fingers through his limp hair. "It was like a long, pointy river. But no canal boats. Remember we went on your boat, Furry-day? There were green hills. On both sides! And a stone house with no roof. And the yellow thing above it. Those boys had been there. They showed me."

It didn't feel like he was making this up, given the fact he seemed surprised at what he saw. "Why did you see that place?"

"I don't know. It was like the stables for me. It seemed important to those boys."

* * *

The driver wore sunglasses, although the slate skies didn't warrant them. Probably some sort of UPDA security staff union rule. Scarlett called him 'Zee' and explained that his anonymising code name was Xenon-12 but that she had always called him by that less formal-sounding moniker. Our drive meandered a circuitous route around Arthur's Seat to a more rural section of Edinburgh. I noticed a drone pacing our car and pointed it out to Scarlett.

"Yeah—it's one of ours. You can never be too cautious. And listen—keep your eyes open when we get inside Angus's lab. I can't say I trust him one hundred per cent, so I'm relying on your experience of nanotech to notice anything unusual. I'll have you watch over the call with Vladishenko too. He's the real slippery one. He enjoys thinking he's toying with me, so arranging a chat is easy."

What a terrible job, where you couldn't trust anyone. I had deep suspicions about Scarlett, and I'm sure she was wary of me. But she seemed wary of everyone.

Agent Zee rolled the car into the cramped forecourt of an unsigned Nissen hut at the periphery of Duddingston village, alongside a new-looking sports car and a pair of identical cruising motorbikes. Although Edinburgh was invisible behind the hill in whose shadow we stood, the hush and countryside here gave no impression of how close the city centre lurked. A tunnel beneath the hill would have made it a 5-minute drive.

"This is the lab?" I asked Scarlett, gesturing toward the Nissen hut. A relic from the last century, Nissen huts had been developed in the First World War as a rapid and cheap way to create a serviceable building for storage and operations. I knew that over 100,000 had appeared in the first war alone, and their design had been copied for Quonset huts in the United States and the larger Romney huts in the UK. This one looked more recent but still several decades old. Shaped like a flipped half-pipe, its corrugated steel arc hulked atop a rectangular concrete pad, like a nightmarish version of a greenhouse. The near end of the semi-circular profile possessed a modern flair, featuring aluminium struts and generous helpings of tinted glass. The door gave no clue as to the purpose of the building, with the stainless steel number 231 its only distinguishing feature.

"Look! A lake!" Grover called.

Beyond a row of hawthorns skirting the Nissen hut's far end, dark ripples on the surface of a small lake reflected the distorted mottling of grey clouds.

A voice cut across our contemplation from across the narrow street behind us. It was Angus's gravel-laden greeting. "That's Duddingston Loch," he said. "I'll show you later. But come over here, there's someone I want to introduce you to, Scarlett."

He beckoned us across, and we crossed the traffic-free street without a glance in either direction, it was so quiet. "This is where Duncan and Darren live. But you've never pigeon met their mother, Delladonna, have you?"

"I don't believe I've had the pleasure," Scarlett replied.

Angus unlatched the gate, and we ducked under a bower of flowering branches to reach the sheltered door to an ancient cottage.

The iron-bound thick wooden door opened a sliver before it flung wide to reveal a memorable woman. Delladonna Donnelly was lighter skinned than her sons and far more imposing. Springs of grey hair with flecks of charcoal descended to frame her strong cheekbones and tall forehead. Her broad shoulders and impression of practised strength were a contrast to the boys' lither frames. She roared upon seeing us, and her lips parted to produce a gleaming smile.

"My word, Angus. You look like a wee cranky troll next to this one! You must be Scarlett, although your boy Angus never telt me how bonnie you were."

Scarlett managed a full facial smile in return, and I realised this was a first for me, seeing any kind of cheerful expression cross her face. "And you, of course, are Delladonna. You know, where I'm from, trolls are a lot hairier, much taller, and, if you can believe it, even grumpier than Angus."

They both laughed. "And that's a fabulous name you have—Delladonna Donnelly. Did you pick a husband just so you could sound like you're a movie star?"

With eyes crinkling at the corners and her hair rippling with fine movement, Delladonna answered, "Child! Nae husband aroun' here. My mamma claims sole responsibility for my name. And I can but *dream* of being a movie star."

The round of introductions extended to Grover and me. We nodded and smiled, unable to squeeze in close enough for a handshake, although I'm not sure Grover was a handshaking kind of person. He studied his shoes for a cue.

The cottage was ancient and seemed to have been knocked onto a slight slant as if nudged by an aggressive neighbouring house in the unknowable past. Although I'm hardly that tall, I had to duck crossing the threshold into the front room, dense with eye-boggling contents. I tried to picture all 6-foot-7 of our friend Chronos squeezing into this place.

As I edged past Delladonna, she patted me on the shoulder and said, "You look a clever young thing to me. But ken what might make you cleverer? Some tea and cakes. Settle yourself over there, and the boys will rustle you up some. You look like a two sugar man to me, am I right?"

It was 1½, but I nodded acknowledgement and sat in the leather-bound wing-back chair she indicated. I glanced around the room, taking in only a fraction of the sights. A soot-stained, wide hearth featured a mantelpiece formed from a broad and darkened beam, the basis for two strata of framed photographs, carved animal figures, and odd human figures formed from entwined twigs. The twins manoeuvred in the kitchen beyond, where I heard the strained whistle of a kettle boiling and the clink of cups. A settee and three upholstered chairs ambushed a low pedestal table carved from a tree stump. My eyes could not settle; everywhere I looked lay intriguing items. One windowless wall was obscured by 37 framed portraits and illustrations. An army of thimbles arrayed haphazardly on a narrow shelf competed for the finest colour, size, or shape. There were at least 60 of them, and I had to restrain myself from taking an accurate count. The panels beneath the chair rail featured inscriptions, wall to wall, with indecipherable symbols. And no room that can conceal a piano for long, but it was some time before I noticed an upright peeking from behind the settee under a round window, criss-crossed with armatures and positioned unusually high on the wall. I packed the images from every glance into my memory so I could ponder them later.

When I looked back to Delladonna, she had Grover's hand clasped between her palms. Like Duncan and Darren, she too seemed to suffer a jolt at the contact, but her response was different. Instead of recoiling, she smiled more deeply and grasped a little tighter. "Child, yes! I see what the boys meant. There's a light in there."

Grover smiled back. "Oh, now I see the horse, proper. I get it."

"Sit down, sit down," she tutted. "You can see that? When we saved Angus?"

Grover nodded. Angus rolled his eyes. "Is it s-s-story time again?" he asked, shaking his head.

We settled in the various seats as tea-making sounds drifted from the kitchen.

"It was just over there," Delladonna began. "Angus was a bairn, only six, and lived 'round the bend in the village. I watched him fae the yard, dawdlin' along in the distance. He was tossin' a thingme up in the air that glittered in the sunlight."

"It was me da's hip flask. I wasnae supposed to play with it, let alone falcon juggle it," Angus said.

Delladonna continued. "And then these two rough-lookin' teens scarpered up to him and snatched it, mid-air. They made him jump for it but kept it just out of reach. One took a few runnin' steps and cast it into the loch before walkin' away, laughing.

"I watched Angus run to the loch's edge, greetin', tears streamin' down his cheeks. He chucked off his shoes and dived in, shorts, shirt, and all. I felt sorry for him and then alarmed when he didnae come up."

"It's deeper than you'd think," Angus added.

Delladonna looked toward her feet as if it helped the memories flow. "I was quicker then, and a much better swimmer. I didnae hesitate, and sprinted across to save him. The sun was bright, and I saw him, flask in hand, tryin' to surface, but his foot was stuck. I dived in."

Angus scowled. "Mind, I can see those boys' faces still— especially the yin ma big brother punched so octopus hard in the nose he sported a black eye for two weeks. But I cannae mind much about being in the loch."

"I swam down to him. Three hard strokes. It was pure Baltic, despite the sun. A pair of mossy rocks pinned his ankle. I don't know how he got it trapped, but he was panickin'. And I couldnae get a good grip on the slick stanes. They were probably too heavy for me, even if they werenae so slippery. Angus went limp, and a cloud of bubbles escaped his lips. But he still gripped the flask.

"I was drained of breath myself, but this little kid made me angry. 'Leave the stupid flask. That's what got you into this bother,' I thought. I ripped it from his fingers and chucked it behind me, giving his arm one last tug before I had to go up for air. It was no use. He was well and truly wedged."

Angus spread his arms wide. "Okay kids, up to now, it's possum believable. I'm nae so convinced about the next part."

"Angus, you were out of it," Delladonna said. "Listen, here's what I saw as I flutter-kicked my way to the surface, still looking down on the trapped boy. The glitter of the flask's descent was in the corner of my eye, and water and bubbles surged fae that direction."

"The horse!" Grover said, nodding.

"Yes! Around here, they're kent as *kelpies*. Water horses. It moved effortlessly through the water and pried a slimy rock away fae Angus with a massive hoof before nudging him to the surface. I swear it buried the flask as I dragged your lad Angus to the shore. I didnae ken anything about lifesaving, but I flipped him onto his stomach and whacked him on the back a few times before he coughed up a lung load of water and started greetin' again."

"We never found the flask either," Angus said. "My brothers dived for it, right squirrel where Delladonna said I was wedged, but nae trace. And I didnae fancy telling me da a kelpie took it, so my brother covered for me. Said he borrowed an' lost it. Took a couple ay lashes for that, he did. Whatever happened, I would have drowned across the road if it hadn't been for you, my saviour."

Delladonna's spirals of hair rippled as she nodded slightly and beamed at Angus. "Och, think nothing of it. Ye've repaid me ten times over the years, and if it weren't for the jobs you give my babies—well, eighteen-year-old babies—they'd be stuck here with me on permanent tea-making duty."

On cue, one swooped in with a metallic tray lined with tea mugs and a typical assortment of Scottish welcome—slices and cakes laced with enough sugar to power an ant colony for a month. I looked at his eyes to see if it was Duncan or Darren, but if it was the former, the dim lighting shrouded his blue eye.

We sipped and chatted, with Angus slipping in a few barbs about the English and how Scottish separation would come quicker than we thought, with the current European upheaval. The twins were warmer than on our first encounter, and we had a side conversation about drone piloting, their part in conducting Angus's experiments. In hushed but excited tones, they recalled a course at a specialist drone pilot school in Manchester. They described their techniques for negotiating tight spaces, and I took their Insta handles so I could get the course details later. It sounded like something I needed to investigate, especially as it was so close to home.

They were so softly spoken I swear they could have a conversation in a library and nobody else would hear more than a hum. Their gentle laughter shared expressions of stifled amusement, expressed without parting their lips.

* * *

Angus described his latest technology as he unlocked the door to the Nissen hut and flicked a switch to light a bank of fluorescent bulbs that ran the length of the ceiling's arc in the open-plan space.

"I call it *reconstructium*. I program the nano units wi' a specific three-dimensional shape, and they work together to ~~sheep~~ reconstruct the thingme if it gets damaged or deteriorates. Come see."

Many questions popped into my mind, but I asked only one before seeing the tech in action. "What's the replacement material it produces to make the repairs?"

"A-ha, Faraday! You have your mother's quick thinkin'. That was the hardest part—figuring oot how to fabricate without expending too much ~~parakeet~~ energy. Also, it has to build itself literally out of thin air."

"Ah—something carbon-based? You pull carbon from the atmosphere?"

"Bingo! It was diabolical to balance how much energy the nano units could gather and the material they could build. I settled on ~~worm~~ a hybrid of solar and kinetic absorption to power them, so the material works outdoors or for any object that gets moved around. Same principle as a self-winding wristwatch being powered by the wearer's arm movements. Not a great idea to rely on sunshine alone if ye're Scots. And the material they spew out is a carbon fibre mesh. Watch this."

Angus lifted a coffee mug made from what looked like hard plastic of an oddly indescribable neutral colour. He raised a cordless drill from the lab desk beside the mug and drilled a hole in its side the diameter of a pencil. I was expecting to have to wait a half-hour for the nano to complete its mission, but it worked with remarkable speed. The hole shrank and disappeared, leaving not so much as a blemish within 4 seconds.

All I could manage was, "Huh!"

Angus grinned as all three of us stood in stunned silence. Scarlett picked up the mug and scrutinised it. "Want to see something even better?" Angus asked.

He held out his open palm, and Scarlett returned the mug. Angus switched tools, using a reciprocating saw's juddering blade to sever the handle from the mug. He lay the two pieces on the worktop.

"This will take much orangutan longer, but watch it start."

I leant forward, my nose inches from the mug. I could see the handle's stub slowly building up and extending. It would take a few minutes, but the mug was regenerating a new handle. Glancing at the severed handle, it too was growing, but tentatively, almost imperceptibly.

"That'll take about six hours to rebuild," Angus said, gesturing at the handle. "The mug will reconstruct its own handle in about twenty minutes. And afore you ask, there's a critical mass of nano units needed. They can't rebuild themselves, and it takes at least ten per kangaroo cent of the set to 'remember' the original shape."

That made sense to me. Nano elements were too tiny to hold much computing power individually, so you needed a matrix of them combined into a computational substrate to do anything beyond rudimentary actions. "So the new mug that gets built from the handle—if you slice it in half, there won't be enough nano remaining to rebuild either part, right?"

"Aye. Got it in one."

Scarlett had jumped ahead of us. "Angus, this is revolutionary. There are so many applications for this. It's unbelievable. You could ship one item made from this stuff, and they could slice it in four pieces at the destination to make four identical copies. If you built a bridge or a building, it would last forever, with no maintenance."

He lowered his chin, shook his head, and looked at her from beneath his eyebrows. "All those things are true, but it's incredibly dear to make the nano units." He picked up the handle and positioned it next to the mug's reforming part.

"Here's the sad part—if I didn't reunite these two butterfly pieces, it'd cost fifty-K to build a new mug for my next demo. My backers are considering speciality uses only."

* * *

We drove only a short way up the road before Scarlett turned to Grover. "Do you want to look at the loch? Where Delladonna said Angus nearly drowned?"

He was staring in that direction out the window and nodded without turning. The three of us made for an odd group, tottering on the small rocks at the edge of Duddingston Loch. "It was right over there." Grover pointed. "But I've never seen a horse go under water before. They don't like getting wet heads. Weird."

My phone rang. It was Newton's number. "Sorry, sorry, brother, I got caught up looking at some amazing nanotech. I should have checked in."

"Nevermind," he said. "Listen, Higgs has a problem. We're going to need some help from Scarlett. Can you switch to speakerphone so she can hear?"

"Give me a sec." I motioned Scarlett back to the idling car where we could escape the wind. "Okay, you're on speakerphone now. Is Higgs okay?"

"Yeah. It's Lars. Is Scarlett on?"

"I'm here, Newton, what's occurring?"

"Higgs's Swedish friend you met in Middle Ides, Lars Janssen? He was camping with Higgs and Dot Pendlethwaite, and they've captured him. Some Scottish independence zealot named McRaven. Ruaridh McRaven."

"Damn. NaCTSO—Counter Terrorism—has been monitoring him. It's not strictly my department because there is no *unusual power* involved, but they believe him to be the leader of an extremist separatist group nicknamed the Tartantula. They have an amateurish banner and everything, featuring an eight-legged tartan spider superimposed on the Scottish flag. They plaster it around Scottish towns, agitating for action. He's only been inciting separatist angst so far. I didn't know he was plotting anything as daft as a kidnapping. And why Lars?"

Newton's voice crackled as static intruded. I looked out the window to the loch's edge where Grover had waded in. Scarlett nudged Zee and pointed, making him hustle from his seat to the loch's edge, ready to help if Grover did anything foolish.

"I need you to get your friends to help," Newton said. "You owe us one for keeping quiet after that stunt with Higgs's science teacher. We both know he did nothing."

I had almost submerged my active suspicion of Scarlett while engaged in the nanotech puzzles thrown around in today's investigations, but as her tone hardened, my bitterness flooded back. Her words emerged clipped, exposing her Icelandic roots. "I owe you nothing," she said. "But I will still help because we need to nail this guy, and I'm not a big fan of kidnapping. Where's Higgs now? What do you know?"

"She's on her way to Edinburgh from Glen Ghuil, but she has no phone. That's where they're holding Lars, apparently."

"Who are *they*? How many?"

"Higgs and Dot didn't see them; they only heard voices. One was this McRaven character—the woman who's driving them confirmed that. They also heard another woman's voice talking to Lars, who is in a cage. Sounded Scandinavian. They said something about the Pentland Hills, Ferndale, and some kind of prophecy."

Scarlett exhaled sharply. "Scandinavian woman? Prophecy? It better not be her," she muttered. "I warned her not to stick her beak into things like this."

Then she spoke in a decisive tone. "Okay, I'm on it. I'll start organising NaCTSO now. We can finalise the plan as soon as Higgs gets in contact. Call us again if she calls you."

I was going to say more, but Scarlett pushed the button to end the call. "You kids are trouble magnets."

Grover was still knee-deep in the loch, not moving. He bent at the waist and rinsed his hands in the dark water before he turned and ambled his way back toward us, wiping his palms dry on his jeans.

Before he and Zee reached the car, Scarlett looked up from her rapid typing on her phone and switched topics. "I noticed those Donnelly boys have been to London a few times. Did you see the stack of youth rail tickets at one end of the piano keyboard?"

I nodded. "Yeah. Eight trips each."

"You counted thirty-two tickets just by looking at them sitting there?

"Well, yeah. I couldn't help but count them."

"I could only see the top one. It was from last week. How do you know they were eight round trips for two people?"

I reached into my back pocket, smiling. "They looked interesting, especially after what you told Newton about the incidents in London, so I didn't only count them—I also snagged them."

CHAPTER 9 - SHREDDER

Newton

"Disco?"

It was unusual that she didn't skitter out to greet me. Normally the key in the lock would alert her, and she would wait to pounce. Since the nanotechnology spill had given her legs some extra spring, her leaps were spectacular, and she had launched from the kitchen to my waiting arms at the front door more than once.

"Where are you, Disco?"

Damn. I saw the ripped back door screen, making plain her escape. A cursory peer around the back garden revealed no sign of our dog. Maybe she was visiting her neighbourhood friend, Antoinette, the French bulldog. With little optimism, I called her name a few times into the dappled garden shadows. Nothing. She had escaped many times before and always returned on her own, so I pushed the residual worry to the background.

An incoming text message distracted me. It was from our family friend Alan Ryder, a local business mogul and president of the Middle Ides Polo Club. He mentioned that one of his polo ponies was missing. Looked like it had broken out of its stable with a few well-placed kicks. Odd. I texted a quick reply and made a mental note to call him later; this seemed like both police and personal business.

A jagged, carved slice of leftover lasagne would do for lunch, and I thought of Higgs and her magical training while I waited the three minutes for the microwave to ping.

It had taken several rounds of frank discussions for Higgs to realise the stork-masked member of the Drowned Cabal was her history teacher—and now my girlfriend—Emeline Grey. That blackheart Beauregarde bore the responsibility for the deep-seated grudge against our family. Even though Emeline had been a part of the cabal, it proved easier than we all expected for Emeline's heart to shine enough for us all to forgive her for not noticing Beauregarde's bleak intenetions earlier. Heck, even Dot was technically part of the cabal, and Higgs's friendship with her never wavered.

Although the practice of magic was a secret undertaking, when confronted, Emeline had freely admitted that she belonged to the cabal of local witches focussed on preserving the natural environment. Their leader, Beauregarde Device, had taken things to extremes and let an ancient family grudge overtake his feelings toward us. Although his actions had nearly killed us, Emeline was so different from him and so offended that things got out of hand that it was easy to accept her apology. Our grandmother vouched for her too, which settled our decision. It was a natural progression that Emeline should use her experience in the magical arts to train Higgs and Dot.

The lessons took place at Pendlethwaite House, or often in our back garden. I tagged along to each one, interested in this hitherto unseen world and my sister's fledgling powers. Occasionally, Lars and I would try to join in, but neither of us had an ounce of aptitude. We formed our own non-magical cabal and enjoyed watching whatever magic the girls could muster.

Dot had some prior training from the erstwhile cabal, and she seemed a better student. Rigorous and graceful, she could muster enough power to make most simple spells work. A cloud of butterflies materialised, a self-excavating hole in the garden appeared, gusts of wind were directed here and there, and other minor miracles whisked in on the back of odd gestures and arcane weaving of natural materials. Many spells seemed to need a physical trigger.

Higgs was the opposite. Multiple sessions ended with her frustrated, unable to latch onto any of Emeline's teachings. Compared to the magic that turned her into a vengeful tree at the gates of the Pendlethwaite estate, the powers in these lessons were trivial. Even Higgs's unconscious magic that repelled the array of mechanical dragonflies in our yard was more than Dot could accomplish. Occasionally, my sister got so frustrated that magic erupted untaught and unexpected. The ashes from a wooden deck chair, incinerated at her fingertips, were evidence of one such episode. And a family of bright pink and nearly weightless hedgehogs roamed somewhere in the neighbourhood after a failed attempt at a location spell to find a teacup that Emeline had hidden in the garden. Emeline told Higgs her magic would emerge on its own timeline and in its own form, but that failed to please my impatient sister.

I wish I had seen her in full fury at the gates of Pendlethwaite House. Faraday described it several times, but my back had been turned to Higgs's transformation during the battle against Beauregarde. But in my moment of deepest need, it seemed like *I* had performed some magic of my own, stemming the torrent of blood from my best friend Chronos's injured leg and saving his life. Emeline told me it was possible I had latent magic. But when we discussed the incident with my grandmother, she said, "Don't be silly, Newton. That was the feeling of Higgs working *through* you. But you are a more important part of her magic than you realize. You need to keep supporting her."

I wasn't sure what that meant at the time, but I made it a priority to be there during the girls' lessons.

The microwave chimed, and I retrieved my plate, shifting it between hands en route to the table to avoid singeing my fingers. I hacked away at the lasagne with the edge of my fork and contemplated the pile of unopened mail before me. It was all addressed to one or the other of my dead parents, and it was a painful reminder of our loss. I shuffled through, ejecting anything that looked like junk mail. That pile would be discarded, unopened. There were bills I knew I should switch to my name that I also knew I would just pay and see another next month still bearing my mother's name. A personal letter to my father invited him to the Romanian ambassador's autumn party. Maybe I could go in his place—it sounded intriguing. As I reached the bottom of the pile, a couriered envelope caught my attention. My mother received other similar items from time to time, even now, but this one stood out because of current events. The return address was in Edinburgh.

The strip of perforated cardboard curled from the envelope as I tore it, and I unfolded the letter within. It was from a Mr Angus MacFarland of Caledonian Nanotechnology, and dated almost three months ago. I made a mental promise to keep on top of the post.

Dearest Alison,

It has been a while, too long really, since we have had any communication. After all that collaboration on the UPSCALE, it seems we've both been busy on our own projects.

I was hoping to meet with you sometime soon to discuss a nano problem that's been stumping me. You know how we worried about the UPSCALE mist being disrupted by powerful magnets? Well, I've been working away on that as part of a military/defence development. Any nano that gets deployed to the field by the military can expect hostile action, and right now, a magnetic field would faze the tech I'm working on, even a pretty weak one.

Have you made progress on converting the manufacture of nano units to materials that are neither ferromagnetic nor diamagnetic? I'm struggling to remove copper, nickel, and cobalt from my designs.

Let me know if we can work together again on this. And use a letter. You know what I'm like with email and phone calls. If it's not the Russians eavesdropping, it's our own government's busybodies. I'm sure if we continue progressing our work together, I can put in a friendly word for your Scottish passport when the day comes.

Regards,

Angus

Was this the same guy who Faraday and Scarlett were visiting? I filed the letter in my mind under the heading of 'coincidence'. But I'm a police officer—coincidence normally means there's a connection that will unfold as you learn more.

I put in a quick call to reply to Iain Vanderkamp's earlier text message. He had been my mother's lab director and now topped Dot, Lars, and my friend Chronos as the most frequent visitor to our house. He and Faraday spent endless hours in the small lab that my mother had furnished, sunk beneath our back garden. Coupled with the notes from the other secret lab at the Ides Giant and his knowledge of Mum's work, Iain could carry on with her side investigations, Faraday at his side every step of the way. With his sponge-like memory and attention to detail, my brother was now at the point where he could make suggestions about how to tweak the constant refinement of the lab's nanotech. I left them to it late into most evenings.

"Iain, it's Newton."

"Oh hey, Newt. I was just thinking about you. Do you know what time Faraday wants me to come over?"

"Unbelievably, you might have to take a day off. Faraday has gone on a side trip with our least favourite UPDA agent. There's been a threatening nano outbreak down in London, and they're visiting some specialist in Edinburgh."

"Yeah, I was afraid something like that would happen," Iain said. "Scarlett visited me too, early this morning. She threatened me into handing over the latest tech that Faraday and I have been improving. It makes sense now—we're developing a nano-killer. It's nanotech that seeks and dismantles any other form of nano units. If she's got an uncontrolled nano outbreak, she may need it. I hope it works properly. And I hope Faraday doesn't do anything stupid. He mentions her almost daily, and nothing he says is flattering or repeatable in polite company."

"Interesting. I'm checking in with Faraday regularly because I don't trust that woman as far as Chronos can throw her. And I'm secretly hoping he gets that opportunity. I'll let you know if I get more details and have questions. But I have one question for you now."

"Sure thing. What have you got?"

"We got a letter from a colleague of Mum's from Edinburgh."

"Was it Angus MacFarland? He's a big player in nano and based up there," Iain asked.

"Wow. Yes—him. Do you think that's who Scarlett is visiting?"

"Almost for sure. He's brilliant, with a side order of weird. I've met him twice here at the Feynman Centre."

"Anyway, he wrote to ask Mum about non-magnetic nano. Was that something she worked on?"

"Yeah, that was a big side project of hers," Ian said. "It's now a pet project for Faraday and me. You know that drone we fly in the empty field at the end of your road? It's got a bunch of electromagnets on it, and we use it to corral and test our magnet-resistant nano units. It's a hard problem to solve, but we're inching closer."

I knew that drone well. Buying it had made a noticeable dent in our insurance pay-out, but Higgs and I agreed it was money well spent, based on how much use Faraday got from it.

My phone vibrated, so I pulled it away from my ear to see the screen. "Beauty, Iain. That really helps. Got to jump to another call now. I'll keep you posted."

I didn't wait for his goodbye. Terrell was calling. "Guv. What's up?" I asked.

"Paperwork, mostly," he chuckled. "But I got you more deets about the case. Lewe grab lunch and I go fill you in."

"I had some lasagne. Want me to bring you a portion? We

can sit at a table in the park."

"Sounds delightful," he replied. "I'll grab tins. Oh—and you've been assigned a missin' person case, too. A kid called Grover Mann."

Oh, come on, Scarlett. You snatched him without even using your UPDA powers to smooth things over? She'd probably done this on purpose, pulling some strings to make me deal with this crap.

* * *

I passed Terrell a foil-covered plate and cutlery in exchange for a can of lemonade. "You know, they should really invent some kinda resealable plastic container for takin' the food away from your house. A real big seller," he said, glancing at me through crinkled eyes.

"I get you. But that invention bypassed our house completely. Mum always mumbled something about plastics breaking down in the dishwasher. So it's a real plate for you, my friend."

"Just kicksin. My mother had fits about stuff like that too. If you couldn't sit down with a proper knife, fork, and napkin, it was all barbaric—may her soul rest in peace."

Terrell opened the can and took a sip as the foil crinkled musically and shifted from the plate under the direction of his fork. "You was good at the scene, Redferne," he said. "No matter how many murder scenes you see in movies, it's always shockin' in real life. You know, I was never scared of horror movies, but Auntie Jade told me about Douens when I was about twelve and it give me nightmares ever since."

"What's a Doen," I asked.

"Supposedly, a Douen is the spirit of a child died before bein' baptised. They appear, wearin' wide-brimmed hats, feet twisted backward, and can lead other children away. I still have that nightmare sometimes, and it vexes me every time I see a straw hat."

I nodded, thinking back to some of my most vivid fears. "Your imagination beats any special effects. That's why the scariest movie scenes are thens where you don't quite see what's happening. But yeah, I'll freely admit the crime scene hit me hard."

Our conversation lulled. I tried to figure out what we had missed that might produce a lead. The clink of Terrell's knife on the plate drifted on the slight breeze that roamed the grassy parkland's terrain. The new skate park, festooned with artful graffiti, rose and sank into the lawns close by. We sat across from each other at a picnic table, one of a clutch that offered a little distance from the banked contours and noisy skateboard wheels but sat close enough for parents of younger children to swoop in and tend to skinned knees or bruised elbows. The teenaged skateboarders normally arrived at lunchtime, and the first few rattled up and down the ramps and attempted tricks, grinding along ledges but mostly attempting shin-bruising board flicks. Hard wheels spinning announced the usual assortment of ragged-haired enthusiasts. They were joined by a rarity—two female boarders. Their ponytails, bobbing beneath helmets, contrasted with the typical scraggle. A portable speaker teetered atop one ramp, bathing the area in current hits.

"I'm assemblin' the dossier for Yulia Antonov's murder. It gonna be a lot of work," Terrell said. "And we tryin' to contact Priti Srinathan's parents. That's our girl from the car park who's almost undoubtedly the killer. I'm pretty good with *who* did it, but lord knows I'm strugglin' with the *why*."

Almost involuntarily, I nodded, feeling queasy as the two dead bodies flashed into my mind. "With you. Teenage emotions run hot, but the ferocity there was beyond belief."

"We'll noodle on it, bounce ideas offa each other. That's how murders get solved," he said. "But that's not the interestin' news. I got hits right away from the Met as I searched the crime database. Some similar real violent cases down there in the last few weeks."

I nodded in silence, not wanting to reveal that Scarlett had told me more than Terrell knew already.

"I been goin' over the scene in my mind. But nothing. No

avenues to investigate jumpin' out. I've requested a call with the officers in charge down London. Got to be some sort of connection."

My mouth was halfway open, and my brain was halfway through a strategy for imparting some of Scarlett's information about the nanotech infestations without over-revealing, when a commotion at the skate park interrupted. Panicked shouts and the rhythms of sprinting feet eclipsed the speaker's music. Although Terrell rose into motion, I paused in horror at the tableau before us.

Ponytail flying up behind her, one girl stood straddling her skate partner with her board clenched in both hands over her shoulder. She brought it down again and again, edge first, onto the cracked helmet of her prone victim.

As the first of the other skaters arrived, she snarled wordlessly, swiping her board in a vicious sideways arc, giving them pause. I was up now too, running at full speed toward the scene. Two more sledgehammer blows to the limp girl's lolling head were followed by the crack of a blow to the forearm of the single skater willing to step into the fray.

I was almost there when Terrell left his feet in a rugby tackle that took him and the skateboard-wielding girl beyond the unconscious form sprawled below. They thumped and skidded on the concrete, the animalistic growls continuing despite his fierce grasp pinning the girl to the concrete. Her abandoned board rolled slowly down a nearby ramp.

"I'm calling an ambulance already, sir," one boy hovering over my shoulder said.

My third body of the day was still alive. Her face was a mess of blood and exposed bone, helmet cracked wide enough to reveal her hair. But her breathing was strong, spraying a patina of blood across her shirt and onto the polished concrete. With a quick assessment, I unsnapped her helmet strap and gently turned her onto her side in the recovery position, supporting her head through the manoeuvre. I didn't want her choking on her own blood but was cautious of neck injuries.

The wail of an ambulance sounded from the hospital's

direction as the radio DJ's voice from the speaker cut over the end of a song, a thread of sanity in the chaos before us. I glanced at Terrell, who still clenched the attacker's wrists. Her eyes widened, and she whipped her head around in terror, saying, "What? Who are you? What did you do to Sandra? Somebody call the police."

CHAPTER 10 - RUSSIAN

Faraday

Scarlett never stayed in normal hotels. "It's not safe. Anyone could be watching, even in your room. And they probably are."

In Edinburgh, the UPDA had a safe house. It was in a CCTV black spot. "We wouldn't want anyone using our own surveillance systems against us now, would we? I mean, our systems security team is top-notch, but there are entire nations trying to hack us."

For a so-called black spot, it was a beautiful location. A two-storey flat in Dean Village. Nestled just below the tourist hubbub of the city centre and Princes Street, it backed onto the Water of Leith. The river streamed its way across a bed of rough rocks to the docks and the Firth of Forth 2 ½ miles downstream. A set of 9 steps punctured the street-facing wall, built from stone blocks of varying size, primarily grey but punctuated with whitish and rosy contrasts. The stairway's edging was red brick, some as chunky as footstools, others mere slivers. Steps led to an arched entranceway that sheltered a thick, black-painted door.

The interior was modern and comfortable. An open-plan kitchen, dining table, and lounge greeted us upon entering, and wallpapered corridors led left and right, each with four bedrooms and a bathroom. Grover pried off his shoes at the entrance, not bothering to untie them. He plopped himself on a grey leather sofa. "Can I watch telly?"

Scarlett nodded, gesturing to the remote control on the side table. From her messenger bag, she extracted a laptop and flipped open its lid as she angled herself against the countertop and waited for it to boot.

"Let's see how our rescue raid is firming up," she said. It felt invasive for me to look over her shoulder, so I sidled onto a bar stool on the counter's opposite side and waited for her to continue. Behind me, Grover and Zee were debating whether to watch football or a nature show.

"It's always complicated, arranging something like this, but I have a logistics lead on my team that could get from a prison cell in Eritrea to his flat in London with nothing more than a pencil, a pith helmet, and a bagful of limes. He's made excellent progress, given all the barriers normally thrown up when you try to engage the anti-terrorism mob."

"So they should be able to spring Lars soon?" I asked.

"Depending on your definition of *soon*, yeah. Not tonight because they'll want to do some recon on the castle and plan how to get him out safely. We're also digging into this Ruaridh McRaven character more deeply. He was on the anti-terrorism team's radar, but we want to assess whether he's got any other surprises in store. I'd say tomorrow night or the day after, our team'll be crawling all over that place."

"I expect Higgs will call soon. She'll be able to give more details. She's pretty observant."

"I'm sure she'll have a thing or two to say to me," Scarlett said, adding a subtle eye roll.

No doubt there, I thought. But if I had temporarily put aside my suspicions surrounding the UPDA and Scarlett herself, Higgs could rein herself in now that her friend's life was at stake. Maybe my apprehensions were undeserved. Now that I saw how efficiently Scarlett operated, it seemed like she only aimed for order. The UPDA wasn't some Wild West posse out to sow seeds of discord.

"Let me talk to her first. She'll be eager for immediate action, but I know my sister. She'll settle."

Scarlett nodded. She raised a finger, and I could see her

attention waver as she paused for her own thoughts. Her eyes flicked to the laptop before she closed the lid. "Looks like everything is lining up. Let me make a quick call."

She paced to the bank of double-glazed windows that looked down to the Water of Leith weaving its way along the flats' curving back wall. Her finger skittered through her phone contacts and triggered a call. I could only hear her side of the brief conversation, which annoyed me.

"Ragnhildur? Please don't tell me you're in Scotland."

The thumb and index finger of her free hand skirted her eyebrows, pinching each temple as she listened to the lengthy reply.

"Don't get wrapped up in this. You need to go home."

The next pause was shorter, and Scarlett's hand flew from her forehead, fingertips pressing against the glass of the flat's rear window.

"Listen. No, listen. I'm still your big sister, and I'll still whip your ass if I need to. Don't doubt that."

I could hear a woman's voice at the other end, rising in tone and volume. I couldn't make out the words, but I guessed it was in Icelandic.

"Yeah, you scared me with that when we were kids. But it won't work now, will it? Just leave."

She didn't wait for any further conversation and killed the call. She shook her head, still looking at the phone screen. "Sisters, eh? There's really no controlling them, is there?"

I agreed, but didn't ask the question in my mind. *Why would you want to?*

* * *

It seemed like Scotland had a giant magnet attached to it. Scarlett's next call was to the Russian nanotechnologist, Dmitry Vladishenko, chasing up Angus's suspicions. Scarlett and I huddled in a bedroom, listening to the call on speakerphone, expecting to have the conversation that way, but he surprised Scarlett by mentioning he too was in

Edinburgh. We agreed to meet in 15 minutes at a coffee shop on Rose Street, a short walk from the flat in Dean Village.

Grover and the driver seemed happy with the idea of pizza delivery and a show about rescuing Australian animals from bush fires, so we left them to it and strolled toward the city centre.

"Why'd you bring the laptop and not the UPSCALE?" I asked.

"We're meeting a Russian. Why do you think?"

Obvious. I should have clued into that myself. It was okay for Angus to see it, since he was its inventor, but it made little sense for the UPDA to show their hand to foreign powers if not necessary. I felt a pang of privilege that Scarlett had let me use it, but then mistrust followed. I'd already seen it in the helicopter after the events at Pendlethwaite House, and my parents were its co-inventors. Maybe I was nothing but an annoyance to her, a tool in her kit that she would discard if it proved unhelpful.

As we made the gradual ascent from Dean Village, I asked Scarlett about the call with her sister. "Sorry for eavesdropping, but you have a sister?"

"Half-sister. Ragnhildur. We were never close, but I think she's tied up in something here, so I warned her off," she said.

"Yeah, I heard that part. Kind of made me glad I don't have an older sister. I don't normally take orders well, but at least when it comes from Higgs, it seems like she's looking out for me, not dictating what I can or can't do."

"Ragnhildur has always been a pest. You'll see if you ever meet her. When she was about nine and I was twelve, she snuggled under my duvet with me one Saturday morning. I thought it was cute until I discovered she had brought the carcass of a half-rotten arctic fox with her. She revealed it by slowly thrusting it between us, past the duvet's top edge. I was nose to snout with it before I realised anything unexpected was happening, and I scrambled away so fast I tumbled from the far side of the bed. She flounced off laughing, leaving the disintegrating corpse in my bed."

I didn't know how to respond to that, so I did what I normally do and said nothing. Scarlett offered nothing more, so we walked on, each in our own contemplation instead of conversation.

We wound our way through the surges of diners, drinkers, and tourists along Rose Street, a pedestrian-only laneway lined with restaurants, cafes, and pubs set a half-block back from where Princes Street opened onto the lush Princes Gardens. Our rendezvous point was a tiny coffee shop called Java, The Hut.

"That's him," Scarlett said as we approached. Her slight nod and upward-looking eyes told me everything I needed to know.

If I had to picture a nanotechnologist, I would imagine someone like Iain Vanderkamp: glasses, bushy beard, overweight, that sort of thing. But if someone told me to imagine a Russian, my mental image would lean toward what I saw here. Dmitri was broad-shouldered and tall. Not quite at the same level as our friend Chronos, but I'd guess 6 foot 5 or 6. He had shaved his blond hair almost to the skin on the sides and sported a crisp escarpment on top. But it was his jawline that marked him. Prominent and making his head look squared-off, it could probably have withstood a sledgehammer blow with little more than a quick head shake to recover.

"Let me do the talking," Scarlett hissed as we drew up to him.

Although dwarfed, Scarlett exuded confidence as she extended a hand to the massive Russian. "Dmitri, long time. What a surprise that you are here in Scotland too!"

A long-fingered hand almost engulfed hers, but he gave it an almost tender shake. His lips didn't smile, but his eyes crinkled with a hint of merriment. His voice was a muted boom. "Vacation. Well, sort of—I brought my daughter to see concert tomorrow. She is eleven."

The preparations for the concert had been clearly visible on our walk here. A massive stage had been fabricated at the end of Princes Gardens, directly beneath the castle's commanding presence. The grey stone walls and parapets surveyed the scene, perched majestic on the hilltop above. Lighting stands and columns of speakers flanked the stage. Temporary barricades lined the streets to control access to the main attendee areas along the verdant expanse of lawns that sloped down from street level to the shadow of the Mound and Castle Rock's basalt buttresses. The Scottish band Piping Hot were the boy band of the day, and this was to be a massive homecoming show.

"Of course. I think they call themselves 'pipettes', these young teen fans, right?" Scarlett asked.

"Sadly, yes." Dmitri shook his head, as parents contemplating their children have done for aeons.

"And Dmitri, this is my associate, Faraday. He's working with me on some nanotech issues."

The Russian cracked a slight smile. "Ah. Redferne? I have heard about you from your mother since you were barely walking. She was brilliant scientist, and I feel her loss, so I cannot imagine what it must be like for you. Following in her footsteps, yes?"

I nodded and held out my hand. He shook it with more vigour than Scarlett had received. "Yes, sir. I'm learning."

When I wasn't in the basement lab with Iain, tinkering with our experiments, I pestered Newton to teach me some of his police investigation techniques. I brought some of these to mind, resolving to watch Dmitri for tell-tale gestures, body language, and pupil dilation as Scarlett delicately probed.

"I don't want to take long, with your daughter waiting. You know I can't reveal too much, but we have had an incident involving malicious nanotech. I want to run it past you and see if you might help identify its origin."

The leading statement wasn't innocuous enough to fool the Russian. Dmitri really smiled at this, his lips parting in a near sneer, a V of lines appearing between his eyebrows. "Come now, Scarlett, you cannot think it is Russian tech used in your adopted country. For one thing, we are quite happy to rely on poisoning, not fancy techno attacks. And second, would we really give away our secrets like that? You *know* I have built classes of devices you only dream of, but we hold them in reserve until we need. Think on this. Why would we show our capabilities now?"

I didn't need any police techniques to figure out that Scarlett had been rumbled at the first attempt. She seemed unfazed, though.

"And would I come to you directly if I thought it was your government responsible? You know I'm not that stupid," she said.

Aha! A double bluff. This was a pleasure to watch, knowing the back story and Angus's comments about the unique parts of the nano in question.

"Take a look. Tell me if you see anything unusual." Scarlett flicked open her laptop on the stand-up table outside Java, The Hut. Dmitri and I each took a flank and examined the ultra-magnified scans and diagrams that revealed the offending technology.

"Are you sure you want to show me this?" Dmitri asked but moved closer to the screen. "Already I can see neurotransmitter bristles, so I know these units latch on to nervous system, likely directly in brain."

I rarely took advice to keep quiet seriously, and I chimed in, "For someone who's not responsible for this technology, you sure spotted that quickly. Seems like you might know more about this stuff than you'd like to admit."

This was not following police questioning procedure at all. Newton probably would have jabbed me in the ribs at this point. Scarlett cast me a glance full of daggers.

Dmitri's hand reached behind Scarlett and provided a hearty slap to my back. "I also recognise distributed computing bus, chemical input receptors, and navigational fins. That's because I am expert, smartypants, not some sort of amateur terrorist."

I bristled and couldn't help but respond. "Well, you didn't mention the oxy-powered fuel cell, the hinge design, or the anti-rejection coating materials."

"I could have, but that stuff is boring. I see you have your mother's intensity. And you would get along well in Russia. We don't mess around with politeness either." He laughed.

Scarlett interjected, "So, what do you think?"

Dmitri rattled off a list of conclusions gleaned from this fleeting glance at a few technical cross-sections of the violence-inducing nanotech. "Well, I'd say it's one unit from a nano swarm which can attach to part of subject's brain and induce neural activity on particular trigger. But think on this: there is no radio-frequency input. It is controlled by subject, not outside signal. It is also not airborne, like your country's favoured but primitive tech. None of those drifting and navigation components are present. You'd need to plant it directly on subject."

"All good. But who do you think made it?" Scarlett asked.

"That is not obvious. There are few players competent enough to make units this professional. The distributed computing alone makes this very complicated project. If we had full swarm and reverse engineered computing substrate, that would be good clue. The software would be revealing. But also, many of components are widely used. It's like Frankenstein monster made from well-known pieces with brief hint of genius thrown in. Looks to me maybe Chinese. Have you checked into Xi Li's work at the Guangzhou lab?"

Scarlett clicked the laptop closed and returned it to her bag. "As always, I appreciate your help and directness, Dmitri."

"You too, my friend. I am sure I will have questions for you someday. And don't forget, offer remains open. Also for you, Faraday. If you ever want to come work at properly funded nanotech lab, let me know. We work on stuff you can only dream of—not chained by the restrictions of pencil-pushing government accountants."

I laughed out loud. It was both a ludicrous offer and an appealing one. I probably shouldn't mention being propositioned by a Russian government scientist on my next passport renewal. "Try to enjoy Piping Hot," I said.

"If my girl loves it as much as I think she will, that's enough for me. I packed earplugs."

Scarlett gave a tacit half-wave as we turned. Dmitri nodded once, glancing down, but did not return the gesture.

* * *

As we skirted the concert preparations to the safe house, I asked Scarlett what she thought of Dmitri's help. "Now, let me get this straight. You knew that if you ranged too far from asking him whether it's Russian tech, he'd be suspicious. So you asked him more directly, but without flat out accusing him, because that would make him defensive?"

"Something like that," she said. "With Dmitri, you have to make him feel like he's the smartest one in the room, so I always let him figure something our right at the start of our conversations. And you did a good job making him flex his expertise too, although I daresay that was an accident on your part."

I laughed at my ineptitude and replied with clear sarcasm. "Oh yeah, of course. I planned that all along."

"But I got next to nothing from that encounter," she added. "My guess is that it's not Russian tech, and he's stumped too without further detail and analysis. That part about Xi Li seems like he's trying to deflect us."

"Could he be working with Angus on something? Is that why he's here?" I asked.

"Maybe. There are only a handful of people in the nanotech field he respects, and Angus is one. I really hope he's not in on the reconstructium that Angus is developing. That's a revolutionary material we should foster in the UK, not reveal to a Russian state-sponsored military lab."

Scarlett swiped us into the safe house. Grover and Zee had inexplicably swapped seats and turned from another nature documentary as we entered. Each had a pizza box in his lap and a can of drink close to hand. "Any left for me, Grover?" I asked.

"We got you your own whole pizza, Furry-day! It's in the oven."

We sat in silence, all watching the animals from the emergent layer of a tropical rainforest. I replayed each of Scarlett's conversations I had witnessed throughout the day. She wasn't only powerful because she had the UPDA's resources at her beck and call. She was in charge for a reason— it seemed every smart little thing she did drove toward a goal. I was glad to be on her side for a change.

But then I jostled myself back into the real world. The world where someone had sabotaged both my car and my father's. The world where the security guard at the Feynman Centre had recorded a mysterious UPDA visit on the day my mother died. Added to that was the attack on my brother and sister by a swarm of mechanical dragonflies and Iain Vanderkamp's troubling recent discovery of nanotech activity at Mum's grave.

And the UPDA's lead agent was sitting right here beside me, eating pizza.

CHAPTER 11 - RAGNHILDUR

Higgs

The Land Rover rattled along the motorway toward Edinburgh, seeming to protest the transition from ruts and rocky tracks to smooth tarmac. It reminded me of rides with Dad in his Jeep. No radio to offset the noise of wind whipping past and through. Despite the twinges of loss, a smile crossed my lips.

Dot asked Ena about what happened earlier at the village shop. "How did you know what I was doing with the nest charm?"

Ena laughed—a hearty gut-driven sound verging on a cackle—and glanced past me to where Dot had leant forward as she asked the question. We sat three abreast on the front bench, Dot and I snuggled to the left to give Ena elbow room as she drove. I had to angle my feet into the passenger side footwell to allow Ena to shift gears. "Och, hen. D'ye think we live in the hills peering at our massive telly screens and wasting time on the internet? You need some more practical skills out here, mind. I've seen your sort of skills before."

Dot paused before phrasing her next question. "What about prophecies? Do you think there's something real there?"

"Well, it depends on the prophet. I do like a good prophecy, though. What have you heard?"

"It's weird. The … person who spoke the prophecy said he didn't know what it meant," Dot said.

"Sounds about right. Anyone that claims to be a prophet normally isnae, and they make up a prophecy to further their own ends. Those fake prophets always explain themselves overmuch."

"This prophecy was about Glen Ghuil. Something about a Viking boy, passing beyond your ken, whatever that means, and ended with, *your new nation will be born, unless he touch the Ghuilin's horn.*"

Ena emitted a musical, "Hmm," as she considered this. "'Beyond your ken' means out of reach of your senses."

A memory flashed into my mind from yesterday afternoon. "Hey, Dot. Remember Lars was trying to get close to that shaggy cow and trying to touch its horn?"

"Way ahead of you," she replied. I didn't feel slighted, but proud of my friend's quiet observational powers. She shared that quality with Faraday; maybe that was part of why I liked her so much. "Lars, Viking boy, horn touching, it all fits."

"So you think that's why Ruaridh took your friend?" Ena asked. "It doesnae sound like him, believin' in prophecies."

I jumped in. "He said as much himself. But the woman there with him seemed to believe it. Seemed like he was humouring her, but had bigger things on his mind."

"Aye, that would be Ruaridh. Self-styled saviour of Scotland."

"Let's say the prophecy is real," I said. "What do you think would have happened if Lars had actually got close enough to touch that cow's horn?"

"Who knows? That's the thing about prophecies: they're dead vague. Seems like grabbin' the horn of a highland cow wouldnae do much, but I've seen stranger."

* * *

I was the beneficiary of some additional coins offered from Ena's unused ashtray to make a call to Faraday from a phone box on the outskirts of Edinburgh. It was reassuring to hear him answer; I sniffled, and my voice wavered after I heard his comforting voice.

"I can't believe you're here," I began. "Newton told you about Lars?"

"Yes, of course. Higgs, Higgs, it's okay. I'm here. I'm with Scarlett now, if you can believe it. She's got everything under control. They're planning a rescue mission already."

I took a couple of deep breaths. Faraday Yes, of coursespoke into the void. "Come on, sis. Just get over here. We have pizza." He gave me an address and general directions from his phone's mapping app.

Before I turned to return to the car, I wiped my eyes on my sleeve. Not that I didn't want Dot or Ena to see my tear streaks, but I felt I needed to be strong for Lars.

* * *

Faraday was there at the kerb when Ena brought the car to a shuddering stop that seemed to presage pieces of shrapnel falling from its underside. I nearly pushed Dot out the passenger door in my rush.

He never really hugged me back, but he accepted it. As I clung to his much taller frame, he whispered in my ear, "It's all good, Higgs. Everything is being planned."

I released Faraday. "Do you have any cash? We should give Ena some petrol money. Oh, sorry, this is Ena McTavish. Our saviour."

Ena smiled and offered her hand to Faraday, who reflexively shook it. "Chauffeur, more like," she giggled. "And there's no way I'm taking money. I've told you girls twice already." She gave a vague sweep of an arm behind her. "Maybe not around here, but where I'm from, we help each other. No questions asked."

Dot snorted at that. "Well, maybe a few questions."

"Aye. A few. I guess that's the price. Look—you are sturdy lassies. I can tell this'll turn out okay, and your friend will be back before you know it. I almost expect to see you two out my windae, ridin' up the glen on white horses. Give that

Ruaridh a slice of tongue pie from me too, the big bully."

I couldn't formulate the proper words to thank her. Instead, I proffered, "Can we have a photo with you, to remember your kindness?"

Dot and I flanked her, and Faraday took a photo using his phone since ours remained uncharged.

"I guess I can't send you a copy," I said to Ena. "But here, take this to remind you of today's little adventure. Lars made it for me, and you should have it." I slipped the multicoloured woven cotton band from my wrist and held it out.

She raised an eyebrow but accepted it with a wry smile. "Tell Lars to come by my croft and get it back for you. Best of luck, lassies."

With that, she spun on her heel and urged the Land Rover back into life, waving out the open window as it roared in a semi-circle and headed back to the glens.

Faraday ushered us up the steps to the safe house door and knocked. Before the door fully opened, I could tell by the flash of blonde hair that Scarlett was across the threshold. I was unsure of how I would feel seeing her again, but that uncertainty didn't last long. My teeth clenched, and I breathed hard through my nose. The unproven but disturbing accusations against the UPDA that Faraday and Newton had debated over the last few months flooded into my mind like a firehose plugged directly into my cranium. The vivid sound of mechanical dragonflies attacking filled my ears, a scarring memory, although my uncontrolled magical powers had thwarted them.

"Higgs, Dot, come in," she said. Her tone, as usual, was neutral, but it sounded condescending and over-sweet to my jaded ears.

"Listen, woman. We're only here because you can rescue Lars. After that, I'm done looking at your ugly mug until there's a court case for our parents' deaths."

Although I'm sure she could have, she didn't retort. She paused there, holding the door wide. Dot tugged at the back of my T-shirt sleeve. "Higgs, let's be thankful now. And don't forget, she saved your brothers from those flaming boars outside my house with that electro-net thingy."

That didn't help. I turned to Dot. "Would you be all lovey-dovey with Beauregarde if he had killed your father but spared you? I'd fight anyone to bring my parents back."

Faraday looked baffled, his mouth an open but wordless void. I knew he was as deeply suspicious as anyone, so it puzzled me that he would be in cahoots with Scarlett for any reason.

It was Scarlett that broke the seething deadlock. "Bite the hand that feeds you, Higgs—it's an all you can eat buffet. But you won't stop me from doing the right thing, and that right thing is rescuing your friend. Please come in. It's been a long day for all of us."

I had some fierce internal words with myself. If I dug my heels in now, would it accomplish anything? Could I use my brewing rage to blast Scarlett to smithereens with some sort of primal magic? And if I did, would Lars be safe? I blew a deep breath through pursed lips, and to Dot and Faraday's visible relief, crossed the threshold.

I still struggled to bite my tongue, dreaming up a whole new dictionary of insults to hurl at Scarlett, but as the four of us moved into the luxurious flat's lounge, it took only nine words to switch my mind to a new and less irate track.

"Hi, Furry-day's sister! Did you come with Disco?" Grover Mann sprawled on the settee was an incongruity that neither brother had prepared me for. Dot seemed as surprised as I, saying, "Wait. Grover? What are you doing here?"

Faraday and Grover answered at the same time. "I'll explain in a bit," was my brother's answer, while Grover said, "I came in a helicopter. We saw an underwater horse and had fish and chips."

That didn't really answer the question, but I felt I should answer him. "No, Disco didn't come with me. She's still at home with Newton. But it's nice to see you, Grover."

"You too. She's coming," he said, turning back to the television.

Faraday waved Scarlett, Dot, and I over to the kitchen area, where we spoke in hushed tones, despite the conversation seeming of little interest to Grover or the man Scarlett identified as UPDA agent Zee.

Scarlett referred to her laptop and gave us a summary of the plan to rescue Lars. It sounded well-coordinated, and under normal circumstances, there would have been no doubt that Lars would be back with us in a day or two. But Scarlett obviously didn't know the complete story. I guessed Newton hadn't yet told Scarlett about our jolting trek along the loch and the mysterious handcuffed blue resident of Castle Ghuil.

"Okay, hold on. I should tell you more about who's at the castle," I said.

"Absolutely! That will help the initial recon unit understand what to look for," Scarlett said. She prepared to take notes on her laptop.

Dot tried to start the explanation. "It's not who, really, it's *what*."

"Even better. Did you see if they had weapons or anything else dangerous? How many were there?"

It was time to blurt out our intel. "We heard only one man—this Ruaridh McRaven. And one woman. But there was something else there. We saw him. Or it. A little blue guy. We could only see him if we weren't looking at him."

"Oh gods, they have an—"

I didn't want to halt the story as it was flowing, so I cut Scarlett off. "Let me explain for a second. He seemed like he wasn't really working with the other two; some kind of weird handcuffs shackled him. And there was magic there too. Not my magic, I couldn't summon it, but something tried to prevent us from leaving the glen after they took Lars. And then it tried to stop us from getting into the castle to save him."

Scarlett covered her mouth with one palm, her elbow resting on the countertop. Her tone was neutral and her voice steady, but it lacked all affect. "What's she done? That's an elf. This changes *everything*."

Faraday's nervous laugh sliced through the resulting silence.

"There's no such thing as an elf. What are you talking about?"

Scarlett remained silent, shifting her palm to cover her forehead and eyes. I took up the conversation thread. "We saw him, Faraday. Only like two feet tall and completely blue-skinned. Scarlett—what's happening here?"

She slowly brought her head up, and her eyes darted around, focussing on nothing. I could almost hear the gears inside her head grinding. "Yeah, they're real. But they always keep to themselves. In Iceland, it's considered lucky if you see one in your peripheral vision even once in a lifetime. They keep to themselves. And you thought the magic that erupted from you when facing Beauregarde Device was something special, Higgs? An elf has a hundred times more magic, a thousand times. There's no way we can compete with that."

Dot leant in and asked a question in hushed tones. "But he wasn't working with them willingly. He gave us the clue that helped us escape Glen Ghuil. It doesn't seem like he's helping them. He's a prisoner, like Lars."

Scarlett went paler than usual if that was possible. "That's not how it works. One condition of their magic is that, if imprisoned, they are compelled to follow their captors' orders. They have to follow any instructions given."

"Like not to leave the castle? Or to stop visitors from walking out of the glen?" I asked.

"Maybe," Scarlett replied. "If my sister said not to let people head out of the glen, the elf could take that very explicitly, figuring it was okay for people to *back* out of the glen. So he's still following orders but being literal about it."

I latched on to the little nugget of new information in that answer. "Wait. Your sister? What's she got to do with this?"

"It's got to be her," Scarlett said. "When Newton told me about the Scandinavian woman's voice you overheard at the castle, I was instantly suspicious. And talking to her didn't make me rest any easier.

"But what I don't get is how she's captured an elf. They are notoriously capture-proof. As you noticed, you can't see them if you look at them directly. And they live in the remote wilderness. Plus, they would surely use their magic to escape if captured. The few times that Icelanders have tried to imprison one, the elf summoned magic to disintegrate whatever cage or bonds bound them. They have powerful, earth-oriented aptitudes. In the 1950s, one enterprising chap dropped a thick, reinforced concrete shell over an elf in northern Iceland, and the little blue guy walked through a melted hole in the steel-reinforced wall less than a minute later. I've seen the weathered dome and the ragged hole—it's still there."

"So nobody has ever captured one successfully?" Dot asked.

"Legend has it there has only been one successful attempt. Long ago, in Norway, a family of trolls cornered an elf in a mountain cave, and they all piled on and pinned her down. Trolls are notoriously magic-proof, and the elf gave up trying to escape and asked what they wanted. Her proposition was to use her magic to get them what they desired, and then they would let her free. The family said they wanted their own kingdom to rule. That's when Iceland rose above the waves, and the elf waved goodbye to the troll family as she pushed them out to sea on an enchanted boat."

"I'm struggling to get to grips with my sister seeing an elf, and now you throw in trolls too?" said Faraday. "If this legend is true, you mean elf magic created a whole new country?"

"I told you they were powerful. And a separate country is what Ruaridh wants now. But look, let's be practical. I need to change the plan. We can't handle this like a simple hostage rescue. It's far more dangerous now."

"So what can we do? How do we stop Ruaridh and your sister from commanding the elf to stop whatever we throw against them?" I asked.

"The only way to stop them is to free the elf. I'll send in stealth forces to get more detail. Satellite photos. Drones. Maybe even some special forces units. Even if the elf detects us, if we can keep our actions secret from the humans, we should be okay. Let me get on to the rescue team and brief them on the new requirements. We'll need some more specialised spying kit. But first, let's see if I can squeeze any more information from my *dear* half-sister."

Scarlett retreated, but only to the hallway to make the call. Faraday, Dot, and I remained silent, straining both to hear the conversation and to pretend we weren't eavesdropping.

"Ragn. Hey, come on. What are you really up to?" Scarlett said. The conversation's other end was barely audible.

"Of course, you don't have to tell me anything, but I figured you normally liked to rub my nose in your accomplishments, no matter how crazy they are."

Another burst of words careered down the line. "Yes. I'd like to hear it in person. Where can I meet you?"

A singular noise sounded, coming from the direction of the river overlook beyond the television. It was a cross between the pop of a champagne cork and the thud of a heavy weight dropped on a gym floor. We all turned to look toward the windows. Scarlett approached the window to peer out, saying to her sister, "What do you mean, you're here?"

Looking down toward the pathway fringing the Water of Leith on the near side and its elegant railings, Scarlett hung up the phone. "Jeez—she's right down there. You stay here. All of you. I'll handle her."

Zee was already up and making to follow Scarlett through the flat door. "No. Not even you," she told him. She swapped her mobile phone for the pass card to the front door that lay beside her laptop, and she scampered out to the riverside walkway. The rest of us, including Grover, formed a phalanx at the bank of windows, taking in Ragnhildur Úlfursdottir for the first time. She glanced up briefly at us, then turned her back, leaning over the railing to watch the river's tumbling flow while she awaited her half-sister.

She was dark where Scarlett was fair, shoulder-length brown hair tousled by the breeze. Despite the distance, that one glance was mesmerising. Her eyes were like an infant's brilliant blue with an azure ring around the iris that you rarely see in adults, prominent even at this distance. They topped by densely-packed lashes and brooding dark brows.

This would have been an ideal time to read lips, but we had to guess what transpired. Scarlett approached briskly along the path, shoulders up and palms wide to either side, saying something inaudible to us. Ragnhildur turned almost casually, still resting one elbow on the railing. She said something brief as Scarlett stopped, hand on hips. There was a flurry of words back and forth between them before Ragnhildur beckoned to her sister to come closer. A hug that looked more genuine from her sister's side left Scarlett looking awkward.

Animated gestures punctuated their conversation; Scarlett waved her arms for emphasis while Ragnhildur's less athletic and slighter frame remained self-contained. Faraday's presence over my left shoulder disappeared, and I looked back to see him at the countertop, replacing the protective film on Scarlett's phone. I raised an eyebrow using the internationally accepted *what the hell are you doing?* arch, to which he responded with the light finger flick that silently screamed, *leave me alone, I'll tell you later.* I watched him smooth the film onto the screen and return to watch the interaction below.

Scarlett clearly dismissed her sister with no paltry amount of anger. The back of her hand waved Ragnhildur away. Her half-sister nodded, eyes locked across the two paces separating them. Patting the top of her own head twice, Ragnhildur disappeared. We heard the strange thunk and pop once again.

I had been angry and desperate, but now a chill seeped deep into my bones. These were powers we couldn't hope to fight. If Ragnhildur had the elf at her command, Lars was deeper in danger than we had thought only moments earlier.

CHAPTER 12 - DEATH CLOCK

Faraday

I suspect everyone had trouble sleeping. The beds were amazingly comfy, and the day had been a long one for all of us, but there was a lot to think about. Long after the rest of us had retreated to our rooms, I heard Scarlett taking calls and discussing plans. With the iceberg of Ragnhildur and the captive elf throwing everything off course, she had a lot of moving pieces to out game.

Despite that, everyone was up early the next morning. I had called Newton late the previous night and filled him in, calling again in the morning to reassure him as best I could. Agent Zee had already prepared a deep pot of bubbling oatmeal, and Grover was spooning it up, perched on the window ledge overlooking the river. Between mouthfuls, he spoke to Higgs, who had a general disdain for breakfast but found the inner strength to nibble some toast with marmalade. "Hey, Furry-day's sister—"

"Higgs," she corrected.

"Yeah, Higgs. Like pigs! Hey, Higgs. I heard you. Last night, I heard you. You said your friend was in a cage. That's not fair. He won't like it."

"Yes, our friend Lars. You know him. He's always running around, sometimes barefoot," she said.

"Oh him! I do know him. He's funny. Can I see your hand?"

Higgs shrugged and held out a palm as if Grover was about

to tell her fortune. I don't think she was expecting Grover to clasp it in both of his hands, one on the palm and one below, but she didn't recoil.

Grover was silent for a moment, then looked away at the river. "Yeah, he sounds like he doesn't like it. But he's in that castle. With the yellow flag. Looks like a good place for horse riding. We should help him get out."

Higgs gracefully withdrew her hand as Grover's clasp slackened. "We will help him escape. Scarlett is going to have her people do that. He'll be fine, I think. And you're right, it looks like a nice place for a horse ride, along the sides of the loch. I didn't see any horses there, only cows. Big, hairy cows."

Grover nodded, entranced, still regarding the river. "A horse will be there soon," he said.

Much of what Grover said was confusing, but we would discover this part to be true.

* * *

Scarlett worked silently on her laptop sat at the kitchen island, drinking a cup of scalding black coffee. She seemed not to notice what would scorch any normal person's mouth as she tapped away. I braved surreptitious peeks at her screen a few times as I grabbed breakfast for myself and Dot and saw some satellite photos of what must be Glen Ghuil with the tiny tidal island hosting Castle Ghuil at the loch's mouth. She had several chat windows and emails open and submitted several complicated forms. She was furiously planning Lars's rescue mission. Furiously in the literal sense, judging by last night's confrontation with her half-sister.

I scraped the dregs from a bowl of oatmeal when Scarlett got a phone call and asked them to hold on while she went to the office room in the safe house. Before the door clicked closed behind her, I said, "Okay girls, let's go for a little stroll along the river."

"But I'm still eating my—" Dot began, but then saw my urgent head flick toward the door. "Done. Good idea!"

The three of us skittered out the door, leaving Grover and Zee glancing over their shoulders at our haste.

As soon as the bulky door thudded closed behind Higgs, I had my phone out, brought up an app, and put it on speakerphone, the volume low enough for us to listen in but no louder.

"I'm trying out one of Ian Vanderkamp's skunk works projects," I said, as the first sounds of Scarlett's phone conversation crackled into life. "It's a special nano-film that works as a microphone and a low-powered Bluetooth transmitter. It looks just like a phone screen protector, thin and transparent. The best thing is that it doesn't change the phone's hardware or software, so the only detectable trace is the Bluetooth signal, which you expect to see from a mobile phone anyway. Clever, eh?"

"It would be a lot cleverer if you shut up so we could listen," Higgs shot back.

"It's mostly working, though. Sound's a little choppy. And look, I have multiple sizes to fit various phone models," I said. I was pulling them from my trouser pocket when both Higgs and Dot roundly shushed me.

We took positions halfway down the front steps, a girl over each of my shoulders. An unfamiliar male voice was speaking. "... new biopsies are lining up with what we saw earlier. Same nano. The lab is working on reverse-engineering the programming now, but it's going to take at least a week. And there are a few cases outside London that seem the same. All young women. All from London. Most have no recollection of what happened, but we're confident it's the same thing, so we have them under medical observation. We'll only perform more autopsies if the aggressor dies. There were two separate cases in Middle Ides yesterday, and one autopsy pending there."

Scarlett interjected here, responding in a succinct, matter-of-fact tone. "I ran the tech by a couple of nano experts— MacFarland in Scotland and Vladishenko from Russia. Nothing concrete on the technology yet, but I have a couple of leads."

"Keep us appraised, please. We received an anonymous letter saying these incidents were only the beginning and that we would receive specific instructions soon. If we want them to stop, there will be precise demands. And we have another guest on the call with an unrelated matter that needs your urgent attention. First Minister, the floor is yours."

A fresh voice spoke with a refined accent, posher than the ones we had heard on our way to Glen Ghuil. Still distinctly Scottish but with softer vowels. "Hello. Agent Thorisdottir, is it? I hope I got that right. It's Fiona Byrd, the Scottish First Minister."

"Yes, your pronunciation is excellent, First Minister," Scarlett replied.

"What I tell you here must be in the strictest confidence, but I understand you have an excellent track record with incidents of national security. There is a particularly Scottish threat in the air just now; let me fill you in."

"You have my undivided attention. Let's see how UPDA can help," Scarlett said.

"Apparently, they're using a *death clock*," Fiona said. "I don't know if it's a device, a computer system, or what, but I know it works. I heard about it through my communication channel with an organisation called the Tartantula. I think you know a wee bit about them already, aye?"

"We do, ma'am. Keeping one eye on them, but they have done nothing overt. Well, not until recently—we're working to free a hostage they took yesterday," Scarlett said.

"Really? They haven't threatened me with that yet."

"We think it's an added way to protect themselves. The hostage is nobody important."

I felt Higgs and Dot both shift and bristle at my shoulders, but they held their tongues, listening intently.

"Well, things are certainly escalating. They clearly have some diabolical plot playing out. This death clock offers them a way to predict a person's precise time of death, down to the minute. They gave us seven examples last week—not the *how*, just the precise time. Two heart attacks, a cancer case, a stabbing, a motorcycle accident, and two others that seem to be natural causes. We could only confirm their accuracy after the deaths. But they gave us another, slated for yesterday afternoon. We had the police pick up that person about thirty minutes before his predicted time of death. Like the others, he had no known connections to the Tartantula. Nothing in common with the other seven either, other than they all lived in or around Edinburgh. The police car was involved in an accident on its way to the station, and the target wasn't wearing a seat belt. Unconscious, he died in the ambulance on the way to casualty, right at the time the death clock predicted. I don't see how even the world's biggest computer could predict anything with that accuracy."

"Wow. That's a handful," Scarlett replied. "I have the germ of an idea about how this death clock works, and I have a few questions. First, what is the Tartantula threatening to do with the death clock?"

"They are using it as blackmail. They want to force me to be aggressive and pursue immediate Scottish separation from the UK. They also warned me not to tell anyone. I can hardly say I'm against independence, but I want it done properly, with the will of Scotland behind me, not blackmailed by some lunatic fringe. Their threat is to release the times of everyone's deaths to the public. They claim they have precise times of death for people in both Scotland and England. They can release a few upcoming deaths to prove the accuracy and then publish everyone's."

"But wait, how is that bad? If you knew your precise time of death, it would make planning your life so much simpler," Scarlett asked. I nodded in agreement.

Fiona Byrd elaborated. "Think about it. Some people will have a lot less of their life remaining than expected and will go radge, trying to cram in as much as they can in their remaining time. Others with too long to live and not enough savings will despair. Parents with children who will die prematurely will look to lay blame. Some folk might take it as a sign they should kill their abusers whose time has arrived. Whole industries, like life insurance, will fail. It may sound like knowledge is a good thing, but in this case, the consequences could be mind-boggling, with many negatives."

There was a silence. The original unknown voice eventually broke it. "Scarlett? Are you still there?"

"Yes, sir, still here. Just taking it in. I get it now. I get it. I don't really think I'd like to know when I'm going to perish."

"It's a lot. Believe me, I know. The last week has been a sleepless blur for me," Fiona said. "It took me several days to decide where to escalate this threat, but I truly need help here. The Tartantula threatened to tell me my time on the death clock. We must do something. Can you think of any next steps?"

"There are only a handful of people that might know how to handle this if my suspicions are correct. It'll be complicated, but I'm on it."

"Thank you, Agent Thorisdottir. I'm relying on your help. The whole country needs your help, and I'm not only talking about Scotland now. I expect daily updates, please."

The nano-film microphone picked up Scarlett's thumb ending the call and then some deep bass rustling from putting the phone in a pocket. I closed the eavesdropping app.

"We'd better actually go on that stroll I mentioned. Let's talk about this crazy new elf magic as we go. I'm lucky to be with my two favourite magical scholars."

Disco

Still, we ran. The first light of day showed the pack we had left the hills. A wide bay swept in, and a surging river fed it. I looked at my companions.

Some had joined the pack in the night but could not keep

up. A badger tried to run with us, but his short legs left him in the distance behind us. Moles and hedgehogs thronged around us when we stopped to drink at a pond, but we had to abandon them. The two kestrels that flew high above us as we ran eyed the mice and rats that scurried around our paws and hooves at the pond but left them in peace.

As we approached the dawn-catching waves at the river's mouth, it was only the birds and the fastest runners that had kept up. My friend clopping beside me, two deer, and a family of rabbits arrived by my side at the sandy shore.

I looked to my right and saw no bridges. No place to cross as far as I could see along the river. The kestrels broke off from their circling. They arrowed along the river, scouting.

Dipping our paws, feet, and hooves in the lapping waters was soothing. Six salmon came to greet us, only half-submerged in the shallow water. After a moment, something larger. A spiral ivory tusk rose above the waves, bobbing as it approached. A bulbous head followed as a wobbling body beached itself beside me. A narwhal, the salmon said. Its head turned with grace, and the tapering tusk swished a triangular divot in the sand, allowing the rabbits to dip their furry feet without danger of a wave soaking them. It locked eyes with me for a lingering moment. Then it heaved itself back into the bay in a series of belly flops. The narwhal circled in the shallows as if waiting for us to join in and cross the bay.

I didn't know what to do. How could we continue our journey? The answer came from the horse. Memories of being transported from one polo field to the next. A muted whinny and we followed along to a lay-by one the road that fringed the bay. A lone man stood on the sandy shore, distant from the only vehicle stopped in the lay-by. It was a lorry towing a dirty silver slot-sided trailer. It smelt like pigs. Lots of pigs.

The horse reared up on its hind hooves. One hoof on the lorry's side helped provide balance while the other scrabbled at some levers at the lorry's rear. One, two, three attempts. There! The trailer's rear door swung open. No pigs remained inside, only their powerful smell. The horse and deer leapt in. I turned broadside to the opening. The rabbits used me like a stepping stone and took double hops to the straw-scattered floor within. The door remained open, but horse teeth the size of dominoes clenched a frayed rope that dangled from the top of the door. It swung lazily and latched shut with a reassuring click. We curled our legs beneath us and rested on the muck and straw-strewn floor, and waited. Even the horse lay down. Kestrel talons scratched the roof as they gripped the ridged metal. The rabbits nestled into a furry circle, their warmth radiating into the arc of my belly where they slept. Soon, a door clunked shut, and the lorry lurched off.

CHAPTER 13 - CLICK

Newton

Faraday and Higgs's reunion dispelled a lingering tension in my body that I could identify only now it seeped away. Nagging doubts about Scarlett's role in our family tragedies left an edge to my lowered tension, but I had no doubt about her competence, only her motives.

Although we had spoken only an hour earlier, I craved contact with my too-distant siblings. I called Faraday's mobile. He answered after one ring. "Newt! We are out for a stroll along the riverbank. The girls and me. Want to talk to Higgs?"

Faraday passed the phone, and I chatted with my sister, picking out the sounds of rushing water and faint birdsong beneath her reassuring and familiar voice. She filled me in on Scarlett's conversation about the Tartantula, the death clock, and the rash of nano-driven violence spreading from London. I had several questions, but most remained unanswered.

"So this elf character. You think he is behind the death clock?" I asked.

I could almost see Higgs nodding, although I only heard her voice. "The First Minister guessed it's some kind of device or supercomputer, but it has to be his magic. Scarlett didn't mention the elf explicitly, but she said she had a suspicion. After she talked to her half-sister and took in what Dot and I witnessed at Loch Ghuil, she seemed worried about his powers. It makes freeing Lars challenging."

"And is she letting you know the details of the rescue plan?" I asked.

"Only bits. The general plan seems good, though. A stealth team will sneak in and remove the handcuffs from the elf. She's confident that once the elf is free, he'll no longer obey her sister, and then conventional forces can swoop in and grab Ragnhildur and this Ruaridh guy while freeing Lars. It's going to kick off tomorrow. I just want to see Lars again and come home. Put a cuppa on for me at dinner time tomorrow, will you?"

I laughed. "Obviously! And I'll add a third sugar because you've had a shock. And what about Grover? His parents are worried sick—they don't know where he is or why he disappeared. I don't really know what to tell them, so I've been avoiding it."

"What? Really? Shouldn't the UPDA handle that? Let me put Faraday on again. See you tomorrow, Newt. Love you."

"Hey," I began when my brother took the phone back. "Can you ask Scarlett to contact Grover's parents? I'm going to report no progress to them and leave it to her to handle. It's her mess."

"She probably won't listen to me. I'm only her pet nanotech expert. Replacing Mum, I guess."

We both paused for a moment. I heard Faraday draw two sharp breaths through his nose before he continued. I knew his self-control techniques, and the next stage would be to press a palm to his forehead to re-centre him as his mind spun to a labyrinth filled with frightening detail but unanswered questions. Constant contact with Scarlett must have been testing his resolve.

I heard no additional breaths, and his voice was steady when he continued. Good—he had latched on to a directed problem to consider. "These girls—are they all girls? It doesn't matter. These people—the ones who are going off in nano-triggered rages—it seems like we know *what* infests them. But we don't know *how* they got infected or what *triggers* the rampages, right?"

"Well, I certainly don't know the who or how parts," I said. "It sounds like they know London is where the nanotech gets introduced. Maybe Scarlett knows more about the *how* and isn't saying?"

"I've got an idea on the how. Or more accurately, the *who*, but I'm not sure yet. What about Terrell? Does he have any idea what triggered the two attacks in Middle Ides?"

"I don't think so. I'll check in with him right after this. And a couple of other things are happening. But don't worry, I've got everything covered here. Granny seems agitated about something, like she feels something happening up in the hills. I'll check in on her this morning. And I lost Disco. She ripped through the screen door and ran off somewhere. I hope that nano she ingested at your jeep accident doesn't have delayed side effects."

"That's unlike her," Faraday said. "She's seemed fine. Faster, obviously, but no other effects. Did you check if she's gone over to see Antoinette?"

"No. Good call. I'll peek in there. And I'll say hi to Granny for both of you. Let me know if anything changes at your end."

* * *

I met Terrell at a folding bistro table outside Blondie's Bakery on the High Street. The slender chair looked over-matched by his wide hips, but I figured the chair would win this round. It would be a different story if my friend Chronos joined us. He'd know better than to settle onto something so insubstantial.

I clutched my takeaway tea with both hands, cutting the cloudless morning's slight chill. Terrell held a coffee and a slice of parsnip loaf. He clearly suffered from the remaining effects of the spell distributed across Middle Ides by the Drowned Cabal; there was no other good explanation for eating the various parsnip-tinged delights from the bakery. I resisted the urge to tell him he was under the influence of magic cast by Dot Pendlethwaite.

"Look, Sergeant, I know you told me to observe and

breathe in the crime scene's little details, but I'm not really getting anything from either attack—other than that I should be a better detective. And it's distracting me from the missing persons case."

He sucked air in through his teeth and gave his head a slight shake. "I not feelin' it neither, you know? I got more info now. A set of special agents from London took the skater girl off us. Gov' wouldn't say what agency they're from. And while stompin' round the place in they big boy boots, one performed another autopsy on Priti Srinathan. Not sure what they found, or what they were looking for. But it's not cricket. Somethin's brewin'."

"Remember when that anti-terrorism squad took control after the school teacher Mr Shinoto blew up his classroom?" I asked. "Seems like that. I wouldn't mind so much if they kept us in the loop, but it's almost like they take pride in shutting us out."

"We're just cogs in the works, Newton, and don't you forget it!" Terrell laughed but shook his head. "But we still do our jobs. Keep thinkin' about those two crime scenes. Sometimes I'll wake up with an epiphany—like the ghosts of crime scenes past, present, and future visited overnight."

"I've heard a mug of tea helps too," I said.

"You're right, there, son. I *knew* there was a reason I came to England."

* * *

A few pieces of the puzzle were before me, but they all seemed to have smooth, rounded edges beyond hope of fitting together. Other pieces were snatched off the table by stealthy, interfering forces. I was the junior detective on a provincial police force, and before this year, I would have accepted my lot with nothing more than mild complaint to myself, or maybe Terrell. But not anymore. I was tired of letting others hold the leash of my destiny. Taking a pointer from Disco, I grabbed the leash in my own jaws—I would demand exercise.

I left Emeline in my grandmother's room, telling them I had a little business to take care of, and called Scarlett's phone from the reception area at the foot of the sweeping staircase.

"It's Newton," I said. "Faraday gave me your number. I have some updates, and I expect you have some for me too since your people are clambering like ants all over my department."

Her tone of voice expressed little, as usual. "Are you surprised? Anyway, what have you got?"

I summarised the updates from the two attacks in Middle Ides. "Maybe it's my DS getting into my brain, but I swear there is something tugging at my coattails here. Some clue I'm nearly missing. What did your team discover?"

"Nothing unexpected. This threat is now number two on the national priority list though, so it's getting attention. The brain biopsy shows invasive nanotech in the subject you found behind Darling House. And the other attack fits the profile. It's more of the same, so I think we need to trace back to the nanotech's source. Faraday and I are chasing that angle down, but I've got my hands full with this Tartantula threat here."

A nanotech attack was only number two priority? It jarred me to realise I knew what number one was—the separatist magic that had kidnapped my sister's friend and threatened to destabilise the nation. But I needed to focus on things I could control.

"Yeah. Higgs told me about the elf. Keep her away from this—I know she will try to help, but this confrontation is no place for a teenager. You'll promise that, right?"

"Of course, Newton. We have professionals to handle this, and my plan will finish these slap-dash separatists playing kingmaker. They aren't organised enough to resist us."

"Sounds like another day or two in Scotland, and then you'll return my family."

"I'm all over this, Newton," she replied. Maybe I imagined the sincerity, but I thought her tone somehow betrayed that emotion.

"I've never even been to Scotland. I'm surprised I don't

hear bagpipes in the background," I said to lighten the mood.

A tangible tingling shot down my neck and across my shoulders. I pulled the phone away from my face as intuition coursed through my every fibre. "That's it, Scarlett! Bagpipes! I'll call you back."

I didn't wait for her reply. I disconnected the call and couldn't scroll to Terrell's number fast enough. I paced half the length of the grand hallway at the Orphanage during the three rings before he answered.

"Gov', it's me. Something jumped to the front of my mind, just like you said it would," I blurted.

"Brill," he replied, ignited by my enthusiasm. "Take a breath. Let's talk it through. What's percolatin'?"

I took a moment to corral my racing thoughts. "Think about the skate park. What triggered the attack?"

"That's an enigma, Newton. Didn't see anythin' to cause that level of violence."

"I didn't see anything, either. But what did you *hear*?"

"Skateboard wheels, I guess. Me chewing lasagne. Birds? I dunno."

I prompted him. "Did you hear music?"

"Oh yeah. They had the radio on."

"I caught the attack's first blur in my peripheral vision right when the bagpipe solo began over that drum 'n' bass beat. Piping Hot—the band on the radio. I think it's called 'Flower of Glasgow'."

"Wait, wait," Terrell said. "I get that hearing bagpipes makes me want to strangle someone, but normally the piper. What's the link here?"

"Hear me out. I'm not linking the music to that attack, I'm connecting it to the *other* attack. Remember—"

My detective sergeant cut me off. "The radio was on in Yulia Antonov's room. Radio One. And the officer in the lounge said the girls were giggling about a boy band. I don't get it, but I see where you're goin'. Hang on, let me check somethin'."

I heard some ambient noise and the muffled thumps of his

fingers tapping his mobile's screen.

"You're spot on, Newton! Lookin' at the BBC playlist on their app. 'Flower of Glasgow' was definitely the song we heard in the park, and looks like the same song could have been playing at Darling House."

"Good. I'm not hallucinating," I said.

"Wait. A song?"

"Yeah, it's like that Doen story you mentioned. Something leading the children away. It may sound like a stretch, but trust me on this, I really think the song could trigger something in these girls. I need to talk to my brother to confirm a few things."

"That's my boy, Newton," Terrell said. "I'm not gonna put the paperwork through just now, but I'm feelin' you. Like that spine tinglin' hits you with some songs—You think that kinda response could be the trigger? While you talk to your brother, I'm going to get the exact times of attacks from the Met Police. See if the London attacks had background music."

I disconnected and popped my head back into Granny's room to tell her and Emeline I had to make one more call. This time to Faraday.

I got right to the point and asked if he thought a sound could have triggered the nanotech in the London attacks.

"Absolutely," he said. "The Russian technologist we talked to yesterday said as much. He identified the neurotransmitters right away—those are the parts that signal your nervous system, causing violent outbursts—but he also said there we no external inputs. The signal to activate the tech needed to come from the host, not from an outside control system. So yeah, a sound pattern could trigger a reaction."

I felt the warmth of finally, possibly, being good at my job. This could solve the mystery of these savage attacks.

"I knew I could count on you, brother," I said. "Fill in Scarlett—get her people to check whether a song could trigger this. It's called 'Flower of Glasgow'."

* * *

Saturday lunch with Granny was a new tradition for Emeline and me. A standing order with the kitchens at the Orphanage provided us with the day's delicacies. We perched with expansive wooden trays on our laps, fitted with recesses for plates, cups, and cutlery, and three finger-holes in the lip at each end for ease of carrying.

Emeline sat in the chair next to my grandmother, who, true to form, had dressed in what she called her 'going out clothes', although she never really left her home these days. Her purple twin set matched a long skirt and caught a matching hue in the marbled frames of the reading glasses that dangled from a silver chain around her neck.

"Angelina, tell Newton what you mentioned earlier. You know, the feeling that's making you uneasy," Emeline said.

I raised an eyebrow and left a silence for Granny to fill.

"I get these flashes," she began. "Two scenes, really. One is dark, about Higgs. It seems like she's in danger, somehow. You should go to her, Newt."

I trusted Granny's intuitions, and this revelation coursed through me in a rush of cold. But I felt I should reassure her. "She's with Faraday now, Granny. I talk to them every few hours. He'll keep her safe. And they'll both be back tomorrow or the day after. What's the other thing?"

"I don't know. It's a lake. Night time. Something unnatural is happening. I can always tell when nature is being twisted nearby."

"Nearby?" I asked. "Which lake is it?"

"It's weird. I don't know. I've been to all the lakes around here when I was younger and able to roam, but I've never seen this one. It feels close, which seems impossible."

I trusted this instinct too. Maybe my grandmother's senses ranged wider as her ability to wander physically diminished. This could be a lake further afield. But Emeline swivelled us back to the first and more personal vision.

"We could do *something* to protect Higgs, couldn't we?" Emeline said. A bangled wrist jingled beneath the loose cuff of her blouse as she reached across to cover Granny's veiny and age-splotched hand. I knew the *something* she alluded to was a spell, these two women sharing a kinship beyond their links to me.

"I'd feel better if we did," Granny replied. "Let me think. We'll need moss and a spider web—Newt can grab those outside. And a fresh twig snapped right from a tree. But what about an egg? Do you have an egg?"

Then her voice took on a sombre tone. "But we'll need some strands of Higgs's hair. We can't get that now, can we?"

I may not have Faraday's eidetic recall, but my police training helped me notice and track things that others might miss. "That's not a problem, Granny. Higgs left a brush on the back shelf of Mum's—I mean our—car. And Emeline can get an egg from the kitchen downstairs."

My girlfriend and I walked together to the front door of the Orphanage, talking in hushed tones.

"If Angelina sees Higgs in danger, we should take it seriously," Emeline said.

"Very. Yes. I didn't want to show Granny I'm nervous, but yeah. I'm going to get Faraday to bring her and Dot back tomorrow. I know they want to be there when Lars is rescued, but they don't need to help in the rescue, and I'm worried Higgs will pull some stunt. I'll get them home."

After splitting up in the high-ceilinged foyer, I scouted the grounds for the prerequisite moss, spider web, and twig. I stretched to grab the hairbrush from my car as a motorcycle rumbled into the car park and skidded slightly on the gravel as it halted beside me.

Removing his black helmet, my best friend Chronos greeted me. That wasn't his actual name—his ID would say he was James McCann—but his colossal size and casual regard for timekeeping made Chronos a far better moniker.

"I've missed lunch again, haven't I?" he said.

"Same as last week. We saved you some," I laughed. "But you need to ride with a tad more caution, no? In your condition?"

I was referring to his artificial leg. Although he was walking well after months of physiotherapy, his dexterity would never be the same as before the motorcycle crash at the gates of Pendlethwaite House.

He slapped me heartily on the back, a forceful reminder of his enduring vitality. "All good, brother! She doesn't want me to tell you this, but Higgs and I have been practising motorbike trials out behind the warehouses on the Ablican road. We have an entire course set up there. I'm as good as I ever was."

"Trials?" I asked. "Like an assault course? How could Higgs help you with that?"

"Well … I didn't say she was *helping* me. I was helping her, more like. She uses the dirt bike you and I rode around on as teens."

I opened my mouth to chastise him, but he knew what was coming. "Don't even start," he laughed. "How hard did you campaign your mother for permission to ride that bike? And she didn't relent until about ten weeks *after* you and I started belting through Nicholson's Woods. I'm way more careful teaching Higgs than you and I ever were."

"She's not sixteen yet. She can't even get a learner licence!"

Chronos spluttered in laughter. "Bro, you were fourteen when you started, so shut it."

That reminder beat any replies from me, so I kept my mouth shut. Only a sigh expressed my big brother protectiveness and exasperation.

"Hey, there's a lot going on in Scotland that I need to tell you about. But right now, Granny and Emeline are going to do a little something upstairs. Want to see some magic?"

CHAPTER 14 - CAGED

Lars

Morsa always told me to be friendly, but maybe this time I was too friendly. In our neighbourhood in Stockholm, she laughed every school lunch hour because I would bring home a different kid—sometimes from my school, other times someone I met as I skipped and cartwheeled my way home from school. She knew every other mother in the neighbourhood from reassuring lunchtime phone calls.

I thought back to yesterday morning. Higgs and Dot were still in their tents when I heard the rustling outside. It was early, but the sun had peeked its shining face above the sides of Glen Ghuil more than an hour ago. I unzipped my tent flap and saw the hairy cows grazing near the little creek.

I pulled on my trousers but didn't bother to put on my shoes. The morning was warm already, and the dewy grass soothed my soles as I jogged toward the cows, trying to look unthreatening. I slowed as I got close.

They were funny-looking things, these Scottish cows. The shaggy hair on their heads seemed unreal, as if someone had snuck up and taped cheap human hairpieces on their bony foreheads. It reminded me of the sheepdog who guarded his flock from the coyote in the Swedish-dubbed cartoons I watched as a kid. The lead cow flicked his head back as I drew closer, the shag parting to reveal both massive eyeballs. Its pupils shrunk instantly, unused to the glare. It focussed on me, unblinking, as it munched noisily.

This one would not move away! She was very calm, not retreating or even shifting her head as I extended my arm. Her nearest horn was within reach. It was rougher than I expected, a mottled brown with ringed ridges marking distinct jumps in thickness from point to skull, like a melting candle that had been lit and relit over a month of dinners.

"Hey there!" a voice called to me, making me snatch my hand back from the cow's horn. It was more than just a friendly greeting—the tone had a slight edge of urgency to it. I had noticed no one else in the open grasses by the stream. The person must have emerged from the woods while I focussed on the cows.

The voice came from a dark-haired, slender woman dressed in lightweight outdoor gear. A typical hiker's outfit. She waved, her eyes friendly and lips curved in a slight smile as she brushed through the grass toward me.

She said something in a language I didn't know. Tried again in Norwegian, which I recognised but didn't know, and then settled into conversation in Swedish. She wasn't a native speaker, but her accent was easy to understand. Oddly, I replied in English. "Yes, I'm Swedish," I said.

She continued in Swedish anyway, although she had started in English. "It's an amazing morning, hey? And look at those cows. They're so calm with you."

When she arrived beside me, her gaze seemed to penetrate through my eyes, and I had to look away from her deeply ringed irises when it lingered too long. As I returned my glance to the cows and raised my hand for another attempt on the horn, she snatched my other palm in hers, and we went ... elsewhere.

* * *

Outdoors became indoors. Coldness assaulted my dewy feet as they pressed against a metal floor. Warming morning sunbeams were replaced with reflected light that shone through open-shuttered window frames and lit the barred cage that now held me in its cruel bosom. The woman released my hand and then disappeared with a pop, re-materialising outside the bars. A red-bearded and cranky-looking man expressed his glee only with a grunting chuckle. "Ah. Our Viking, I presume, lassie?"

"Swedish, he says," she replied, then nodded my way. "We might as well get familiar. You'll be here a while. I'm Ragnhildur Úlfursdottir, and this is Ruaridh McRaven."

I had moved to their side of my cage and was about to grip and shake the bars to test their strength when I glimpsed another figure. I hadn't noticed him at first because of his size. He stood fully erect under a table, and his blue skin concealed him well in the shadows. "Sundalfar, I am. Sundalfar. Caged too." I tried to inspect his appearance in more detail, but found he disappeared when I looked directly at him. This was odd, but I found I coud see him just fine if I looked at something beside him. With concentration, the finer details of his appearance became apparent in my peripheral vision.

His gangly forearms rose to display a set of handcuffs, wispy and metallic. "Socks. You need socks. Human feet. Always so cold, so cold they are."

Somehow, my right hand clutched a pair of blue woollen socks. "Um ... I'm Lars Janssen. Can you let me out now, please? I need to find my friends. They'll be worried."

Now that the blue guy had planted the suggestion, I couldn't stop thinking that, yes, my feet *were* cold. I really should pull on the thick socks before the cold crept any higher. I sat on a plush, cobalt blue sofa that I swear was not on the far side of the cage a moment ago.

"Settle, lad," the Scottish man said. "You're going naewhere any time soon. Want a biscuit?"

Sundalfar nodded in morose agreement from beneath the table, hunkering on his bony heels. As I lifted my feet to pull the socks all the way up, a blue tartan carpet rolled out to cover the cold metal cage floor.

* * *

I paced the confines of my cage throughout that morning and afternoon, occasionally rattling the lock, to no avail. The small blue man wandered the wood-framed building, standing on tippy-toes to peek out the windows when Ragnhildur was outside. She and Ruaridh largely ignored me, offering me lunch, which I refused, and a mug of water, which I accepted.

Ruaridh talked endlessly on a massive phone handset, organising something I couldn't quite decipher. Ragnhildur took Sundalfar outside for a while, and their distinct voices floated back through the open windows on the warming afternoon air. She ran him through a series of instructions for mysterious procedures. Footfast. Scatter. Elevate. Something called 'mirror me'. The odd little creature responded with exasperation to most of these instructions. "Yes, mistress. Sundalfar knows," he would say, or, "Rules. Rules. Rules. Obey the rules. Free me?"

Later in the afternoon, I heard a series of popping sounds— the same noise that had accompanied the transition from our campsite to my cage. Sundalfar slipped through the half-open door to the building, his bare, elongated feet slapping the boards as he crossed to me.

He lay on his back on the floor beside my cage and let out a sigh that sounded too human to have come from his alien lungs. "Sundalfar is sorry. Sorry to the boy. A prophecy made the cage."

I whispered, afraid that Ruaridh would stomp in and do something unspeakable to me or my fellow captive if he caught us conspiring. "What do you mean, a prophecy?"

"Sundalfar told them. They didn't ask. Just told them. Thought it would make them angry. Free Sundalfar, maybe.

A Viking boy will roam the Glen,
He must not pass beyond your ken.
Your new nation will be born,
Unless he touch the Ghuilin's horn."

"What, they think *I'm* going to stop whatever they're planning? That's silly. I think the prophecy should be about my friend Higgs. She can do magic, like you. Hey—can you do another prophecy? Is Higgs coming to rescue me? Or maybe you could magic me out of here, back to my tent?"

Sundalfar took on hushed tones too. Not really a whisper, but a quieter version of his gravel-tinged lilt. "Higgs. Girl with elf hair? With other magic girl?"

I nodded, smiling inside about the elf hair reference. It was almost as if Sundalfar had felt an aftershock from Dot's spell that had everyone in Middle Ides admiring Higgs's hairdo. "They came. Sundalfar had to keep them out. But showed them how to escape. Get help. Not allowed to help the boy, though. Must keep you in cage. No cows. Never cows. Not near. Sundalfar keeps everyone out of the castle. Must. Until free."

I realised where they were holding me. The cage must have been inside Castle Ghuil. I had an oblique view of ragged stone walls that belonged to the castle that looked so tiny from the head of Loch Ghuil. Outside, I heard Ruaridh's gruff tones. "See our guest inside? Have a chat with him, in case you need to do you're stuff wi' him, the later."

A pair of twins entered, opening the door wider than when Sundalfar had squeezed through. They looked a little older than me, springs of short dreadlocks swinging at their temples. They walked with the closeness of a lifetime spent together and dragged chairs close to the cage.

"Hiya, Blue," one said to Sundalfar. "All good? What would you normally do on a Friday night?"

The awkward creature pulled himself to a sitting position, hugging his knees. "No Friday. Not us. Every day of the year is special. Special things on each special day. Today Sundalfar should help fish down the waterfall. Stay friendly with the water. Should be free."

The other twin spoke. "Nae long now, mate. Ragn said she would let you go once we've made the deal. When we're independent, aye?"

He faced me now, offering an extended hand through the bars. "You too, mate. Ruaridh's dead nice once you crack through his cranky shell. He's just superstitious, keeps bletherin' on about some prophecy. You'll be comfy until he can let you go. I'm Duncan, by the way. This is Darren."

I tentatively accepted his handshake, which he continued for a little too long for my liking. He looked me right in the eyes the whole time, giving me the same uncomfortable urge to look away as when I first encountered Ragnhildur in the meadow.

As he withdrew his hand, Darren offered a fist bump between the bars. "Anything we can get for you, brother? A blanket? Any snacks? Ruaridh keeps enough food here for a month, with loads ay snacks."

I was quite hungry, and although I had barely met these two, it seemed a better idea to accept offers from them than from my direct captors. "A cup of tea would be nice. And something on the side would be good too. How long, do you think, until they let me go?"

Darren retreated to another room while Duncan answered. "Maybe a week. Nae mair than two. Things are happenin' fast, the now." I heard the click of a gas-powered stove igniting and the oscillation of a kettle being filled.

Ruaridh's thick frame blocked a significant amount of light as he leaned into the door frame and called to Darren, "Add us to the round too, aye? Ragn and me."

I could see Ragnhildur's shadow on the grass outside, but she wasn't in my direct line of sight as she and Ruaridh continued their conversation. "Ferndale has definitely had enough time to settle. Sundalfar has given me a really long list already."

"Brill," Ruaridh began. "It's time to start the death clock tickin' on the Sassenachs. Let me give missy one more chance before we go large."

He palmed the oversized phone handset, connecting a call. "Okay, son, relay me through to her, please."

There was a delay before he continued. "Fiona, it's me again. I'm looking for progress. The time for bein' a dafty is over."

He paused here and listened for a good while. "Naw, naw, nae good enough. I'm goin' up the chain now. Turnin' the death clock on for England. Expect a call from the PM any minute now."

The phone's shadow dropped from his ear, and he pressed a button on it before bursting into a deep laugh. "I can feel it now, eh lads? A braw day dawnin' for Scotland."

I sipped at a giant mug of tea and nibbled my way through eight or nine biscuits as the twins chattered with Ruaridh. Ragnhildur remained outside, sunning herself. Sundalfar huddled beside me, head bowed. I slid to the carpet on the cage floor, putting my back against the bars nearest him. Without turning, I whispered, "Higgs will come back. With help. She'll get you out of here too, friend."

The twins returned to the grass, and after a call from Ragnhildur to Sundalfar, with a dry crackle like a burst of static electricity, they disappeared. The shadows lengthened, and my eyelids closed as I stretched on the pliant sofa, the drone of another phone call coming from somewhere out of sight. I tried to imagine Higgs's face, and it left an unpleasant taste when I couldn't remember every single detail, every eyelash, every cinch at the corners of her mouth when she laughed.

The scrape of a chair's feet across the floorboards drew me from my reverie. Ruaridh pulled a chair alongside the cage, and I smelt leather, sweat, and a hint of earthy cologne.

"Listen, lad," he began, "I cannae say I really want you here. It's something the elf said, you ken? We're no gonnae hurt you, so relax. It willnae be long before Scotland will rise again under its own rule. Ragnhildur brought us the power to do what we want, but quiet-like, see? It'll be the quietest revolution you never heard of. Once it's settled, you can stroll out ay here, nae bother."

I let a moment's silence hang in the air before responding. "But I read my morsa's newspaper sometimes. Why don't you just wait for the next referendum? It seems like that's the best way to become independent."

"Aye. Tried that. Snatched away fae us. Propagandists,

right? Naw—this time we're gonnae make sure. If you cannae lever the people to persuade the politicians, lever the politicians."

He reached through the bars and clapped me once on the shoulder; a strong whack, but filled with the spirit of camaraderie, not malice. "Lots ay good biscuits here. Give us a shout whenever, lad."

* * *

It was long past midnight when I finally managed to sleep. Not for a lack of comfort, though—the plush sofa and blue tartan blanket were nicer than my bed at home. It was my racing mind that kept me awake at the end of a very long day. Would my captors' cordiality turn vicious? How long would it be before Higgs and Dot alerted the police and rescuers arrive? I was confident Newton would pull some strings and spring me free. Probably tomorrow morning.

As I drifted off, I felt the dream that haunted me most nights since Higgs's Granny told us the story of the Pendletoad, lurking in the hills above Middle Ides, concealed beneath the waters of Ashoton Pond. In my dream, Granny wasn't supposed to betray the secret of the massive toad's location, and it rose from the depths, clomping its corrupt mass down the hillside to take its revenge on her.

Newton

"A duck egg would have been better," my grandmother said as she surveyed the materials arrayed on her meal tray.

Emeline shrugged. "They don't have a range of duck eggs in the kitchen downstairs. Just your normal chicken variety. I've used them before."

Granny shook her head. "Kids these days, eh Chronos? It's

all about instant gratification."

He laughed. "Tell me about it! But how about this? You can use this feather that was poking through your duvet and jabbed me in the cheek."

With a flourish, he presented the fluffy, stunted fan of an eiderdown tuft to Granny.

"Ooh! That'll work," my grandmother said.

Chronos smiled, his glee infectious. "See, Newt? I'm magic too!"

Emeline and Granny got to work assembling the spell. They snapped the twig into three segments and created a triangle with overlapping ends, reminiscent of a squat letter A. The pat of moss rested atop with the still dew-laden spider web draped across. The strand of Higgs's blonde hair from the brush needed to be tied around the egg, fastening the near-weightless duck down to it. This proved difficult.

"Why does she have to have such short hair," Emeline complained. "It's going to take some tiny fingers to tie the knot after it's circled around the shell."

Chronos angled in his massive cranium to get a closer look at the problem. His cheeriness continued as he delivered an intentionally over-acted line. "Stand back, amateur spell casters. Leave this to the expert."

Instead of trying to tie a knot in the hair around the egg with fingers that were more used to heaving unruly club patrons onto the pavement than displaying fine motor skills, he placed the egg and feather aside. Taking a hair, he tied a skilful half-hitch, closing the ends into a full loop. Positioning the feather inside the loop, he slid the egg inside. It was a perfect fit, and he lay the egg gracefully onto the blanket of the web.

Granny cackled. "What would we do without you, dearie?"

"Not a lot of magic, obviously," my friend replied. "I'll stand back now though, just in case."

Emeline unscrewed the salt cellar lid and handed it to Granny, who had the twig, moss, web, and egg sandwich on the tray before her. "You do it, love. My hands are trembly these days," she said.

"Double triangle, right Angelina?" After a nod of acknowledgement, Emeline poured six trails of salt, surrounding the eggy apparatus with a pair of overlapping triangles that formed a six-pointed star. The six salt trails' junction points bulged higher than the rest of the pattern. Emeline made a complex set of gestures that I couldn't track before fanning open her palms above the egg as if to warm them on a fire. The salty junctions re-organised and levelled themselves, and the whole star became slightly crisper. Every stray crystal mustered into perfectly straight lines.

She clasped her hands together, then knelt on one knee before my grandmother's wing-backed chair. "Shall we?"

My grandmother, the oft mysterious Angelina Redferne, did not raise her gaze from the pile of natural materials but placed a hand, palm up, on either side of them. Emeline placed a palm gently in each offered hand, bowed her head, and closed her eyes.

Without thinking about it, I held my breath. Chronos was motionless and silent beside me on the edge of Granny's bed. After five or six seconds, the spider web shed its dew, which ran in aimless rivulets toward the salt star. The margins of the web's polygonal shape fluttered as if in a localised breeze, cradling then wrapping the egg.

My grandmother looked up at Emeline, then squeezed her hands. "Grand," she said. "I think the duck feather really worked."

"Let's hope Higgs doesn't need the protection," Emeline added.

Without ceremony, Emeline scooped up the spell materials and dumped them into the rubbish bin near the door. Granny set the tray aside. "Now, James darling, was that your motorcycle I heard outside a few minutes ago? The sound reminded me, I heard that exact noise in the background of a lake I've been dreaming about."

Ruaridh

Sitting alone on the shore, gazing out to sea, skipping loose pieces of shale across the lapping waves wouldn't accomplish much. But I needed calm, and places like this were my sanctuary.

Everything I had said and done over the last three years lined up precisely with Scottish independence. But was that really what I wanted? For all my bluster, I remained unsure. I knew what felt right in my yearning heart; that we were a people apart from the English. We deserved the right to protect the wild beauty of our lands without suffering suggestions borne of ignorance from some bugger in London. But mentioning 'we' sometimes felt hollow. Those city folk in Edinburgh and Glasgow often pissed me off even more than the Sassenachs. Was I really striving for them too, only to feel *their* interference when the inevitable independence arrived? I imagined the supreme and bitter disappointment.

And it was unclear whether we really were a people apart; I probably shared ancestors with our caged Viking lad. Half of Scotland and the north of England were descendants of coastal raiders from Scandinavia. And my entire time at university in Glasgow—hadn't I spent those years pining to be up here, away from the glib attitudes of the central belt dwellers? In a place where three strides out the back of the croft could transport you to a world hidden from the southerners? One that pulled at your heartstrings using the power of mist, the muted splendour of autumn heather, the familiar pitch of the hills, or a fleeting glimpse of a proud stag?

Could I hide the fact from myself that it wasn't about Scotland—more about just the North? Bloody southerners, trampling our lands and polluting our ears with their inane banter. Why'd the elf have to utter that prophecy? The lad Lars seemed sound and blameless; a better prophecy would have mentioned two meddling English girls.

Glancing up the slope to Ena's croft in the distance brought to the fore thoughts of a simpler life, a less angry existence. I should have never left the glen. I skipped another sliver across the turbulent waves at the entry to the boat channel.

It was my anger that took me from here to that accursed boys' school near York. If I had held my tongue, kept my fists down, Father wouldn't have trundled me off there. The things I didn't care to remember would never have been done to me. A flash-memory of the shadows in the corner of the woodworking shed made my heart thump audibly. But the accelerating anger ultimately sprung me free from the torment of that twisted boarding school. It was expulsion that delivered me back to my mother, my motherland, and the visceral joys of this familiar landscape.

I snapped back to the present situation; ruminating on the past had never done me any favours. Our ally from even further north needed more consideration. It was so easy to accept Ragnhildur's offer of the elf's power. She was like a lost kitten meowing for attention. Specifically, the attention of an ally with a mission. I think she expected to flaunt her power when Scotland was a proper nation again, pulling strings behind the scenes. But she underestimated my temper. I'd kept it in check in front of her so far, but maybe it would be her that triggered it with a careless or misinterpreted remark. Perhaps the ungrateful rabble in Edinburgh or something as senseless as an awful night's sleep. But a flare of rage would erupt from my gorge eventually, as it always did, and I'd toss aside the power of the elf like a pirate scuppering his precious galleon to spite the encircling armada. She'd have nothing left. No power. Not even the right to remain in our new nation.

I patted my vest, reassured by the firm shape secreted away in the inner pocket. My insurance against the Icelander. The key to a pair of handcuffs.

It wouldn't be long now before independence. Maybe that calm could tame me.

CHAPTER 15 - PIPING

Higgs

The map of Glen Ghuil consumed the entire kitchen island at the safe house. The corners of two sellotaped-together pages dangled over one rounded marble edge.

Scarlett gestured with the tip of a pencil. "A team of two Black Ops troops will curl around the shore from the south. They'll use a rowboat to maintain absolute silence and will enter the castle through the sea-facing portcullis. Thanks for confirming it's stuck in an open position, Dot."

"What's that thing?" Grover asked, pointing to a haphazard arrangement of three rectangles, nowhere near where the rest of us were focussed.

"It's a house, Grover," Scarlett replied. She didn't immediately return to describing her plan but elaborated. "In Scotland, they call it a *croft*. It's like those little farmhouses on the Peaks road, right above Little Ides."

Grover nodded. "Okay."

Scarlett returned to the outline of Castle Ghuil. "Once the Black Ops team is in position, the drone operators on the glen's slope above the castle will pilot a set of drones in. The first one will drop a nano-net; you saw one in action at Pendlethwaite House. That will knock out any tech and token magic inside the castle, but I highly doubt it will affect the elf. The team on-site will already be in motion—armed with gas-powered industrial bolt cutters. They will get to the elf and snip off the handcuffs. Once he's free, his obligation to obey my sister will end, and we can drop gas canisters from the remaining drones and sweep in with conventional forces. We'll have a helicopter scramble from just out of sight over the brow of the glen."

"Do the on-site team know they can't look directly at the elf if they want to see him?" Dot asked.

"And what about the gas? It won't hurt Lars, will it?" I asked at almost the same time.

"All planned for. The enhanced-vision visors the team wear may be able to spot the elf—we obviously have little experience with that—but I checked with the operations team, and the visors allow good peripheral vision. The pair selected for the mission have been appraised they may need to work that way. I'm hoping the elf will help us and cooperate fully. And the gas is an anaesthetic—it will put Lars to sleep, but it won't do anything more than make him groggy for a couple of hours after he wakes. We'll get him out safely, Higgs."

I figured this was a good time to use the knowledge we got by eavesdropping on Scarlett's call. I approached the topic from an oblique angle so as not to expose Faraday.

"When Dot and I were listening in on Ruaridh and who we now presume was your sister—"

"*Half*-sister," Scarlett corrected.

"—half-sister, yes. They were talking about a 'kick-the-bucket list' and it sounded like the elf was going to magic someone to death named Roderick Simpson, or something like that, at two-thirty-six this afternoon. How do we know the elf isn't just going to obliterate the forces attacking the castle once your half-sister sees the nano-net descending?"

"I can't say with one hundred per cent certainty that won't happen, but the scholars in Iceland have a pretty good handle on elf culture and behaviour. Although they're elusive themselves, there are several quasi-religious elf sites in the country's remotest parts, and we can decipher parts of their language and wall inscriptions, although I'll admit they are better at our language than we are at theirs. There are some very clear codes of conduct that govern elf life. One of their tenets is not to kill anything. Not each other, not animals, not even people that threaten them. There has never been a recorded case of an elf killing a human, recently or in legend."

"So what do you think they were talking about? How is this Rod Simpson going to die?" I asked.

"I have no idea," Scarlett said. "Maybe that's part of Ruaridh and Ragnhildur's plot. I wouldn't put it past *them*."

"That's *bullshit*." Faraday slammed a fist on the map. A second and third slam followed, as I knew they would, honouring his standard number of repetitions. He struck the map at the last place I saw Lars, I noticed. "Of course, you know about the *death clock*. You're filing daily reports to the Scottish First Minister about it."

Faraday, Faraday. For all his mental gymnastics, he could be so naïve. Once again, I sprang into the breach to save him. I raised my eyes to meet Scarlett's. Her normally pale cheeks were attempting to match her namesake colour. "Look, Scarlett, we overheard you talking this morning. We're only trying to help you figure this out."

Her voice rang out, tense, her words clipped. "Well, you are *not* helping much. This is agency business, so get your beaks out of it."

Grover perked up at this. "Beaks? Yeah, we're going to need worms soon, too."

Dot snorted at this. If she had been drinking milk, surely some would have dribbled from her nose. "You're an odd bird too, Grover. Where's your beak?"

Scarlett's flush faded. After a moment of uncomfortable silence, she continued in her customary, even tones. "Let's set that aside. The raid will go down tomorrow afternoon, but we need to tackle the second problem. Newton has a theory about the violent incidents that have erupted in London and Middle Ides. He thinks a specific sound pattern triggers these young women into violence. A pattern encoded into the recent hit song by Piping Hot."

"Is that really the trigger?" Faraday asked.

"It checks out. We can't verify every case, but in more than half, we know there was music playing at the times of the violent outbursts, and, from either the music devices or from radio station records, we can tell that "Flower of Glasgow" was playing around the right time."

Dot looked at me side-wise. "So you think *a boy band* is responsible for the attacks?" I asked.

"Probably not. But their music, yes. Whoever created the nanotech implants coded them to react when a certain sound arrives at the victims' ears."

I pondered this for only a moment. "Well, I don't know about the rest of you, but I won't be able to stand it, waiting around here for the rescue mission to start. We should go to the Piping Hot concert tonight and see if we can collect any more clues. If nothing else, we'll get to see what all the fuss is about."

* * *

Dot and I reclined on the sofa across from Grover's perch on the windowsill. Summer sunlight illuminated his rounded shoulders and beamed down on the trees overhanging the Water of Leith that we knew meandered below our line of sight. Behind us, Scarlett fielded calls, putting last touches to the operational plan for the rescue mission and securing us tickets to tonight's concert. Faraday's legs stretched out toward Grover along the deep sill, his shoulders propped against its right-hand edge, partially obscured by the television screen. He fiddled with the UPSCALE, sliding the walrus tooth along its impaling rod as he stared enraptured at its screen.

"I can see your icons lit up again," he said. "You are a golden tree, Higgs. Grover has his animal symbols, and Dot, yours is a parsnip. I couldn't see you two on the screen while you were in Glen Ghuil."

Dot glanced over. "Maybe the elf was blocking it somehow?"

I don't know why it took so long for that idea to blossom.

"Yeah—that would explain why our magic failed!"

Grover glanced between Dot and I as we spoke. Dot addressed him, "Hey, Grover. How do you do your magic, talking to the horses?"

His brows narrowed in a V between his eyes, magnified by his oversized lenses. "It's not magic. I learnt it from the puppy next door when I was little. You just watch what the animals do, and you'll know. You should try. They can't speak, but they still *talk*. Mummy is allergic to dogs, so we can't get one. But then they took me to see the polo ponies. They always want to talk, so I stay with them now. They are all friendly, even the cranky grey one, when you get to know them. Same with people. You don't need to use all those words. Just watch, and touch, and smell."

"Can you teach *me?*" I asked.

He scarpered over to kneel before the sofa, tucking his limping leg beneath him like a portable stool. "I think you can do it," he said. "Let's try."

He offered one hand, inviting mine, so I held it loosely. Somehow he seemd to come into sharper focus when I looked up from our clasped hands. Dot scooched in at my side and her light breathing teased my ear as Grover held open his other palm and jiggled his arm, causing his sleeve to ripple. From the cuff crept a sizeable praying mantis. It manouvered its way to his palm and reared up, as if examining me.

This display was unusual in several ways. First, I was pretty certain that preying mantises were not native to the UK, so I'm not sure how Grover found it. Second, did Grover keep the insect up his sleeve at all times? I'd never seem any suspicious moving lumps in his jumper. And third, did it really just nod at me?

"Okay Higgs, look at him. I call him Perry, but he doesn't have a real name. They don't use names, I guess. Does he seem hungry?"

I struggled to imagine how I'd know that. I wasn't even sure what Perry might eat, but he looked like his front legs were built for capturing prey, so I reckoned he ate other insects. "I can't tell, Grover. How can I communicate with him?"

"Just look closer," Grover urged. "If he was really hungry, his shoulders would pull back his front legs a little, in case any food appeared in front of him all of a sudden."

I wasn't sure what the normal resting position of a preying mantis should should look like, so maybe Grover just used pure observation and attention to the small details of animal movement to draw conclusions about what they might do next. Could that be it?

"Also, he's not thinking about food, he's thinking about you, Higgs."

A surge of information, like a burst of emotion rather than coherent thoughts passed from Perry to me. But not directly. I felt the surge of warmth flow into me via Grover's and that was entwined with mine. A highly distorted view of my own face came first, consistent with the perspective from Perry's position below and to my left. This was followed by a weaker image of Grover's also-distorted face, as if the preying mantis was comparing a memory of Grover to its view of me through multifaceted eyes.

"See? Perry is thinking about whether you look like me, but can't quite decide. I knew you could do it, Higgs."

I laughed at his confidence in me, but was pretty certain the power was all his, and I just basked in his proximity. "Thanks, Grover, I'm glad you could show me," I said. Perry the preying mantis extended a languid foreleg toward me, then shimmied off, clinging to the back of Grover's hand before disappearing into the sanctity of his sleeve.

"And once you know an animal, they will be your friend forever, unless you do something to hurt them. Like the ponies. And Disco. You can call them if you need them."

Grover gave a few angular nods, looking up and to the right at nothing in particular. "Yeah, like Disco. She's been running a long way."

* * *

When Scarlett announced she had backstage passes for us, Faraday insisted she get two more for the Donnelly twins. He wanted to figure out more about what they were doing during their trips to London.

None of us had much to wear for concert-going. Faraday and Grover had no choice—they wore what they had dressed in yesterday morning. Dot and I should have worn our 'travelling clothes' from the journey up, which were more presentable than the layered activewear we'd sported for the camping expedition. Sadly, those clothes lay lonely in our tents at the head of Loch Ghuil, so we just freshened up as best we could and blitzed our clothes using the hair dryer for a few minutes.

It was a short walk to the end of Princes Gardens where the stage stood on struts, presiding over the open space below, but sunken slightly below the pavements and shops of Princes Street. Although it was early evening, the summer sun still smiled from over our shoulders, picking out the mottled vegetation on the rocky base supporting Edinburgh Castle, looming large above the stage.

Sensitive now, I noticed two Tartantula flyers posted along our path to the concert: one on a bus shelter, the other affixed to a post box. I tore them off as best I could, leaving glue-laden shreds and vague Scottish flag patterns, but no message from the organisation that had taken Lars.

The powerful spotlights suspended from an array of lighting rigs flicked on and off in test patterns, and the squawk of guitar techs tuning instruments drifted from speaker stacks across the gardens. We showed our backstage passes and left another pair for the twins at the entrance behind the stage. The gate wardens ushered us into an area frenzied with uniformed security, caterers, and clipboard-armed organisers scurrying about in final preparations for the show. Admittance and directions to the VIP lounge came from a yellow-jacketed and barrel-chested man with a Caesar-like wreath of hair and a squiggle of translucent wire dangling from his earpiece to disappear beneath his collar. It had several quilted sofas, overflowing catering trays of fruits and snacks, and a direct side view of the stage. A small drum kit and a couple of acoustic guitars lingered in one corner.

Scarlett had done her homework. She recognised Piping Hot's manager from the record label's website. "I'm going to see if I can get some details about the record's production out of him. Maybe figure out if anyone added some kind of programmatic sound. Here come the Donnelly boys—you hang with them," she said, strolling off with a paper plate ringed with celery sticks that restrained a trio of rolling grapes.

Faraday waved the twins over to the sofa where he had staked his claim. Dot perched on the sofa's arm beside him, and I leant in from behind it, resting my chin on my crossed arms.

Before the boys reached us, a call of, "Youse alright? Ready for the show?" slapped us from the doorway facing stage left. A straightened arm against one edge of the frame propped up a lithe figure that leant against the doorway's other edge. The young man's hair swept from his brow in a drooping teardrop shape with its tip several inches above his left ear. It clearly required professional styling and a heck of a lot of product to stay aloft. His trousers were a patchwork of leather strips, mostly red, forming a modern interpretation of the Stuart tartan, and he wore a tank top that looked sewn from an actual Union Jack.

Dot laughed in joy at the spectacle. I stood, and the twins looked back over their shoulders in a mirrored motion worthy of a dance troupe.

"It's ma hair, right?" the newcomer asked. "My wee sisters laugh harder than you did and keep trying to flatten it. The stylists chuck a fit when I have to return for a touch-up. Och, the agony of the entitled pop star." He sauntered over, his trousers audibly creaking.

Dot stood too as he approached. "I'm sorry. Your outfit is amazing. It's just so … *unexpected*. I was imagining you'd be older, assuming you're in the band."

It was his turn to laugh. "Ah. A non-fan, I see. That's why

I enjoy popping into the VIP afore shows. It's dead unpredictable who'll be here. Could be my Nan, maybe some corporate bigwigs, but totally different crowd than the pre-teen screamers out front. And yeah, I'm Tam. My publicist would have you call me Tam Thunder, but the lads fae down the street here where I took my highers would call me Tam Ovens. I'm the drummer. And yeah, if you're in a boy band, seventeen is mid-career. I'll probably retire by twenty-two and appear on some dingy reality show by thirty."

"No disrespect, Tam—and charmed to meet you," Dot said. "I get what you do, but I'm not really into this poppy sort of music."

"Okay, let me warm up a bit and figure you out at the same time. Come perch your lovely self over here." Tam turned his back to us and strode to the drum kit in the corner, selected a pair of sticks, and motioned to the nearest armchair. He seemed fixated on Dot, but I opted myself into his invitation and sat on the chair's arm while Dot nestled in.

Tam cinched the round seat up a fraction, then elided into two long drum rolls on the snare. He paused and scratched an eyebrow, the drumstick tip in that hand pointing skyward. Looking at Dot's face the whole time, he said, "Maybe this?" and burst into a frenzied attack on the few drums in the kit. The bass drum thumped a steady line beneath an aggressive rhythm punctuated by cymbals kept in constant motion. The sticks were a blur, evoking a space for a heavy guitar riff soaring overtop. He paused and gripped the two cymbals to quell the echoes. An eyebrow raised in Dot's direction.

I glanced at her face, seeing a scrunched-up pair of sneering lips and her hand teetering thumb, pinkie, thumb, pinkie in the universal sign of 'maybe'.

"Aye. Got it now," he said and eased into a syncopated rhythm with the sound of silence emphasising the teasing backbeats. Danceable, for sure.

Glancing over Dot's shoulder, I saw the Donnelly twins trying to teach Grover some dance moves, keeping time to Tam's drumming. Their instruction wasn't very successful, but all three were laughing.

Dot nodded. "That's much better. I'm more of a reggae and ska girl."

"Brill," Tam said. "My first band at school was called the Gendarmes, and we dead wanted to be the Police. But of course, nobody can be the Police, except the Police. So here I am."

Across the VIP lounge, the band's manager called over from where he still stood with Scarlett, "Tam—better get ready. You're on in ten!"

"Well, lassies, duty calls! Will you be back here after we're through? If so, I'll swing by for sure."

I had to interject to cover Dot's speechlessness. "We're never going to get another chance to see tartan leather kecks, so yeah, come find us."

Tam saluted us with the pair of drumsticks, which he pocketed before backing out and heading to find his bandmates.

I elbowed Dot. "Can you be a wingman if you're a girl?"

She regained her normal composure. "Sort of. Let's go see what these twins are like, wingwoman."

Faraday was deep in technical discussion with the Donnelly twins when Dot and I sidled up.

One twin was explaining something, using languid swoops of his hand and arm to emulate a drone's flight path. Grover stared at them, enraptured. "—and you can program the professional drones we use to follow a path between up to sixteen 'beacons'. They're tennis-ball sized rubber devices— you can plant them ahead of time. Makes it dead simple to fly the drone along a complex route."

The other twin turned our way as we approached and offered a smooth-skinned hand for a fist bump. "I'll save your brother the introduction since he's already pointed you out to us. You're Higgs. And Dot, aye? I'm Darren."

"*Enchanté*," I said, in self-mocking tones, providing the required over-accentuated fist rebound. "And it's a good thing you introduced yourself. I'm not confident Faraday would have fulfilled that duty without prompting. He seems to be droning on over there."

Dot and Darren both laughed, their disparate hairstyles rippling in contrasting wavelets. "I take it you're not super into Piping Hot either?" Dot asked.

They both answered with the same reply, a fraction of a second apart, providing their own reverb effect. "Nah, no really."

"We're glad you invited us, though. Thanks for that. It's not every day you get to get this view of a concert, eh? But the bagpipes are over the top, no?" Duncan asked.

Faraday scooted himself up to perch atop the sofa's backrest, at eye level with the rest of us who stood. "I read that bagpipes are classified in some ancient law not as musical instruments but as instruments of war."

Darren chuckled. "I cannae really disagree, judging by the so-called music that comes out of them. But it sounds like some Sassenach law to prevent us from playing 'em in England."

"Do you ever go to any concerts down our way, like in Manchester?" Dot asked, flicking her gaze between the Donnelly brothers' faces. "I've only been to a couple."

"We go through to Glasgow, mostly. Most tours stop there," Duncan said. I found myself drawn to the eerie lightness of Duncan's one blue eye. I tried not to make it obvious, but was not sure I succeeded.

"How about London? Do you go down there for any events?" Dot asked.

"Nah. Only been there the once, to a club night," Darren said. "There's plenty up here to keep us entertained."

Scarlett swept up and waved a second tag hanging from her lanyard. "I have an opportunity for you to geek out, Redferne. The band's manager over there gave me two passes to the sound and lighting booth. Want to head over?"

"What kind of question is that? Let's go," Faraday replied.

The flood of a thousand conversations flowed to us from beyond the stage. "Sounds more interesting out there than backstage. Want to mingle a bit, boys?" I asked the twins.

They smiled and led the way.

"Come on, Grover, you're with us," Dot said, offering the crook of her arm to the confused-looking stable boy, who nonetheless hobbled forward to accept it.

CHAPTER 16 - POLLUTANTS

Newton

It was an incongruous mix of war council and stress relief. Emeline, Chronos, and I sat in woven-fibre folding lawn chairs in the backyard of what I still thought of as my parents' house. Motes of dust and clumps of pollen hung in the air, picked out by the warm summer sunshine gracing the back garden.

"Hey, look. There's one of those hedgehogs Higgs accidentally charmed," whispered Emeline, pointing to the back line of shrubbery. Airborne, it nosed through the verdant leaves and ripening berries of the shrub, its pink spines making camouflage impossible.

"Seeing one cracks me up every time," Chronos said. "Look at him, floating there like some sort of party balloon."

It was hard to say if the mutated hedgehog was happy with its lot. The near weightlessness allowed it to forage high in the bushes, where other hedgies would never dare climb. I'd seen the pink ones cavorting with other normal hedgehogs before, so they weren't ostracised. Maybe they were proud of their uniqueness.

I tinkled the half-melted shapes of ice cubes from side to side in my glass. "I feel a bit paralysed right now. Higgs and Faraday are far away in the hands of a woman I don't really trust. Not to mention Grover. My guess at the trigger for these attacks lines up, but I'm left waiting on Terrell and Scarlett for more details. And when Granny feels there's something up, it's nerve-wracking. She knows more about the goings-on in the area than all of us combined, even though she barely leaves her room. The spell to protect Higgs makes me feel a tad better, but what about Granny's visions of the lake? She says she doesn't know where it is, so how can we investigate?"

"Yeah, that's weird," Emeline said. "She's roamed every nook and cranny around Middle Ides at one time or another, so it makes little sense that she feels it's close if she's never seen it before. Maybe it's part of her fogginess—could she have visions of a place but forget she's been there before? It's not like there are any *new* lakes around here."

A call from behind us interrupted our musings; it originated somewhere around the side of the house. "Newton, are you back there?"

Chronos stood and crossed the patio, with only a hint of a lurch in his stride. He was finally moving freely, although I knew if he ran, it required considerable concentration, and the abrasion where the new leg met his stump would leave residual signs of his exertion. "Oh, hey Iain," he said, as he rounded the corner. "Come on back. Want a drink?"

"No thanks, I'm grand," Iain Vanderkamp replied. "I knocked at the front door, but I thought you might be back here, taking advantage of the sun. Oh, hi Emeline!"

I don't think I had ever seen my mother's former nanotech lab assistant Iain wearing shorts, although he visited Faraday on a near-daily basis. It somehow seemed incongruous to have such a bushy beard and wear shorts, as if nestling your face in hair also required you to always protect the rest of the body in warm clothes.

"Listen, Newt, I discovered something," he said, pulling up another lawn chair to sit directly beside me and pressing the home button on a handheld tablet computer. "Something about your mother's grave." I knew he had been pursuing his own suspicions about the incident that preceded my mother's death, when UPDA agents had visited the lab at the Feynman Centre. "Can I show you? Here?"

I took his question to refer to Emeline and Chronos,

although he looked only at me. "Ha—yes. This is Middle Ides, remember? Everyone knows everything about everyone, sooner or later. But yeah, these two are fully up to speed with my misfortunes, so don't hold back on their account. What have you got?"

"Well, you know I lowered a couple of probe tubes into Allison's grave site, right? And I used her nano-detection device to have a look. It was my hunch that something happened in the lab to trigger her aneurism. That it wasn't purely natural."

"Yeah—I know you confirmed there was *something* still active there," I said. "Did you decipher anything else from the readings?"

"Sort of. By accident, almost. Your mother's anti-nanotech experiments that Faraday and I have been perfecting need some better signalling and marshalling technology, so I ordered some kit to try. Don't tell anyone because I got it from this website in China, and I don't think customs would be too happy about things like this being sent into the UK, but whatever. The readme for the nanotech bits' signalling system describes the protocols for communicating with it from a computer system. Look here, in this schematic. It's completely different from the signalling that we use in the lab—that all follows a British and American standard. But I recognised parts of this protocol right away. They were the same as the faint signals I detected from inside Alison's grave."

"Wait," Chronos interrupted. "You mean to say that some sort of Chinese nanotech infected Mrs Redferne?"

It sounded weird for anyone to call her that, but Chronos had been coming to our house since we were toddlers, and some old habits don't fade.

"Well, I *ordered* it from China," Iain said. "And the technology was new to me. But it was *built* in Russia."

Later, I wished I had paid attention to the Russian implication, but at the time, my mind shot off in another direction, picking out Iain's phrase 'new to me'. It echoed something Emeline had said earlier.

"Hold that thought, Iain. Emeline, you said there aren't any new lakes around here. But that's not strictly true—there is a new body of water. Ferndale. Higgs heard them mention that name at Castle Ghuil."

"Oh my goodness, yes," she said. "Of course! Ferndale reservoir! It's not a real lake, but they completed it within the last ten years, so Angelina would have only ever seen the valley in the hills above us, not the reservoir."

An unnatural link was falling into place between the Tartantula's actions in Scotland and my grandmother's visions. My friends and I stood at once and made our apologies to Iain.

* * *

I packed Faraday's fancy drone into the back of the jeep, cradled in its padded case in case we needed it for reconnaissance. We were back at the Orphanage sooner than we strictly should have been if I had followed my police instincts and obeyed speed limits. I explained to Granny about the reservoir and waited impatiently as she got herself ready to leave her home.

The jeep's hard top, still badly scratched from Faraday's accident in the spring, kept the wind noise to a tolerable level for speaking as we ascended the winding road into the peaks above Middle Ides. Emeline and Chronos asked more questions about the reservoir, but we failed to arrive at any conclusion. Exploring the scene seemed the only way to discover more.

As we topped the slight rise and the flooded valley now known as Ferndale Reservoir came into sight, Granny peeked between Chronos's muscular shoulder and my less impressive one. "This is it. It's what I've been seeing. But not in daylight like this—I see it under a full moon."

The reservoir provided water for much of the surrounding area, its pipelines snaking through the hills as far as Manchester and Sheffield. Two rivers had been dammed, forming a deep V-shaped trough, submerging the valley and a pair of former farmsteads. The road we sped along crossed a narrow point of the reservoir on a new multiply arched concrete bridge.

I slowed and steered the jeep into a lay-by with a scenic view across the reservoir's calm, dark waters to the hills and higher peaks behind. In the winter, they might feature snowy caps, but in the height of summer, all were green meadows and blooming patches of bushes, punctuated by an occasional moss-laden boulder.

We stepped from the jeep to the grassy verge that sloped to the pebble-strewn margin of the reservoir's smooth surface. Crickets sang to us as I took Granny's arm and helped her navigate to the water's edge. A warm breeze raised an armada of ripples and faint lapping sounds at the point where land became lake.

"It is eerie. Something's not right," Emeline said.

Chronos chuckled. "Remind me not to go on holiday with you, Miss Grey. I couldn't think of a better day or a nicer place to spend it."

I felt nothing untoward, but Granny seemed to side with Emeline. "Let me feel the water," she said to me, using a voice barely audible even in the near-silence of our rustic surroundings.

I settled Granny into a seated position on the grass, and we removed our shoes and socks. Even at the height of summer, the water was cool on our toes as we waded into the shallows. I held Granny's elbow to steady her, and Emeline was alert at her other shoulder.

"Give me your bracelet, dear," Granny said to Emeline. "No, the copper one."

Emeline handed over the copper circlet, dense with Celtic knotwork but smooth at its edges from years of use. "What's your idea, Angelina?"

"Not sure. Checking something," she said cryptically. She shooed away my hand for a moment as she released a wider gold circlet from her right wrist, but then sought my balancing grip again as she held both trinkets in her left hand and bent to dangle them in the reservoir water. She mumbled a few things that I failed to make out as the bracelets hung there, half-submerged.

Were they moving of their own accord, or was it my grandmother's subtle finger motion that guided them? I'll never be sure. But after about twenty seconds, she straightened suddenly, and her voice rang hoarse and cavernous. "There's something in here."

All she could tell us was that some sort of malign magic was at work—she had no specifics other than something in the reservoir, somewhere. Some creature.

As the others slid their socks on, I was already unpacking the drone. Although not as expert as Faraday, I was adept enough to fly it in open terrain like this. I turned on its camera, checked the battery levels, and set it off. It ascended straight up at first before I moved it out across the water's surface. Criss-crossing the reservoir multiple times, the four of us crowded around the control console but saw nothing unusual, even as the drone reached the far shore, its whine almost imperceptible in the distance.

Granny lost interest after a while and returned her gaze to the reservoir. "Look! Over there!"

Her head faced the distant arches of the bridge, but her arm stuck out at a right angle, pointing to a small stand of trees on the water's far side.

I looked but saw nothing in the direction she pointed. Nor in the place she seemed to stare. I navigated the drone toward the trees. Maybe her vision had picked up something I missed, although that seemed unlikely given her age and eyesight.

"Emeline, do you see it? Right at the water's edge, by those pines?" she asked.

"No. I don't see anything," Emeline said.

Chronos shielded his eyes with a hand at his brow. "Me neither."

I continued to coax the drone closer, but still nothing unexpected appeared on the video monitor.

My grandmother chided nobody in particular as she continued to stare at the bridge but point at the other bank.

"Don't *look at it*, silly, just *see* it."

Emeline was the first to catch on, turning her head to face the bridge. "What the …? It's massive! And massively hideous! Is it a fly?"

Chronos and I finally caught on and the fearsome sight leaked into our peripheral vision as we turned our heads away but focussed on the cues coming in from near the trees. A fly the size of a delivery van blocked our view of the trees on the grassy far shore. It wasn't like a house fly. An almost spherical body weighed down six multiply articulated legs that depressed the turf beneath. It seemed covered with fur, coarse and mottled silver like a grizzly bear's. Its wings were nearly transparent and comically small; flight seemed like an impossibility. But the most striking features composed its face. Eyes like disco balls glistened in dark and multifaceted menace, ringed by sparse, thick lashes the length of blackened reeds. A proboscis curved out and down into the reservoir waters, a tube of misshapen and hardened enamel that would dwarf even Chronos if we dared approach it. Those orbs seemed to stare at us, unblinking, its nozzle an unmoving malice in the reservoir.

I turned to look at it directly, and the horrendous blowfly disappeared. The pines were visible again, but this time I noted the six depressions in the turf where I knew in my mind a horror stood. My hands darted over the drone's controls, sweeping low through the space where I once again saw the fly as I tilted my head to peer indirectly. The drone's video picked up no trace of the bloated insect.

"We'd better leave," Granny said with a quaver from behind us. That was not an invitation we needed to hear twice.

CHAPTER 17 - HINGE

Higgs

The anticipation was growing as the security guard released us into the general crowd at the far right-hand side of the stage. Agent Zee took a position outside the gate so he could watch Scarlett's bouncing ponytail as she and Faraday made their way to the mixing booth. People had sardined themselves more aggressively than the last time we had peeked out, but the pack remained navigable. The twins led the way into the crowd, veering off to the higher ground to find freedom away from the thronging pre-teens inching as close as they could to the stage.

"I still cannae see the appeal, crowdin' up to the stage when the better sound and chiller atmosphere is a wee bit further back," Duncan said.

Dot smiled, one corner of her lips twisting higher than the other. "Well yeah, but you aren't looking to get the lead singer's sweat on your arm and then swear to never wash that part of your skin again."

"True, true. There is that," he agreed. "But you also get the full effects of the light show from back here too."

Grover reached out to touch Darren's long-sleeved black shirt. "But you can make your own light show!"

Both twins turned a shade too quickly to look at Grover. "What do you mean by that?" Duncan asked.

"You know. The thing. He can make the light. And you can

make people really, really scared."

It was Darren's turn to question. "Who telt you that, Grover?"

Taking a half step back, Grover put his hands in his pockets and pulled his head into the lee of his shoulders. He looked at Dot, then at his shoes. "Well. You did. At the office. Remember?"

I put an arm around Grover and searched the twins' faces for a moment before speaking. "Grover—are you saying these boys can do magic? Not tricks. Real magic?"

"I don't know what magic is. They can do things. Like you and Dot can do things. But different things."

I could see the flickering tell-tale signs of a conversation headed in the wrong direction. Nostrils flaring a little. Clenched jawlines. The twins rising a fraction, shifting weight onto their toes. All indicators that Newton taught me to watch for in an escalating situation. But Dot diffused it.

"We get it, lads. We share that with you. I'll show you something. But hold up your jackets to keep any casual eyes away from what I'm going to do. Best not attract unwanted attention, eh?" she said.

We all huddled in close, and the twins obliged, grasping their lapels and expanding them out like bat wings to shade us all. Grover stood between them, opposite Dot and me, a conspiratorial grin brightening his sallow features. In the newfound shade, Dot held her left hand aloft, at shoulder height, fingers and thumb curled, as if around an invisible billiard ball. I knew what she was going to do as I'd seen her rehearse it in the back garden at my house several times before. She lightly licked two fingers on her right hand and stroked them three times along the tendons that accentuated the back of her upheld left hand. She said an inaudible word, deep in her throat, and then opened her palm to reveal a dark and lovely butterfly. It flexed its wings twice before she directed her gaze and gave a slight nod in Darren's direction. The wings fluttered, and the butterfly rose, only to settle again almost immediately on Darren's shoulder, sheltered by the raised jacket.

We all laughed, and the tension fizzed away. "Och, it's like that, is it? Aye, okay. How's this?" Darren said.

He closed his own palm gently around the butterfly, put the cage of fingers to his mouth, and puffed a single breath inside. He lowered his jacket, cast the butterfly into the air, and it swerved off, fluttering its black wings.

"Bit unimpressive," I said. "I thought Grover said you could do real magic."

Duncan chuckled. "Just watch," he said.

As if on cue, the butterfly's outline became limned with a shining orange before the glow bled across the breadth of its wings, bursting into light. Grover's mouth hung open as the self-illuminating butterfly wove in erratic flight over the crowd, wings now outlined in green light and its body glittering deep red.

"And I'll show you my real party trick. Each of you pluck out a hair for me."

Dot was hesitant but followed my lead, a small yank and a complaining, "Ouch," producing one of her long dark strands. We handed our specimens to Darren. He took each in turn and tied them into loops, breaking off about half of Dot's strand to make a circle of about the same size. He glanced to either side, checking for prying gazes. Finding none, he clutched the strands together in his fist and again blew a lungful of air into a gap formed by his curled index finger and thumb. After two or three seconds, he opened his fist to reveal brightly glowing bracelets formed from our own hair and handed them to us. Mine pulsed with golden light, and Dot's cast a glittering deep purple glow.

"Put them on! We're at a show, after all."

He had a trained eye for sizing too. The fragile loops could pass over our hands and onto our wrists without danger of snapping but fit snugly enough that they wouldn't slip off. They cast an amazing amount of light despite their slenderness. It didn't seem possible that a single strand of hair could be so luminous.

With the iridescent butterfly still visibly ascending over the crowd's centre, a cheer went up as the lead singer of Piping Hot, Peter Piper, sprinted to the middle of the runway that extended from the stage into the crowd. "Edinburgh, we're *home!*" he shouted into the mic, raising his arms to cheers of adulation that reverberated from the castle's rocky promontory. In spite of ourselves, Dot and I threw our arms into the air with the rest of the fans, our circlets glowing in the half-dusk of a perfect Scottish evening.

Faraday

I clipped the laminated mixing booth pass to the lanyard sporting my VIP pass and waded behind Scarlett into the crowd. The mixing booth rose above the closely packed concertgoers' heads on a scaffolded plinth. Agent Xenon-12 took a few steps after us, but a slight wave from Scarlett made him linger by the gate to the VIP area. He took up an observational stance, hands clasped together in front of his black jacket.

If you were an eleven-year-old Piping Hot fan, what do you think the best concert viewing position would have been? If you guessed the ideal perch was on the shoulders of a 6 foot 6 Russian nanotechnologist, I'm pretty sure you'd be right. Scarlett spotted Vladishenko and pointed in his direction as she changed course and parted a tangent through the sea of teenagers.

"Olga, say hello to Scarlett—she's from Iceland—and Faraday, who is English. I knew his mother very well," Dmitri Vladishenko boomed as we reached his position. His daughter beamed a week-brightening smile at us, her wispy white-blonde hair catching the last angling rays of daylight from her aerie atop her father's shoulders.

She called out what sounded like 'pre-viette' in a sing-song voice but which I knew was the Russian word привет meaning 'hello' and likely spelled 'privet' in the Latin alphabet. "I am pleased to meet with you," she said, spacing out the English words.

"They'll be on soon," Scarlett said. "Are you excited?"

"Da! Da! Very much excited! My early birthday present, right, Opa?"

"And more interesting than I thought, already," Dmitri said. "I watched them test drum riser mechanics. It rises, spins in arc, and can angle forward. And you know what I realised?"

"That you should have been a drummer instead of a nanotechnologist?" Scarlett ventured.

"Ha! How do you know I do not in my spare time? No, no, think on this. I watched drum riser tilting forward on its massive hinge, and I figured out something that was bothering me about schematics you showed yesterday. The nano hinge. Remember how components needed to angle themselves, once anchored in host, so they could communicate in mesh? And they had unique hinge design that I mostly ignored?"

Scarlett glanced my way. I nodded. "Yes—that was a key design feature of the system. What about it?"

"I've seen it before, that hinge. In sample I collected myself, last year. It's component of mist you emit from your CCTV systems. Your nano-detecting tech. That is only time I have seen same style of joint. It is ingenious. Surprised it wasn't designed by Russian, but I know it was not."

Scarlett clenched her jaw. "Damn! I wish that wasn't so helpful, but it means the world to me, Dmitri. We owe you a favour."

"I'll expect one." He smiled.

"And I don't mean to be rude, but I really have to move on this information. Enjoy the band, Olga!"

Scarlett pulled out her phone and moved away from Dmitri and his daughter, looking for a gap in the crowd. I waved to the Russian and his smiling daughter as I followed.

"It wasn't my mother who designed the hinge, was it? It was Angus," I said.

I received a nod, blonde ponytail bouncing as Scarlett spoke into her phone. "Control? Yes, it's Thorisdottir. I need an arrest made right away. Special forces, not locals. Target is Angus MacFarland from Caledonian Nanotech in Edinburgh. He's not particularly dangerous himself, but he may have an array of unexpected defences. Nobody tells him anything until I get there to interrogate him. I'm sending authorisation through the secure channel app now."

"You're brilliant," I blurted out but then felt sickened by my hypocritical turn. This was the woman that I still half-believed had betrayed and killed both my parents. I needed to finish this unsavoury business and catch her duplicitousness. These were my missions, and I focussed. I took 3 deep breaths and pounded my right thigh with the bottom of my clenched right fist 3 times.

"We know *who* unleashed this," I said. "We know *why*—it's all part of the separatist blackmail you're trying to hide from us. Let's finish the job and confirm Newton was right about the *how*. Seems like the violence is triggered by something added to a Piping Hot song."

"This time, *you* can talk. Try to wow the engineers with some tech chat and see what we can figure out," Scarlett said.

She followed me this time as I wove my way to the mixing booth riser, shoes crunching an occasional plastic water bottle. I apologised 11 times for accidental foot-treadings as we navigated the increasingly dense crowd.

Flashing our passes got us into the mixing booth. The lead sound engineer and the lighting techs leaned back in their chairs, chatting. Strangely, an illuminated butterfly fluttered overhead. I dived in immediately when they turned at our arrival in their sacred space. "Hi guys, I know you'll be busy soon, but I wanted to say how privileged I am to get a look at your setup. That's a *massive* line array configuration out there today."

The sound engineer nodded, raising an eyebrow. "You're into this stuff? That's refreshing. And yeah, it's a luxury to run an outdoor concert. We can use enormous banks of speakers in the line array without having to worry too much about echoes and reverberations like we would in an arena or concert hall. Bit of bounce back from the castle rock there, but nothing serious."

"And how many channels are you running? It looks like you have fourteen mics," I said, gesturing at the marked-up strips of gaffer tape above each channel on the massive mixing board, illuminated by a horde of flexible LED lamps.

"Yeah, our boy Peter Piper likes to roam around a bit. And all the lads sing here and there. Gotta get in those multi-part harmonies to live up to the boy band ideals!"

I could see that there were sliders controlling pre-recorded backing tracks labelled things like *back.synth*, *back.percussion* and *underflow.1*, *underflow.2*, and *underflow.3*. I struggled to figure out how I was going to ask what each of those tracks contained when Scarlett's side conversation distracted me.

She was talking to another person I hadn't noticed at first, who hung at the back of the booth. He wore his scraggle of hair tied back in a messy ponytail beneath a grey combed-wool flat cap. "So you recorded the entire album?" she asked.

"Aye. The lads have worked with me from the beginning. I run a wee studio down by the port in Leith."

Annoyingly, Scarlett had found the right line of inquiry even while letting me run the show. She wasted no time in panning the gold nuggets while I waded in silt. "What about all the background tracks, the stuff that noobs like me wouldn't realize are there? Do you make that part of the music yourself, or does the band do it all?"

"Aye, smart question, there. It's a bit ay both. We layer on multiple guitar tracks, for example, but I play some low-level synths, and on some tracks, there are non-musical bits and pieces, like spoken word or samples of everyday sounds. It's bizarre in a way to come to this show, 'cause I'll hear some of my own sounds. Braw, but cringey at the same time."

She was closing in for the killer question. "What about 'Flower of Glasgow'? Any interesting little flourishes on their current hit song?"

The recording engineer considered the question, nodding and scratching the side of his nose. "Loads of piping in that one, but I've recorded whole pipe bands before, so that was pure dead easy. And you'll hear some drum 'n' bass beats beneath the solo—lower down but still pretty audible."

It seemed like he was going to stop there, leaving us dangling with no further clues, but then he perked up, eyebrows raised in impressive arches and lips pursed. "And the record company sent in their own weird synth track underneath that. It's passing inaudible. I didnae think it added much, but they were insistent. See if you can hear it under the bagpipe solo when it arrives. An' I saw the guys that biked the sound clip in from the record company here earlier. There they are, way over there. Those twins with the short dreadlocks."

Things in the booth sprang to life as Peter Piper dashed forward on the stage outside, grabbed the mic, and started a frenzy. The sound and lighting engineers rolled their chairs up to the boards and computers and triggered the lights and sound levels with practiced, almost languid flicks of their control sliders and technical equipment.

The security guard who let us into the booth waved and nodded to us. It was time to leave the professionals alone. But Scarlett was in action too, pulling an earpiece from below the lapel of her blouse and speaking into a microphone along its cord. "Zee? It's the twins that helped trigger the nano attacks. Don't let them out of your sight." She stood tall, waved her right arm, and showed their position with an arched arm and pointing finger. I saw the crowd ripple as Zee waded against the current like a black-suited salmon toward Higgs, Dot, and the twins.

I had a foot on the riser's top step when Scarlett whispered aggressively in my ear, "We've got to stop the show. I can't have them play that trigger music in a crowd this size."

But the bouncer's vinyl-jacketed arm was already encircling her back, ushering her from the booth. She turned to him, her face only inches away from his, and drew out a leather-framed ID card. "I'm stopping this concert under the authority of the

UPDA," she shouted, lunging toward the mixing board.

From my position on the lowest step, I froze and watched. The bouncer outweighed Scarlett by at least double, and he easily held back her lunge. "Easy, lass. Time for you to go." Scarlett snarled, face flushing instantly. "UPDA. Seriously. If the concert doesn't stop, people may die."

"I dinnae ken what UPDA is, but I'm fae the CU," the bouncer said, getting a constricting grip on the back of Scarlett's collar. Her earpiece dangled wildly, and a button popped from her blouse.

"CU?" Scarlett replied in a puzzled tone.

The bouncer laughed. "Yeah—see you, lassie!" He threw her clattering down the metal steps where she knocked me into the clearing behind the mixing riser where the stage view was obstructed. As Scarlett and I lay befuddled and grass-stained, the bouncer, still laughing at his own joke, clicked shut the door to the booth.

From the stage, I heard Peter Piper belting out introductions, punctuated by an unsurprisingly high-pitched response of cheering fans. "The bass fiddleman, Randall Radiation ... the man with the sticks, Tam Thunder ... and on guitar and pipes, Mr Malcolm McChord!"

CHAPTER 18 - FLOWER OF GLASGOW

Higgs

Over the screams of the fevered early teens surging toward the stage lip and the cheers of the audience straddling Princes Gardens and gawking from every building, side street, and even the castle walls, Peter Piper took command.

"Edinburgh! We're home!" The reverberations from the shopfronts along Princes Street and the rise opposite rang with excitement. Malcolm McChord belted out the guitar refrain from "Sweet Home, Alabama", which I only knew from my father's mandatory Saturday night sing-a-longs when we were little. This generated a deeper-voiced wave of chuckling from the crowd's fringes.

"Lads, we cannae leave it for the encore, can we? This is 'Flower of Glasgow'!"

Dot's new admirer Tam raised his sticks overhead, clacked them together four times, and set the song's tide in motion.

As the band slowly built their crescendo, two young women danced over to the twins, arms in the air. We could tell they had met before because each had a glowing twist of hair bouncing around a forearm as they moved. They leaned in, wedging shoulders between us and the twins. London accents unmistakable, they spoke loudly to be heard over the crowd. Waves of chestnut hair cascaded around the olive complexioned face of one of them. "What you doin' here? You said you was from Scotland, but I thought it was me imagination when I spotted you," one said.

Dot stiffened beside me. These twenty-somethings with their casual elegance, full makeup, and boundless exuberance brought our camping clothes and provincialism into sharp relief. An earring hoop that could nearly have doubled as a netball ring dangled in my line of sight. I struggled to identify the reason for my extreme irritation but shrugged that question away and raised an eyebrow in Duncan's direction. He shrugged as the second woman held up her wrist and gestured toward it with a nod of her head that rippled a blue-tinged asymmetric bob.

"Look! Still glowin' after a week! Amazing! When are you lads in London again?"

As the music continued behind us, Dot yelled to me above the guitar crescendo. "That's us shut out now, eh?"

"Let's just enjoy the show," I replied, half-turning from the twins to face the cut-and-parry of lasers and the rhythm of the drums. Grover's head bobbed to my left, and Dot leant in on my right. I patted Grover's shoulder for reassurance as I spotted Agent Zee shoving through the throng toward us.

Zee had almost reached us when Malcolm McChord settled his guitar into its stand and took up his bagpipes. I caught a counter-current of motion in my peripheral vision and saw Scarlett elbowing her way between annoyed-looking concertgoers with Faraday urging her forward. Was that dirt on her face? I nudged Dot and nodded toward the crowd's centre, to Scarlett and Faraday's advance. Her brows drew in.

As the first strains of piping erupted over a pounding undercurrent of rapid drumming, I heard Duncan Donnelly call out behind me, "Bro. Better stand back."

I craned my neck around, still maintaining a gentle grip on Grover's shoulder. I saw Duncan pulling Darren forcefully back from the two girls, a space opening between the two pairs. With his other hand, he shoved Dot away from the women. He forced her back a step, and Grover grabbed Duncan's wrist in a show of defence that was swatted away. In my right ear, I heard Scarlett shrilling, "Take them! Take them now!"

Puzzled, I pulled Grover closer and felt Dot pressing in from behind me as Zee barged past, an outstretched arm scything between the two women as he almost swam between them to reach the twins. Scarlett was closing in fast but stumbled momentarily. Faraday crashed into her back and threw her further off balance.

Then the music triggered the nanotech deep within the two women.

I had never seen any person—or any animal—transform from relaxed cheeriness to full combat mode in a heartbeat. Both young women pulled their lips back, exposing teeth clenched in primal snarls. One already had a handful of Agent Zee's hair as she fell back, pulling him down. The other kneed him in the face as he toppled. I glimpsed mixed surprise and confusion on Zee's face as he collapsed into a mass of writhing arms and legs. Somehow, a broken bottle was already in her hand, and she plunged it downward three times before a flying Faraday tackled her, and the glass flew from her hand, glinting red in the gathering gloom. The pair hit the ground with an impact I felt through my soles. The bagpipes played on as the twins retreated, averting their gazes from the melee and fleeing as fast as the crowd would part for them.

I guess wrestling with Chronos must have instilled some deep-seated fighting instincts in my brothers. Faraday had the blue-haired girl's face forced into the detritus of plastic bottles and food wrappers with his forearm. He leant in with his full weight as she tried to wriggle free with determined ferocity. Dot dived and pinned her legs, taking a couple of vengeful kicks to the ribs in the process.

The other woman continued to punch and kick at Agent Zee from beneath his bulk. He had one of her arms pinned beneath a knee and fended off blows from the other arm while he leant into her chest with an open palm. Blood flowed freely from a gash from his brow to his chin, splattering the face of his assailant.

"Zee! Zee!" Scarlett's voice echoed the cries of the surrounding crowd that had backed off, forming a ragged circle around the eight of us. It was the first time I'd seen her lose her cool.

The bagpipes and their drum 'n' bass substrate gave way to Peter Piper's soaring vocals, and both women went limp in an instant.

For that frantic twenty seconds, I was numb, but the look in Duncan's eyes as he turned and fled stoked the ember that burned forever inside me. I took two running steps to the edge of the space around us and swung myself onto the railing that partitioned the concert crowd from Princes street, bringing myself to a shaky but balanced position atop its chrome tube. About fifty metres away, I picked out the wave of dreadlocks as the twins sped through the audience's thinning fringes.

They approached the outstretched limb of a proud maple as I felt indignation and rage erupt from deep within me. Leaves sprung from the backs of my hands and my scalp tingled with electricity. My eyes narrowed to slits as I willed the tree to help me. A thick tree bough softened and raised in a swirl like the backstroke of a coiling whip. The twins looked up, then cowered.

But the limb froze in that position, and the leaves withered and dried on the backs of my hands. Although my anger flared, the magic seeped away like the last half-spray from a depleted spray bottle. Granny had warned me I needed Newton to fuel my magic, but I guess I never really believed it.

Medics pushed through the crowd toward the now calm scene of the fracas behind me. The twins scuttled out of sight, still running.

* * *

We used the VIP lounge as a makeshift war room, emptied of anyone else while Piping Hot played on. An ambulance had whisked away Agent Zee. Stab wounds to his shoulder and forearm accompanied the lacerations on his face; he was a bloody mess but had been lucky to avoid any life-threatening injuries.

We pushed two sofas into conspiratorial range. Dot, Grover, and I still nestled together. Dot had two muddy shoe prints on her shirt where kicks had landed while she helped Faraday pin down the short-haired woman. Although I tried to comb them out with my hands, a plethora of dried leaf fragments remained woven deep in my hair, diaspora from my quelled magic. Scarlett's cheek featured a scuff of dirt, the result of her topple from the sound booth. Faraday was the least sullied. "Play everything back one more time, Faraday," I urged.

"All the nanotech points back to Angus MacFarland and the Donnelly twins. The Russian guy Mum worked with noticed a nanotech building block in the substance used in the attack. It's one of Angus's signature inventions. Newton was right—once planted, it messes with the victim's mind, making them go berserk when triggered. And that signal is a sound embedded in the Piping Hot single, right under the bagpipe solo. We know the Donnellys delivered the sound clip and had the recording engineer add it to the track."

Scarlett interjected here. "We tried to stop them playing the song today, but the bottom of a bouncer's boot put a stop to that. There were two other incidents in the crowd during that song, so the nano infestation is wider than we'd hoped. But I've already put wheels in motion to have that part of the song remixed and re-released to every radio station and streaming service. That should be done by the end of tomorrow to mitigate the risk of more incidents. We'll have to hope the copies we can't update, like CDs and vinyl, aren't in the hands of anyone infested already."

Dot massaged her ribs. "And it was the twins that were the nano distributors too, is that what you're saying?"

"Almost certainly, yes," Faraday said. "They're obviously very persuasive—they even had me liking them, and you know me and people. Seems like they had multiple trips to London, where they met and infested several unsuspecting young ladies. I found their stack of used train tickets, and you encountered two victims first hand."

"Their party trick is a big draw," I added. "Darren makes these glowing bands out of a strand of your own hair. Those girls that flew off the handle during 'Flower of Glasgow' each had one."

"Well, they don't *both* have them anymore," Dot said. "I pulled this off the wrist of the one Faraday and I tackled. Thought it might be useful." She emptied her pocket and dangled the still-glowing circlet from her muddy hand.

Faraday shot a venomous look in Scarlett's direction. "And this is all part of the blackmail effort against the Scottish First Minister that you haven't properly told us about yet."

Scarlett sighed. "Yes, yes. But outstanding work, all of you. Look, we've planned the raid on Castle Ghuil for tomorrow afternoon. We'll neutralise the death clock and any further threats from the elf. And we now know the what, why, who, and how of the nano attacks. It's only a matter of time before we pin down Angus and the twins."

Grover had been swivelling to watch each of us in turn as we spoke as if a spectator at some verbal tennis match. "But what about the bad thing that's going to happen to that running boy?"

He said a lot of strange things, but this made me nervous, and a physical pang surged through me. "Lars? Our friend from Middle Ides?"

"Yes. Lars. The boy with the blue eye is going to do that thing to him now. I saw it when I grabbed his hand during the fight."

Thing? Thing. I remembered Grover's description of Duncan's power from earlier when we were charmed by Darren's luminary theatrics. "You said he scares people? Lars is tough enough not to let some trick frighten him. He's already in a cage."

"It's not scaring like that, Higgs. He can see what scares you the *most* in the entire world. And whatever you think of, he makes it real. When I touched him just back there, I noticed him thinking about how the power works. How he rubs the charcoal along his arm and the back of his hand. Like a skeleton hand, then when he touches you, he can see what you are frightened of, deep down. And once he sees it, he looks back inside himself, wraps it up with his power, and lets it flow back into you.

The power even scares him, that boy, a little too, even though he doesn't use it on himself. When he first learned how to use the power, he was mad and used it on someone at his school. Whatever that kid imagined, he never came back to school after that. It was sort of an accident, but it's not gonna be an accident when he uses it on Lars."

I felt like I was going to suffocate. Tears welled up my eyes but stopped short of trickling down my cheeks. "Scarlett, you've got to stop them before they get to Castle Ghuil and use their powers on Lars. You'll get them soon, right?"

"I'm all over it, Higgs. But we don't have trackers on them yet. Or Angus. He keeps slipping our surveillance. If we think they're headed to Glen Ghuil, I'll update our surveillance net. It may help."

Scarlett moved over to the corner near the drum kit and murmured into her mobile. She was back in control after the rare moment of vulnerability when Zee fell, and we left her to her organisation. Faraday shifted over to the sofa to join the three of us and put his arm around my shoulder. "Come on Higgs, be positive. You've seen the UPDA at work. There's nothing we can do that they can't do better. Trust the process."

I turned and looked deep into his eyes, wiping away the welling tears. "Do *you* trust her?"

He looked away. "Damn. I see your point. But I don't want you to do anything stupid."

"He's our friend, Faraday. Yours too."

The music paused, and I heard Peter Piper call into the microphone, "We love you, Edinburgh! We're Piping Hot. Good night!"

With our side view, we saw the four of them back off the stage, waving to the torrent of cheering and applause. As he passed the VIP lounge, Tam Thunder stuck his smiling face across the threshold, towelling his sweaty hair into a more sustainable swept-back look. "Hey Dot, Higgs. I'll only be a minute—you'll hang here for a wee while yet, right?"

Dot nodded rapidly, and Tam whisked himself away backstage.

He was back in about three minutes. No more leather trousers or tank top, this time he wore black jeans, a crisp white button-down shirt, and a pair of polished Chelsea boots. His still-damp and dishevelled hair lent an edge of tiredness to his refreshed look. "Where are you staying? I'll walk you back."

Faraday sneaked a quick glance my way, and I read an entire paragraph into it, if not a novel. "It's all good, Faraday," I said. "We know the way back to the Dean Village. Shall we stop for a bite on the way, Tam?"

My brother paused, then nodded. "Looks like you're with me and Scarlett, Grover. We'll start walking once she's off the phone."

"Will Zee be there to watch telly with me?" Grover asked.

Faraday slung an arm around the shorter boy's shoulders. "Probably not. But I'll watch with you. It's Saturday, there should be something good on."

Dot ran quickly to the loo before rejoining Tam and me. He ushered us toward the backstage exit. "It's better, walking," he said. "The crowd'll take an age to disperse. Randall and I came here on motorbikes because it'll be ages before a car can pass along these streets. We'd planned a quick exit, but I can trek back for my bike later, nae problem."

"Give me one second, Tam," Dot said, turning to me as we approached the stage's rear gate. She whispered as she brought up the map app on her mobile.

"Higgs, I used the finding spell in the bathroom stall just now. With the glowing hair band. I can see all three of them! The girl is in a hospital bed over *here*, but I can also visualise where Darren is, probably because he infused the hair strand with his magic. He's skirting around the city centre from his mother's place in Duddington, heading west. I feel another motorbike in front of him which I suspect is Duncan."

"They could be on their way to Castle Ghuil already?" I

hissed.

"Looks like it, yeah, once they can get on the A road. I should go back and help Scarlett track them."

"Scarlett will just want to stick to her plan. She doesn't care about Lars being frightened, she only wants to stop the Tartantula. She can keep to her plan, but it's not *her* Lars, it's *my* Lars. Sorry … *our* Lars. Let's intercept them. I failed when I had my chance, but I'll stop them this time." I wasn't sure how I would overcome the lack of power when Newton wasn't around, but I'd figure that out. Maybe Dot could power me, somehow.

Dot was a planner that complemented my drive. "Er, Tam? There's something *really* important we need to do. You said we couldn't get a car anywhere near here, but how would we get to the closest taxi? We can run. We're dressed for it."

"Including a pair of boot prints on your top, I see," Tam said, grinning. "The dancing's mair violent than it looks from the drum riser, I guess. But as I said, it's only fit for walking out of here for the next hour."

She leant in beside him, pointing to her phone. "We need to catch these guys on bikes. They're riding across here just now, and we think they're heading west out of town. Know of anything that would let us catch them up?"

"I could take one of you on my bike. We can probably catch up to them if we're quick. I have an extra helmet."

"We both need to go," I said, sounding more demanding than I'd hoped.

Tam scratched an ear. "Randall's bike is here too. Let me get both sets of keys from our security guy over there, and I'll see if I can find Randall. He can take you."

I pointed to the pair of motorcycles parked in the shade behind the stage. "If you can get both sets of keys, let's not waste time—I can ride the second one myself."

Tam looked at me with a half-smile and raised eyebrows. "Um, okay? Why not? Helmets on. You show me where we're headed, Dot, and you follow us, Higgs. You're sure you're good on a bike?"

I nodded grimly, trying to look confident. The bike was way bigger than the one Chronos had trained me on. And technically, I didn't have a licence. But it was for Lars.

If my parents or either brother could see me, I'd be pulled off the bike and given a tongue lashing that didn't bear thinking about. But there was no turning back now. Tam and Dot were already gliding toward the gate.

CHAPTER 19 - STALKERS

Higgs

Randall Radiation had a much bigger head than mine. His helmet jiggled and threatened to slide down over my eyes, its chinstrap dangling idle. I cinched it as tight as it would go and rolled the motorcycle forward off its stand. It sounded simple enough to ride in the wake of Tam Thunder's bike as it negotiated the pedestrian-clogged roads ahead. Dot's helmet turned to check on my progress as she gripped the pillion passenger handholds beneath her.

I stalled the bike initially, but restarted it and spurted forward to follow them through the gate. This bike would need taming; it was twice as powerful as the one Chronos taught me on. I took a deep breath and concentrated on the spinning rubber of Tam's rear wheel.

Throngs filled the pavements of Princes Street, and the strolling, scurrying, and erratic dancing of the dispersing concert crowd made the roadway a conveyor belt of hazards. The low-speed progress suited my bike trials skills even though the weight of this machine was double my previous experience. We wove through the surging diaspora with snakelike progress, my front wheel mirroring Tam's every twist as if on an invisible tether.

A pack of drunken revellers flowed like an amoeba onto the roadway in front of me, momentarily separating my bike from Dot and Tam's as they headed through a gap in the traffic control barricades, aiming for the turn that would take them on the ascent across the North Bridge to the old town above us on the right. From there, I knew we would circle back, skirt the castle's far side, and escape the crowds before intercepting the Donnelly twins on their westward journey.

Tam's bike edged further away, while I only inched along, avoiding interlopers. The gap between our bikes widened. Two police officers lunged into that gap, confronting me as they attempted to control the crowds. I was forced to stop.

"You cannae come through here!" one bellowed at me, blocking my progress.

"I'm just—"

They both shook their heads and positioned themselves so I couldn't proceed without flattening at least one of them.

A stone's throw ahead, Tam had stopped and steadied the bike with his right foot on the tarmac. Both helmets pointed in my direction. The twins were slipping from our grasp with every passing second.

I urged Dot and Tam to continue with a frantic overhead series of pointing gestures. Dot tapped Tam on the shoulder and pointed the way. They headed off, picking up speed as the crowd dispersed ahead.

But I didn't mean for them to continue without me. On the contrary, I was more determined than ever to vent my rage on the twins. In three spasmodic bursts, I turned my bike in a tight circle, unused to the extra power and mass.

It was only a short distance back to the dipping roadway to the train station, nestled in the valley beneath the North Bridge. I revved the bike and navigated the slope down to the station's entrance, whisking past protesting pedestrians. I shouted as I rode—incoherent warnings to stay out of my path as I coaxed more speed into my circuitous path and tried to figure out where the horn was located. An occasional brush of wing mirror on fabric as I veered too close to an oblivious walker left a trail of protests and insults in my wake, but I didn't care. My only aim was to not bowl anyone over.

Past the station entrance, the road rose slightly, but another barricade blocked the curling rise of the cobblestone road that would reunite me with Dot and Tam on the High Street above. With this option removed and negotiating my way back through the concert crowd's clogged heart to head west looking like a job measured in hours, I had no obvious choice. I would have to leave it to Dot to trace and stop the Donnellys.

Although the bulk of the people departing the concert and heading southward chose to clamber over the barricades and ascend the picturesque arc of shop-lined roadway, I spied a couple opting for a more direct route to Castlehill above us— they ducked into a steep-stepped nook, turning sharp right at the barricade. The stone steps of one of Edinburgh's ancient pedestrian 'closes' was good enough for them, so why not me?

This ill-planned decision resulted in probably the first ever trip up the stone stairs of Advocate's Close on a motorcycle. Hopefully, it would be the last.

I approached the entrance to the close with momentum, my rear wheel gliding, disobedient, across the yellowed cobbles of Cockburn Street as I banked right. The long shadows of dusk obscured the entrance to Advocate's Close. What seemed like a reasonable idea from a distance seemed lunacy now that my front wheel was on the bottom step. But the benefit of lunacy is that its practitioners rarely back down. Nor did I.

The instincts that Chronos had honed as he forced me across countless random obstacles on the smaller bike kicked in. I throttled in just enough to give the bike power to lurch up each stone step without losing control and alignment. Like the ratcheting jerks of a roller coaster climbing to its first drop's apex, the bike leapt from one stair to the next.

I got the hang of the climb, rising from the saddle on the foot pegs and focussing on the steps, each with its irregular span, when I encountered my first problem. The couple I had seen diverting into the close were only a few steps ahead. There was no concealing the juddering whine of my engine as I clattered from step to step, so they turned in surprise as I closed in from below. They realised their best option was to become as close as possible to two-dimensional along the wall of the close, given that it was barely wide enough for two people to pass.

I dared not slow down—it would have been almost impossible to ascend again from a dead stopbut I slowed a little, since I could not pass them without my handlebars skewering one or the other. With two steps to spare, the man yanked the slight woman into a fortuitous niche formed by the back door to a flat that spilled into the close. I called an apology as I roared across the landing they huddled beside.

The next obstacle was a ninety-degree bend in the close as the stairs turned south, yearning to reach the Old Town High Street above. I needed to take the corner without losing velocity.

With more speed than I expected, I shot into the bend. My front wheel spun up the wall in front as I struggled to swivel the bike, but I wrestled it into the turn. A stone ceiling enclosed the close from this point upward, a claustrophobic arched tunnel leading to its ultimate exit street-side. Then disaster struck.

Although I had the bike pointing in the right direction, I hadn't the agility to re-point the front wheel, and it landed at an angle on the next step, immediately wrenching to the left. The handlebars ended up pointing directly left, wedged at the stony base of the next step's rise. My forward motion stopped, and the engine raced as I struggled to hold on to the handlebars and accidentally gunned the throttle.

This inadvertent extra power was ultimately what saved me from toppling over backwards. The front wheel returned from its side journey up the close wall and bounced as the shock absorbers sprang back. This bounce freed the wheel and cleared the next step, but I had to both lean way forward over the bars and straighten them at the same time. My chest took a bruising blow from the handlebars, and my open helmet left my nose inches from the madly spinning front wheel.

How I remained balanced, I'm still not sure, but I shot from the upper entrance to Advocate's Close still half-dangled over the handlebars. My sprawl was lucky because otherwise, the low frame at the top of the close would have decapitated me.

My good fortune continued as I blitzed across the wide pavement and onto the cobbles of Lawnmarket. A man held his two young children back from the brink of my path, probably alerted by the revving engine noises blasting up the steps.

There was no immediate traffic for my bike to collide with, ending my pursuit prematurely, but as I rebalanced myself and turned westward to face the approach to Edinburgh Castle, a second bike pulled alongside me. I had burst from the top of Advocate's Close as Tam and Dot sped along Lawnmarket. I could hear Dot hooting with joy even over the engine's roar and the rumble of tires skimming cobblestones beneath us.

Tam gestured to take the left fork ahead, and we glided down the road that skirted the castle's other side. The stage would be directly through the rock from here. Dot held on with her left hand while her right held her mobile phone with its map open and the loop of illuminated hair that maintained her connection to Darren Donnelly.

We sped out on Queensferry Road, leaving Edinburgh and heading westward toward Glen Ghuil. Instead of taking the motorway, Tam steered us onto the smaller roads that flirted with the south bank of the Forth as it ventured out to the North Sea. The twins must be nervous about apprehension, taking a less obvious route. My hands verged on cramping as I gripped the handlebars with far too much force, but I had never ridden half as fast as I was now, and my nerves wouldn't allow an iota of relaxation. But still, I followed, hoping with Dot's every glance screenward that we narrowed the gap with our quarry.

I considered our options for when we caught up to them; the planning part of my brain apparently had left this detail intentionally vague. What were we going to do, run them off the road? Overconfidence made me believe that my magic would somehow leap into this void of uncertainty, but I couldn't imagine concentrating on magic when I could barely loosen either hand from their vice-like grip on the bike.

I had thought little more than this when we started to close in fast on two motorbikes. As the distance between us shrank, I could see it was the twins, a few tell-tale inches of flapping dreadlocks blurring their helmets' bottom edges.

Luckily, my magic didn't seem to need any planning. As I thought about what might befall Lars, I pictured him cowering from the twins in whatever confinement held him. But there was no escape for him without intervention. It was up to me to protect him, and that time was now. I opened the throttle and glided past Dot, her pale complexion ghostly behind the helmet's visor. Speeding up, I left Tam's bike to pull in behind me as I sidled up to the trailing Donnelly brother.

A feeling like internal fire flared in my left arm. Three thick vines grew in unnatural abandon from my wrist, coiling and reaching in a flurry of erupting leaves toward the handlebars of whichever twin dared ride beside me. He turned his head a fraction toward me, and I imagined his terror behind the tinted visor. He picked the wrong girl to mess with.

Tendrils of the vine caressed the near-end of his handlebar, looking for purchase. But just like at the concert, when I stood on the railing, the flame of magic within me failed without warning. The vines retracted at speed, none having reached their target. A big black boot extended toward me and kicked the frame of my motorcycle. Wobbling at high speed across the darkened road, my bike dipped into a ditch while the back wheel bucked me high into angled flight toward the flanking trees.

CHAPTER 20 - FLIGHT

Faraday

The hubbub of 10,000 conversations from the dispersing crowd infused the area between the castle and Princes Street. Grover and I were ready to leave the VIP area when the girls left, but Scarlett was making a series of calls and checking her phone for progress on finding Angus and the Donnelly twins. I ushered Grover to the drum kit, and he attempted to build up a rhythm. It was only semi-successful, but it occupied him. The sofa gave me some distance from both Scarlett's murmurs into the phone and the erratic snare drum strikes. I considered what was within my power; how could I help put the finishing touches to the plotters' capture?

A glance at the wall-hung phone in Delladonna's cottge had etched her number into my mind along with every other detail of her home. I rang. I was never good at opening chit chat, so I got right to the point when she answered.

"Hi Ms Donnelly, it's Faraday. From yesterday."

"Och hi, petal. The boys are out just now."

I figured as much. "That's okay. I really wanted to talk to you. Listen—this won't be easy."

There was a brief silence. "What've they done now? They were in such a hurry after the concert. They were only here two minutes before they left on their bikes. I had a bad feeling."

"It's not really them; it's Angus," I said. "Well, they're involved, I mean, but Angus is exploiting them. There's this thing, this nanotech, and he's making them infect people with it, down in London. Some people have died."

Another long silence followed. "I'm not sure I want to hear this, but tell me anyway," she said.

I drew in a deep breath and launched into the short version of the story. "Can you call them? They're clearly in trouble, but I'd like to see them get out from under this shadow before they do anything worse. I'm worried they may use their powers against our friend, who is being held at Castle Ghuil."

Delladonna growled like an enraged feral dog. "That Angus! After everything I've done for him! I'm gonnae take my hand of his face when I catch up to him. Give me a sec, I can't stretch the phone far enough to see if he's over the road."

There was a slight clatter as the phone dangled and I heard a door being wrestled open in the background. Delladonna returned a moment later. "Lights are off there, and I cannae see his fancy car. A few gadges poking around the hut, like. Are they yours?"

I wasn't sure what a gadge was, but I replied instinctively. "Scarlett has put out a bulletin, so there are people looking for Angus. And your lads, too. We want them stopped before things get worse."

Delladonna's voice was a lament. "I'm such a fool. Angus took the boys under his wing, away fae the wrong crew. I always knew that Angus was full of venom, but I figured he only used this independence lark to let out the spite and fear knocked into him by his father. I should've seen he was moving the boys from common trouble into more sophisticated manipulation."

I felt for her. My interactions with the twins made me believe they were good at heart—they'd taken to Grover, too, including him when others mostly ignored him. But they'd also done unforgiveable things with their eyes wide open.

Grover's affair with the drums had ended, and he sidled up beside me, pressing his ear to the other side of my mobile phone so he could hear too. I allowed him this awkwardness as I figured out what to say to Delladonna. I didn't want to reveal any of Scarlett's plans, but I knew my mother would have wanted the opportunity to fix things if any of us were in a mix-up like this. "Listen. Darren and Duncan are in a lot of trouble, I can't dispute that. But they aren't in any danger right now. If they head to Castle Ghuil and get tangled up with Ruaridh and this Tartantula nonsense, none of us can protect them from what might happen. You've got to get through to them, get them to surrender. Tonight. Can you do that?"

A wrenching sigh came across the line. "Aye, I'll try. They were never ones to do what I ask direct, like. I hope what I tell them sinks in, but they only learn by doing, not by listenin'. Maybe they'll realise this is a mistake before they ride it all the way to its miserable end. I'll try, Faraday. If I hear their bikes come back, I'll call you. Maybe someone their own age can talk some sense into them."

I ended the call and rubbed the phone screen against my trouser leg. Was there anything else I could do?

"Higgs and Dot are on motorbikes, too," Grover said.

I looked into his earnest, spectacle-magnified eyes. "No, no. They're walking back with that Tam guy. The drummer from the band. Let's get Scarlett, and we can go back too, watch a show on telly."

Grover shrugged. "Okay," he said and bounced off the sofa. "Wouldn't it be good if Disco went up there, near that castle? Then we could see her tomorrow."

Higgs

Although there is an eternity to think about things after being thrown from a motorcycle, there is remarkably little time to act. Luckily, this is something that most people never learn. I was not so fortunate.

I flew through the warm night air, the River Forth shimmering in the moonlight to my right and a pine-fringed farmer's field dead ahead.

I was a foolish little girl and should have listened to Faraday's pleas and allowed Scarlett's forces to handle the Donnelly twins. Instead, I had, until recently, piloted a motorbike too powerful for me at inadvisable speeds, chasing a rock star and a pair of murderous magic-wielding magicians across an unfamiliar countryside. I deserved the wake-up call of a kick that divorced me from the bike and catapulted me here, about to cannonball to my death in an anonymous turnip field. If by some grace I survived to make mistakes in the future, this was the type of blunder I swore to avoid.

The last image in my mind before plunging into the pointy, unwelcoming pine branches was Lars. I didn't deserve him as a friend. He definitely didn't deserve the wrath of Duncan Donnelly, who I had failed to stop. I thought not of the impending pain, not of my brothers or my best friend Dot. I dwelt only on the idea that I would never see Lars again. Strange.

My aerial trajectory was about to enter a turbulent phase. It looked like I would avoid the tree trunks in the double row of bush-branched pines, allowing my body to scrape through for a full face-plant in the turnips.

But the first impact in the branches wasn't as harsh as I expected. A patch of brittle and diseased branches at my entry point halfway up the first tree did little more than scratch me, desiccated pine needles sloughing away as I shot through. If anything, they slowed me slightly.

I also escaped the thickest boughs as I continued my spiral. A clack on the back of my helmet signalled a thick branch passing behind me. My small surge of involuntary preservation magic parted a dense patch of branches, leaving me with no more than a carpet of resin-coated needles latched onto my clothes with gummy resolve.

When I cleared the second row of trees, I was still a good two storeys above the field, and the full moon crossed my field of vision as I rotated. My neat spiral morphed into a cartwheel as I slowed unexpectedly. A new stickiness that covered me from face to feet joined the gummed pine detritus. I had struck, been momentarily pinned, and then plummeted from a massive spider web, its strands as thick as twine and as broad as the rug in our lounge at home. The bike dangled above me, springing back in the tangled embrace of the webs.

Disoriented, I tumbled straight down in a new rush of acceleration after the momentary pause in the web's clutches. From this height and rotating like a rag doll flung away in a tantrum, there were going to be a lot of broken bones, but I had a moment of clear optimism that I would not die after all. I visualised myself in a hospital bed, leg raised in plaster, tended to by Dot and a rescued Lars. And Chronos—he owed me after all the visits to the hospital to see him following the battle at Pendlethwaite House.

The impact arrived mid-vision. I landed flat on my stomach and cried out in agony. But only because I felt an obligation to cry out. For some reason, I still breathed, despite expecting to have every last ounce of wind knocked from me. I pushed myself into a press-up position on my amazingly unbroken arms and legs. I jiggled my oversized helmet free, knelt, and felt myself all over with frantic palms. Uncommonly sticky, yes, but nothing more serious than a few scratches on my hands and forearms. I laughed hysterically but paused as I surveyed my resting spot. Somehow I had landed on a bed of springy moss as deep as the fanciest mattress, covered by a layer of feathers. Impossible feathers. Each was the length of my arm and curled like a saucer to hold a pond of fluffy down. As I stood, one feather remained cupped to the resin and web criss-crossing my back. I must have looked like a crazy runway fashionista as I scanned nervously for signs of a massive duckling.

"Higgs! Higgs, bloody hell! Sit down, you must be in shock," Dot called in a rising voice as she cast aside her helmet and stumbled across the field to me.

I had never been happier to see my friend. She jumped at the sound of the wrecked motorbike crashing down from the web and burst into tears as she rushed to my side.

"I'm perfect, Dot. Somebody must be watching out for me. Come here!"

By the time Tam pushed through the tree branches and jogged across to us, Dot and I were both laughing and dancing in circles. "Looks like we're gonnae need an Uber," he mused, surveying the wreckage. "And a muckle great wet wipe to get that gunk away."

CHAPTER 21 - RESERVOIR

Newton

"Higgs, it's gigantic, the size of a van. But let's leave the mostly invisible fly to one side for now. Are you sure you're okay after your accident? You didn't bang your head? How can that be?" I asked over the phone.

Higgs's steady voice had the hint of a smile. "I told you, Newt, I'm all good. Scarlett and Faraday had to fetch me in the car because the motorbike I rode has given up the ghost, but I've only a few scratches. I somehow landed on a really thick patch of moss. And some *giant* feathers."

I called across Granny's room to Emeline and Chronos. "Em, it worked! Higgs landed on moss and feathers." Putting the phone back to my ear, I continued with Higgs. "What about a spider web? Was there a web?"

"What? Yes! Did you do that? Never mind, I know the answer. I owe you. Again."

"Just promise you'll hang back when they rescue Lars. I can't take any more of this long-distance worrying," I said.

"By this time tomorrow, it'll all be over, Newt. We can come home. Let me put you on speakerphone—Faraday wants to update you."

A fizz of ambient noise interrupted as the phone switched modes and Faraday spoke. "Newt, you were one hundred per cent right about the music. Nailed it. Those twins I told you about planted the nano onto unsuspecting girls in London, and they also brought the triggering sound clip to the recording studio. Scarlett's got the UPDA purging the malicious sound from all the online copies already."

"I knew it!" I said. "Not sure I can tell my sergeant that I'm the hero, but that doesn't matter."

"And the raid is all planned, she's got—"

Grover interrupted Faraday. His voice rose in pitch as the words tumbled out. "They're so mean. They're going to do it to Lars. Right now. Making the scary thing. They should stop."

My heart dropped low in my chest as I heard the anguish in Higgs's voice without being there to comfort her. "No, no, not Lars. When I see him again … Granny, can we stop him?"

My grandmother craned her neck to get closer to the phone, and I carried it over to her seat near the rear window as she spoke. "What's happening, Higgs? Who's doing something to Lars?"

"It's one of those damned twins. He has the power to bring someone's deepest fear to life, and he's using it on Lars as a sort of punishment. It's all my fault, and I need to stop it."

"I don't think we can," Granny began but was interrupted by Chronos, who shot up from his spot on the edge of her bed. He rushed to the window. "What the hell was that?"

It was a sound I had heard once before: the deep bellowing of what sounded like a massive toad.

Dot's voice sounded distant at the other end of the line, but its urgency was unmistakable. "Lars, no! Not the bloody Pendletoad. Higgs, Lars is fine, but Middle Ides isn't. Remember he told us about his nightmares?"

"It's supposed to stay in Ashton Pond," my grandmother said. "This is bad. Terrible. It took a whole cabal of witches to create it, to protect the original Pendle Hill coven's drowned bodies. But it never strays from the pond, and it sounds like it's—"

"Right there!" Chronos pointed to the brow above the Ides Giant's chalky outline inscribed in the hillside.

The blowfly at the Ferndale reservoir was grotesquely oversized, but the Pendletoad was a whole new order of massive. Its glistening body, lit from behind by the full moon peeking through a gap in the clouds, would dwarf a lorry. It pushed aside a tree as it positioned its squat body at the hill's summit and surveyed the Orphanage with lumpen, blinking eyelids that sprayed water droplets skyward.

It croaked again, twice, rattling the window pane. With deliberate thuds of its black webbed feet, the Pendletoad advanced down the hill, preceded by its unwavering stare at my grandmother's room.

"The only power that can turn this back from Middle Ides lies miles away in Edinburgh. We need Higgs's magic to stop the toad." My grandmother said this a bit too calmly for my liking. Was she giving up? Maybe we should run. Or should we stay safe in the Orphanage? This was well beyond the policing manual's scope.

Chronos spoke quickly, not daring to take his eyes off the advancing amphibian. "I can't just heave this guy out like some drunken idiot at the club. What can we do, Newt?"

"Worms, James. Get some worms," Granny said. Chronos looked confused but backed to the doorway, then turned and ran down the hall toward the front entrance. "And Higgs, you need two live fish. If you can't be here, and Newton can't provide his battery for your magic, we'll connect the two."

"A simpatico tunnel! Brilliant," Emeline cried. "I'll get things ready."

Higgs called out through the commotion. "Granny, what? I don't know what this simpatico tunnel thingy is, but where am I going to get two live fish? It's almost midnight."

"I know some," Grover Mann mumbled in the background. "Out there."

"In the river? Show me."

The call deteriorated into clattering and rustling. Scarlett shouted unanswered questions in the background. Faraday panted when he next spoke. "They're in the river behind the safe house. Grover and Higgs. It's waist-deep, but the current is not too powerful. They aren't in danger, Newt. I'm going in too. Hang on."

I heard Chronos taking the steps back up to us two at a time, his new gait lending his footfalls an uneven cadence. He rushed into Granny's room, hands covered in tarry earth.

"Worms! Lots in here. My god – the toad is springing down the hill, headed right for the Orphanage!"

Aside from a quick diversionary glance when Chronos returned, we were glued to the spectacle before us. With bounds that shed water and bits of uprooted vegetation from the toad's roughened hide. The monstrous beast made the long slope of the hill seem insignificant. Intense eyes ringed with fierce intention zeroed in on Granny's window, unwavering even as the colossus was airborne.

Granny and watched the fearsome toad rear up on its scum-encrusted hind legs to rest a foot adorned with suckers the size of dinner plates on the Orphanage's roof. Slates scraped above us and showered past the window. A thunderous croak shook the building, and the Pendletoad's nostril slits vented wide, splattering the window with chunks of black-flecked mucous. Shouts from other residents let us know this was not just some waking nightmare.

Granny patiently waited for the croak to subside so we could hear once again. "Newton, love, you are the battery that powers Higgs's magic. Stand there, take the worms, and imagine you are bait. Think *hard*."

Front feet on the roof left bulging armpit flab to frame the toad's squat head right at the level of our window. The grotesque, lump-ringed eyeballs glared at Granny, pupils dilating from saucer-sized to dinner plates as they focussed. It was as if the Pendletoad felt that all rumours of its existence were circulated by her and her alone. A dark gleam of vengeance simmered behind the terrifying stare.

My grandmother gestured to the ring of bedsheets that Emeline had been tweaking into a crenelated circle on the floor beside the wingback chair. I cupped my palms, and Chronos deposited two fistfuls of wriggling dirt. Despite fearing to tear my defensive gaze away from the Pendletoad, I scrunched my eyes closed.

Then the window smashed, and everything went to hell.

Higgs

Despite the summer air, the Water of Leith was cold. I wasn't sure if I could feel my legs.

"Here they come," Grover said, pointing downstream.

Ripples, distinct from the water's normal flow across submerged rocks, tracked the approach of two large salmon.

"What do I do, just grab them and lift?"

"Don't grab them—hold them gently. They're friendly. And leave them in the water, or else they will be angry."

The fish turned and darted away slightly, but I felt a surge of magic. Not from within, but the tingling that I felt when Dot's magic lessons elicited her power beside me. Grover submerged his face in the flowing river, and the salmon swung around again and wavered their way toward me, one beside each leg, swimming languidly against the current.

With a gasp, Grover splashed his face from the water. "They're ready," he said. "Be gentle."

I squatted slightly, reaching down to the level where the fish wove patient patterns. It surprised me how warm they felt as my fingers conformed to their muscular curves. As soon as I made full contact and felt the reassuring touches of Grover on one side and Faraday on the other, I knew what to do. I shut my eyes and told the fish to find Newton and his worms.

A starry, whirling tunnel irised open behind my closed eyelids, and I searched for Newton at the other end as my salmon looked for their bait. Where was he?

Newton

Smithereens of glinting crystal shards arced through the room as the window shattered under the force of a clenched toad fist the size of a washing machine. As I learned later, everyone else covered their faces when the assaulting blow approached, but I stood broadside to the window with my eyes clenched shut in concentration, taking a dozen small lacerations to my cheeks and forehead. I must have had my mouth open because I coughed out a fragment of glass after it tore a strip from the inside of one cheek. I tasted blood.

Of course, there was no way I could stand entranced while this carnage unfolded. I blinked my eyes open to see my grandmother's chair tossed aside, Emeline knocked to the floor, and Chronos grappling with one of the two toad toes that curled around Granny's midsection. The other two toes braced against the outside sill, and a single, fathomless toad eye loomed just beyond, scrutinising its prey. Each throbbing toe displayed the characteristic raised lumps commonly mistaken for warts, and the one Chronos attempted to pry loose was significantly longer than the other clutching appendage.

Despite the constriction, Granny threw her still free arms overhead, and two rings of fire gleamed from beneath the sleeves of her twin set. "Not now!" she chanted, rotating her arms in tight circles.

The sleeves burst into flame, revealing the bracelets beneath that roared and hissed with coruscating fire like pulsing furnaces. "Not now, Pendle. We're busy!"

A deft shake sent the wreaths of flame past her wrists and into the grip of each palm. She brought the brands down with force, one onto each encircling toad toe. The foot recoiled, taking the wooden window frame with it as it fled the room, leaving us with a view of one heavy-lidded eye and a partial view into the Pendletoad's cavernous maw.

Chronos smothered the sleeves of the smouldering twin set with swarming hands, finding Granny's arms amazingly unscathed beneath. She held the blazing rings aloft, staring at the single visible eyeball considering its next move from beyond the window.

"Newton, dear," she said. "Get back into that circle. You are bait and need to act like it. Think like it. You and Higgs are our only hope."

I realised I had stepped out of the sheet ridge, so I leapt back within and closed my eyes, wondering how to think like bait. I felt nothing; no magic. A groan snuck from Emeline as she stood, a tinkle of glass shards dropping from her clothing. Then I heard a sound that was hard to describe. It was like a cross between a slap with a wet fish and a titanic anchor reeling out into the ocean.

I couldn't help myself. I opened my eyes again to a sight that will haunt my dreams forever. The unusual sound was the Pendletoad's blackened, rubbery tongue slashing through the smashed window to lash and latch onto Granny and pull her back into the church of its slavering jaws. Chronos tried to save her, but the clutching tongue's impossible strength and stickiness wrenched her from his grasp. I caught my last glimpse of her purple outfit and outraged face as the primordial jaws snapped shut, and Granny's bracelets clattered to the sill, extinguished.

How dare this monstrous creation of long-dead witches snatch away my grandmother? She'd never hurt a thing! Anger flared within me as Chronos leant on the sill, shouting something and clutching my grandmother's shoe. Then I knew how bait felt—victimised by some gigantic creature that snatched everything away. I closed my eyes once more and let my feeling guide me.

Almost immediately, I heard Higgs's voice inside my head. "I'm here, Newt. I know it took Granny. Open your eyes so I can see through the tunnel."

My eyes shot open, and I sprang, two-footed, to balance on the window sill beside Chronos. The motion came unbidden, as if someone else moved my legs.

"It's open, the simpatico tunnel. I can feel her," Emeline

screamed from behind me. "Let her work though you, Newt."
I felt her hands on my shoulders as if they were a part of me,
but a part that dwelt in another county.

The Pendletoad returned to its natural crouch, extracting its
right leg from the Orphanage's roof. Its sucker-adorned foot
slapped the turf below, leaving a craterous divot in the grass. I
didn't know if a toad could look smug, but this one seemed to
attempt it, lips tightly sealed.

My vines snaked unbidden down the rough stone rear wall,
reaching the grass in mere moments. Wait. I had *vines?*

"What's happening? Newt—Higgs is doing something." I
wanted to answer my brother, whose worried voice crackled
from the speakerphone that lay somewhere behind me. But I
couldn't. Layers of bark littered my face, and my lips wouldn't
part.

Chronos called out from beside me, "It's working, Faraday!
Whatever Higgs is doing. Newton is trying to save Angelina.
Go on, Higgs!"

My arms were rigid, and my roots bored through the carpet
into the wooden floor beneath me. Tendrils caressed Emeline's
arms as she leaned into me from behind, murmuring in my ear.
My vines multiplied, snaking and seeking past the garden below
and across the field beyond in a surge of deep green, red-veined
leaves. The grass rippled in a tempest despite the windless
warm night air.

The moon broke fully through the clouds, illuminating the
affront to reality that was the Pendletoad as my questing vine
tips reached a pair of moonlit feet carved into the limestone
hill. Perfect—that was far enough. Energy flowed through the
tunnel, down into my roots, and out through my lengths of
vine. Animating energy.

A noise like some colossal strip of Velcro being torn loose
sounded from the hill's face. Clods of earth splattered the grass
below, and the Pendletoad rotated its hideous head to peer
over its right shoulder. No longer a hill carving, the Ides Giant
rose to one knee. It was still formed from the whitest stone,
but now lived as a moving, towering, three dimensional figure,

dwarfing both the Pendletoad and the Orphanage. It moved like a stiff man, the outlined edges of its form as thick as a tree trunk and reflecting moonlight as it rose into action. The parts of the giant that had been grass as it lay on the hillside were now empty space and we could clearly see the ruined hillside through its open torso. Bolders torn from the hill served as makeshift eyes. The carved and stylised nose hung suspended beneath. My vines no longer clung to its feet—the reanimation work felt complete and now I had a rudimentary connection to the giant. It seemed to have some volition of its own, but needed the direction that Higgs and I could provide.

A toad of that size could take a truly amazing hop. Leaving four-toed impressions in the grass that would take a year to fade, the toad sprang, aiming to clear the Orphanage and head toward the town centre. But the incredible bound halted mid-air as a glowing white limestone hand snatched it from on high, gripping its sides firmly but not squeezing it to oblivion. The Ides Giant's stony feet pressed down on my vines, and its club dangled from its free hand, grazing the base of the hill from whence it had torn itself.

None of us said a thing as an eerie silence replaced the cacophony of the preceding chaos. No words could express what our eyes beheld. Long an observer of Middle Ides life, the carving of the Ides Giant now had a life of its own. The stony colossus knelt on one knee, its sculpted crown glistening in the moonbeams that penetrated its mostly open form. An inadvertent nudge scored a gouge in the stone wall of the Orphanage that would remind us of this night forever.

With a gentleness that betrayed its size and crude outline, The Ides Giant resettled the wriggling Pendletoad onto the field and palpitated the toad's sides using blocky, rectangular fingers. With reluctance, the toad's lips parted, and a ball of mucous shot from its cruel jaws to smear my vine bed. A boulder-sized clot rolled a quarter turn on the grassy field below before coming to an oozing halt.

Angelina Redferne, my amazing grandmother, clawed her way loose from the ball of toad phlegm and rolled onto her back, coughing and clutching her sides. Strands of ick surrounded her as she broke the eerie silence of our jointly-held breaths and said weakly, "That's the worst hospitality I've ever seen."

"You're okay?" Chronos shouted. "I don't believe it! I'm coming down."

"Wait. I think my ribs are broken. But before you call an ambulance, I had an idea while I was in *there*. That disturbing fly that's abusing our land. If you wanted to scare off a giant magical fly, what do you think would frighten *it*?"

* * *

As Chronos thumped down the stairs, my vines retracted, leaving me with two bark-laden forearms and rigid, finger-shaped stumps. The squiggling worms thrived in one wooden palm.

Chronos rounded the corner of the Orphanage with one of the resident medical staff sprinting beside him in a starched white uniform. She skidded, then disappeared from sight with a panicked scream.

Chronos retreated and reappeared clutching her free hand—the other helda green first aid kit. "No, trust me, it's fine. We need to see to Angelina."

With tentative footsteps, Chronos's companion overcame her terror and skittered across the grass to where Granny sat, holding her ribs. I think my grandmother's calm somehow infected her benefactor. She knelt and brushed toad mucus from Granny's face, asking whether her spine and neck felt okay, as if there wasn't a hill carving grappling a monstrous amphibian a few paces away.

Chronos leant in and spoke to Granny briefly, but she waved him away. He shouted back toward our shattered window, "Newt, Em! We have a mission. Jump in the jeep, and I'll ride my bike around back here. See if you can get your new chalky friend to follow me."

I needed Emeline to drive the jeep, given the immobilised

state of my oaken arms. Chronos straddled his motorbike between the toad-gripping Ides Giant and the insignificant pair of humans easing their way across the moonlight grass. Granny brushed off a miasma of toad goop and looked almost cheery, one arm draped around the now-splattered white coat of her companion, and the other clutched like a bandolier around her ribs. She hobbled away, urged onward by the nurse, nodding my way and directing a dismissive wave at me with the back of her hand. Emeline drifted the jeep around the corner of the building, leaving a wake of upturned turf like a pair of black scars in the dim illumination. I took that as a signal that she was well enough without us, and that we had bigger fish to fry. Or a bigger fly, in this case. Most curtains on this side of the Orphanage twitched, and a host of incredulous faces surveyed the bizarre scene. Tongues would wag with hard to believe tales during visiting hours at the Orphanage tomorrow.

I looked down at the intertwined forms of the worms in my boughs and felt drawn into their motion. As I focussed, it was as if I shrank to their scale, then moved inside them. The tunnel between Middle Ides and Edinburgh sprang into focus, a kaleidoscope of colours forming a twisty pipe between me and Higgs. A coursing stream of blue energy swizzled along the tunnel ahead of me, and a returning blaze of green power flowed from Higgs to me. I could see my sister, standing waist-deep in a river flowing between the well-kept steps and flowering window-boxes of quaint grey-stone tenements.

"Higgs, you have to stop soon. I don't know about you, but I can barely feel my legs," Dot was shouting.

But Higgs was oblivious, concentrating on the tunnel and channelling her magic through me.

Although I couldn't see him, Faraday's voice floated through the tunnel. "Dot, get out of there and wait on the bank. I'm coming in. You too, Grover."

"I'm okay," Grover said. "The fish aren't cold in the water, and they are helping me and Higgs feel warm too."

Splashing noises came from somewhere behind Higgs. "Ay! This water isn't very summery," Faraday said.

"Wait ... water! Dot—was it Ferndale and Pentland that Ruaridh mentioned when you were at the gates of Castle Ghuil? And he said something about starting his plans in England?"

Dot's voice was further away now. "Yeah, I think so."

Faraday continued. "Scarlett. Check again on the death clock victims. Didn't you say they were all from around Edinburgh? And is Pentland a reservoir too, like Ferndale? Check your phone."

I couldn't hear Scarlett's reply, but a few moments later, my brother continued. Once again, his brilliance had drawn the threads together to sew up the answer.- "That giant fly at Ferndale. It's obviously part of the elf's magic because the fly is only visible in peripheral vision, like him. But it's poisoning the drinking water, priming people with the magic that allows the elf to predict their times of death. They started here in the Pentland Hills Reservoir, affecting everyone around here. After that, they moved on to England, at Ferndale."

That's my boy; I really needed to tell him how proud I was of his brilliance. But not now. "Higgs?" I said, not sure if she could hear me.

"Newton? I lost sight of things at the Orphanage for a while. Is everyone okay?"

"Yes—you did it. The Ides Giant has the Pendletoad in his massive stone hand, and he saved Granny. But we want to take him up to the reservoir. Are you strong enough to carry on?"

"I'm perfect, Newt. But aren't you getting tired?"

My arms felt tired, but I figured that's the way trees felt all the time. But now that she mentioned it, I was feeling weak. "No, I'm good," I lied.

"Okay, brother. I love you. Wow! I can see everything again now—the Giant really is giant when he's standing up. Here's how you're going to get him to follow Chronos ..."

* * *

The Ides Giant lumbered after Chronos, who bumped his way

straight up the hill, bike engine protesting. Emeline carved another set of tracks in the grass, and we took the road, intersecting Giant, Pendletoad, and my closest friend as the Peaks Road coasted toward the reservoir. Emeline later told me I sat slumped for the ten-minute trip, examining the worms at close range and muttering. The jeep pulled into the lay-by where we had ogled the bizarre blowfly, and I opened my eyes and looked to my left where Chronos blazed along a walking trail through the forest on the far side of Ferndale Reservoir. I could see the fly's globe-like body now that I had an indirect view.

Knocking trees to the ground as it waded into the forest, the Ides Giant strode with thudding steps that landed only once every three seconds. It carried the Pendletoad like a rugby ball, clutched beneath one poorly drawn arm.

The motorbike's journey sent echoes skipping across the water's surface, subsiding as Chronos halted a short distance from the fly, whose musket-like proboscis still pulsed at the waterline. The fly's mottled body threw off a deep blue light, and its undersized wings thrummed frantically as the Ides Giant approached. If it wasn't so frightening, it would have been comical to watch the fly's eyes bulge, expanding to double their original multifaceted diameter as the Giant and its captive approached. But its nose remained in the water, compelled in its mission.

The Ides Giant had dragged its club, the size of a house, all the way here. Our return trip would reveal several scars in the Peaks Road's tarmac that would need urgent road crew attention, cracks criss-crossing its surface from inadvertent club strikes. He pulled himself to his impressive full height as he halted a pace short of the pulsating blue fly. One stony foot sank into the mud at the shoreline, while the other kicked away a small boulder before splintering a picnic table. The Ides Giant stood braced on the bank, ready to attack the fly.

Soundlessly, the Ides Giant raised his club high and swung it viciously down in an underhand arc, leaning in like a polo player straining in the stirrups to contest a loose ball. Impact!

Chaotic sound erupted, sending a shockwave across the water to lap at our shore. The club exploded as it struck the fly's blue orb of a body, fragments of stone scattering along the beach. The fly's eyes narrowed to slits momentarily at the unthinkable impact, but the blow failed to dislodge it. Its impossible snout remained rooted.

"Oh, come on!" Emeline shouted beside me. "You carry a toad all the way here, and then you want to *swat* the fly? This proves once and for all that the Ides Giant is definitely a man, although he's not anatomically correct."

I heard Higgs's voice inside my head at the same time. "We're in control, Newt. Make him use the toad."

I concentrated on the worms, and more blue energy flowed away, followed by a corresponding surge of green. Higgs's magic filled me, and I directed my attention to the giant, who stood pondering the club's stump in his hand as if he held something unexpected and puzzling, like a lobster.

He flung the stub of stone, as big as our jeep, into the reservoir. Water cascaded away from its entry point as if a depth charge had exploded. With his hand free, the giant snatched at the fly as its eyes bulged further, and its glow escalated to a brilliant blue.

I tried to project, "NO!" and that seemed to work. The giant paused mid-stoop, hand poised but not touching the fly, which was a good omen. Stalled in his lean, he rotated his head. A grinding noise shuddered from his neck as he faced me. If he had any eyebrows, one would have been raised.

From the deep recesses of my mind, a thought sprang forth—where the heck was Disco? She'd been missing for a full day now, making this the longest spell she'd ever disappeared. The giant took my break in concentration to continue his attack on the fly. He turned back to his unnerved prey and extended his hand closer.

Higgs's scolding rattled around the inside of my skull. "Newt, focus! I can't do all the work here!"

Through the tunnel, I heard Grover's nasal intonation. "He's worried about Disco. Newton, Disco is okay. She's with her friends. I see her now."

I'm not sure how he knew where Disco was, but I was less sure about everything as magic came into play. Grover's words gave me a degree of solace. Maybe Disco was visiting his bulldog friend Antoinette. I refocused on the task at hand—the Ides Giant needed tactical help.

More power coursed through me, and I made an idea blossom in the Giant. He straightened to his stiff but colossal full height. He retracted his hand from temptation and his head darted in several directions, eventually settling its gaze on the Pendletoad as if he only now realized he was carting around a lorry-sized monster.

The toad had long since stopped struggling, and its obsessive stare zeroed in on the giant fly. As the Ides Giant cupped the Pendletoad in his hands, almost gently, I thought I saw the ghastly hint of a human smile on the menacing toad's lips. Then it struck.

I had encountered the tongue's nightmarish texture up close when it had ensnared my grandmother. I could picture its sticky and slimy surface as it rolled out like a musty carpet and slithered beneath the magic-spawned fly's rotund belly. The tip slapped across the hairy back, thr tongue's underside sticking to a crescent of the fly's body from top to dangling underbelly. The tongue pulled taut, its muscular end tugging the insect. Six rickety legs braced as they scrabbled for purchase on the muddy shore. Six troughs grew deeper, ploughing the land as the fly oscillated, pulsing with an icy light. Nevertheless, it clung to its mission, the stony nozzle of its proboscis anchored in the water.

A thunderous croak crossed the water to us, partially stifled by the Pendletoad's own straining tongue. The moon's reflection blurred in the ripples, and the sparking sizzle of electricity railed against the croaking as the fly's magical energy surged up the tongue toward the threatening maw. It was almost impossible to remain looking away from the spectacle, but Emeline and I knew that if we looked directly, the fly would disappear from our view.

Chronos reversed his bike further from the site of the titanic struggle, his heel and prosthetic leg straining against the soft earth shaded by the tree line.

I willed the Pendletoad to pull. Higgs pulled too. Her presence as she worked through me warmed me like a smoky bonfire.

The crackling sparks of the fly's wrath flew from the Pendletoad's tongue like fireworks approaching its fearsome snout. The toad braced its webbed feet against the Ides Giant's curling fingertips and tugged at the corruptor of Ferndale reservoir. The magical counterattack reached its snarling lips.

With a *thok* that shook the trees and echoed from the hills backing the reservoir, the fly separated from its lodestone nozzle of a proboscis. The Pendletoad's tongue entangled the fly's body as it flew across the gap and landed with a gurgle in its foetid mouth. Swallowing, a pulsing blue energy shone through the Pendletoad's mottled skin as the fly slithered down its throat and into its flabby guts. Three or four pulses flashed as silence fell across the area before the unnatural light faded.

As my arms shed their bark and the worms fell from my grasp into the gravelly earth beside the jeep, I saw the Ides Giant stoop once again, releasing the Pendletoad with a thud. Extending its hind legs and leaping away, the toad looked back over one shoulder at the Ides Giant, eyeballed Chronos for a moment as if our friend might make a tasty additional snack, then careened into the forest, croaking as it headed toward Ashton Pond.

The Ides Giant stood tall, raised his heels as much as his blocky feet would allow, and looked over the tree tops back toward Middle Ides. Spinning, he strode in that direction, leaving pockets of devastation where his paces struck.

I was tired. Exhausted. I heard some distant croaks and retreating footfalls as I slumped into the jeep's passenger seat and shuttered my eyes. A motorbike roared into life somewhere, and I heard Emeline speaking into my mobile phone.

"Yes, Faraday, it worked. The Pendletoad has wandered off,

and all that's left of this infectious fly is its ten-foot-tall nozzle sticking out of the reservoir ... No, he's walked away too, now that the simpatico tunnel has collapsed. Headed back to his hill, no doubt. Is Higgs okay? ... Super. Excellent. Get her into a warm bath. Grover too—they're probably both as exhausted as Newton ... Okay, will do ... And we've had enough of relying on Scarlett to take care of you. Executive decision. I'll drive to Scotland while Newton gets some sleep in the back."

CHAPTER 22 - MARSHALL

Faraday

Despite the previous night's frantic activity, we were all up early, nervous about the impending rescue mission in Glen Ghuil.

Scarlett wore camouflage-patterned military fatigues as she hauled a hard-sided case of unlabelled equipment into the hall, preparing to decamp to the mission control centre outside Glen Ghuil. "I *finally* got permission to take you all with me. I vouched for your behaviour and only convinced them because of the help you have provided already. But no funny stuff, right? My reputation is riding on this. See that suitcase over there? Grab whatever outfit will suit you best. The sizes are all I could arrange at brief notice."

Higgs dropped her shoulders in relief. She had been working Scarlett *hard* for permission to be there when they freed Lars. Dot took immediate charge of the uniforms—she hoisted camo trousers and jackets from the suitcase and held them up in front of Grover and me for sizing.

"Shush, everyone," Higgs blurted in clipped words, pointing at the television. "Listen, Dot, that's his voice!"

I snatched the remote and increased the volume. A news presenter was in discussion with a disembodied voice on a crackling phone line. The caption read, 'Voice of Ruaridh McRaven'.

The presenter asked an open question, her voice a melodic

mix of strong vowels and an occasional rolling R.

"… as you have said before on this very show, Dr McRaven, you are deeply invested in independence but have little time for the machinations of the Scottish National Party. How do you reconcile those two feelings?"

Higgs and Dot furrowed their brows in synchronized listening as the rough depths of McRaven's voice answered through a crackle of static. "Well, Carol, it's plain to see the will of the Scottish people is to control their own destiny. But see how the SNP is all chat, chat, chat? They're more concerned wi' infighting than accomplishing their real mission. We're Scots, for goodness' sake. Never conquered and not runnin' from any confrontation. Take a stand, folk. Nae mair chat, let's see action. Nae nonsense!"

As the reporter thanked him for his time, Higgs thrashed her fists against the back of the sofa and let out an animalistic growl. "How can he be on telly? He's a bloody criminal, not some splurge of colour to counter the stupid, bland answers politicians give. I can't wait to see him in handcuffs."

Dot ran a soothing hand along her shoulder. "We're almost there, Higgs. His ragtag Tartantula can't stand up to what Scarlett's planning."

My mobile rang, and the soothing, familiar voice of Iain Vanderkamp reminded me there were matters in Middle Ides to consider. It seemed a week or a month or a year since I had been at home, working on my nanotech experiments with Iain. "Iain, hey! I met 2 new friends—well, people—up here who put me onto a professional drone piloting school. Wanna sign up with me? It looks really useful. And their drone is amazing."

"Yeah, sounds good, Faraday. Let's look into it," he said. "But listen, I found something important. It's about the data from your mother's grave …"

Iain filled me in on how the nano that caused my mother's aneurism originated in Russia. He talked about requesting another autopsy, but a red mist descended over my brain, and I ended the call as quickly as I could without being rude. Well, without being ruder than usual.

"Scarlett?" I called.

Something about my tone of voice alerted Higgs, who shot her head around to face me as she pulled up her too-baggy fatigue pants. Scarlett was snapping shut a second case in the hallway as I approached her. In our canal boat at Little Ides, I had despaired and wilted at the news of Higgs's kidnapping. But I promised myself that it wouldn't happen again, that I would stand strong in the face of adversity.

"When my mother received a mysterious visitor on her last day at the lab, some type of unknown nanotech infested her. *Russian* nanotech."

I thought I uttered that first part calmly, but I knew the next part came out in rising tones and with a hint of a growl. Higgs was already beside me, cradling my elbow.

"You used some kind of *experimental* Russian technology, and it killed her? And one of your own agents? Was Vladishenko in on this? You seem to be pretty cosy with *him!*"

Scarlett returned my stare, unflinching. She took a breath before answering as I clenched my fists at my sides, and Higgs turned her touch into more of a grab. "Faraday, we've been through this. I didn't send anybody to the Feynman Centre. Your mother's death was a tragedy, but I worked *with* her, never *against* her."

"That's a LIE! You're angling for a job with the Russians. I heard it with my own ears—he offered you a career over there!"

There were no words left. All that remained of my logic was to lunge at her. Agent Zee wasn't there to protect her traitorous arse now.

I tried to twist out of my sister's grasp as I sprang at Scarlett, but she's stronger than she looks. Unable to evade Higgs's grip on my elbow, I spun part way around and failed to reach the target of my rage. Higgs insinuated herself between my flared nostrils and the icy impassion of Scarlett, who had not flinched or broken eye contact.

"Faraday! Parking, parking!" Higgs said, using her quiet but firm tone reserved for drilling the most important information through my shell. "This is not something for *now*. Now is for *Lars*."

With two hands on my chest, she coaxed me to take two steps away then return to the lounge where Dot and Grover stood dangling shirts and jackets as they froze during the encounter. "Faraday, this should fit you," Dot said as if nothing had happened.

I threw myself onto the sofa and seethed. Behind me, I heard Scarlett placing a call. "Hi. It's me," she said. "I need to rule something out. Can you check we didn't authorise any *activity* in Middle Ides in April of this year? Some sort of mechanical dragonfly attack and the placement of a trailer hitch designed to cause a vehicle accident? Yes, thanks—tomorrow is good."

She called over in a louder voice, but I refused to turn and acknowledge it. "I'm double-checking, Faraday. But it wasn't me."

* * *

With Agent Zee still in the hospital after the attack at the concert, Scarlett drove the SUV herself. Grover took the front seat, which excited him no end, while Dot, Higgs, and I sat in the rear. I simmered and fiddled with the UPSCALE as we drove.

Chronos called from the Redferne jeep's passenger seat. Apparently, Newton was still asleep in the back seat, and he and Emeline had taken turns driving through the night. I told him the position of the advance base for the attack on Castle Ghuil and told him to meet us there.

"I can't wait to see my horse friend again," Grover said from the front seat. He stared out the side window at the rise and fall of heather-clad hills as we left the motorway to join a twisting local road, addressing nobody in particular.

* * *

The term 'advance base' sounded much more glamourous than its reality. A pair of military personnel shunted aside a heavy wooden road barrier to let our SUV pass along the final mile or so of winding road to an olive canvass tent that brimmed with guy wires on the most level expanse of grass along the approach to the head of the glen. The bus stop where Higgs and Dot met Ena McTavish was around the next bend.

We joined 8 other camo-clad staff in the tent where 3 tables sat in a neat row, stacked with rubber-clad computer systems and portable monitors. A radio system crackled to life occasionally. True to our promise, the four of us stood together in the tent's back corner, observing and chatting in hushed tones. We tried to be as inconspicuous as possible, but we still received an occasional glance that screamed '*interlopers!*'

Although there was nothing to see—and we left the tent to strain our eyeballs skyward—the first action was a pass over Glen Ghuil and its castle by a high-altitude reconnaissance aircraft. Well, that's what Scarlett called it, rather vaguely, but I suspect it was an unmanned aerial vehicle—a military drone. A UAV would have been able to navigate the patchy layers of cloud with more agility than a manned aircraft and offer more opportunity for clear lines of sight around Loch Ghuil.

At Scarlett's behest, the team begrudgingly allowed us to see some camera footage. The new construction of the chalet inside the castle grounds stood out in the aerial shots, and they zoomed in on the loch head where the girls and Lars had abandoned their tents.

"Look!" Dot said, pointing and bouncing on the balls of her feet. "I can see the spots where Higgs and I wer affected by the ... erm ... trouble." She avoided mentioning magic or the elf in front of the military staff. She was such a clever and sensitive girl—I would have blurted out entire paragraphs of cringeworthy secrets if I had been in her shoes. Well, maybe not—I'd be in such anguish squished into size 7's that I wouldn't say anything.

Dot pointed out several highlights along the loch. "We ran toward the bus stop from our tents along the main path, went into the woods around *here*—I think we were on this rise on the loch's far side for a bit too. See how you can look directly along at Castle Ghuil from there? And then we were at the front gate. Oh, also back there on the castle's seaward side. The not-so-secret entrance. It's high tide now, but the causeway to the castle was above water when we were there."

Scarlett conferred with the mission leader. "No unexpected civilians on the scene? Any issues?"

A slight shake of a head of grey-cropped hair from the man in charge of our advance base lent him an air of quiet confidence that he reinforced with his reply. "We always knew civilian presence was a possibility, but it doesn't change our mission parameters. The frogmen who are approaching now know to watch for this situation."

"There are *frogmen*?" Grover asked me. He used a more subtle than usual level of volume, and I answered him in quieter tones.

"It's just an expression, brother. They are military forces that arrive underwater, in diving outfits so they can swim in from the sea without being noticed. Normal men. Or women. They will be the next to arrive on-site, and they will sneak in through the portcullis—that's like a gate over a small river from the sea that goes inside the castle."

"So they are going to sneak in and rescue Lars from those naughty boys?"

"Sort of. They are mainly trying to free this elf thingy that Higgs and Dot saw. He's in handcuffs inside the castle, and if we can free him, then the bad people inside the castle won't be able to use his magic against us. Then it will be easier to swarm in and rescue Lars and make sure those boys don't scare anyone ever again."

"That's a good plan," Grover said. "Can we see a video of the frogmen?"

"I don't think so. We are going to listen to that radio over there and wait for them to tell us they cut off the handcuffs."

Grover plodded to a side table and grabbed 4 more biscuits, offering the rest to us when he returned. I took 1, but the girls declined, leaving Grover to deposit crumbs from the other 3 down the front of his fatigues, testing their camouflaging ability.

They gave the order for the frogmen to leave the rowboat just beyond the crinkle of the coast that hid them from direct view of the castle. From their, their journey dispatched them like a pair of missionary mermaids toward the castle. We waited, ears alert for the next message over the radio.

Instead, a satellite phone buzzed, and after a perfunctory greeting, one of the military staff held it up and motioned to Scarlett. "It's for you, ma'am."

Now our ears strained further, trying in vain to hear the conversation on the other end as Scarlett spoke.

"Yes, gov'," she began. "Proceeding to plan so far. Oh … hello, First Minister … What? No … But that's what we're doing—we can neutralise the Tartantula here within the next thirty minutes. All we have to do is … It's a form of magic, sent through the reservoir systems … Yes, both up here and at Ferndale. I can take care of both problems in one go—I only have to free the elf … Yes, I *did* say 'elf' … No, in Snow White those are dwarfs, and that's just a story… Of course magic is *real*, that's what I'm trying to help you with … But … Yes, First Minister, I understand. Thank you."

Although her voice sounded calm on the call, she still broke a chunk of casing from the ruggedised military satellite phone when she slammed it onto the table. "Idiots! Bloody idiots!" she yelled before turning to the commander, and in a more civilised tone said, "Call it. First Minister's orders. And Downing Street."

Nonplussed, the commander nodded to his staff, and some frantic typing into nearly silent dampened computer keyboards followed. The commander waited by the radio, receiver in hand, waiting for contact from the frogmen. I counted. It was only 38 seconds later that he repeated into the receiver in a soft voice, "Abort, abort. I repeat, abort."

With the curt reply of, "Roger that," the raid on Castle Ghuil came to a miserable end.

Scarlett knew what was coming and waved directly at Higgs and Dot as she spun on her heel and left the tent. We all followed and arrayed ourselves around her as she leant on the SUV door furthest from the tent. For once, she looked as exhausted as she must have been feeling for the last two days.

Higgs was looking redder by the minute. "Scarlett, come on, you can't call this off. What about Lars? You promised."

"I know. It's both wrong and unfair. They don't know I can fix this and how close we are." Scarlett left a dent in the SUV door with the back of her clenched fist. "But it's above me now. The Scottish First Minister is getting cold feet, but now the Prime Minister is across this whole thing too. It's not much of a secret now the Tartantula is advertising the death clock and picking off victims across Cheshire and Yorkshire. They're pressing this independence crap at both the Scotland and UK level, it seems."

"So we didn't get rid of that damned fly in time, I guess?" Higgs asked.

"Obviously not. The death clock spell must have made it into the water systems already. Who knows, there may be other flies at other reservoirs. But the bottom line is that they want to negotiate with Ruaridh now instead of storming in. They're worried he might release a full list of deaths if he's taken out. They've ordered me back to UPDA in London so I can help with the negotiation and planning of the next steps. Some sort of joint forces operation where UPDA is just a participant. Don't they know I've given everything to be in a position to stop threats like this? There's nobody better equipped to handle this."

"Call them back," I said. "Use your persuasion powers to reassure them the mission will succeed!" I sounded whiny, even to my own ears.

Scarlett opened her mouth several times to speak, but aborted each response, crestfallen. She looked glumly at her boots. "No. We're done here. I can drop you off in Middle Ides as I fly back. In a few days the bigger team will have this sorted out."

Flabbergasted, we piled into the SUV, not knowing what else to do.

"Imagine what Lars's mother will think when she finds out," Higgs said, a steady flow of tears rolling down her cheeks. "She'll think it's *our* fault he was captured. We don't even know how long it will take to rescue him!"

I was glad that Grover had taken the front seat again. My arm snaked around Higgs's shoulders as her head drooped, and it was met with Dot's arm curling in from the other side. "We'll help him," she said. "With your Granny and Emeline—there are *things* we can try."

Higgs could not reply, her tears accompanied by anguished gasping.

"They'll be here soon. We should wait," Grover said, looking rearward past our 3 huddled shapes, as we left Glen Ghuil behind us and approached the barricade and the open road beyond.

Disco

The two kestrels screeched and pecked at the lorry roof. It was time. We were close. We had nearly left the lorry too early, near the city with the castle in the middle. But then a new destination became interesting. The long lake with the falling-apart castle and the waving flag. We waited a few hours more until we were close enough to run there.

The horse shimmied upright. She turned to face the lorry's rear doors and hooves stepped carefully backward until she neared the wall of our space. The driver was just beyond. Deer and the uncountable rabbits moved aside to make way for the horse, thronging inside the lorry's doors.

I yipped. The horse kicked and kicked, banging on the front wall. The driver *must* be able to hear that.

Yes—it was working. The lorry slowed, turned slightly, and

stopped. We heard the man open and close his door, and footsteps echoed alongside us, unseen. One car passed us. The man talked to himself as he slid the bolts that would open the rear door. We readied ourselves for escape. The horse took a few steps forward, waiting right behind the deer and the furry mass of rabbits.

Rabbits frothed out as soon as the door opened a crack. The man shouted something, and the door swept wide. I jumped. Right over the man's bald head. He ducked to avoid the deer and the leaping horse.

We knew which way to go and moved like a river. We leapt the metal road barrier and ran into the thin bushes bordering the roadway. With a keening cry, the kestrels lifted from the lorry roof and followed our course.

The deer were natural pathfinders, and we followed their lead into the hills. I stopped and looked beyond my friend the horse and saw the driver still standing in the distance, staring after us and scratching his head.

We were almost there. Only a few more hours of running, and we would see the castle. I had to protect the pack.

Higgs

Teardrops cascading onto the desert of my disappointment, a familiar and somehow comforting sound urged me to raise my chin and look along the twisting roadway toward Loch Ghuil. Ena McTavish's Range Rover trundled along the single-track road, slowing to a stop where Dot and I moped. The window rolled down in a series of jerks, and the familiar spray of hair appeared before the musical notes of a sympathetic voice.

"Och, you wee flowers, come here and tell Ena what's happened."

She gave a friendly wave to the two military personnel that

looked like they might leave their post at the road barricade to question her. "It's okay, boys, it's just me. I live up there on that hillside, so nae need to worry someone wasnae doing their job at the other barricades."

Dot and I leant our sorry-looking faces through the window, both our chins settling on the lip of the glass. "It's your friend, isn't it?" Ena asked.

I didn't have the power to speak without blubbering, so I just nodded. "They were just about to rescue him, and then everything got called off," Dot said.

"Now listen," Ena said. "See what I have here on my wrist? The woven bracelet you gave me. If anything bad had happened to your friend, I would have felt it here. Have a touch, you'll feel it too."

Dot and I reached out in unison, rubbing the fibres between thumbs and forefingers. Was it unnaturally warm? It was hard to tell, but I took solace in Ena's confidence, anyway.

"Aye, he's good. Just missing you two, no doubt, but I feel he'll be back with you soon. And he's with Ruaridh. The man may be a fanatic, but he's no a psycho."

I managed a small smile. "Thanks, Ena. I'm feeling a little better already." Dot nodded agreement.

"Look. If it's any use, I'm keeping an eye on the Glen. Mind I'm looking down on that castle and if you ever need my help, you two can think of me, and I'll be there to help. Like just now!"

Dot actually laughed a little at that. The mirage of a rattling Range Rover had appeared just when we needed some comfort. And it wouldn't be the last of the aid that Ena would offer; there was another crucial intervention to come.

CHAPTER 23 - REINFORCEMENTS

Newton

We drove through the night, only to be prevented from travelling the last mile to Glen Ghuil. To be correct, Emeline and Chronos drove through the night. I curled beneath a blanket in the jeep's back seat, so exhausted from channelling Higgs's magic that I didn't notice the blanket was three-quarters dog hair and only one-quarter wool. I don't even remember Chronos lifting me from the passenger seat into the back. Comatose dreams filled my head, full of darting salmon, worms, and a multicoloured tunnel spinning me toward Castle Ghuil.

I checked in with Terrell. Although it was Sunday morning, I was still working with him on an active murder case, so weekends meant little. However, he seemed resigned to our police work being trampled by the big boots of the London team. I promised to be back by Monday lunchtime, which he accepted, provided I promised to bring back some shortbread.

Confronted by the road barrier, we rolled down every window and tried to negotiate our way through. It was imperative that we rejoin Faraday and Higgs after what seemed like a month apart, but was only three days. Lars disappeared Friday morning, but the ferocious pace of activity since then made it seem longer than two days. Manning the blockade were no-nonsense military types who rebuffed every mention of

Scarlett or my siblings. Because the mobile signal had faded to nothing ten minutes prior, we knew there was no hope of calling ahead. There was nothing for it but to pull to the shoulder and wait for them to emerge, hopefully with Lars in tow.

I was still groggy and hadn't heard the latest news, so Chronos and Emeline filled me in as we leant against the jeep's tailgate, warming and cooling as the clouds and sun tangoed above us. We passed a flask of warm-enough coffee between us as we waited.

Chronos gave me an aggressive, impromptu shoulder massage, his massive fingers pressing deeply and offering me no choice but to wake up. "Alan Ryder texted me from the hospital. He's with Angelina. She's in wonderful spirits and charming the scrubs off the doctors and nurses, but she has two cracked ribs. They'll keep her in overnight to make sure there's nothing more sinister, like internal bleeding. I guess that enormous ball of toad spit, despite being the grossest thing I've ever handled, protected her in the end."

"And what happened to the Ides Giant and the Pendletoad? Please tell me they didn't rampage off through town," I said.

Emeline answered, "The landscapers at the Orphanage will have their work cut out for them. There are deep footprint divots all over the hill and the field below. Both toad-shaped and blocky giant prints. Then there's the broken window in Angelina's room and the trail of slime across the grass that was drying into a greyish film when we got back."

Chronos erupted into a belly laugh. "And *somebody* left a series of tire diggies in the grass. I inspected them, and they looked like jeep tire tracks to me."

Emeline waved him away. "I thought I saw a series of motorcycle skids carving their way up the hill. Did you see *those*? Anyway, the Ides Giant returned and soaked back into the hill. He's noticeably closer to your mum's shed, and he no longer had his club. His crown seems to be at a different angle. But he's got both arms raised in victory. Although he has very primitive facial features, I kept imagining him smiling in the moonlight."

"The toad went back home, too," Chronos added. "We heard three long croaks roll over the hill from the direction of Ashton Pond. There has been enough new weirdness to keep every tongue in Middle Ides wagging for six months. I don't know how any of our activity can be explained away, no matter *how* charming your grandmother is."

There was no need to settle in for a long wait. A black SUV with tinted windows approached from the other side of the barricade and was waved through without even a conversation by the carbine-armed attendants. It looked set to speed away but jolted to a stop beside us.

The rear passenger side door burst open and Faraday leapt out, stumbling in his haste. "Newton! You're here! Brother, are we glad to see you."

To be fair, nobody in the SUV looked glad about anything. I clapped Faraday's shoulder in passing but leant into Higgs, whose tear-streaked face pressed into my shoulder in a deep hug.

Dot's voice was flat as she looked me in the eye and flicked hers toward Scarlett in the driver's seat. "They called it off. The rescue mission. Lars is still out there, at the castle."

Scarlett hadn't so much as glanced at me yet. She looked like she was trying to pulverise the steering wheel in her white-knuckled grip and her taut jaw muscles knotted behind her ears. Releasing the wheel, she whacked it with her palms and whirled. "They're clueless! No idea what they're in for, Newton. I can't believe they called it off. He's got them doing *exactly* what he wants, that Ruaridh McRaven. We should have eliminated the bloody Tartantula a long time ago. I'd run up the Glen and drag him out by his gnarly beard right now if I didn't think they'd hang me for treason afterward."

Higgs had composed herself enough to speak now, and she pulled back from our hug. "We don't need the UPDA, Newt. Let's get Lars ourselves. Now that you're here, I can feel my magic coming back. And we've got Dot and Emeline too. We have to do *something*."

Dot's eyes widened. "What about the *elf*, Higgs? You've seen what he can do. And even my easiest spells weren't working in the glen, remember?"

Faraday crowded in behind my right shoulder, and Emeline and Chronos looked on from outside the window that Grover took delight in rolling up and down. Nobody knew what to say. There was a pause, and then Faraday spoke.

"Look, we won't make good decisions hanging out here on the hard shoulder. Can we have more time, back at the safe house, Scarlett, so we can figure things out?"

She nodded, paused in thought for a moment, then said, "I've got a better idea. That devious prick Angus is still out there somewhere. We know he's got the full inside scoop about what's occurring at Castle Ghuil. Let's see if we can't flush him out."

* * *

Chronos and Emeline swapped over to the SUV. I noticed they let Grover remain in the front seat; I guess he was enjoying himself too much, and Chronos shoehorned himself into the back. Faraday drove the jeep, and some of our shared anxiety faded as we slipped into the comfortable pattern of cruises around Middle Ides earlier in the summer, brothers in front, Dot and Higgs in the back. Only Disco was missing.

It took almost the entire drive back to Edinburgh to complete the picture. The goings-on in the glen, Faraday's encounters with Angus, the twins, and the Russian. The frightening conclusion to the motorcycle chase, the merits of Piping Hot, and the hyperbolic events in Middle Ides. Our reunion spurred wave after wave of sharing, and by the time we arrived in Duddingston Village, we had an inkling of a plan.

Although Scarlett drove at a conservative pace along the winding road through the village, the SUV curled abruptly into the small car park beside a Quonset hut, blocking in a parked Mercedes sports car and skidding to a stop.

"No way it can be this easy," Faraday said. "That's Angus

MacFarland's car. I thought he would have hightailed it by now – the twins must have aerted him."

He parked behind the SUV. There was no way the Mercedes was leaving without our cooperation.

The Caledonian Nanotech lab was unlit; if Angus was inside, he hadn't turned on the overhead lights. "My optimism is fading. He's probably not here," Faraday continued. "I wouldn't drive my own car if I was him, either. Too easy to spot."

"He's *definitely* not here," Dot said. "Because he's over *there*."

Sure enough, Angus was with Delladonna, both of them peering in the afternoon light across the lane from the open doorway of her cottage. Scarlett stamped across the tarmac, followed closely by Chronos, as always ready for action.

"Buddy, you've got a hell of a lot to answer for," Scarlett called.

Angus raised his palms and retreated a half step. "Scarlett, Scarlett. H-h-h-hang on a wee minute, we n-n-need to talk here."

The four of us leapt from the jeep with various degrees of grace and jogged across in Scarlett and Chronos's wake.

Delladonna positioned herself between Scarlett and Angus. "Just a moment, darlin'. We all know what Angus did, and you can have him, but not until he's helped convince my boys to get away from that Ruaridh. I won't let them get hurt."

"Aye, I can get them out, Delladonna. I'm probably the only sheep one they'll trust after the happenings last night. I can negotiate with McRaven. And look, Scarlett, I shouldnae have done all that stuff with the nano. I got camel swept up in Ruaridh's enthusiasm, and you know I'm a sucker for his way of thinking. I needed to apologize to Della here about dragging her starfish bairns into it before giving myself up. Make amends, like."

Scarlett stared down Angus for long enough to make him physically squirm. "Talk to the twins and get them out of there. Get them to ride out of the glen and turn east. I'll have a unit waiting there to take them into custody. After that, cut the call, and you can improve your chances of leniency in court by telling me *everything*. But if you so much as drop a vague hint about us to McRaven, my friend Chronos here informs me he'll stick his prosthetic foot so far up your arse it'll void his warranty."

"Look, I ken I'm rumbled. But I owe it to Delladonna and the boys to get them tuna out of this unharmed. They're only kids still, really. I shouldnae have drawn them into my schemes in the first place. But I'll need my satellite phone—it's in the boot of my car."

Scarlett extended a palm. "Keys."

She passed them back to me, and I jogged over to the Mercedes, popped the boot, and extracted the hard black case with a phone icon on it. I made sure it was as advertised before handing it to Angus. The handset was blocky, with an extensible antenna which he pulled to its full length before dialling a very long number. As he waited for a connection, he held a finger to his lips as if we might not already know to remain silent.

Delladonna put her ear to the back of the phone as Angus spoke so she'd hear when one of her sons got on the call.

Someone picked up the call, but we heard only a half conversation. "Och, hello!" Angus began. "I was expecting Ruaridh, but that's okay. I'm glad to hear your voice, Ragnhildur. I just wanted to say puffin I need to talk to either of the twins. Puffin. Are they around? Puffin."

Delladonna's eyes wandered. Either something weird was being expressed by Ragnhildur, or she was waiting for a reply. Maybe the phone had lost connectivity.

Angus continued to hold the phone to his ear. "Ragn? Are you still there?"

I heard the *pop-thud* combination for the first time, but Faraday and Higgs must have recognised it immediately. A small gust of wind swept past us as Ragnhildur appeared, right beside Angus. Her fine facial features marked her as a close relative of Scarlett's, dark and ruggedly beautiful where Scarlett was smooth-skinned and white-blonde. Strangely, one of her hands was a deep indigo, as if she'd held it in an ink reservoir.

Unfazed, Chronos was quick to action. He knocked the satellite phone into an arc across the densely vegetated garden, and his hand strained around Angus's neck, pinning the smaller man to the door frame's rough-hewn upright. His prosthetic leg slammed into the Scotsman's foot, bringing a clenched wince in response.

With his prey pinned, he faced Ragnhildur, who shrugged in a way that was much too calm for my liking. She was almost close enough for a headbutt and seemed unperturbed. "I heard the *unsafe* word, Angus. Looks like you *do* need rescuing," she drawled.

"I have no idea where you came from or what you think you're doing here, but this boy is *mine*. Back off now, love, or you'll regret getting involved."

"This is my sister, Chronos," Scarlett said with a sigh. "And she's backed by magic from her pet elf. There's not much any of us is going to do to stop her."

"Quarter-sister." Ragnhildur smiled, taking Angus's quivering hand in her blue palm.

Ever the logician, Faraday had to express himself. "Wait— you can't be someone's quarter-sister. Only full- or half-sister. You don't have four parents and share only one of them with Scarlett."

"That's where you're wrong," she said. "I'm twice the woman she'll ever be."

He walked into that one! But Ragnhildur had more scores to settle. "We're all together in this. The Tartantula, Ruaridh, Angus, and your sons, Delladonna, despite you trying to turn them against us. Angus here may have wanted to say goodbye to you, but our mission is nearing completion. Freedom!"

The sound of her laughter hung in the air after the now-familiar pop took both her and Angus away. Chronos grasped nothing but air, and his prosthesis clunked to the flagstone.

Delladonna's eyes welled up, and a single tear broke free and raced down her cheek to splatter on the flagstone at her feet. "That black-hearted bastard! He got them away fae the trouble they tangled themselves in two years ago, and I swore he'd fix things again now. So much for saving his life. And I ken what's next, Scarlett. You're gonnae tell me Duncan and Darren will be taken out with the rest of that damned Tartantula."

Scarlett dipped her head and raised her brows as she looked somewhere near her feet. "We were supposed to sweep in today, although that's now on hold. But yeah, it'll probably happen soon."

Delladonna turned her back and slammed her door shut with a reverberating thud. Nobody moved for a long moment until Scarlett broke the silence. "I need to get back to London. Come on, let's go."

"No," I said. "We're done with you. Again. I'll take care of everyone here. Your job is to call me *immediately* when you've prepared an alternative plan to rescue Lars. I'm expecting that by *tonight*. And you can pay for our hotel while we wait."

She shook her head twice and exhaled deeply. "Unbelievable. What do I need to do to show you I'm on your side? Here—take the entry card to the safe house; you shouldn't stay in a hotel. It'll be tight, but there are sofa beds. And you're going to have a hard time getting seven of you in the jeep. At least let me drive you back there before I go."

Faraday rattled a set of keys over my left shoulder. "We've got *two* cars now."

Scarlett shrugged and brushed past us on the way to the SUV.

"But hang on," Faraday called. "You want us to trust you? Show us the results of your queries back to the UPDA about Mum's death and my accident."

Scarlett pirouetted to face us, slipping out her phone as she did so. After a few taps and swipes, she exhaled sharply. "For the sake of our fathers. They've cut off my access to our systems. I can't see anything."

Faraday closed the gap to her before anyone else had moved. "You lying bitch!" he shouted. She made only half-hearted efforts to fend him off and he shoved her so hard by the shoulders that she managed only half a recovery step backward before landing with bruising impact on the pathway. Faraday leant forward, right arm raised and fist clenched, falling on her.

The blow never fell. Faraday remained suspended at an angle, mid-fall. As usual, Chronos was the first into action, and clenched Faraday's bunched shirt-back in his hand, halting his attack. "Easy, lad. I feel you, but this won't help."

Scarlett scrabbled backward then lurched to her feet again, dusting leaves and dirt from herself as she regained her composure. Higgs flew to Faraday's side and glared at Scarlett as Chronos lowered my brother to the ground. I noticed his hand hovered near Faraday's collar in case there was another lunge coming. Bouncer's instinct.

"She lying and hiding everything from us, Higgs," Faraday mumbled. His voice was twisted and anguished, the colour of rust. "Won't show she's not involved in Mum and Dad's deaths. Won't explain how Russian nanotech got into Mum's body. And now, she won't stand up and continue the rescue mission. She doesn't even *care* about Lars."

That was the wrong thing to say to Higgs.

Scarlett was turning, and one hand unlatched the gate. She was saying, "Newton, I'll call you later," when it happened.

A length of densely leaved vine lashed from Higgs's extended arm and bridged the gap between her and the gate in an instant. The vine was as thick as her arm, covered in black bark, and gnarled into twists and tiny offshoots. Scarlett got up a hand to protect her face, but the vine looped around that wrist and then her neck.

Unable to speak, her face erupted in shades of purple, and her eyes pleaded for mercy. Chronos this time stood frozen, and Emeline and Grover stood to one side, mouths agape. I knew it was my time to intervene.

"Higgs, no! Stop! This is not the way."

Still the vines constricted. Scarlett toppled onto her face, barely breaking the fall with her free hand. I knew that somehow I was the battery supplying Higgs's magical powers.

I focussed within myself and concentrated on stemming that flow. I remembered the flow of energy through the sympatico tunnel, and tried to imagine it reversing course, returning from Higgs to me.

My attempt failed. If anything, the power coursed from me in ever greater pulses. Scarlett's body twitched where it lay on the pathway.

Behind me came the sound of metal clicking on metal. "Not on my watch," boomed Delladonna's commanding voice. "She may help my boys yet. So let ... her ... *go!*"

My head whipped around. She wore thimbles on each finger of her right hand, clicking them in a pattern so fast that I could not follow the exact movement. The length of vine turned to ash, suspended for an instant before collapsing to the pathway in a snake of cinders. Higgs snatched her now fleshy arm back as if she'd received an electric shock. It's a good thing these flashes of magic were summoned in a quiet yard in a quiet corner of Duddingston village. Granny had warned Higgs many times about keeping any spells discrete, but I don't think wisdom was intruding on her decision-making process right now.

Nobody stopped Delladonna as she strode to Higgs and embraced her from behind. The grey coils of her hair cascaded over my sister's shoulders as the older woman muttered near her ear. "She may deserve it, I dinnae ken, but you need to hold back. We may still need her help. Simmer, lassie, simmer."

Dot joined the cluster too. My siblings and the two witches huddled as Scarlett spluttered and struggled to one knee. She massaged her neck where welts danced with rising bruises on her pale skin. As she stood unsteadily and hobbled through the gate, Higgs spoke quietly and to no one in particular. "Screw it. We'll rescue Lars ourselves."

All of us nodded. It was unanimous.

CHAPTER 24 - ROGUE

Faraday

Few groups would have needed a second journey from Edinburgh to Glen Ghuil on the same day, but we were on a mission of our own devising this time. In retrospect, the mission couldn't accurately be called *devised* because we had no proper plan when we set off from Delladonna's cottage.

Newton drove the jeep this time, with me beside him. Dot, Higgs, and Emeline scrunched together on the back bench. Grover perched on the cases in the rear, worryingly unrestrained by any seat belt, his tousled hair appearing in the rear-view mirror occasionally. Chronos was excited to get behind the wheel of Angus's two-seater Mercedes, and Delladonna rode shotgun.

We spent the long drive attempting to formulate a feasible plan. I half turned in my seat so I could see everyone and tried to visualise our attempt to free Lars. We didn't care so much about Ruaridh, Ragnhildur, or the Tartantula, but we knew that neutralising the elf magic was mandatory.

"Okay, what have we got that we can use?" I asked.

Dot was a planner like me, and she got stuck in. "We aren't sure any of our magic will work. Last time Higgs and I tried some real simple stuff in the Glen, it fizzled out. Probably Ragnhildur has the elf stopping any magic."

Higgs cut in. "But maybe now that Newton is here, I can get through that block."

"Mmmmaybe," Dot replied, "but I don't think we can count on it."

"I brought the drone," Newt said. "Could we use that to look inside the castle and see what they're up to while we sneak up?"

"Good idea," I said. "And I moved 11 anti-nano flasks across from the SUV, so if we get attacked by any of Angus's nanotech, we can try cracking them open to protect ourselves. I'm guessing Angus is at Castle Ghuil now, right?"

I rummaged in the glove box. "We also have a pair of binoculars, a roll of duct tape, 17 cable ties, 11 plasters—which will be handy only if we face a skinned knee or a thistle jab—and a half-used squeezy bottle of bug repellent."

Those were our only resources. It didn't seem like we had much going for us, except for the element of surprise. Eventually, we decided upon a strategy of sneaking along the loch, checking out Lars's location using the drone, and then having Chronos sneak through the portcullis to snatch both Lars and the elf. It was unclear how Chronos would open the cage that confined Lars, but we had to hope a couple of tire irons and his strength could spring the lock. Even without a proper plan, our commitment left no space to turn back now.

Because our phones wouldn't work in the glen, we figured Emeline could stay at the roadside and leave to get help if any of us raised our arms overhead in an X. We also figured there was no way we would stop Delladonna from moving down the glen with us. That was probably for the best; she might persuade Darren and Duncan to switch sides.

"I'm coming too!" Grover called from the back. I'd almost forgotten he was with us until he stuck his head up between the girls' shoulders. Then he slouched and disappeared from view again.

In a conspiratorial voice, Newton asked me, "Can he really do magic too, Faraday? Will he be able to help us?"

I shrugged. "I don't know the answer to either of those questions. He can definitely do *something*. He summoned those fish to help open the simpatico tunnel somehow. But we can't really count on him helping us with anything specific." I called out in a louder voice. "Hey, Grover. You know your special abilities? What do you think you can do to help us get Lars back?"

His head popped up once again. "I'll get some animals to help. They always want to help, but nobody ever asks them. And I'm good at finding things. I'm not strong like your friend, but I have the silver thing from underwater. Maybe it can do something."

We agreed to pause and reconvene at the spot where the barricade had blocked our way earlier. As we snaked along the last stretch of road to the head of Glen Ghuil, the Mercedes blew past us as if we stood still. The top was down, and we caught trills of Delladonna's laughter as her hair rippled in gravity-defying waves on the air turbulence above their seats. In the distance ahead, the brake lights sparked into life as the sports car slowed. As Newton braked, a motorcycle approached from behind, matching our speed and pulling alongside. The helmeted rider waved to us, and the only one of us not too puzzled to wave back was Dot.

"Really, Dot? Really?" Higgs said in mock shock.

"I texted him as we left Edinburgh to say goodbye. I may have mentioned Glen Ghuil, but how was I to know he'd ride up here?"

The rider stopped ahead of us at the rendezvous point and dismounted, removing his helmet. Tam Thunder's hairdo was less coiffed than when we first met him but no less wild as it sprang from his helmet. He grinned. "What a coincidence, Lady Pendlethwaite. And greetings, Redfernes. It's a pleasure."

Chronos and Delladonna joined us, and we went over the skeletal plan. As expected, Delladonna insisted on joining us for the approach. "There may be a thing or two I can do to help. And I may have it in me yet to send my lads to the naughty step."

There was also the matter of how Tam would figure in our plan, now that Dot seemed to have ensnared him. "I only meant to say goodbye, in case I didn't see you again," she said.

"I don't want you getting roped into our weird battles."

Reluctantly, he agreed to remain with the cars at the head of the glen, ready to get help if needed. "I ken the X signal, but how's about if you give me an overhead Y, I'll bring my bike down the loch and rescue you? Can you at least make me feel like I'm doing *something* brave?"

"Deal," Dot agreed.

We crept our three vehicles to a point just shy of the opening to Glen Ghuil. A good viewing point in the long grass revealed the glen's narrow expanse with a view along the loch to Castle Ghuil and the open sea beyond. The bus stop where Higgs, Dot, and Lars had alighted only two mornings ago stood in lonely solitude beside road's sweeping arm to our right.

I double- and triple-checked the drone. Fully charged. Batteries in the control handset good. The anti-nano-nano flasks that Iain and I had loaded with our prototypes were ready to slot in as a payload. I patted them in their foam sleeve in the thigh pocket of my fatigues to double-check.

We were as ready as we were ever going to be. Newt embraced Emeline in a drawn-out kiss, and Dot gave Tam a perfunctory hug and a regal wave as she rejoined us.

Newton took the lead, and the rest of us prepared to follow him, but he paused to let a car pass along the road behind us before we embarked on our improbable mission. The car slowed, and rubber popped gravel nuggets aside as it stopped on the shoulder. From the black SUV's lowered window, a familiar voice called out.

"You'll probably try to kill me again, and I *know* I'm a fool to help you, but here I am."

We all turned to look at Scarlett and must have looked puzzled. "UPDA be damned. We all know they're making a mistake by not letting me take out that bloody elf. They may have locked me out of all the systems, but I still have a few, shall we say, *tools*."

We still stared, nobody expressing the confusion we surely all felt, considering our last interaction and the deep violet series of ugly bruises that circled her neck, a striking contrast with her ivory skin and camouflage fatigues. She must have taken the lack of response as acceptance because she jumped out, popped open the back hatch, and slotted 2 cases into a strapped harness she hoisted onto her back. Begrusgingly, I admired her confidence.

Dot looked down at her own ill-fitting outfit and broke the silence. "Well, we kind of *look* like we're a team. Let's march."

Scarlett handed me the UPSCALE to balance the case I held in my other hand. Higgs gave her a lingering glare but then turned to join the rest of us as we entered the glen in the patchy, angling sunlight of a beautiful Scottish late afternoon.

We passed the bus stop and soon arrived at the campsite. Dot ducked into a tent and pulled out a pair of shoes.

Bless her optimism. She shrugged, saying, "Lars is going to need these to hike all the way back, isn't he?"

Higgs pointed lochside, past where the three tents remained pitched. "Don't forget what I said about the magic that drew us along the glen. Maybe it's still in effect. We can probably use that to get closer to the castle, but it may stop us from entering the front gate once we get there."

Each absorbed in our own thoughts, we headed into the magical jaws of the Tartantula.

CHAPTER 25 - ADVANCE

Newton

We knew our chances of accomplishing anything were slim, but I drew a deep breath and committed to leading our raiding party with optimism and as much rigour as we could muster. I didn't utter it aloud, but it was comforting to have Scarlett with us. I hoped her experience would outshine anything I'd learnt at police college. Regardless, I took the lead as we left the campsite.

Looking back at our ragtag company, I saw five of the seven in military fatigues and caps, a holdover from the aborted earlier mission. Chronos looked his usual self—black jeans, black T-shirt, and one black boot. He wore his bladed prosthesis which was better suited to action, but gave him some trouble in the soft turf with its smaller striking area. He had the most physical ability of any of us, so I hadn't a single strand of doubt where he was concerned. Delladonna had changed at her cottage into hiking boots, some brown leggings, and an olive zip-up top, so she too blended in well with the surroundings other than the grey spring of tied back hair that caught the light now and then.

The baleful eyes of a quartet of highland cows followed us as we approached the stand of trees near the loch's headwaters. I followed the narrow hiking trail's beaten earth, but I heard murmuring behind me after I passed the cattle and broke the treeline. I turned to see Dot and Higgs approaching a cow, making soothing sounds. It exuded an air of unperturbed grace and allowed them within wooing distance. They stroked its shaggy flanks, and Higgs slid a hand down one curving horn. "For Lars," I heard her say, as they retreated and rejoined the back of our snaking troupe.

A little way into the trees, Higgs called from the rear. "Newt, let's try doubling back toward the road now. This was one spot where Dot and I got transported on Friday."

I motioned for everyone to form a line behind me. "Follow closely, everyone," I said. "If the magic takes us closer to the castle, let's hope we all stay together, like Higgs and Dot did. Let's run, in three … two … one!"

I set off at a moderate jog, with muffled footfalls behind me. Sure enough, as if encountering an unexpected break in the canopy overhead, a change in the ambient light signalled we were no longer beneath the trees. The loch lapped close on our left. Realising we had a direct line of sight to Castle Ghuil, I instinctively crouched and stopped, raising a fist to halt my companions. When I looked behind me, our group was still intact, and everyone crouched, awaiting my next move.

"Let's try again," I called in a soft voice. "Higgs, you go first, and we'll follow. Stay low!"

Rotating a half turn, we prepared to follow my sister away from the castle. She counted us down from five with her upraised arm.

The disorienting switch happened again, but this time we didn't arrive together in our neat line. We ranged in a wide arc, facing the walls of Castle Ghuil, about a hundred metres away from it. The walls before us looked black with the sun low on the horizon behind it, and long shadows spread our way like spilled ink. The crenelated tops glowed in the sunlight, and the open gate spilt out a patch of golden light to break up the shadows. Low tide revealed the tidal causeway's sandy and seaweed-strewn glory.

Exposed once again, we all fell to the ground in synchrony. Faraday was the only one of us who reappeared on the main hiking path to the castle, so he dived off to one side and found the safety of the long grass like the rest of us. Swarms of midges took to the air as we invaded their habitat. Crickets scattered.

"I brought everything else—why not the bug repellent?" I heard Faraday mutter from his position slightly to my left. His hand fluttered in a cargo pocket of his baggy fatigues, and he pulled out the small pair of binoculars. He craned his neck and squinted back toward the road. "I can see Emeline and that Piping Hot guy. Looks like she's using the zoom on her phone camera to watch us."

He pocketed the binoculars and was turning on the UPSCALE as Scarlett shuffled, prone, at high speed and took a position in the grass between Faraday and me. To my right, waving grass signified the other four shuffling their way closer too.

"Let's have a look at the UPSCALE, Faraday," Scarlett said. "The nano part won't help us up here where we have no detection clouds, but maybe the magic tracker can tell us something."

Faraday adjusted a few controls on the unit's side, and some symbols appeared on the screen. As he zoomed in, I noted the loch's contours and the outline of the castle grounds at its mouth.

"Nice, it's working!" Faraday said. "Well, sort of. The symbols fade in and out. The elf's magic must affect the magic traces, which explains why it couldn't track Higgs when we checked from Middle Ides. Now that we're closer, the signals must be stronger. Look—here's where we are. I can see Dot, Higgs, and Grover's icons. This one must be Delladonna, I haven't seen it before. There's Emeline back at the road. And something up on the hillside to our right, a wavering question mark."

Faraday chimed in. "But look at this: the UPSCALE must have detected Ragnhildur using the elf's magic, either at the Water of Leith or maybe outside the Donnelly place. I can see two icons inside the castle grounds. Look at the magnitude marker on that one—it's got to be the elf. And the other one has the same icon but with a much lower magnitude. Maybe residual magic on Ragn?"

The symbols were drifting slightly on the map. It looked like they were in the open ground in the castle's central area, but we knew from the surveillance and from Higgs and Dot's experience that there was a new building inside the walls that wouldn't be on the UPSCALE's map. We knew Lars was likely still in the cage that he mentioned when Dot and Higgs overheard him two days ago, but we knew nothing of its composition or its precise location.

"This is good," Scarlett said. "We can use this to guide Chronos to the elf. Let's show him how to use it."

I waved Chronos closer, and he crawled behind us and scootched in between Scarlett and me. As Faraday explained how to understand the UPSCALE in a stage whisper, Grover rose to a crouch and scuttled behind us, across the path, and down to the loch's edge. He ignored my quiet calls as he removed an item that flashed silver from a pocket inside his camouflage top and filled it with water. A flask. It would be sea water here at the loch's mouth, so I didn't understand why he'd want to do that, but this was not the first mysterious thing Grover had done, so I left him to it and hoped the Tartantula wouldn't spot him from the castle.

"That's right, you've got it," Scarlett said to Chronos. "Scoot along the shore now. Keep as low as your bladed leg will allow. You see the inlet mapped behind the castle, just *there*? It leads through a gate into the rocky base, and the folk from the Scottish National Trust that we spoke to when planning the raid told us it leads to a set of stone steps. They ultimately emerge onto the lawns inside the castle right about *here*."

I patted my oldest friend on the shoulder. "When you hear either commotion or one of Higgs's famous wolf whistles, that's your cue to snatch the elf, get him out of the handcuffs, and pry Lars loose while we keep Ragnhildur and Ruaridh busy. Got the tire irons?"

Chronos lifted the hem of his jeans to expose his prosthesis. It had the tire irons from both the jeep and the Mercedes strapped to it with duct tape. "Should be a light ten minutes of work, and then you're buying the pints." The energy of his wide grin lingered even after he crouched and ran past Grover along the shoreline.

Scarlett slung the two cases from her back onto the grass before us. "Okay, everyone, it's time to cause some chaos."

She flicked open the first case. She had explained it contained some high-tech surveillance and combat devices, but I hadn't expected them to look so familiar. I glanced at Higgs—she blanched, too.

CHAPTER 26 - FLUTTERING

Faraday

We crept within striking distance of Castle Ghuil without being detected, it seemed. Chronos was in position on its opposite side. We were ready to create a diversion to cover for him. I'm not sure what Grover was doing mooching around in the shallow waters, but I had more interesting things that needed focus.

The gates to the castle lay directly ahead across the rock-strewn, sandy isthmus laid bare by the low tide. The half-ruined fortress roosted on a slab of gnarled and vegetation-covered rock layers. A massive nugget of granite that looked like it could have arrived from space or been flung across the sea by an angry Irish giant. The path led to the sand and then resumed with a steep climb on the tidal island before it culminated at the half-open wooden gates.

Scarlett opened the cases that she had described earlier as 'automated surveillance and combat devices'. The cases contained moulded foam inserts that protected the items within. First, she popped a control tablet from its recess, flicked open its angled stand, and powered it up. A detailed control application appeared on screen, and she made adjustments in an interface that showed a world map. It was akin to the mapping function on the UPSCALE. She adeptly zoomed into Castle Ghuil.

"We'll send the full force of these recon and attack units

into the castle," she said as she removed 32 mechanical insect replicas from their protective niches. Each was the size and shape of a dragonfly. Up close, you could see their mechanical structure, but a casual glance wouldn't reveal their technological nature. They were effective replicas of natural creatures.

I looked at Newton and Higgs, who lay prone in the waving grass on Scarlett's other side. "Hang on. These look like the things that …"

Newton and Higgs nodded in unison. "These infernal machines attacked us in our own home in the spring," Higgs snapped.

Scarlett glanced quickly at each of us. "As I said before, that wasn't me. We copied these from the Russian military. Anyway, we'll investigate that later when I get my system access back. Let's focus on the plan."

I fought back a lump that rose in my gorge, parking the rage-inspiring questions about Scarlett and the UPDA that filled me again. I let my mind revert to the technical details. "What's their assignment, and how do you control them? There are too many to pilot individually."

She nodded. "True. You give them operational parameters. In this section here, I've already defined the area they are going to investigate. They use artificial intelligence software to act like a real swarm, co-operating only loosely but all with the same destination in mind. And over here, I've set a second phase for their flight mission. When I see their camera footage, I'm going to select some targets for the attack. That's how I'll tell them to go after Ruaridh and Ragnhildur but ignore Lars and the elf. I'm pretty sure any direct attack on the elf will fail, so I'd rather concentrate on our human opponents."

I noticed Scarlett didn't mention the Donnelly twins. I figured they were potential targets too, but she didn't want to rile up Delladonna.

Newton cut in. "When you say 'attack', what weapons do they have? Is it those little darts that flew at Higgs and me?"

"Yep. Micro-darts. Each insect is armed with ten darts,

some carrying anaesthetic tips that render targets unconscious, and others have a powerful incendiary fluid that can set fires. Effective against both people and objects. And of course, they all have cameras and microphones—those multifaceted eyes aren't just for show. We'll be able to see all thirty-two signals here on the screen and listen through these earpieces. They can see above, below, and almost three-sixty around themselves."

Scarlett fanned the dragonflies before us on a stony patch of earth unimpeded by the tall grasses that hid us. Newton staged our mega-drone alongside them, in case we needed it too for any reason.

"What are we waiting for? Let's mess these idiots up!" Higgs hissed.

Scarlett pressed the 'Start Mission' icon and confirmed the attack. The dragonflies flapped, the blur of their wings accompanied by a realistic buzzing one might hear on any warm summer day.

"That's amazing," I said in hushed reverence. "Not even a hint of electric servo motor whine."

The dragonflies unmoored themselves from gravity in 2's and 3's, lifting gracefully before nosing down and speeding toward the castle walls. Scarlett's hands were a blur too, picking out the most interesting video feeds. All six of our heads nestled close, so we could observe the surveillance unfold.

The first footage of the castle interior appeared as the initial wave of dragonflies rose above the castle walls. Ragnhildur and one twin stood near the open door of the Tartantula chalet, talking. It looked like their conversation included someone indoors, unseen from this height. Scarlett and I had an earpiece each, and she selected a drone to move in closer and focus its parabolic microphone toward Ragnhildur. We picked up scratchy snatches of speech.

We discerned Ragnhildur's first. She was calling through the doorway, with one twin nodding and listening at her side. "According to Sundalfar, yes. Something took out his ability to pump the spell into the reservoir at Ferndale, but the one in Pentland is still going strong. He says he's got enough strength now to deploy to another water source. Do you want to go to Ferndale again, or somewhere else? England or Scotland?"

A gravel-laced reply came from within. It must have been Ruaridh McRaven. "Whatever our wee blue pal did at Ferndale, it's well workin'. He says we can pick from over two million Sassenachs already. No need to return there. How about London? It's dead easy negotiatin' with them lot instead of tryin' to convince that dunderheid Fiona Byrd. They dinnae seem to give two hoots if Scotland separates. I thought blondie *wanted* independence, then she gets all greetin' about the *citizens* when I pushed her, ken?"

Another voice agreed from inside the hut. Angus. "Aye, work the English. They dinnae give two piles of cockle crap if Scotland comes or goes."

"Agreed," Ragnhildur said. "Let me look at the map and see where Sundalfar should insert next. Gods, as if the midges weren't bad enough, now there are dragonflies hovering about."

She looked right at the camera and into our remote eyeballs but then glanced away. Angus emerged, blinking his crinkle-edged eyes in the bright light.

Scarlett's fingertips danced on the control pad, swapping cameras to give us a multi-angled view of the building and its occupants. We could see them from above and at ground level in split-screen. "Watch closely, Faraday. Here's where you need to work fast to adjust the mission priorities. See that low-flying unit there? He's got a good line of sight into the building. I can't see Lars, the second twin, or the elf, but if we fly low, we can target Ruaridh through the doorway."

She opened a targeting window with a bull's-eye style cursor and quickly selected targets. Ragnhildur, then Ruaridh, Angus, and finally, the visible twin. Anticipating a comment from Delladonna, she said, "It'll only anaesthetise them. We're not using the incendiary darts. Don't worry."

One of the thumbnail videos from a high-flying dragonfly briefly showed something of interest before it dipped to get a better firing angle. I wasn't sure what I'd seen, so I looked away and replayed the image in my mind. "Scarlett, can you rewind that video in the top left corner? I think I can see Lars."

With a tap and a swizzle, that video cycled back. "Look! Right there, behind the chalet. See the cage? And that haircut is pure Lars. They have him out back. Perfect—he's between Chronos and the back of the building."

"Nice. That's one target acquired," Scarlett said, as she focussed to prepare the attack pattern. A few more flicks on the tablet, and she declared we were ready. "Okay, Higgs. Ready to whistle for Chronos?"

My sister nodded. Scarlett clicked the icon marked 'Rally and Engage'. The panorama of camera views transformed to momentary chaos as several dragonflies sped to new positions.

Angus, still squinting, shouted in alarm. "R-R-R-Russian drones! Everybody g-g-get down." He flung himself to the ground as Scarlett's tablet lit up with indicators of dart fire.

The cameras clouded with bursts of propellant gasses, and the darts' flight patterns cut feathery lines through the floating residue. Darts raced, imperceptible, to their targets. Ragnhildur and the twin alongside her hadn't reacted; they looked higher into the sky. I guess Angus's warning wasn't specific enough for them to suspect the dragonflies.

The darts should have struck all four targets multiple times, but our cameras picked up a series of deep blue flashes, each one resulting in what looked like a semi-transparent soap bubble. Inside the bubbles, the dragonfly darts hung, suspended. The bubbles floated on the breeze, popping on the chalet sides or whisking above its roof. Scarlett's finger bent backwards as she cancelled the attack orders. It seemed futile to waste ammunition given the magical defences at work.

"We're under attack," Ragnhildur raged. "Whoever's doing it doesn't know the elf is watching over us. Morons." Angus shoved himself to a crouch and retreated into the cabin. Ragnhildur pulled back, scanning the scene from a half-concealed position behind the door frame. The Donnelly twin obviously felt empowered by the elf magic's offer of invulnerability and stepped forward 4 paces. His brother edged past Ragnhildur and joined him. Their heads swivelled almost in unison as they scanned the grounds for any other signs of attack.

This dashed any embers of hope that our attack would work. The twins were alert and would see Chronos if he came up the steps at this point. Any further attack by the dragonflies seemed pointless. Whoever's fingers gripped my shoulders reacted the same way—I felt them dig in as our failure became apparent. The pre-Scarlett plan of rushing the gate and letting Chronos dash in during the confusion reverted to being plan 'A'.

Higgs slapped Scarlett on the back, spurring her fingers back into action from where they hovered, paralysed. "Lars ins't inside. Burn them out," she demanded.

Swipes and taps played across the screen like music. "Good idea, Higgs," I said. "Maybe they haven't told the elf to protect the property."

Dot pushed closer to the screen to see the finer details. "And Sundalfar seemed like he was obeying only to the minimum degree. He wants out of there as much as Lars."

Scarlett marked several areas on the wooden building and re-engaged the attack sequence. We all held our breaths through the disorienting blur as the dragonflies recalibrated their attacks. In the earpiece, I could hear Ragnhildur shouting instructions to the elf.

"Sundalfar, destroy those ungodly dragonflies. And sense around the castle for intruders."

The puffs of dart flight were visible as the dragonflies fired again, this time aiming at the roof, walls, and door of the building that insulted Castle Ghuil's ruins. No blue bubbles appeared this time.

An odd, semi-strangled and high-pitched voice crackled across the audio channel.

"Mistress! I hear mistress, I hear. Those are two things Sundalfar can do. Must do. Must do. And elf needs to know which one to work on first. All must be clear. Be clear."

Impatience laced through Ragnhildur's reply like acid.

"Argh! Dragonflies first, you idiot!"

I couldn't see any results from the second volley of darts. The incendiary attack hadn't worked either, so I figured it was little loss when the cameras all went dark on Scarlett's screen. The elf made swift work of Scarlett's weaponry. Newton and I sprang up as one, prepared to rush the gate on foot.

Higgs's voice was quiet but tinged with darkness, a dagger aimed Scarlett's way. "So much for your precious *tools*."

"Did you see any blue bubbles this time?" Scarlett pushed out a short barking laugh. "Give it a few seconds. Duck back down, you fools. You'll see."

She was correct. Although our recon was now crippled, through the open gate of Castle Ghuil, I saw the chalet roof burst into violent gouts of flame.

A minor victory. We rose and charged the gate as one.

Shadow Over Loch Ghuil

CHAPTER 27 - FOOTFAST

Higgs

It seemed strange that I could outrun the rest of our motley party. I had the shortest legs, but maybe the head start helped. The grass rasped past my calves as I raced in a bee line toward the gate. It took a couple of attempts for my fingers to press my tongue into the right shape as I sprinted, but I managed three explosive and shrill whistles while still running. If the flames leaping from the wooden building hadn't alerted Chronos that all hell was breaking loose, he'd know now.

I had a good line of sight as I closed the gap to the gate. I spotted the corner bars of a cage peeking from behind the chalet. Angus and Ragnhildur blossomed from the doorway, shoulder to shoulder, turning to assess the flames. A third figure that could only be Ruaridh McRaven hurried them to the cropped grass. He looked a little different from the photos we'd seen, but the weatherbeaten crags of his face and the wiry red explosion of his long beard made him instantly identifiable. The lurching figure of the handcuffed, knee-height, blue-skinned elf followed, his elongated feet slapping at the earth. I lost sight of him as he moved into my main line of vision, but I knew he was among our adversaries, invisible.

Ragnhildur issued more commands. My feet pounded the sandy isthmus. Did Faraday take into consideration the tides, so we didn't arrive at a time when we'd have to swim across? I expect he did.

"Sundalfar, what the hell?" Ragn said. "Put out the damned fires."

He pointed a multi-jointed, spindly finger at the hut's roof, which verged on an inferno already. "I tell you now. I telled you before. I probably be telling you again. Earth. Air. Only. If I break the pacts, I die. No good, no good. Fire is for trolls. Only trolls. Sundalfar cannot help. And water is for the others. We cannot speak of them. Never. Air and Earth only, mistress. Only. You should free us, mistress. Free us now."

Visible through the gates, the twins turned and ran toward us in unison. They took turns calling alerts to their trailing co-conspirators, who swiveled their attention to the six of us approaching across the sands.

"Incoming!"

"Magic, too. It's the Redferne girl and her witch friend."

"And Scarlett. Those drones were *hers*."

"Mum! No, Mum! Go back. You cannae get involved."

Past the elf at Ragnhildur's knees and behind the backs of the Icelander and her two separatist cronies I saw Chronos running toward the cage behind the flame-engulfed building.

Ragnhildur grabbed the dome of Sundalfar's mottled scalp and forcibly turned his face toward us. "You will not ask any more questions, elf. Footfast. Now. Everyone that's not one of *us*. Footfast! Do it!"

The others had caught up to me, except for Delladonna, who lagged, still negotiating the twisty path to the sand. The elf's oval eyes seemed to stare only at me. A pair of blue shoulders shrugged, the blurring handcuffs shackling his wrists visible between two outstretched hands.

Then we all stopped running. My legs still attempted to propel me to the edge of the island proper, only steps away. But my feet refused to lift from the ground. Newton, a pace behind me, fell to a three-point stance, leaving a handprint in the sand before righting himself. We all looked down at our recalcitrant feet, but none budged. Behind our adversaries, I saw Chronos had bounded almost to the cage and was scrabbling for his tire iron, but judging by his ungainly position, the footfast spell anchored him too.

Ragnhildur's cackle was a dentist's drill to our ears, its shrill tones aimed at Scarlett. "You again, sister? Of all people, you should have convinced these amateurs to stay away. You can't win against someone with the power of an elf unless they are exceptionally stupid. And you know best of all how smart I am. For example, I can tell you aren't here on a UPDA mission. They'd never let you lead a sloppy attack like this. What happened? They wouldn't believe you when you started talking elf nonsense? With our little blue friend, this land is ours for the taking. Negotiations are well under way to cover our tracks as the genuine power, and that insignificant First Minister will be a puppet on our strings by the end of this week. You can stay with us and watch the progress first hand."

She laughed again, harder, her face ugly as it tried but failed to contain her contempt. I caught movement from the corner of my eye, and it took all my discipline to avoid turning my head for a full view. Grover was moving. Not along the shore, but across the deeper waters separating the mainland from the tidal island where Castle Ghuil rose. He wasn't swimming, but juddering across upright, his waist rising and falling below the waterline as he progressed. He held the flask above his head as if trying to keep it dry. And somehow, he still held it at the perfect angle to reflect sunlight straight onto the side of my face. He bobbed slightly as if he rode a fully submerged horse and made rapid progress toward the far shore.

More words spewed from the castle gate. Angus wasn't as confident as Scarlett's half-sister, but had some gloating of his own. He called from Ragnhildur's side, "See that crap Russian tech you Komodo dragon tried against us, Scarlett? Tranq darts, eh? You shouldae asked me for the perfected version of that weapon. Wanna see it?"

I looked at my companions, still helplessly struggling to lift either foot. Delladonna, on the higher ground behind us, had her arms raised in a Y, shrugging her shoulders to the sky in an emphatic rhythm, looking back along the loch.

Angus grinned as he took a handheld control from his

pocket. "See you inside the cage. Nighty night!"

CHAPTER 28 - ATTRACTION

Newton

Our half-baked plan wasn't working. Not that I'd ever had much confidence in it. Our best weapon was one that Scarlett introduced at the last minute, and our secret raider had slunk behind enemy lines but froze mid-sneak, rooted to the ground like the rest of us. Any moment now, one of our adversaries would turn and see him, hulking and guilty, behind them. Only Grover was somehow still in motion.

The little blue-skinned elf's pointy ears retracted against his scalp as he cocked his head and peered skyward. Angus fiddled with a small device he had retrieved from an inner breast pocket, a crooked smile slashed across his face.

From the crumbling parapets rose an aerial armada of what looked like paper airplanes—shiny silver paper airplanes decked out with tiny engines and other apparatus dangling from their rigid wings. "Lookie, lookie!" Angus called. "Your Russky fake dragonflies can only cruise a few hundred metres. These wee cheetah beauties can drift almost indefinitely."

Scarlett sneered beside me. "Yeah, but mine are *scarier*. Come get me, little airplanes!"

Angus reddened. "I used the same dart system. When will you find out if I'm using the anaesthetic darts or the warthog fiery wee nippers? Oh, the suspense!"

Although all of us but Delladonna and Grover stood stranded in the shadows cast by the low-riding sun, the drifting planes glittered intermittently above the castle. They looked like smooth aluminium foil constructions, fine metalwork lining their wings. Metal ... there was something about metal and nanotech in the long, unopened letter from Angus to my mother.

As usual, Faraday reached the same conclusion, but ahead of me. "Ahem, my turn with the toy," he said, giving the drone control that hung limp at my hip a 'come hither' signal with his curling fingers.

Yes, of course. We had our own drone, didn't we? And it was ready for take-off on the mainland behind us, primed for flight. It may not have had the anti-nano flasks loaded, but it probably had Faraday and Iain's magnetic experiment ready to go. I lobbed the controller past Scarlett to my brother's outstretched hand. He wasn't the most dextrous of athletes, but his anticipation offset a sub-optimal throw. He flicked on the unit, and the drone's whine rose behind us a second later.

Meanwhile, the lazy airplanes looped and split, two or three angling directly toward each of the six of us on the isthmus. It would be only moments before the hiss of compressed air released darts at us. Only Grover and Chronos, still undetected, would be spared the first salvo. I shuffled back and forth, offering more than a stationary target.

The twins objected to the trio of darting planes that angled toward Delladonna, almost in unison. "Angus, leave Mum out of this!" one said, while the other spluttered and gestured in her direction.

I thought back to the mechanical dragonflies that had attacked Higgs and me through the rear window of our house earlier this year. Although I didn't realise it then, Higgs neutralised the darts and repelled the nanotech with her magic. Maybe it could blaze through again and protect us from Angus.

Delladonna ducked just in time as Faraday's drone whizzed past, rising as it crossed above us, making an unusual sound. It was a combination of sheet metal being flexed and a timpani being tuned. As the drone blared its *wow-wow-wow*, the planes all wobbled. The now familiar *phhht* of firing darts spattered from the planes even as they faltered from their paths in the passing drone's magnetic field.

Scanning my companions, we all seemed to have avoided dart impacts. Then I saw Scarlett—five or six darts quivered in an angling line across her chest, puncturing her camo jacket.

Faraday was pallid in concentration as he swung the drone through the castle gate, making the twins duck just as their mother had. The drone arched up, flipped, and returned in a dive over the castle wall toward the tiny, looping planes that reestablished their flight paths around us. The Donnelly twins followed the progress of the whirring drone's graceful flight, nodding in silent approval at the skill involved.

From the corner of my eye, I caught a glimpse of Grover, who had progressed through the water to the castle's midpoint on our left. He was dismounting into the shallows, holding aloft a silver flask. Dismounting? How do you dismount from the sea? I couldn't spare a second to consider this weirdness, and my attention snapped back to the drone battle overhead.

Faraday had slowed the quad-copter to a steady hover, and the nearest clutch of glistening airplanes cartwheeled across to adhere to a small cube suspended below the much larger drone. The drift of each plane grew erratic as Faraday wove a zig-zag through the squadron. Plane stuck to plane as the powerful magnet came within range. A few more darts fired harmlessly into the sand and water before every one of Angus's remaining emissaries hung jumbled beneath the drone.

With a few deft flicks, Faraday's nimble fingers directed the drone out to sea in a graceful ascent that ended in a sharp dive and not so graceful plunge into the waves. As the redundant drone control dangled from his hand, my brother raised his chin toward the enraged nanotechnologist. "I see you haven't figured out how to remove ferrous materials from your fabrication rig yet, Angus."

I spared half a look at my brother's face as I watched Scarlett slump to her knees, her feet still fixed to their positions in the sand. He looked so proud of himself, stood paralysed before our enemies.

"And you can stop tryin' to hide in plain sight, ya great cockwomble." Clearly, Ruaridh had spotted Chronos.

CHAPTER 29 - INDEPENDENCE

Faraday

A burst of righteous energy coursed through me when I dispelled Angus's nanotech planes, sending them to a saltwater death. Although our feet clung immovable to the terrain, for a few fleeting instants, it seemed we had the upper hand. Then reality slapped me awake. We remained helpless in the subjugated elf's magical grasp.

Ruaridh faced Chronos, frozen in mid-sneak on the lawn inside the castle's foreboding walls, within an outstretched arm's length of Lars's cage. Scarlett, punctured with nanodarts, had fallen to her knees and her arms shook in spasms. Dot, my siblings, and I clustered on the sand, Higgs almost on the pebbled beach of the castle's island, but nobody was quite close enough to assist Scarlett. All we could do was watch in horror as she jerked repeatedly, head bowed.

Ragnhildur barked orders, perturbed by Chronos' proximity to the caged Lars. "Sundalfar! Move the cage away! Put it somewhere else on the island. Now!"

There was no debate from the elf at this command. A popping sound accompanied the disappeance of the cage.

"And make him magic those stupid cows away fae the new spot!" Ruaridh bellowed. "I'm no gonnae find out prophecies are real just now."

Sundalfar hopped from foot to foot, circling Ragnhildur as he gave an animated reply. "The island, mistress. No cows can

253

come on it *already*. Hear me. Hear me. And you told me the spell should hold *even when it's not, not, not an island*. When the water is low. All done, mistress, all done already." Ragnhildur shook her head in scorn, seeming to resign herself to the flames.

I had almost forgotten about Grover, but his voice called both through the air and somehow directly into my mind. I slowed my sprint and glimpsed him on my left. He remained a step or two beyond the water's edge, now at the hip of the isthmus on the mainland side. "I see Lars. His cage is on the beach!"

Grover pointed with his entire arm beyond the castle's corner, toward the place where Dot and Higgs must have first encountered Sundalfar. He gripped a silver flask in his hand that reflected a slanting sunbeam directly into Higgs' face. Only Grover could see the cage, due to his superior vantage point, but it was reassuring to know he was there.

Turning to make sure Higgs had heard too, I read her face like a map. There was a clear path to Lars. She visibly strained her legs in a cycle. Useless. All she would want was to get to the castle's base and skirt around the beach.

Closer at hand, Scarlett had stopped jerking and was fully upright again. Her arms retracted into her jacket, and she shook it off. "Dammit, more speed less haste, woman," she said to herself in a quiet yet scolding voice. Jacket off, she fumbled to undo snaps at her shoulders and hips, and a heavy vest flopped to the seaweed strewn tidal remains at her feet, leaving her dressed in a white vest.

She looked up at our shocked faces. Instead of perishing in some gruesome series of mortal twitches, she was merely rushing to separate herself from the darts. "Flak jacket. Standard issue," she said.

I felt aggrieved for a moment that we hadn't been issued bulletproof vests too. Given how much I hated her, I felt oddly relieved she was still with us.

As Grover shook seawater from his soaked camo trousers, still out of the line of sight of our adversaries, Chronos bellowed from the castle grounds above and ahead of us. His voice was clear and commanding, not the sort of tone you'd expect from a person immobilised by magic amid hostiles, but something we all expected from our friend. "Cockwomble? You can't best me at schoolboy insults, you scraggle-chinned weasel. Care to say something more insulting right to my face, you coward?"

Ruaridh vibrated with contained fury and strode briskly to Chronos. Unsurprisingly, he took up a position a fraction out of arm's reach, confronted with a colossus a head taller than him. Despite the distance, the spittle flying from Ruaridh's lips was noticeable as he raged. "See you, pal. You're the one glued to the floor in the middle of *my* house. In the middle of *my* country. You should shut your Sassenach gob before I shut it permanently."

Chronos chortled, which brought Ruaridh a threatening quarter step closer. "I think you'll find it's *our* country, wee man."

The space between them wasn't close enough for a swung fist, but Ruaridh was close enough for Chronos to act. He shifted his weight to one side and kicked Ruaridh with his prosthetic leg's blade, a sweeping blow straight up to the crotch. As Ruaridh doubled over, our oldest friend followed up with a head butt to the bridge of Ruaridh's nose. Blood exploded from both nostrils and mixed with the ginger beard as he stumbled backward and landed awkwardly on the grass.

Chronos tried to angle in for a finishing move, but only one of his feet was free from the footfast spell; the other remained anchored. Instead, he straightened and dusted his shoulders off. "That kick didn't do as much damage as I thought it would," he mocked. "I should've known you were dickless."

Ruaridh snarled at the elf who peered at him from behind Ragnhildur's thigh. His voice came out as an anguished croak. "I thought you said their feet were all stuck!"

Chronos laughed again, louder. "My foot is somewhere in a medical waste bin, mate. Like all your plans, this one had an obvious flaw."

Sundalfar capered to regard Ruaridh from the relative safety of Ragnhildur's other flank. "True! True! Sundalfar does exactly, *exactly* what he's told. Be clear, hear me. Clear."

Ragnhildur pushed the elf gently away in annoyance. One Donnelly twin and Angus helped Ruaridh to his feet, but he remained bent, massaging his inner thigh and pinching the bridge of his nose with the other hand. Blood dripped freely to the grass from his swelling face. There was a long moment of inaction where nobody seemed to know what to do next. It was Ruaridh's muffled and nasal command that broke the deadlock.

"I've had enough of this Icelandic magic and knock-off Russian tech. Let's show them some proper Scottish hospitality. Duncan—put the frighteners on 'em so they'll be compliant when Ragn uses the elf-magic to touch them and pop them into the cage."

Ragnhildur swept wind-tousled hair behind her shoulder. "With their feet held, I think I can safely get close enough for Sundalfar to bring them with me to the cage. But why not scare them a bit? Let's try my big sister, shall we? I know what frightens *her*. Do your worst, Dunc."

Angus hung back with Ruaridh, but the twins and Ragnhildur ambled through the gate and approached our position on the sand with exaggerated nonchalance. Duncan withdrew a stick of charcoal the shape of a stubby cucumber from a pouch in his trouser pocket and drew broad skeletal lines on his arm, leading from the bottom of one rolled-up sleeve to split and follow the contours of each finger. He scuffed a foot backwards on the dirt as if leading up to a bullish charge. Sundalfar followed but halted at the mossy line where the castle gate would settle when closed. He seemed constrained by his captors, unable to leave the castle grounds.

I saw Higgs turn her head a fraction to the left, where Grover continued his trek in the shallows, moving toward Lars's cage. She shooed him along with a flicking motion of her fingers, still held close to her side.

This was either not subtle enough or Darren Donnelly

caught Grover's movement without the prompt. Dreads wobbled as Darren's gaze settled on the previously unseen intruder. "Grover, mate—where are you heading? Come join yer pals, here. It's okay, you're a friend, we won't hurt you. Only tryin' to keep you safe." Darren beckoned, wide-armed, to Grover, who stood ankle-deep in the lapping waves. A half-hearted gesture of the flask toward the castle's seaward side revealed Grover's hesitancy.

His brother ignored this, intent on Scarlett's face. He advanced past Higgs and took a position 2 or 3 paces from where Newt, Scarlett, and I squirmed against the hold of the footfast spell. He squinted, staring into Scarlett's defiant eyes, and fretted with something in his pocket. I only realised I held my breath when the burning desire to exhale built up to an intolerable level, and I breathed out sharply. He reached out with his skeletally illustrated arm and although Scarlett recoiled to the range her fixed feet would allow, she could not evade his touch. She parried his attempt to place his palm on her forehead but he grabbed her wrist instead. He held it only long enough for her to twist and spring free of his grasp, but it seemed sufficient for his spell to take effect.

"It's done," Duncan said to Ragnhildur, spinning away from us and scuffing at the charcoal, brow furrowed as he turned. His shoulders slumped as he loafed off, ascending the path to the castle gate with heavy feet. Higgs called to his retreating form as he passed her. "Traitor!" she spat.

Ragnhildur smiled at her half-sister, an unappealing twisting of her lips that held more malice than warmth. She said nothing, but Scarlett responded to the silence with wrath. "Nothing's happening. See? I'm not scared of *anything*."

Ragnhildur sucked her teeth and spun on a heel to join Darren, still trying to coax Grover over. "We'll see about that," she said.

A patch of scrubby brush shook beside the pathway's ascent to the castle. Fish flopped onto the sand of the isthmus. A small shriek sounded from Delladonna behind us.

From the brush near us crept a weasel, skittering over the

shore's small rocks. There was something unnatural about the way the weasel moved. It was the colour of driftwood and mold, its fur matted and only vaguely attached to its emaciated and desiccated body. One leg was inoperable, pointing directly out from a shambolic shank. As it lurched forward, we could tell this weasel had died a considerable time ago, but some arcane power compelled it toward us.

The weighty fish flopped along the sand, also heading our way. It had a green and scaly head trailed by a skeleton picked clean by carrion feeders. Blackened and hollow eye sockets shed maggots as its body writhed. Soon several compatriots from the sea joined it, all in various states of decomposition. Slimy trails and scales glazed the sand, all radiating in our direction.

A headless grouse lurched across the seaweed behind us, heading toward Dot. Half-bald with its remaining feathers threatening to shed at any moment, it left a veering line of three-toed tracks in the wet sand.

To my left, the carcass of a deer strained to free itself from the dense bracken at the castle rock's foot nearest Grover. Its front two legs pushed in repeated jerks and its single remaining antler scrabbled at the overgrowth pinning its hind legs to the earth. Powerful exhalations accompanied each burst of effort. And behind us, a stag, adorned with clods of heather advanced on Delladonna, accompanied by a troop of shredded-eared rabbits.

We had all seen magic before, but nothing on this scale and nothing this frightening. Almost as if choreographed, we each tried again to uproot our firmly-moored feet, but the attempts were as unrewarding as before. Newton cursed and Scarlett had coiled into a foetal position. Although it was unfair, I think we were all depending on Higgs to fight this magic with some of her own. But based on the narrow escape from the Pendletoad, accomplished without the dampening effect of the elf's counterspells, I put the chances of success at less than 10 per cent. Our best hope was that these creatures were just some illusion, but the experience with the toad made this unlikely too.

"Higgs, you can do this," Dot called in a wavering voice from close behind me. She crouched in preparation to fend off the shambling grouse, now accompanied by a pair of decomposing snakes.

My sister crouched, burying her fists in the sand. Buds appeared and flourished on the back of her neck and peeked through her hair. A guttural cry came from her lips, unintelligible.

The dead of Glen Ghuil appeared on the ridge near Delladonna. Newton extended both arms toward Higgs, and I thought I saw wavering air between them, the transfer of power almost tangible.

A meek, throaty voice floated across the hushed scene, the only other noises the lumbering of long-dead animals and Higgs's primal snarls. "Must. Sorry, young girl. Must stop you. It's one of the rules. Can't break the rules. No."

Sundalfar placed his palms on the moss beneath him, and a blue glow raced through the earth and stones to Higgs, whose sprouting blossoms withered and fell in a shower around her.

CHAPTER 30 - ARISE

Higgs

The stench of death preceded the disintegrating animal army's lurching mass. Ragnhildur was almost within my reach when she turned and raised an eyebrow at a hyperventilating Scarlett. "See? It scared you silly then, and it still gets you now."

I wanted to snatch her annoying hair and drag her beneath my knee for a round of pummelling. The feed from Newton lingered, and my magic surged and leapt, only to retreat into my core under the watchful clench of Sundalfar's counter-charm.

The castle gateway framed the diminutive character as he shrugged at me and held out his bound hands once again, the handcuffs whirling with an odd energy. Something stirred there that remained difficult for my senses to appreciate.

I remembered that Chronos still had his tire irons, so I motioned surreptitiously with my eyebrows and the backs of two dangling fingers, willing the elf to understand that Chronos could free him. He seemed to understand, glancing over his shoulder then sloping out of view behind the gate before sidling toward Chronos, scanning from side to side as he moved to obscure his intended destination.

Amid rasping breaths behind me, Scarlett struggled to pull herself together momentarily. "Duncan's power—it's to scare you, not hurt you. Stay calm," she muttered to herself. Then she whimpered as the resurrected weasel approached. She resumed gasping for air.

I didn't mention aloud the attack of the Pendletoad, but Newton must have been thinking of it too. That wasn't exactly a harmless bad dream. The small birds and mammals that approached us were undoubtedly sinister, but they didn't scare me in the same way as the larger corpses. They looked like a good swat would knock their moldering carcasses to bits. It was only the bigger reanimated creatures I worried about—the stags that appeared in greater numbers on the ridge and a pair of sharp-beaked sea eagles too plundered of feathers to fly but still sporting threatening beaks and claws.

We had a little time until those bigger animals closed in, but there was no obvious technique to defeat them. Especially with our feet anchored. Duncan shuffled to the castle gate, casting wistful glances at his mother. Once there, he turned and jogged halfway down the sloping path before pausing, torn between loyalties.

Darren was still trying to coax over Grover who now stood, indecisive, in the shallows at the side of the castle. He seemsd to be unaffected by the Footfast spell, taking hesitant steps toward Darren then moving away to ward Lars. "Look brother, I can protect you fae them monsters. Come to the castle, Grover," he called. I noticed that a tailless seal had beached itself and splashed toward Grover from behind, and a second deer carcass joined its sister in a series of three-legged hops.

Grover shook his head and removed his glasses as if reducing his vision would promote a corresponding increase in bravery. "No. Lars is my friend." He pointed to the castle's rear flank, to the place I couldn't see but trusted held Lars. Grover trod in a series of artful hops along the shoreline, veering to avoid some minor threats I could not make out from this distance.

Scarlett spat words at Ragnhildur's back like a thrown dagger. "You're just doing all of this because of Faðir. Because he didn't love you like he loved me. Release us, and we'll leave you in peace. You can have this barren land."

Ragnhildur whirled, still close enough that I saw her nostrils flare and her neck redden. Her voice had the iciest tone I'd ever heard from a human throat. "You wolf bitch! That's where you're wrong. I only had you scared because it's funny. But I'm doing *this* because of Faðir. Sundalfar!"

The elf paused mid-stride, looking side-eye at Ragnhildur as if he'd been rumbled in his plot to conspire with Chronos.

"Enough of this playing, elf. Make these corpses kill my sister. Kill them all."

Ruaridh cleared his throat and raised a finger to point at Scarlett. His mouth opened, but no words tumbled forth. Instead, he looked at the blood from his nose that had caked the valley between thumb and forefinger and let his arm drop to his side and his mouth ease shut.

Sundalfar held his head in his handcuffed hands. "But. But. Mistress, hear me now. You know—"

"Yes, you can't kill anyone. I know. Let me be *very* clear. Give these animals the strength to remain in one piece and the teeth, hooves, antlers, and talons to rip humans apart. There's no rule against that, is there?"

Sundalfar hung his head lower, not daring to peek between his clenched fingers. "No rule. Gods, no rule. Sorry. Sundalfar is sorry. Children. Sorry."

The horde of encircling dead pulled themselves a little taller, eyes or eye sockets shining with the same blue luminance that crackled around their remaining teeth, claws, hooves, and horns. They moved with renewed purpose. Dot punched the rotting grouse away, but it righted itself and advanced again. The two deer charged at Grover.

Darren spun to face Ragnhildur. "Call it off, Ragn! This isnae the deal. See Grover, he's done nothing to anyone, ever. Nor has Mum."

Duncan also turned. "Yeah—that's our mother there." He sprinted down the path toward Delladonna on the rise behind us. At the same time, Darren carved an intercept path that would take him between the advancing deer corpses and Grover.

Ragnhildur snarled. "I've had enough of you two softies

too. Sundalfar, tell these ingrate magicians when they are going to die."

The elf sagged to his knobbly blue knees. "Mistress. The two ingrate magicians die this afternoon. At the same time." A motorcycle roared somewhere behind me as I tried and failed once again to release my magic.

CHAPTER 31 - DERAILMENT

Ruaridh

I was like a neutral observer to my downfall. I'd fought back the rage when that one-legged prick baited and tricked me, resisting the urge to raise my fists or retaliate in some more violent manner. He may outclass me in a fair fight, but he still had one foot pinned to the ground. But when I should have asserted my will, when I should have stopped Ragnhildur from her murderous change of plan, my anger shook me from within, and I remained silent.

The blood from my nose had dried into Rorschach blobs on the back of my hand. My own blood was not an unfamiliar sight, but it brought back unpleasant memories. The fights at school, when my stuck-up southern classmates ganged up on me. The times in the woodworking shop, alone with the headmaster who thought it a lark to vent his twisted frustrations on a kid that nobody would believe. I couldn't exact vengeance then, but was that ancient ember what gnawed at my human decency and stayed my hand when I should have raised it to prevent this current atrocity?

No. We could accomplish our goal of Scottish sovereignty with no deaths. That was my plan all along—harness the power of the elf to bring about a bloodless revolution. And I owed no favours to the rabble before me, but there was no need for this. They could all be in the cage with a tap from Ragn and a touch of the elf's magic.

The rage boiled up, uncontrollable. But a distant part of me realised it wasn't rage at the audacity of our attackers. It was directed at being unfairly diminished. How dare that Icelandic interloper call the shots here? This is my dream, my scheme, my future. She couldn't just use me in a show of strength to crush her sister.

My voice rumbled from deep within, a sharp bark of an order. "Ragnhildur! Stop this nonsense, now! This is my show, and I willnae have the blood of these innocent folk on my hands. Tell the elf to call off Duncan's horrors and get these fools caged, like we originally planned!"

Ragnhildur didn't even bother fully turning. Instead, she cast me a withering glance down her nose, eyes half shut as she cast them from my boots to my cap. "Piss off," she said. "This isn't your show any more, it's mine. You'll get your independence from England, but never from me."

Turning to face the rabble beyond the castle gates, she spoke casually to Sundalfar. "Elf. Footfast again. This time on Ruaridh."

A wordless, twisted scream echoed from the castle's curtain walls as I attempted to lift my feet from the grass.

CHAPTER 32 - THIMBLES

Higgs

Dot, my brothers, and I flexed and stooped, scattering the smaller shambling animals away. Scarlett didn't even pretend to defend herself; she huddled and covered her ears, eyes clenched shut.

Darren lunged between Grover and the approaching deer as their glowing blue hooves raised to strike. Duncan crossed the isthmus and sprinted halfway up the slope but would not reach his mother in time to defend her from being impaled on the horns of a once-majestic stag, now reduced to a horror-show shadow of its former self.

I craned my neck to watch the disaster befall Delladonna as if in slow motion. Duncan took lunging steps up the rise as the stag lowered its glowing horns and powered from its rear hooves in a murderous strike. Delladonna held up a forearm in a gesture that I could tell would be useless.

Duncan cried out in anguish as the attack unfolded, unable to arrive in time. "Mum, no!"

The bellow and growl of Tam Thunder's motorcycle engine burst across the ridgeline as he swept past Delladonna with inches to spare. His right boot kicked out, striking the stag in the neck. The motorcycle's full kinetic energy met the antlered head, wresting it to an unnatural angle as the bike shot past.

Unbalanced and careening at high speed on the slope's scrub, the bike rose to a perilous balance on the front wheel, the rear wheel visible above Tam's fluttering hair, casting off globs of earth as it spun furiously. The glowing antler tip had punctured the small windscreen and torn the stag's head from its collapsing body. For a moment, as Tam wrestled with the bike's balance, the stag's head swivelled on its trapped antler, and two surprised faces looked directly at Dot—one with the flying mane of a Scottish pop star, the other a grizzled and decomposing nightmare.

Poised to topple, Tam righted the bike at the last moment, its outraged rear wheel clattering back to earth and launching the bike down the slope once again. The stag head dislodged and spun off on its own trajectory toward the shore.

Duncan prepared to tackle the second stag, now at his mother's side. On the shore to my left, his brother had already diverted a hoof strike with a flailing forearm, protecting Grover, who clutched his flask overhead for protection.

Delladonna shrieked, "Turn them off, Dunc! Make it stop!"

"I'm trying dead hard Mum, but I cannae stop it. Sundalfar's blocking me." Duncan braced for the next attack.

I heard a clacking sound that tugged at the harp strings in the back of my mind, but I failed to place it as I watched the motorbike throw up a wall of sand to our right. Tam powered through a tight turn, wheel spinning shells, wet sand, and bits of corpse in a wave away from us. And from Dot in particular, I noted, apparently still playing the role of her wingwoman.

Thimbles! The clacking sound was Delladonna's thimbles weaving a syncopated pattern from the wild motion of fingers raised high above her head. She bowed, eyes hidden behind her curls, and closed her eyes, oblivious to the ring of horns that threatened her and her son.

Lightning struck her imploring, thimble-clad hand. But not normal lightning. It was a rusty orange, and it crackled not from the sky but along Glen Ghuil. It struck the thimbles, halted, and gathered power, fizzing more energetically with each passing second.

A fiery ring of bristling orange energy burst from the thimbles, encircling both her and Duncan, pushing the corrupted animals back. A second ragged ring rose above Delladonna's red-lit hair, and a subtle gesture propelled the coursing electricity in an arc that expanded and settled around Darren and Grover, severing the reanimated seal's bloated corpse into two writhing halves. The third ring descended onto the beach, raging out from the fringes of our position, driving the monstrous attackers back, leaving only a handful of floundering corpses to contend with inside the ring. Tam dismounted beside Dot, leaving the engine idling and kicking at anything that wriggled, limped, or skittered with glowing teeth along the sand. The footfast spell did not seem to affect him.

Through the crackling orange barrier, I saw Angus approach the gate, looking down on the carnage. Ragnhildur held her position halfway down the castle path, stepping back as the raging ring of energy expanded toward her. Sundalfar crept closer to Chronos behind them all, taking comical tiptoe steps despite the crescendo of crackles from the defensive rings sizzling around us.

But then the same stifling counter-charm that quelled my surging magic extinguished parts of our ring. The lightning still erupted down Glen Ghuil from what must have been Emeline's position to Delladonna's skyward-thrust thimbles and arches of energy powered the three coruscating loops protecting us, but they protested, and gaps appeared in their borders. The energy paled and turned blue.

With a fizzle, the ring protecting the sand-locked six of us dissipated, and the link between Delladonna and Emeline disappeared in a puff of smoke that drifted on the light breeze. The same thing repeated a moment later with the barrier protecting Grover and Darren. The herd of deer that had assembled while we enjoyed protection advanced in unison, eyes glowing blue. Only the ring surrounding Delladonna and Duncan remained intact, half-orange and half-blue, as she wrestled with the elf's counter-spell. The presence of friendly magic had buoyed me, but as it was beaten back, my desolation returned. I thought of Ena's appearance at the roadside just when we needed her—twice—and wished she were here to offer some reassurance now.

As the protective ring around Delladonna also fizzled into nothingness, a second stream of lightning, this one a more brilliant yellow, triangulated on Delladonna's thimbles, joining the orange one. This second stream came from a small house on the glen's margin, now illuminated by the yellow energy. The three protective circlets sprang back into life, once again forcing a retreat from our dishevelled attackers. The revitalized barrier rings had shades of both orange and yellow as the two magical sources channelled through Delladonna's thimbles.

I remembered Ena McTavish reassuring Dot and me as she drove us away from the glen what seemed like years ago. "Around here, we help each other, nae questions asked," she had said. The memory fortified me. I nodded to myself, pulling myself to full height and standing defiant, my mind racing to discover what action I could take to spring us from this trap.

Tam pulled two snakes from Scarlett's hunkered form, but she seemed not to notice. Rivulets of darkening blood spattered her white vest where she refused to defend herself from the ghastly adversaries. She rocked slightly on her anchored feet, whimpering.

Beyond the rings, complete circles of the dead assembled, waiting for the next lull. And the lull approached with near certainty. Blue veins of magical power slithered down the rock from the castle, increasing in intensity as they reached the circle protecting us. Once again, the fire crackled orange, yellow, then patchy blue before fading. All three circles winked out of existence, leaving a single fireball of energy that darted to Grover's flask, still positioned to protect his face. The flask burned with intense golden light before the fireball abandoned it. It burned an arching path over our heads, briefly lit a pair of darting kestrels, and finally landed beyond the treeline on the mainland. The forest absorbed the energy, and the fireball contracted and disappeared.

Darren and Duncan grabbed a pair of menacing antlers each, and Tam remounted his bike, revving the engine. Clods of rotten flesh spattered our feet as the army of rotting flesh leapt into the gap left by our former wards.

I locked eyes with Dot, thinking this might be the last day I spent with her. Why did we have to come to the shores of Loch Ghuil? I didn't even like camping.

An oddly joyous voice sounded behind me. "They're *finally* here," Grover shouted.

CHAPTER 33 - DOWNHILL

Disco

It was a sign. The ball of light rose from beyond the castle below us. My friends, the kestrels, absorbed part of its light as it passed. Beside me, the horse trapped the ball in the tufts of its braided mane. It shook. Some kind of juice spattered over us all. The hooves beside me glowed with golden light. Ready, we surged from the forest in leaps and blurs.

The rabbits bounded ahead, so I ran faster. My teeth felt hot. I saw golden horns in my peripheral vision. The deer.

Newton, Faraday, and Higgs were below me on a patch of sand. So was Higgs's friend. The boy from the horse house was further away, near the water.

Some bad-smelling animals gathered and moved in fighting stances. There were other people there too. I ignored them. I had to protect the pack.

A badger was about to bite Higgs in the leg. From halfway down the hill, I jumped. Farther than I had ever jumped before. We all jumped.

Higgs tried to push the badger away, but it was too strong, and its teeth sank into her leg. Before it tore off a chunk of flesh, I landed on it. Well, I landed *through* it. My jaws tore a hole in the back of its skull. The force of my landing broke it into damp shards of bone and bad-smelling skin.

Three rabbits saved Faraday from being trampled by a pair of ragged-looking deer. One rabbit bit a deer leg clean off.

My deer friends rampaged among the bad animals, hooves flying and antlers tearing rotten flesh. The kestrels screeched and plummeted from the sky in attack. A motorcycle swirled and wove as I leapt again and again. My fur couldn't shed the slime and stink of rot. I was protecting the pack.

Newton

The blue veins of Sundalfar's power pulsed from the castle gate in conduits beneath the earth, corrupting the magic that protected us. As the golden-tinged ring collapsed around us and the hungering horde surged into the vacuum, I heaved one more time at my anchored feet. If I couldn't move, it meant failure to protect my siblings—a destiny thrust upon me when murky forces had killed our parents. Strain as I might, neither foot would budge. Two drooling rows of blue-lit badger teeth opened wide and lunged for Higgs, just out of my reach. I had failed.

From my right, where the sloping path from the mainland to the isthmus yielded to a line of trees, golden points of light bounded. A whippet that looked remarkably like Disco leapt in a grand arc from mid-hill, clearing the heads of Dot and Tam Thunder toward Higgs. The jagged point of a broken antler heading for my face veered off and stabbed the sand at my feet as a screeching, golden-taloned bird grazed my cheek and fended off the reeking stag. The creeping horrors that ringed us shuddered with impacts like a cavalry charge—except animals from the British countryside led this onslaught. Rabbits raged at our attackers. Kestrels swooped and raked faces and eyes. Deer horns twisted and tore through fermented flesh and corrupted bone.

Most fearsome of all was a hammer-hoofed horse. It shouldered the ranks of the moldering army aside, rearing and striking. This was the most unusual way to solve a case. On a stretch of battle-scarred half-land, half-sea in remote Scotland, I located Alan Ryder's missing polo pony. I also found our missing pet. How in the world had they arrived here in time to save us from Ragnhildur's malice and elf magic?

The sights, sounds, and smells of the melee crowded my senses. Darren Donnelly lay sprawled on the rocky shore at Grover's feet, the head of a decapitated stag clutched by an antler. A pair of protective, golden-horned deer paced the vicinity, repelling the dwindling attackers that dared approach Grover. On the ridge, Duncan Donnelly swung a gnarled tree branch to defend his mother. An uncountable number of rabbits darted and leapt and swarmed in their defence. Delladonna continued her thimble work, sparks juddering forth and igniting shambling carcasses that evaded her cadre of furry warriors.

Closer to hand, Tam's motorbike had carved a sandy trench where the protective ring had burnt earlier. He circled and circled, booting interlopers that tried to cross the line. Faraday hadn't succumbed to the panicked paralysis I feared; he brushed off small attackers absentmindedly as he stared through his binoculars at the scene inside the castle. A few smaller animals limped and slithered toward him, and a flapping fish swiped at his ankles, but he seemed not to notice.

The biggest change was Scarlett. She unclasped her ears, looked at the progress toward clearing the reanimated army, and stood tall. She glared at Ragnhildur, who teetered open-mouthed near the castle threshold. Scarlett's bare arms shot skyward, and her biceps flexed as if demonstrating a power that her little sister could never overcome. Her vest and arms were bloody. A clothesline of weasels dangled from each outstretched arm, picked at by the graceful leaps of rabbits. Sand laced her hair, which fluttered as she threw back her head and raged, a wordless battle cry reverberating off the castle walls. She strained to lift her leaden legs from their pinned positions.

Ragnhildur spared a glance for Ruaridh, even as the older man cajoled her. "It's not too late, lassie! Just put them in the cage. Nae more nonsense!"

She shook her head and turned to locate her blue-skinned captive, spotting him crouched beside Chronos, who was prying at the handcuffs with the tire iron from the jeep. "Sundalfar! Shame on you! You will help me *now*. Mirror me. Like we discussed earlier."

She turned her back on the elf and waved dismissively at Angus. "Deal with that crap, man."

She stooped and stepped to Ruaridh. He tried to grab her by the hair, but she was far quicker than him, and ducked his flat-footed attack to pull a small but vicious-looking serrated knife from the top of Ruaridh's high woollen sock. A staccato series of popping sounds rebounded from the castle walls, and I knew we were in deepening trouble.

CHAPTER 34 - MULTIPLY

Higgs

Despite having no coherent plan beyond Scarlett's dragonflies and Chronos sneaking around back, we had thwarted death more than once already. If Chronos could pry Sundalfar loose from the handcuffs, the upper hand would be ours. The remarkable appearance of Disco, Alan Ryder's missing horse, and their animal companions had decimated the shambling forces that assailed us, and they darted here and there, continuing to prevail.

But the elf's magic, commanded by Ragnhildur, again proved superior to anything we could throw at it. She brandished a vicious *sgian dubh*, the famed 'black knife' that Scotsmen carried tucked into a sock. Its profile, with one serrated edge and one flat edge joining in a wicked pointy tip, caught the angling sunlight coming through the open castle gate. "I'm coming, quarter-sister! I'll finish the job myself."

With a series of pops like a chorus of Champagne corks, Ragnhildur advanced down the rocky path toward us, multiplying with each step. First there were three of her, then nine, then I lost count. By the time she reached the sand, they easily outnumbered us, each one armed with an identical knife, their wild-eyed anger boiling further with every step.

Most burst toward Scarlett, who crouched into the best combat-ready position she could, given her fixed feet; her blood-drenched arms raised, fists at chin level. Being closest to the castle gate, two enraged copies of Ragnhildur ran at me, knives slashing. One mirror image winked briefly out of existence to appear a pace back to avoid Tam's roaring bike, but the other one stabbed downward at my chest. I raised a forearm to block the falling blow, but with momentum, gravity, and possibly strength on her side, the best I could hope for was a vicious puncture instead of being torn from sternum to hip.

I was correct. My forearm did little to blunt the attack's force. A whoosh of air in my left ear accompanied the blade's speedy descent. The heavy impact collapsed my arm and struck my chest at nearly full force. The impact knocked me to the sand, bent backwards at the knees like a spring-mounted figurine, lungs emptied by the blow. I reeled, trying to breathe and clutching the point of impact to stem the inevitable spurt of blood. Oddly, I found no blossoming wound. My camo top was unpierced, and all I felt was a few shards of broken plastic littered in the area. I gasped and tried to make sense of the scene above me.

Later, Faraday told me how he had saved my life. As the mirrored Ragnhildur rose to strike, he threw the only thing to hand—the drone control. At first, he thought it was going to strike me in the back of the head, but as I raised my forearm, I recoiled from the expected blow and shifted to my right. The device sailed past my left ear—the whoosh I recalled hearing—and smashed into the descending knife. Point struck controller, scattering shards of plastic but jarring the *sgian dubh* from that Ragnhildur's grasp. The only thing that hit me was a knifeless fist.

As I lay on my back, struggling for breath, I watched in horror as the marauding troop of Ragnhildur duplicates winked in and out of existence as our defenders tried to halt their progress. They easily avoided the desperate leaps of Disco and the rearing horse's flailing hooves. A dagger was buried hilt-deep in the horse's side, and rabbit blood splattered my face as a halved long-eared corpse struck me. Dot screamed as a knife blow descended, only cut short by the rasp of metal on metal when Tam's bike swirled to a stop beside her.

Despite the panicked undertones, I could tell from the excitement in Faraday's voice that he had an idea. "Higgs, I need you. I know what to do, but I can't do it myself." I hoped it wouldn't be the last idea he ever had.

CHAPTER 35 - RECONSTRUCTIUM

Faraday

Scarlett squared off against one of the Ragnhildurs. Was it the real one? Was there even any way to tell? Although her immobilized feet took away the combat advantages I could see she would have in a fair fight with her sister, she managed to hold her own. She turned slightly away to take the brunt of a kick on her flexed upper leg and ducked beneath a vicious backhanded knife swipe. As the knife returned, Scarlett parried an uppercut, the blade piercing her forearm and remaining embedded there. She looked shocked, but her disarmed opponent retreated 2 steps, snarling.

Something within me realised we were all under attack, but I ignored that, treating it as background noise. I knew our only way out of this was for Chronos to pry the handcuffs from Sundalfar's wrists. I watched through my binoculars as he strained at the tire iron, the blue form of the elf winking in an out as I looked slightly to the other side of Chronos. I felt a few nips and a distant pain in my ankle but quashed those sensations as I noticed the remarkable handcuffs.

Scarlett had told us that imprisoning an elf for anything beyond a few minutes was impossible because the elf would use its magic to escape. With air- and earth-grounded powers, making a cage that could resist their ability to escape was a conundrum unsolved until now. As I watched Chronos's powerful cranks of the tire iron, a realisation dawned. Even in the shaky peripheral binocular view, the metal of the handcuffs was insubstantial but continually resolidifying. As if it was regenerating under the strain of Chronos's torture and the elf's innate unmaking magic. *Reconstructing itself.*

This was the combined power of the trio leading the Tartantula: Ruaridh's drive for separatism, Ragnhildur's knowledge of the hidden magic of Iceland, and Angus's invention of nanomaterial that could defy being broken down. That twisted bastard wasn't going to outsmart me. I'd already defeated his armada of dart-throwing mini-planes, and in my pocket, I had several vials of anti-nanotech. A puff of it would destroy the communication between the nodes of the reconstructium manacles and allow Chronos or Sundalfar himself to break them. I only needed to smash a vial at Sundalfar's feet, and this would be all but over.

This left only one minor problem to solve. How would I get the vial from my hand, through the gate or over the castle wall, to the place it needed to go? If anyone was going to save us, I knew it would be Higgs.

As she turned to my call, I explained her mission. "I need to smash this vial of nano on the elf's handcuffs. Use your vines to get it there. You can do it!"

Higgs clued in right away. Scrabbling to her knees, she closed her eyes. "Lars, we're coming!" she screamed, then called for support. "Dot, Newton, you need to help me."

Dot threw a handful of sand into the air, and the particles drifted off, defying gravity in a cloud of golden glow. They settled on the pulsing blue veins of Sundalfar's energy, dimming them. Tam's bike burst into a defensive weave, disrupting the mirrored Ragnhildurs' infuriated lunges.

The golden grains of sand hardened around a flowing channel between Newton and Higgs. The blue veins of magic suppression, although weakened, pulsed beneath the sand, working against the girls' magic. A few wisps of vegetation peeked from Higgs's sleeves and collar, alternating with gold and blue pulsations.

A moment later, the crackling streams of lightning sizzled

across Glen Ghuil. First, the air between Grover's uplifted flask and Ena McTavish's croft on the hill sprang to life, writhing and spitting energy. The popping trail of sparks from Delladonna's outstretched thimbles and Emeline from the top of the loch joined in, skirling trails homing in on the flask's supercharged outline.

A wave of power flowed from the scintillating flask to Newton and from there through the crystalline cloud to Higgs. The blue in Higgs's leaves drained away, yielding to a brilliant gold. From her left hand, a vine sped to my outstretched palm, encircled the flask of nanotech, and launched toward the gate.

Angus planted his feet, ready to block this new threat with his body if needed, but that defence was in vain. The tendrils of vine wove protective coils around the glass vial before coursing from Higgs and bumping across the rough ground to the gate's left side. The lead tendril ascended the castle wall at incredible speed. It pulsed with golden light, tinged only slightly by the blue elf magic. It disappeared over the crenelated parapet as an excited yipping sounded from behind me. Disco bounded after the path of the speeding vine tip, taking the ascent to the castle gate in a single bound and torpedoing between Angus's legs to skid on the castle lawn behind.

All the leverage Chronos could muster seemed to have no effect on Sundalfar's handcuffs. The toughened reconstructium would not be persuaded by a mere tire iron and a large dose of muscles. In anger, Chronos flung his tire iron, and it ricocheted off Angus' shoulder. Our adversary dropped to a knee, cursing and massaging the point of impact, his gaze tracing Disco's run.

Still alert to the possibility of a Ragnhildur duplicate slipping past Tam's rampaging bike, I watched the vine advancing across the lawn. It slowed as it approached Chronos and Sundalfar. The golden glow faded and became corrupted with blue. The vine's tip shed leaves and uncoiled from its precious cargo. Progress across the lawn halted, and the tendril corkscrewed straight up, turning a deep indigo before leaving only a dusty plume to blow away in the breeze. The sizzling lightning faded to an eerie silence, punctuated only by the scrabbling motorbike and Ragnhildur's attacks. The vial hung in the air for a moment, then fell. It had come to within a handful of paces from its intended destination, but would now plop unbroken to the grass.

Higgs collapsed, exhausted. Dot and Delladonna cried in anguish while Tam skidded to a stop, and Duncan Donnelly rolled down the slope, a snapped stag antler protruding from beneath his collarbone.

Inside the castle walls, Chronos drew out the second tire iron, ready for whatever might come next. Angus knelt with a puzzled expression at the smoky trail and falling vial. Ruaridh's blood-soaked nose dripped and he worried at his beard with both hands. He twisted his hips above his emplanted feet to follow the only remaining motion—our whippet's snaking sprint.

In a high-velocity turn, Disco sent clods of grass into the air, leaving veering divots in her wake. She leapt in a perfectly timed and graceful sweep. Spittle-encrusted jaws gently cradled the vial, snatching it as it fell. Her fur shed ichor from the undead army; it was marred with burrs and thistledown from her journey and sand from her battle on the beach. She bore down on Chronos and Sundalfar.

The speed of her approach left neither man nor elf time to react. Four tracks in the turf illustrated her skid. Although we couldn't hear it from our position, I could tell that Disco bit down on the vial as she halted, shaking her head at the elf's outstretched hands.

For a moment, it seemed like nothing was going to happen, but then Sundalfar leapt away from Chronos, arms raised in a V above his head in a cloud of dissipating black vapour.

The mirrored images of Ragnhildur became two-dimensional for an instant before fluttering away like a human-sized deck of cards in a hurricane. The knife in Scarlett's forearm shrunk and blew away, leaving a gushing wound. With her other arm, she punched the remaining, real Ragnhildur under her jaw. Finding her feet suddenly free, she sprang on her sister, knocking her back and pinning her to the sand with one knee.

A few remaining undead animals took their last staggering steps before collapsing in carrion-feeding ruin. Darren Donnelly groaned where he lay, trampled at the feet of Grover Mann. Duncan had been the most mobile of us all, ignoring both the undead antler that had pierced him and the elf-freeing escapade inside the castle. With the mouldering remains of the antler sloughing away from his wound, he lolloped through the gate and slammed his charcoal-etched arm against Ruaridh's back. The bigger man was pushed slightly off-balance, but recovered, realizing his feet were now free. Ruaridh turned to face an enraged shout from Duncan whose momentum forced him to the grass. "Let's see what *you're* frightened of, old man."

Feet free, Ruaridh retreated out of my view, ignoring Duncan's collapsed form and beckoning Angus as he limped along. The wounded horse clopped listlessly to Grover and nuzzled the favourite stable boy like a long-lost friend. Dot crawled to Higgs. Tam shut off the motorcycle and rushed to their aid. Newton's reassuring arm fell across my shoulders.

There was a moment of silence before a dark thought struck me: the anti-nanotech. It had worked perfectly, released by Disco's jaws in the right place at the right time.

But nanotech also laced our dog's body after the earlier incident in Middle Ides. My gaze swivelled to the castle interior where Disco lay like a heap of jelly, unmoving.

CHAPTER 36 - PROPHECIES

Higgs

I felt limp as if someone had drained my blood and replaced it with maple syrup. At least I could let my legs lay flat now, my feet no longer fixed to the sand. I was so exhausted I failed to realise this meant Faraday's ingenious idea had worked. Wet sand pressed into my cheek, my eyelashes. Shouts reached me as if from a ship distant in a gale.

Words without meaning crept along the hallway of my right ear, treading lightly. My hand hung a million miles from my body, yet I felt someone rubbing it. A tingle of love and attention. It could have been a second, a minute, or an hour before the words coalesced into meaning. It was Dot.

"Higgs? Can you hear me, Higgs? You did it. Sundalfar is free. Let's get to Lars."

Lars. Yes.

It took an effort just to open one eyelid. I saw Dot kneeling over me and the floppy coif of Tam Thunder hovering behind her. I tried to ask if Lars was okay, but all that came from my sandy lips was, "Hmpffff."

The most difficult push-up ever took me only to all fours. "Help me," I managed.

Dot gingerly brushed sand from the left side of my face, and Tam circled to my other side, lifting me with one arm beneath the crook of my knees. I clung with one arm around his shoulder and the other dangling listlessly.

"This way, around the side of the castle," Dot said, close at Tam's side.

I squinted as the sun struck my face. It wasn't bright at this late hour, but we'd been in the shade of Castle Ghuil's walls for so long that it was a shock to emerge into the light. Grover's enthusiasm jostled me further awake as he joined our group.

"I told you they were coming. Did you see Disco's jumps? She was amazing. And I put Darren onto the horse because he's hurt. A deer stepped on him. And I rode on the underwater horse. Did you see that? It came when it saw that man's flask, from when he nearly drowned as a little boy. Look, there's Lars!"

That last sentence forced my eyes open again. Sure enough, an iron cage perched on a flat rock behind the castle, one edge verging on the sand. Inside it, Lars laughed uncontrollably at the sight of us. "Higgs, Dot! You came! I knew you'd come."

He burst into tears, still smiling and laughing in bursts.

Our progress was slower than my brothers'. They burst past us in a sprint to the cage, followed by Scarlett, pushing Ragnhildur before her, the younger woman's hands bound behind her with a set of tightly zipped cable ties. "They're getting away!" she called. "Stop them!"

A powerful-looking motorboat bobbed in the waves beyond the cage, engine not yet running. Angus pushed away from the rocky channel with a long-handled mooring hook.

Ruaridh pointed at us as the boat floated away from the end of the channel that emerged from the castle's belly. It must have been moored beyond the portcullis where we first laid eyes on Sundalfar. They had fled down the staircase that Chronos had snuck up earlier. Why didn't Chronos stop them?

"See that elf prophecy," he shouted in a nasal tone due to his swollen nose. "It never came true. Nae silly cow in sight, eh? You cannae stop the Tartantula! We're still free, and free of that scheming bitch Ragn's treachery, and I have all the death clock names and dates Sundalfar told us safe in here." He patted his jacket pocket.

No longer constrained to the castle, Sundalfar capered in his slap-footed gait onto the foreshore, followed by Chronos, who cradled something in his arms. He gingerly laid Disco's grimy, limp, and unmoving body on the slab of rock at his feet.

Graceless, I swiped at Tam's arm until he lowered me to unsteady feet. I staggered first to Lars, overlapping his hands on the bars with my own and touching my forehead to his. "I missed you, Lars. Don't wander off again without me, eh?" My leaden arm found the strength to wipe away one furrow of tears from his cheek, leaving a sandy residue in its place. Then I half stumbled, half crawled to Disco.

Chronos had settled our brave dog onto her side, tongue lolling from her flaccid jaws. Her legs splayed at her side, but they were clearly wrong. Instead of the strong angular form of a racing dog's legs, they were gracefully but unnaturally curved into lazy squiggles, as if they were noodles, not bone and sinew. I fell with my face in her unbreathing chest and closed my eyes, too shattered to cry.

Ruaridh continued to fume, turning his ire on Delladonna, who supported Duncan. "And *you*, woman, you raised two traitors, you ken? And big Dunc's magic didnae work on me at all. There's nothing for me to be afeared of here. Enjoy their deaths, woman. I heard the elf call them out earlier."

Chronos threw the tire iron to Tam Thunder. "Make yourself useful, lad. Spring Lars out of that cage."

Grover faced the waves rolling onto the beach near the cage and exclaimed, "I *wondered* when you would get here. It's a long way around."

A narwhal leapt from the shallows and slid across the sand on the slick seaweed. The tip of his spiraling tusk came to a stop just inside the rusting cage. Lars stepped to that side of the cage and cradled the narwhal horn in one palm while it regarded him with its inscrutable gaze. He turned and shouted to the passengers of the bobbing boat. "Prophecy *this*, you bullies!"

Dot clapped once and laughed. Sundalfar slapped his feet alternately on the slab, repeating the prophecy in an accusatory

tone, orb-like eyes fixed on Ruaridh.
"A Viking boy will roam the Glen,
He must not pass beyond your ken.
Your new nation will be born,
Unless he touch the Ghuilin's horn.

Never said it. Never said cow. Hear me. Cow only in your mind." The elf laughed too, a raspy eruption from somewhere deep within or beyond.

Ruaridh blanched visibly, despite the beard that obscured most of his face and the flat cap that shaded his brow. Maybe Duncan's spell had worked after all. This was the thing he'd feared since the words of the prophecy first escaped Sundalfar's lips. His voice wavered. "Enough—we're outta here. Where's the keys, Angus?"

Lars punctuated that question with a piercing peal of laughter, verging on hysterical. He pulled a ring and its dangling prize along the length of the narwhal's rippled horn and jingled it aloft. "You mean *these* keys?" A pair of keys dangled from a ring encircling his pointer finger. "The waves are pushing you back to shore. I'm looking forward to finding out what happens when you get closer to our friend Chronos."

Was this the prophecy in action? Or Grover's magic? Or just a mischievous narwhal investigating a glittering object on a boat moored under a castle? Maybe some of each—I was too drained to care.

I observed all this from my vantage point at Disco's side. Faraday joined me and arranged Disco's jellified legs into their proper shape. "It was the nanotech, Higgs. She saved us all, but it attacked her too," he whispered. Newton stroked her head, picking bark, sand, and blades of grass from her fur.

The blue-skinned elf squatted down between Disco's legs and peered into my half-averted eyes as if they were tunnels to some forgotten treasure. "Can you bring her back, Sundalfar?" I asked quietly.

"Not allowed. Never. No killing. No bringing back. Rules. Rules, I tell you."

The waves lapped. The boat drew closer. Dot murmured to Lars behind me, and I heard Tam working at the lock. Grover urged the narwhal back into the sea.

"But I know who *can*," Sundalfar said. "You help me. Young girl. Helped me. I will help your dog. And tell the mother something. Tell her. Tell her I only saw the magicians die, not the boys."

An odd whine sounded from the loch, growing louder. Although Disco was almost as long as Sundalfar was tall, he could cradle her in one elongated, spindly arm, and he lifted her carefully but easily. As the whine grew, he carried our dog, our sister, our conspirator. He ventured past the cage where Tam stumbled back as he sprung the lock, past Grover and the shimmying narwhal. We all took a step back as a colossal yet somewhat comedic fly alighted on the shore. It was second nature now to look slightly to the side so we could see both elf and fly. The massive insect was a duplicate of the one I had seen through Newton's eyes at the Ferndale reservoir, but a deeper indigo in colour. Sundalfar scaled its bulbous, near-spherical flank one-handed, his palms and the soles of his feet sticking to it as if by Velcro. Saddled between its ridiculously tiny wings, still cradling Disco in one arm and grasping a handful of terrifying, coarse fly hairs with the other hand, he urged it into the air. The fly lifted slowly above us.

"I will summon you, young girl. Summon. When you need me. When things are ready. Remember," Sundalfar called down.

The fly sped off and was soon a speck on the horizon, heading north.

I lay down again and closed my eyes. Delladonna's thimbles caressed my cheeks. After a moment, she reassured my brothers, "She'll be okay. The magic makes you dead exhausted, but not dead. But my boys need medical help, and I dinnae ken how it's going to get here. Can your lad here ride back on his bike and get someone? Dunc's shoulder's punctured, and Darren's had his ribs trampled. I used some wee charms to stop the bleeding, so I cannae see their wounds killing them, but you heard the elf as well as I did."

"About that," Faraday replied. "Sundalfar said that he only saw the magicians die, not the boys."

Delladonna choked out a throaty laugh at the revelation. "Mind this, boys," she called to her twins, who sat back-to-back a short distance away, avoiding any sudden movements that might jar their wounds. "I gave you magic powers at birth, and I sure as hell can take them away. This is gonnae both save and punish the two a' you." Her thimbles clinked as she walked back to their position.

Delladonna had seen to Scarlett's stab wound as well. A throbbing welt marked the spot on each side of her forearm where the knife had stabbed through. Blood caked the back of Ragnhildur's hair where Scarlett had ground a sopping knee into her spine. A resigned expression plastered Ragnhildur's face as she watched the boat bob closer to shore with each cresting wave.

Ruaridh stamped twice, pulling at his beard. "If it wasnae for your bitch sister, none of this wouldae happened. I told you to deal with her early on, but you underestimated her, hen. Bloody incompetence all about me."

Angus spluttered at his side, failing to enunciate anything coherent in his own defence. Ruaridh balanced on the bobbing boat's lip, reached into an inside pocket of his jacket, and pulled out a revolver. He pulled back the hammer and aimed it at Scarlett. Everyone froze. Everyone except Faraday.

He was the last person I would expect to protect Scarlett, after all we suspected she'd done to us. Maybe it wasn't about Scarlett, but pure instinct that took over. As Ruaridh pulled the trigger, Faraday sprang from his crouch beside me, throwing himself between the pistol's barrel and Scarlett's already bloodied torso.

Smoke puffed from the barrel, followed by a short length of wooden doweling. A flag unfurled in a jerk beneath it. On the tattered piece of cloth was Sundalfar's smiling face. Ruaridh cast the pistol into the sea in disgust. Faraday picked himself up from his heroic sprawl. He and Scarlett looked at each other, both with raised eyebrows, before Faraday quickly looked away and rejoined Newton and me.

When Angus tried using the mooring hook to push the motorboat away, Chronos snatched it from his grasp, almost pulling the Scot into the sea with it. He planted an end of the hook's pole on the rock, standing like a lancer awaiting a joust.

"This is your last chance to call me Sassenach." He grinned. "The mayhem starts in about ten seconds."

CHAPTER 37 - UNMISSING PERSONS

Newton

Friend of my parents and familiar presence in our lives since we were kids, Alan Ryder sat in the chair on the other side of my Granny's hospital bed. "The Strathclyde Police trailer driver tried to tease the details out of me when he dropped our pony at the stables. I guess he was just given an address, but no explanation. I just laughed and made a few comments about horse smugglers. Not sure if that's even a thing."

Granny laughed at that. "My uncle Memphis once stole a donkey from the neighbour's farm and tried to ride it to London," she said. "He was twelve and only made it as far as Bishop's End before the donkey quit moving and lay down beside the cart track where it refused to budge."

She bristled at being kept in the hospital and had insisted we take her back to the Orphanage because she was feeling much better, but we awaited her discharge papers. "And did they fix up my room already?" she asked.

"They have," I said. "New window. They're working the slate roof today, to fix the damage up there. And visitors shaking their heads and talking in hushed tones is the new departure protocol up there. I talked to one gentleman that was visiting his mother. I think her name is Margaret? Two doors along from yours? Anyway, she seemed convinced that she'd seen the Ides Giant come to life and heard weird croaking noises. But he was having none of it."

Granny giggled at that, and Alan raised an eyebrow. "You know," she said. "I swore the night nurse to secrecy. When your man Terrell came around to see me, Gwendolyn was here checking in on me. He asked her what was going on when she tended to me behind the Orphanage that night. You know what she said?"

Alan smiled. "Obviously not that there was a life-and-death struggle between a magical toad the size of a small house and a hill carving brought to life."

"Not exactly. She said that kids were riding their dirt bikes up and down the hill and that ball lightning had struck the building, knocking me into a miracle landing on the grass outside. Ball lightning! I'd never even heard of that, and asked one of the nice orderlies here to look it up on the Internet."

I shook my head in disbelief. "Terrell will not believe that for a minute. He's probably figuring out a third explanation now, because the truth isn't very believable and no offense, but some of the resident witnesses at the Orphanage have credibility issues."

"And how much did you tell him about events in Scotland?" Alan asked.

"He's pretty open-minded, so I gave him a mix of half-truths. I said that Lars had been kidnapped by a cult and they knocked him out with a herbal potion. And that Higgs, Dot, and Grover had convinced Faraday to travel up and use his gadgets to bamboozle the inept kidnappers. Of course they kept all this from me, and only called when they needed a ride home. Typical teenagers. I don't think he bought all of that, either, but he's patient enough to let me tell him the full story when I'm good and ready. We also went together to visit Grover's parents. I had to apologize profusely for Higgs taking him with her on the camping trip without talking to them directly. Lars, Dot and her have been over at the stables a lot, hanging out with Grover, so I think the parents are balancing the newfound camaraderie against whatever Grover has been telling them. He's been talking mostly about Disco, apparently."

A lump in my throat blocked any further words, and tears welled but didn't quite spill My grandmother clutched my hand in both of hers. "Disco was a brilliant part of the family, so always remember that. And it's okay to cry, Newton. Your father stayed in his room for three full days when our pet goat died, and there's still a small tombstone for Vilhelm, up by Ashton Pond."

CHAPTER 38 - DIPLOMATS

Higgs

Three weeks later, two limousines and a beaten-up Range Rover jostled their way down the cobbled slope of the Royal Mile in Edinburgh. As the slope petered out past the Scottish Parliament, the gates to the Palace of Holyroodhouse opened before us, footmen tending to the gates. We had all been offered limo rides, but Dot, Lars, and I rode instead in Ena's mud-clad vehicle that had swept us away from Glen Ghuil the first time. Tam Thunder was the guest of honour, and rode shotgun.

Scarlett and Agent Zee emerged from the first limo, while the second emptied like an overpopulated clown car. My brothers followed Emeline, Chronos, Delladonna, Grover, and Grover's parents. Even now, the Manns looked shell-shocked; it was going to take more than a couple of weeks to recover from the case of their missing son transforming into a tale of magic, nanotech, and a cross-country journey involving a menagerie of land, sea, and airborne animals.

It was hard to stop Grover from referring to the events that we felt obliged to keep hush-hush. Luckily, he expressed so many random ideas it seemed safe to assume people would take any of his exclamations with a healthy dose of scepticism.

The Queen's footmen ushered us into a plush reception room where the First Minister of Scotland waited for us. We were flattered to be received in a royal palace, even if there were no royalty in residence just now. Her beaming smile welcomed us, lighting up her lined face beneath a blonde fringe. Fiona Byrd greeted us each warmly, embracing us in turn, a message of gratitude tailored to the role each of us had played in the struggle at Castle Ghuil. I wished Disco was with us. She probably would have sniffed out traces of the Queen's corgis that lingered in the palace.

The Prime Minister stood beside Fiona Byrd and shook our hands as we finished with the First Minister. After the formalities, the First Minister beckoned us into a semi-circle and her gaze alighted on each of us as she spoke.

"You know there is no way we can properly thank you for what you've done. Although we may want Scottish independence," she began. I noticed a slight eye roll from the Prime Minister at this point. "This is not the way it should ever happen, driven by some lunatic fringe. I can tell you that Ruaridh McRaven, Angus MacFarland, and several of their associates are already imprisoned for terrorism. Their trial details will be classified, of course. We are still working on a compromise for your sons, as you know, Ms Donnelly. And we have deported a person of Icelandic origin.

"In lieu of the public recognition that we can't really give you, I am presenting you each with a sovereign seal." She handed each of us a transparent case containing a broad silver coin the size of a water biscuit, engraved with the Queen's head on one side and a thistle on the other.

When she reached Newton, she handed him a second coin. "I understand your grandmother was unable to join us via video call today, so I trust you can make a suitably formal presentation to her on our behalf."

"Well, she didn't say she was *unable* to join in a video call. But she did use the words 'newfangled', 'unnatural', and 'interfering with tea break' when I described it to her," my brother replied. "But of course, she'll treasure it. Thank you, First Minister."

She continued, addressing us all. "Each of you has a unique ID number inscribed on the Scottish side. If you ever need the

Scottish Government to help you, *ever*, call the first ten digits of the number and tell them the remaining digits on the coin to identify yourself. Whatever help we can offer will come your way."

Faraday glanced across at Scarlett. "There are some reports I'd like to see if it's not too much trouble," he said.

Fiona smiled and glanced at the Prime Minister. "Send me the details. I'll see what we can do."

"And I smashed up someone's motorbike. Could you replace it?" I asked.

Fiona smiled at that. "Your eldest brother asked me to take care of that already."

Grover turned to his mother and said, "Oh yeah, Mummy. Do you have the thing? For Higgs?"

She nodded and pulled something pink and woolly from her handbag. Grover took it in both hands and brought it to me, offering it at arm's length. It was a hand-knitted winter toque with a frilly chin strap. "I asked for a medal for Disco, too. I put it here in the hat that Mum made for you. It's going to be very cold when you see her, so you don't want to get cold ears."

I welled up, thinking about the last time I had seen Disco, cradled by an elf and leaving the shores of Loch Ghuil. I sniffled but couldn't find any words as I accepted the hat and Disco's coin. I held his hand in mine, but Grover looked puzzled.

"She means to say thank you, Grover," Dot replied on my behalf.

"Oh, okay," he said. "But don't be sad, Higgs. The animals all had an adventure, just like us. And Disco will have another, I think."

After a brief spell of less formal chit chat, comparison of fading bruises, and open conversation about the contretemps at Loch Ghuil that we couldn't have in any other company, we ambled as a group back to the waiting cars. As we emerged into the evening sunlight, a raucous tune sprang to life. Bass, guitar, soaring vocals, and a bagpipe solo charged us with smiles and laughter. It was a tune most of us had not heard before, but it would soon blare from radios all across the still-United Kingdom. The tartan-clad trio hammed it up, rooster-stepping across the palace forecourt as far as their portable amp cords would allow.

"Drums! The song needs *way* more drums," Tam shouted, laughing. He grabbed Dot's hands and danced her right up the bonnet onto the roof of the limo.

As the reverberations faded, Scarlett sidled up to Faraday but kept a moderate distance. "Wait till you see where we're going for dinner. It's just outside the castle gates, which sounds like it might bring back bad memories for all of us, but the ancient building and the menu are amazing."

* * *

The late Scottish summer dusk gave us a last look at the fair face of Edinburgh. Tam had to leave dinner a little early to board his tour bus, and the rest of our crew piled into the limos to head to the airport. Dot, Lars, and I said our farewells to Ena McTavish.

"That's us, Ena," I said. "We're hiring a car from the train station, but it's a fine night. We can walk there."

"You're nae taking the 'copter back to Middle Ides wi' the rest of that lot?" she replied.

Dot chuckled. "Our last vacation was slightly ruined, as you might remember. We're going to the Isle of Skye this time."

Ena looked at her side-wise, cocking a whorl of an eyebrow. "Ye're no camping, are ye?"

"Hells no," I said. "Five-star hotel this time. Fiona's paying."

"Och, hen, don't bother yerself with a hire car. It's a ways but I'll drive you there."

Dot, Ena, and I continued in unison. "Around here, we help each other." Our shared laughter radiated on the warm evening air.

Lars opened the Range Rover's door for Dot and I to slide into the back seat. "Can I sit in the front, Ena? I have a story to tell you about a toad, and it may take a while."

LAST WORDS

Thank you for reading *Shadow Over Loch Ghuil*. If you enjoyed the story, leaving a review is a good way to let other readers know how to follow in your footsteps. I appreciate your feedback.

Higgs, Faraday, and Newton will return in *Whispers Under Middle Ides*.

A magical artifact poised to cause unthinkable destruction is hidden somewhere near the town of Middle Ides. A shadowy global organization known as The Revision is poisoning the land with sinister devices to further their ambitions.

As the forces of magic and nanotechnology collide again, the Redferne siblings must decipher the signs and intervene to prevent an international disaster.

Join the Redferne family and their tapestry of friends and enemies in *Whispers Under Middle Ides*.

Join my mailing list and find more at
www.pattisontelford.com

Pattison Telford lives in Toronto, Canada, with his wife, two quietly magical sons, and snaggle-toothed dog. Previously living in Scotland, England, and Australia has armed him with a considerable range of slang words and insults. He grew up playing basketball and has spent far too much time sitting in front of computer screens in his job as a Microsoft IT Consultant.

CPSIA information can be obtained
at www.ICGtesting.com
Printed in the USA
BVHW030906110821
614178BV00001B/87